HIST

OF THE

SCOTTISH REGIMENTS

IN THE

BRITISH ARMY.

BY

ARCH. K. MURRAY, ESQ.,

MAJOR OF THE NINETY-SEVENTH LANARKSHIRE VOLUNTEER GUARDS.

Published by Request of his Brother Officers.

GLASGOW:
THOMAS MURRAY AND SON.
1862.

CONTENTS.

TTT

INDEX TO PLATES.

PREFACE.

In the present Work, the Author, without pretending to submit anything very startling or original, has endeavoured to gather from the records of the past such facts as may enable him, avoiding the tedium of detail, to present to the reader a brief and, it is hoped, at the same time, a comprehensive narrative of the origin and principal events in which our Scottish Regiments have so largely and honourably been distinguished.

It is wholly foreign to the purpose of the Author in any way to overlook the valorous achievements of the English and Irish Regiments in Her Majesty's Service, which have alike contributed to build up the military renown of the British Army; he only trusts he shall receive that same charitable indulgence, in his present undertaking, which in like circumstances he, with every right-hearted Scot, should cordially extend to brethren of either a sister land or sister isle. It is in these pages, as a Scotsman, he ventures to give expression to the nation's gratitude and honest pride—awards, in the name of friend and foe, the meed of praise justly due to the brave soldier who has fought his country's battles in almost every land—ofttimes victoriously—at all times honourably.

The Author gratefully acknowledges the assistance freely

rendered him in this compilation by many Officers of the
Regiments described. He feels also considerably indebted to
many very valuable works, on the same and kindred subjects,
for much of his information. Unfortunately, many of these
volumes are now very ancient, others nearly extinct, and
nearly all so expensive as to fail in answering the purpose of
the present Work, by bringing before the public, in a cheaper
and more popular form, the records of those heroic deeds,
the narrative of which *ought* to be as "household words,"
infusing a thrill of living patriotism and loyalty into the soul.

It is hoped, as the grand result of the Work, that Scotsmen, considering the rich legacy of military glory bequeathed
them by their heroic forefathers, specially registered in these
Scottish Regiments, will be more impressed with the duty
devolving on them to maintain and emulate the same. Whilst
these records may afford knowledge, it is also hoped that they
may awaken a larger sympathy and deeper interest on the part
of the people in those, their brave countrymen, who so well
represent the nation; and if circumstances preclude us from
accepting the "Royal Shilling," and so recruiting the army,
let us be ready to accept, for the expression of our thoughts
and feelings, that grand channel which, in our time, has been
revived as the exponent of the people's patriotism and loyalty
—*the Volunteer Movement*—whether as active or honorary
members, giving effect to our sentiments, and demonstrating,
"by *deeds* as well as *words*," that we are in earnest.

INTRODUCTION.

NATURE has been aptly represented as a fickle goddess, scattering her bounties here and there with a partial hand. Some spots, like very Edens, are blessed with the lavish profusion of her favours—rich fertility, luxuriant vegetation, warm and delightful climates. Some, on the other hand, which have not so shared the distribution of her gifts, represent the barren wilderness, the sterile desert, the desolate places of our earth —entombed in a perpetual winter—a ceaseless winding-sheet of snow and ice seems for ever to rest upon these cold, chilly, Polar regions: or parched, fainting, dying, dead, where no friendly cloud intervenes, like the kindly hand of love and sympathy, to screen the thirsty earth from the consuming rays of a tropical sun. But, as if by "the wayside," we gather from the analogy, that as in the world of man there is a Scripture proclaiming comfort and blessing to the poor and needy—whilst it tells the rich how hardly they shall enter into "life"—so in the world of nature there is an over-ruling, all-wise, all-just Providence, "Who moves in a mysterious way," making ample amends in the result upon the peoples of these climes, so as yet shall cause "the wilderness to rejoice." Thus we find that lands enriched by nature ofttimes produce a people who, rich in this world's good things, acquired without much

effort, allow their minds to become so intoxicated with present
delights and indolence, as to fail in cultivating the virtues of
the man.   Too frequently the fruits are these—ignorance,
lust, passion, infidelity, and general debility. Whilst the barren,
dreary wilderness, the bleak and desolate mountain-land—
like the poor and needy upon whom Nature has frowned—
enjoy the smile of Providence "in a better portion;" for there,
amid a comparatively poor people, are nurtured all the sterner,
the nobler, the truer, the God-like qualities of the man, the
soldier, and the hero. There, too, hath been the birth-place
and the abiding shrine of freedom—the bulwark and the bas-
tion of patriotism and loyalty. Ascending higher, these—the
peoples of the rejected and despised places of the earth—have
ofttimes begotten and been honoured to wear the crowning
attribute of piety. Turning to the history of Scotland or of
Switzerland, for illustration, and taking merely a military
retrospect, there it will be found. All centuries, all ages, all
circumstances, are witness to the bravery and the fidelity of
their mountain-soldiers.

Scotland, the unendowed by Nature, has been thus largely
blessed by Nature's God, in yielding a long line of valiant and
illustrious men. Perhaps no nation engrosses so large and
prominent a place in the temple of military fame—none can
boast so bright a page in the history of the brave. Her stern
and rugged mountains, like a vast citadel, where scarce a foeman ever dared to penetrate, have been defended through centuries of war against the advancing and all but overwhelming
tide of aggression; besieged, too, by the countless hosts of

Tyranny, they have still remained impregnable. Her wild and desolate glens, like great arteries down which hath flowed the life-blood of the nation, in the living stream—the native and resistless valour of her clans. Her bleak and dreary heaths have written on them one dark history of blood—" the martyred children of the Covenant." Faithful unto death; " of whom the world was not worthy." Her crown oft crushed beneath a tyrant's heel—her freedom trampled on—her people betrayed—all lost but honour. Unscathed, unsullied, she has triumphed, and still lives to write upon her banner, the mighty, envied, and thrice-glorious word, " Unconquered."

Armies have a very ancient history. Their origin might be traced to the very gates of Paradise. When the unbridled lust and wrathful passions of man were let loose like Furies, to wander forth upon the earth, then it was that lawless adventurers, gathering themselves together into armed bands for hostile purposes, to live and prey upon their weaker brethren, constituted themselves armies. Passing down the stream of time, through the Feudal Age, we find one among the many greater, mightier, wealthier—a giant towering above his fellows—exercised lordship, levied tribute, military and civil, over others as over slaves. These were the days of chivalry, —the Crusades—when cavalry constituted the grand strength of an army. Here we might begin the history of cavalry as an important constituent in armies, were such our purpose. The comparative poverty of our ancient Scottish nobility prevented them contributing largely to the chivalry of the age. Almost the sole representative we have of our Scottish Cavalry,

is the Second Regiment of Royal North British Dragoons, or
Scots Greys—a most worthy representative. The wars of the
Interregnum in Scotland—the times of Wallace and Bruce—
when the feudal lords had nearly all either deserted or betrayed
her, introduce us to a new force, more suited to the independent
character and patriotism of the Scottish people—the formation
of corps of infantry, or armed bands of free burghers. These
were the fruit, to a large extent, of the Magna Charter in
England, and of the struggle for liberty in Scotland. Hence
the wars of Edward the Black Prince with France, distinguished
by the victories of Poitiers, Agincourt, and Cressy, may be
viewed not merely as the epitome of the triumphs of England
over France, but more especially as illustrating the success of
this new force—represented in the English yeomen, burghers,
citizens, and freemen—over the old force, sustained in the
chivalry, the cavalry of France. The result of these successive defeats, we find, was most disastrous to France. The
jealousy and fear of the nobles and feudal lords had denied the
people the use and the knowledge of arms; so that when themselves were defeated, France was ruined—since they could
expect no support, as in Scotland, from an unarmed and
unskilled people. They had done what they could to quench
rather than foster the spirit of free patriotism, which in the
nation's extremity should have been the nation's refuge—the
soul burning to deliver their land from the yoke of the
stranger. In not a few cases, the French rather sympathised
with, as they sighed for the same blessings of our free-born
English yeomen. Here we would mark, respectively in the

English and Scottish armies, the first formation of that branch of the service for which the British army has ever been specially distinguished—*the Infantry.*

Our reader is no doubt aware of the calamitous results which flowed from the short-sighted policy of these privileged orders—the old feudal lords; whose love of a petty despotism laboured to postpone the day of reckoning "till a more convenient season"—and so refused the timely surrender of those privileges and that liberty which the growing wealth and intelligence of the people claimed. Long, bloody, and unavailing civil wars have desolated and vexed many countries as the consequence; and in France the contest attained a fearful crisis, and the people wreaked a cruel retribution in the awful horrors of the Revolution.

The increasing importance of commerce, and the growing desire for wealth in preference to the uncertain and doubtful lustre of the battle-field, induced men to gather themselves together, not as formerly for war, but rather for the prosecution of trade; thus constituting themselves into trade-unions, communities, burgherates, free townships. Disowning the bondage of feudalism, as a system peculiarly adapted for war, and hostile in its spirit to a more peaceful vocation, they sought and obtained, in their earlier history at least, royal protection. Independently of their engagements and allegiance to the throne, these trading communities, aware of the restlessness, rapacity, and necessities of the old feudal lords around them, formed themselves into trained bands of free yeomen, or sort of militia, for the purpose—first, of defending their own industry, property, and lives; and, secondly, for the service of their sovereign and country in times of need. These are amongst the earliest ideas we have of a regiment. At an earlier age, we find many of the monarchs of Europe retaining in their service a body of foreign guards, specially entrusted with the defence of the royal person, so often threatened through the ambition of the nobles and the turbulence of the people. In nearly every instance these were composed of Scottish emigrants, driven from their country by the cruel and desolating wars which then disturbed her peace, and had proscribed many of the honourable and brave. We know no exception in which these corps of guards have not maintained the Scottish character, nay, been specially distinguished for the valour and fidelity with which they fulfilled their duty. Thus originated the First Royals, or Royal Scots Regiment of the present British army. The free citizens, continuing to prosper and proportionably growing in power and influence, gradually insinuated themselves into State affairs. As they grew in wealth, so unfortunately they increased in pride and arrogance, forgetting altogether their early humility. They essayed to be a political as well as a trading community. Having overthrown the power of feudalism, they threatened to shake the foundations of the throne. These murmurings speedily awakened the royal jealousy, and broke in upon the peaceful harmony of their hitherto successful alliance. The prosperity and support of these freemen had elevated the might and majesty of the throne, with which they had been early leagued, and these together had compelled the old feudal nobility to

exercise their rule in something more of a constitutional way.
Gladly, therefore, did these last avail themselves of these dissensions to restore their long-lost power. Uniting with the
crown, whose interests were more peculiarly their own, they
called upon their still adherent tenantry to muster around
them; and thus commenced the sanguinary civil wars, already in a previous paragraph referred to, between king and
people, which have devastated so many lands. These tenantry, thus raised, ultimately taken into the royal pay, as
regiments, have gone far to constitute the armies of their
several states.

In conclusion, we would remark, that the wars of the past
have been as it were *material* contests—wars of matter rather
than of mind—by which we mean that *might* has been understood as *right;* not as now, when *right* is acknowledged as
might. Formerly it was he who excelled in physical strength
and prowess that was crowned victor; now-a-days the appliances of mind, the inventive genius of man, have so improved
the art of war, that upon these the result of the contest must
largely depend. Skill and science, developed in a thousand
ways, are the weapons with which our battles are to be
fought and won; and this, too, at a time when man has been
dwarfed in his bodily might by the bloody and protracted
wars of the past, and enervated by the ease and indolence
found in cities, so as to be no longer able for a contest as
of old; and so the providence of God steps in to supply
the vacuum occasioned by decay, and from the rapid march
of civilisation, and the wonderful development of the mind,

represents to us a better state of things—the triumph of the *mind* of the present over the *matter* of the past. The victories of the battle-field are being superseded by the triumphs of the Cabinet. The first Napoleon conquered by the sword— the present Napoleon conquers by superior craft and intrigue, whilst we, as a nation, are sitting by to register with an occasional growl his successes. It has been the knowledge of these facts—this new system of warfare—that has aroused the nation to see its danger in time; to feel that " our glory " is but an ideal security; to know that steam and electricity have comparatively bridged the sea, and so done away with our best defence; to learn that the inventions of men comparatively equalise combatants. It has been the knowledge of these things, along with indications of a coming struggle casting its shadow before, that has called the nation, with one enthusiastic voice, to arms—in our present *Volunteer force.*

HISTORY OF THE SCOTTISH REGIMENTS.

SECOND ROYAL NORTH BRITISH DRAGOONS,
or
SCOTS GREYS.

CHAPTER I.

> "Come fill up my cup, come fill up my can,
> Come saddle my horses, and call out my men;
> Unlock the west port and let us gae free;
> For it's up wi' the bonnets o' bonnie Dundee."

EARLY HISTORY—COVENANTERS—BATTLES OF DRUMCLOG AND BOTHWELL BRIDGE—ARGYLE'S REBELLION—THE RAID OF THE MACDONALDS—FLIGHT OF JAMES II.—DUNDEE'S REBELLION—BATTLES OF KILLIECRANKIE AND CROMDALE —MASSACRE OF GLENCOE—1660–1695.

THE page of history presents to us many dark scenes of oppression, where one man, trampling upon the rights of another, and disregarding the heaven-born principle of charity, has sold his brother in o bondage. Nay, more, (as especially illustrated in the case of Spain groaning beneath the thraldom of the Papacy), some men have even succeeded in en-

slaving the mind; stopping up with vile trash the avenues of
knowledge, and so defacing and ruining that mirror of
the intellect which reflects so much of its Creator, which
originally bore the impress of divinity, and was moulded
in the likeness of God. But the pride of the human heart,
and the unhallowed passion of man, stay not here, but have
attempted more—to subdue the soul—but in vain. It is possible to fetter or destroy the *body*, nay, it is even possible to
enslave, or annihilate in madness, the *mind*, but it is *impossible* for man to bind the undying *soul*. Nevertheless, it has
been the infatuation of tyrants, deluded by false creeds, in
many countries and in many ages, to seek, but in vain, to
usurp the dominion of the *soul*. The *soul*, like "the bush
burned but not consumed," lives still, lives for ever, defying
the fires of persecution, the wasting famine, and the devouring sword. It comes forth scatheless, purified, living;
having shaken off the corruption of earth, it appears clothed
in the garments of immortality. There can be no better testimony to the suitableness of the true religion to meet the wants
of man than this—that whilst all others have proved themselves to be so many systems of tyranny, bereaving man of
his beloved liberty, the religion of Jesus is free, and is always
to be welcomed as the herald of civil and religious liberty;
wherever its blessing rests, its benign influence is felt, and its
glorious light shines.

It was in such a time as this in Scotland, when the iron
will of Charles II., already oppressing the persons and the
minds of his people, aspired to the dominion of their soul

and conscience, by calling upon them to introduce into
their simple forms of worship a host of objectionable
mummeries, savouring of Popery, and threatening thereby
to corrupt the purity of the Presbyterian faith. In vain
they petitioned for liberty of conscience and protested against
these intrusions. Persisting in the introduction of these
idle rites, and denying redress, the monarch preferred plung-
ing the nation into all the horrors of civil war, rather than
depart from his purpose. To enforce these requirements
the king raised in Scotland two troops of Life Guards, afterwards disbanded; a regiment of horse, known as Claverhouse's
Troopers—

"The bonnets o' bonnie Dundee;"

a regiment of Foot Guards; a regiment of foot, now the
Twenty-first, North British Fusiliers; and, in 1678, two troops
of dragoons, which, increased by the addition of other troops
in 1681, constituted the *Royal Regiment of Scots Dragoons*,
now known familiarly as the *Scots Greys*. The corps was
originally commanded by Sir Thomas Dalziel, who in 1681
was appointed the first colonel of the regiment. He was
always a staunch adherent of the House of Stuart, had been
taken prisoner at the battle of Worcester, but escaping from the
Tower, served with distinction in the Russian army during the
Tartar wars. Returning to Scotland at the Restoration, he was
employed by the king in enforcing his will upon the Presbyterians, and he discharged his duty with all the scrupulous
exactness of a soldier. To the Covenanters he has left a most
unenviable memory—as a monster of cruelty, devoid of mercy.

His eccentricities, especially in regard to dress, often excited the merriment of the Court, and created quite a sensation amongst the juveniles of the metropolis. He died in 1685.

The early history of the Royal Scots Dragoons is painfully and intimately associated with the sufferings and trials of the Covenanters—a page in our history which, would the truth admit, we would gladly omit. The ignominious duty imposed upon this gallant regiment, of hunting down the Presbyterians, and the cruelties which they were called to witness, sometimes to inflict upon their unhappy brethren, must have been extremely harrowing and repulsive to the feelings of brave men. Along with a troop of horse, a troop of the corps was present in 1679, under Graham of Claverhouse, at the battle of Drumclog, where they were defeated, with the loss of twenty men, by the superior numbers and desperate valour of the Covenanters, as also from the unsuitableness of the ground for cavalry to act upon. The result of this overthrow was a general rising of the disaffected and oppressed—a motley and undisciplined army was speedily assembled, better in the use of the tongue than the sword; and as always happens where that "unruly member" is in the ascendant, proved the precursor of party division, and in the end brought ruin to the good cause in which they had embarked. Foiled in an attack upon Glasgow by the retiring royal troops, especially the Royal Scots Dragoons and Scots Foot Guards, the Covenanters took up a strong position behind the Clyde at Bothwell Bridge, and there awaited the attack of the royal army, now advancing from Edinburgh under the Duke of Monmouth. Failing in effecting an accommodation, the battle was commenced by the Royal Scots Dragoons, supported by the Scots Foot Guards attacking the bridge, which, defended with great bravery, was only relinquished when the ammunition of the defenders was exhausted. The loss of this most important post, as well as the divisions already prevailing amongst the Covenanters, soon produced a panic which lost the battle, ruined for the present the cause of liberty of conscience, and served to add nearly ten years more to their sufferings. In the pursuit, the troopers of Claverhouse took a cruel revenge for the defeat of Drumclog, upon the broken and flying remnant.

The Royal Scots Dragoons continuing to be employed in the humiliating work of persecution, were often roughly handled by the Presbyterians, especially at Ayr Moss on the 20th July, 1680, where a desperate *rencontre* took place.

The Earl of Argyle, a nobleman of great merit, and for some time enjoying the esteem of his sovereign, being suspected of a leaning to the Nonconformists, or Covenanters, at the instigation of the Duke of York was arraigned for treason, and, accordingly, condemned to death. Escaping to France, Argyle returned in 1685, and landing with a force of 300 men in Argyleshire, summoned his clansmen, and endeavoured, with little success, to raise the Presbyterians, and so, setting up the standard of rebellion, threatened to dethrone James II., who but lately had succeeded his brother in the throne. After much fruitless manoeuvring, he advanced into the Lowlands, but was met by the royal troops, including the Royal Scots Dragoons, near

Dumbarton, under the Earl of Dumbarton. Attempting to
retreat in the darkness of the night, his guides betrayed him,
his army fell into disorder and disbanded, whilst he himself
was taken prisoner and afterwards executed at Edinburgh.
On the morrow, the Royal Scots Dragoons, assisted by other
troops, attacked a considerable body of the rebels under Sir
John Cochrane, which still remained together in the neighbourhood in a strongly fortified position. After hard fighting, in
course of which the dragoons dismounted and fought hand to
hand on foot, and after the loss of many officers, among whom
were Sir Adam Blair, Sir William Wallace, and Capt. Clelland,
also Lord Ross wounded, the rebels were driven back and
ultimately dispersed.

On the death of Lieut.-General Sir Thomas Dalziel, in 1685,
Lord Charles Murray, afterwards the Earl of Dunmore, and
son of the Marquis of Athole, one of the original officers of the
corps, was promoted to the colonelcy.

In 1688 a part of the regiment was called upon to interfere
on behalf of the Government—unfortunately on the wrong
side—in one of those unhappy broils which, as the dregs of
feudalism, still so sorely distressed the Highlands. The
Macintoshes having despoiled the Macdonald of Keppoch of
his estate, during his temporary absence in the Highlands,
the Macdonald, on his return, taking the law—as was usual
in those days, specially amongst the clans—into his own
hand, and taking an ample vengeance, redeemed his own.
The Royal Scots Dragoons were sent to the assistance and for
the release of the Mackintosh, who had been taken prisoner.

In retaliation they were inhumanly ordered to destroy all that pertained to the Macdonald—man, woman, and child. Although such instructions were quite in keeping with the character of the Court, happily it was about the last exercise of a power ever rioting in such acts of merciless cruelty.

The close of the same year brought the Prince of Orange to our shores, to deliver the land from the bondage of the Stuarts who had so grievously oppressed it. To meet this emergency, King James had drawn together to London and its neighbourhood the whole reliable forces of his kingdom. Amongst these were the troops of Scottish Life Guards; Claverhouse's regiment of horse; Dunmore's regiment of *Royal Scots Dragoons*; the regiment of Scottish Foot Guards; and two regiments of Scottish Foot—in all, 3,765 men from Scotland. After a seeming show of resistance, and much manœuvring in the vicinity of Salisbury, the monarch, dreading the wrath of an outraged people, fled to France.

"Conscience makes cowards of us all."

When the Prince of Orange, as William III., ascended the vacant throne, he found many of the troops inclined to dispute his authority, especially the regiments of Royal Scots Horse and Royal Scots Dragoons; which still remained together under the command of Viscount Dundee, and with the characteristic loyalty of Scotsmen, would still have maintained the cause of an unworthy and exiled prince, the degenerate representative of the Bruce of Bannockburn. The tact of the new monarch succeeded in winning the sub-

mission of the Royal Scots Dragoons; but the Royal Scots
Horse, deserting, followed Dundee into Scotland, took part
with him in his subsequent rebellion, and so, sharing his fate,
have been lost to the British army. The Earl of Dunmore,
declining to serve under the new king, was superseded in
the colonelcy of the Royal Scots Dragoons by Sir Thomas
Livingstone, afterwards Viscount Teviot—a Scottish soldier
of distinction, who came over from the continent with the
prince.

To stem the torrent of rebellion which the return of Dundee
to Scotland had excited—especially among the Highland clans,
nearly all of whom were devotedly attached to the Stuarts—
the Royal Scots Dragoons were ordered to return to Scotland.
Throughout the succeeding campaigns the regiment behaved
with signal fidelity and gallantry, with the exception of some
few of its officers who were found guilty of treasonable intercourse with the rebels — having a sympathy with their old
comrade in arms, Viscount Dundee. Amongst the arrested
were Lieut.-Colonel Livingstone, Captains Murray, Crichton,
and Livingstone. The royal forces under the command of
Major-General Mackay, included, besides the Royal Scots Dragoons, many regiments since known to fame—Lord Colchester's
Horse, or the Third (Prince of Wales') Dragoon Guards; Berke-
ley's, or the Fourth (Queen's Own Hussars) Dragoons; Sir
James Leslie's, or the Fifteenth (York, East Riding) Foot;
besides a considerable body of Dutch troops under Colonel
Ramsay. Dundee was joined at Inverness by Macdonald of
Keppoch and his clan, thirsting for revenge because of the

atrocities committed upon them and theirs by the soldiers in the previous year. After much time spent in marching and counter-marching in search of, and pursuit of, each other, the two armies met at the Pass of Killiecrankie, when the death of Dundee, in the moment of victory, virtually ruined the Jacobite cause. The Royal Scots Dragoons, although not present at that disastrous battle, had previously distinguished themselves in a skirmish with a body of about 500 High-landers, chiefly Macleans, who, defeating with great loss, they dispersed, and, dismounting, pursued among the rocks and crags of the mountains. In the following year, the rebels still continuing in arms, under General Canon—who on the death of Dundee assumed the command—and being recruited by a body of men from Ireland under General Buchan, took up a strong post and awaited the attack of the royal forces at Cromdale. Here, on the morning of the 31st April, they were suddenly attacked by Sir Thomas Livingstone, at the head of the Royal Scots Dragoons and other troops, and, amid the darkness and confusion, totally defeated and dispersed with great slaughter. The scene was one of consternation and horror, and had it not been for the merciful intervention of a mountain mist, as if to befriend her own children in their day of calamity, would have proved even more fatal to the flying enemy. In this action the Royal Scots Dragoons took a gallant part. This victory was quickly followed by the relief of the castle of Abergeldie, then besieged by the Highlanders, where two troops of the Royal Scots Dragoons utterly routed the rebels with great carnage. Unable longer to sustain such a hopeless struggle, the clans tendered their submission to King William, which was accepted.

But the triumph of the Government was stained by a deed of barbarous cruelty and sin, which remains a blot on the page of British history, known as "the Massacre of Glencoe." The Macdonalds of Glencoe having failed to tender their allegiance within the prescribed time, although they had done so a few days afterwards, the whole were treacherously murdered in cold blood, whilst peaceably sleeping, by a party of soldiers from Argyle's regiment, who had been received and hospitably quartered among them as friends. This inhuman action has been vainly attempted to be excused, and all authorities have alike endeavoured to escape the responsibility. We gladly record that the Royal Scots Dragoons were not called to take any part in the matter; and their colonel, Sir Thomas Livingstone, although then Commander-in-Chief in Scotland, has been fully exonerated from blame by Parliament.

CHAPTER II.

" London's bonnie woods and braes,
I maun lea' them a', lassie;
Wha can thole when Britain's faes
Would gi'e Britons law, lassie?"

WARS OF THE SPANISH SUCCESSION—REBELLION OF 1715—
SEVEN YEARS' WAR—1693-1793.

OUR last chapter closed the dark record which unhappily
clouds the early history of the Royal Scots Dragoons, and it is
with pleasure we turn from the record of these unnatural and
suicidal wars to narrate the nobler deeds of the regiment on
a nobler field. The accession of William, Prince of Orange,
to the throne, is not to be regarded merely as the triumph of
the Protestant party, but as involving the dawn of freedom to
an oppressed people; as the guarantee of liberty of conscience;
and as the harbinger of peace, especially to distressed Scotland.
In 1694, the Royal Scots Dragoons, accompanied by Cunningham's Scots Dragoons—now the Seventh (Queen's Own)
Hussars—and associated with the First (Royal English), the
Third (King's Own Hussars), the Fourth (Queen's Own
Hussars), and the Fifth (Royal Irish Lancers) Dragoons, were
sent over to the Netherlands against the French. Here they
represented the nation with credit, especially at the siege of

Namur, until the conclusion of peace, four years afterwards, permitted their return.

Unfortunately, the peace was not of long duration, and afforded but a short respite, during which the regiment was remounted on grey horses, as a *corps élite.* The question of the Spanish succession rousing the ambition of France, the flames of war were again rekindled. Accordingly, in 1702, the regiment was called to maintain the honour of their country on the plains of Holland. The earlier campaigns were chiefly made up with a variety of sieges—Venloo, Ruremonde, Stevenswaert, Liege, Bonn, Huy, Limburg, &c., in all of which the regiment had a part. Lord Hay, afterwards Marquis of Tweeddale, this year (1704) purchased the colonelcy of the regiment. The daring spirit and rising genius of Marlborough, who then commanded the British army, aspiring to something mightier, turning his eye towards Germany, selected a grander field of action—planned a campaign, which, taking Europe by surprise, fell like a thunderbolt upon the foe, and produced the most glorious results. The soldierly bearing of the Royal Scots Dragoons had already attracted the keen eye of the Commander-in-Chief, and won for them this tribute to their fidelity and worth, inasmuch as they were selected to be his own body-guard. They were, moreover, destined to lead the van, or, at all events, to assume a first place in the memorable actions of the campaign. Their firmness and valour helped their great commander to a great renown, as they were honoured to share with him the dangers and the glories of the campaign, and so " win laurels that shall never fade." Not less brave, although not so favoured, were the gallant troops which accompanied the Royal Scots Dragoons in the marvellous march from the Netherlands to Germany, and who alike contributed to the success of the expedition. These comprised the First (King's), the Third (Prince of Wales'), the Fifth (Princess Charlotte of Wales'), the Sixth (Carabineers), the Seventh (Princess Royal's) Dragoon Guards, and the Fifth (Royal Irish Lancers) Dragoons; besides the infantry which followed, including the Foot Guards, the First (Royal Scots), the Third (East Kent Buffs), the Eighth (the King's), the Tenth (North Lincoln), the Fifteenth (York, East Riding), the Sixteenth (Bedfordshire), the Eighteenth (Royal Irish), the Twenty-first (Royal North British Fusiliers), the Twenty-third (Royal Welsh Fusiliers), the Twenty-fourth (Warwickshire), the Twenty-Sixth (Cameronians), and the Thirty-seventh (North Hampshire) regiments of Foot. Marlborough having successfully accomplished with rapidity and secrecy this masterly manœuvre, and united his army to the Imperialists—hardly allowing the French and Bavarians time to know, far less to recover from their surprise—immediately prepared for action. The assault upon the French lines on the heights of Schellenberg, and the consequent capture of Donawerth, was the first event calling forth the bravery of the Scots Greys. But this was but the precursor to a more decisive blow. On the 13th of August the French and Bavarians were encountered in the vicinity of the village of Blenheim. The struggle was a severe one. The Greys and other troops attacking the village, which was strongly occupied by

the French, for long waged a very doubtful conflict; but at
length, by indomitable efforts, they succeeded in driving back
the enemy, and cutting off their retreat—twenty-four battalions of infantry and twelve squadrons of cavalry surrendered. The campaign closed with the siege of Landau.
Having delivered Germany from the immediate presence of
the enemy, Marlborough withdrew the British army into
winter quarters in the Netherlands. The only action of importance which falls to be recorded in the succeeding year is
the victory of Helixem, where the same redoubtable British
cavalry successfully attacked and broke in upon the French
lines.

A mightier achievement awaited the arms of our "gallant
Greys" in 1706. At the battle of Ramilies, after much hard
fighting, the regiment succeeded in penetrating into the village
of Autreglize, inflicting a dreadful carnage, and were honoured in receiving the surrender of the French "Regiment du
Roi," with arms and colours. Amid the trophies of the day,
the Greys are said to have taken no fewer than seventeen
standards. At the close of the battle a very curious circumstance was brought to light, affording an illustrious example
of woman's love, fidelity, endurance, and heroism. Amongst
the wounded of the Scots Greys, a female (Mrs Davies) was
discovered, who, donning the habiliments of man, had enlisted
in the regiment, braved the perils of Schellenberg and Blenheim, that in this disguise she might follow her husband,
who was a soldier in the First (Royal Scots) Foot, then with
the army. Her case at once excited the interest and sym-

pathy of the whole army; and awakening the generosity of the officers, especially of the colonel of *her* regiment, she was restored to her true position as a woman, lived to be of considerable service as envoy to the army, and at her death in 1739 was buried with military honours in Chelsea Hospital.

In the autumn of this eventful year, the Greys were called to mourn the death of their colonel, who had been with them throughout the war, and who was cut off by fever in the midst of a bright and glorious career. He was succeeded in the colonelcy by the Earl of Stair. About the same time the regiment was authoritatively designated the Royal North British Dragoons, and in 1713 was further registered as the Second Regiment of Dragoons.

It is superfluous to say that, at the battle of Oudenarde, in 1708, the sieges of Lisle and Tournay, and specially at the battle of Malplacquet in 1709—where, thrice charging the French household cavalry, they ultimately broke through that magnificent and hitherto invincible corps—as well as at a variety of minor engagements, the Greys maintained their high character. On the peace of Utrecht, in 1713, they returned to England loaded with the honours of war.

In the following year, the Earl of Portmore, a distinguished one-eyed veteran, was appointed colonel in room of the Earl of Stair—retired.

The rebellion of 1715, in Scotland, in favour of the Pretender, again called for the service of the Greys, who, with a firm fidelity, continued to discharge their duty to the king—notwithstanding many pressing temptations to desert. Whilst quartered at Stirling, they dispersed gatherings of rebels at Kinross and Dunfermline. With the Third (King's Own Hussars), the Fourth (Queen's Own Hussars), the Sixth (Inniskillings), and the Seventh (Queen's Own Hussars) Dragoons; also the Third (East Kent Buffs), the Eighth (the King's), the Eleventh (North Devon), the Fourteenth (Buckinghamshire), the Seventeenth (Leicestershire), the Twenty-first (Royal North British Fusiliers), the Twenty-fifth (King's Own Borderers), and the Thirty-Sixth (Herefordshire) regiments of foot, in all 4000 men, they were present at the drawn battle of Sheriffmuir, where the enemy mustered fully 10,000 men. The royalist army was mainly saved from utter defeat by the dauntless valour of the Greys, who, repeatedly charging the cavalry and right wing of the rebel army, succeeded in driving back and ultimately dispersing them, so as to counterbalance the success of the rebels on the left. Although forced to retreat for the time, the royalists, recruited by other regiments, were soon able once more to assume the offensive, and, notwithstanding the presence of the Pretender himself, ultimately dispersed the rebel army. A second attempt, aided by a Spanish force, in 1719, met with the same firmness, and fared no better. The rebel army, encountering the king's army—including the Greys—at Strachell, were completely routed.

Meanwhile the regiment was permitted to enjoy its laurels in peace. In 1717, General John Campbell had been appointed colonel of the Scots Greys, in room of the Earl of Portmore—resigned.

In 1742, France, Prussia, and Bavaria having leagued together for the destruction of Austria, George II., espousing the cause of Austria, in person, led an army of 16,000 British through Flanders into Germany. Of this force the Greys formed a part, under the command of their own chivalric monarch. The battle of Dettingen, in 1743, was the first event of importance in the war, in which the Greys were engaged—successively charging and defeating the imposing line of French Cuirassiers, and thereafter the magnificent array of the French household cavalry; capturing from these last a white standard—a trophy which never before had been taken by an enemy.

The army having been withdrawn into Flanders, and placed under the command of the Duke of Cumberland, achieved nothing of importance until the disastrous battle of Fontenoy, in 1745, in which, although no very prominent place had been assigned the Scots Greys, they nevertheless suffered severely —especially in the loss of their gallant colonel, General Campbell. He was succeeded in the colonelcy by the Earl of Stair —reappointed.

The rebellion of 1745, in Scotland, occasioning the withdrawal of a large portion of the army, the following regiments were left behind to make head against the overwhelming hosts of France:—the Second (Scots Greys), the Sixth (Inniskillings), the Seventh (Queen's Own Hussars) Dragoons; the Eighth (King's), the Eleventh (North Devon), the Thirteenth (1st Somersetshire or Prince Albert's), the Nineteenth (1st York, North Riding), the Twenty-fifth (King's Own Borderers), the Thirty-second (Cornwall), and the Thirty-third (Duke of Wel-

lington's) Foot. These were aided by a few regiments of
Dutch and Hessians. Taking advantage of these circumstances, the enormous masses of the French under Marshal
Saxe were advanced, with the intent to overwhelm this handful of brave men. The attack was accordingly made at Roucoux, but failed; although the British general was forced to
retreat, which was accomplished with success, notwithstanding
the immediate presence of a foe greatly superior in numbers.
It was the intrepidity of the British cavalry which rescued
the army from destruction.

The following year the Earl of Crawford was appointed
colonel in room of the then deceased Earl of Stair. He was
an officer of very extensive military knowledge, having served
in many of the continental armies, as a volunteer, with credit.

The bloody and glorious battle of Val, fought in 1747, and
which may fitly be considered the closing event of the war,
exhibits in bold relief what may well be esteemed as the
crowning achievement of the Scots Greys. Towards the close
of this desperate fight, the regiment was ordered to charge.
Notwithstanding their resistless bravery and accompanying
success, by which the French cavalry were broken and lost
four standards, these fortunate results and glorious trophies
were dearly won, not merely because of the numerous casual-
ties which the regiment was called to mourn (157 killed and
wounded), but on account of the loss of that which to a
soldier is dearer than life itself—a standard. It fell into the
enemy's hands in the confusion of retreat.

On the conclusion of the peace of Aix-la-Chapelle, in 1749,

the regiment returned to England. In the following year the
Earl of Crawford dying, the coloneley of the regiment was
conferred on the Earl of Rothes, but exchanging into the
Third (Scots Fusiliers) Foot Guards in 1752, he was succeeded in the command by General Campbell, afterwards Duke
of Argyle.

On the breaking out of war with France in 1758, whilst a
newly-raised light troop of the regiment was engaged with
other troops in successive descents on the French coast, viz.,
St Maloes, Cherbourg, and Lunar, the remainder of the regiment was sent to Germany, to aid in the liberation of Hanover from the French yoke. Under the command of the Duke
of Brunswick, the Greys were present at the battles of Bergen
and Minden, but it was not until the assault upon Warbourg
that they seriously encountered the enemy. Their conduct on
the occasion is well described by the Commander-in-Chief
when he says they performed " prodigies of valour." At
Zierenberg the battle was decided by a brilliant and successful charge of the Greys and Inniskillings. A variety of
manœuvres and skirmishes continued to agitate the conflict in
the following year, in all of which the regiment upheld its
reputation. The peace of 1763 at length released the regiment from the turmoil of war, and permitted it to return home
and rest awhile upon its honours.

It is interesting to observe that in nearly every instance
the Royal Scots Dragoons shared the dangers and glories of
the conflict with the Royal Irish or Inniskilling regiments of
dragoons. It is still the same. Scotland and Ireland, side by

side, are to be recognised fighting their country's battles. It is an ancient and happy alliance which, strengthening with years, has been of signal service in the past, is blessed in the present, and promises to be of further use in the future.

In 1770, on the death of the Duke of Argyle, the Earl of Panmure was advanced to the colonelcy, and on his death, in 1782, General Preston was appointed colonel, but he in turn passing away in 1785, made room for General Johnstone.

These were times of peace, and afforded no opportunity for these venerable soldiers to distinguish their stewardships. The succeeding chapter introduces us to more stirring times.

CHAPTER III.

"O Fame, stern prompter of most glorious deeds,
What numerous votaries attend thy call!
For thee the poet sings, the hero bleeds,
And warlike kings bid empires rise or fall."

THE REVOLUTIONARY AND CRIMEAN WARS—1793–1862.

IN 1793 the restless and aggressive spirit which sorely troubled France, developed in the Revolution, once more plunged that nation into war with Britain: nay, not only so, but sending forth her revolutionary incendiaries charged with the subversion of all constitutional government, and seeking to poison the minds of almost every people, her ruthless and frantic demagogues virtually declared war against the whole monarchies of Christendom. Accordingly, a British force, including a portion of the Greys, was sent to the Netherlands under the Duke of York. These were chiefly employed in the sieges of Valenciennes, Dunkirk, Landrecies, etc., which preceded the double battle of Tournay, fought on the 10th and 22d May, 1794. The Greys and the other British cavalry easily routed the newly-raised horsemen of the Revolution, which were sadly degenerated from the splendidly-equipped cavalry of the old monarchy—long the terror of Europe, and most worthy foes. The utter bankruptcy of the French nation prevented them from equipping or maintaining a powerful cavalry, and, in consequence, we find the armies of the Revolution at that time very deficient in this branch of the service. Notwithstanding the excellence of his troops, the Duke of York found his position untenable, with such a handful, against the overwhelming hosts of France, which were being daily augmented by a starving crowd which the Revolution had ruined, and so forced into the army as the only refuge in those unhappy times. The British, retreating into Germany, reached Bremen in 1795, whence the Scots Greys shortly thereafter returned to England.

Notwithstanding the continuous and bloody wars in which our country was engaged during the next twenty years, the Scots Greys were allowed to pine in quietude on home service, until the campaign of Waterloo called them to take the field.

In the meantime, we take opportunity to enumerate the series of colonels who successively commanded the regiment during this interval. The Earl of Eglinton, appointed in 1795, was succeeded by that brave and distinguished officer, Sir Ralph Abercromby, who fell in the arms of victory on the 28th of March, 1801, at the battle of Alexandria. On his death, the colonelcy was conferred on a no less distinguished officer, Sir David Dundas, who continued to command the regiment until 1813, when, exchanging into the King's Dragoon Guards, he was succeeded by the Marquis of Lothian. This nobleman dying in 1815, made way for an able and accomplished soldier, Sir James Stewart, who, retaining the colonelcy for the lengthened term of twenty-four years, lived to be the oldest general and the oldest soldier, both in one, in the British army. In 1839, Sir William Keir Grant was appointed colonel. As if worthily to recognise the heroic daring of the regiment at Waterloo, it has continued to be commanded by veterans who have earned their laurels in that proud field of fight. Lord Sandys was appointed in 1858, but only enjoyed the honour for two years, when death laid him low, and he was in turn succeeded by the present colonel, General Alex. K. Clarke Kennedy, C.B., K.G. The history of all these brave officers is replete with deeds of heroism, and it would have been truly a pleasant duty, had our space admitted, to have recounted somewhat of their achievements.

During the years of their home service, a part of the regiment was present at the imposing ceremony accompanying the burial of England's Naval Hero, Lord Nelson, in 1805. They were also present at the great review in Hyde Park in 1814, when the allied Sovereigns visited England after the Treaty of Paris.

The following year witnessed the escape of Napoleon from Elba, his return to France, and the general and disgraceful desertion of the French army to their old chief. This untoward event at once arrested the retiring armies of the allies, and recalled them again in haste to Paris. The promptitude and harmony of the measures adopted by the Cabinets of Britain and Prussia enabled their armies forthwith to take the field, and so stemming the returning tide of French despotism, for ever crush the might of the tyrant whose restless ambition, like an evil spirit, had so long troubled Europe. They

were honoured side by side to fulfil the first and last act in
the short but decisive campaign which followed. Six troops
of the Greys were ordered to the theatre of war, and, landing
in the Netherlands in 1815, were brigaded with the Royals
and their old comrades the Inniskillings, under Sir William
Ponsonby. Anticipating no immediate attack from the French,
and the better to obtain supplies, the Duke of Wellington had
disposed his army as a chain of posts to watch the movements
of the enemy. While separated from the Prussians, under
Blucher, both armies narrowly escaped destruction. The
immediate and personal presence of so able and enterprising
a General as Napoleon, at the head of a powerful and well-
appointed army — consisting largely of the veterans who,
smarting under the disasters of a previous year, burned for
revenge, or of those who, so unfortunately for their chief, had
been too long incarcerated as garrisons in the distant fortresses
of the Oder and Vistula, but who, released on the conclusion
of the late peace, gladly welcomed their old commander, and
followed him to the field with high hopes to retrieve the
defeats of the past—the immediate presence of such an army
rendered the position of the allies one of considerable danger.
On the night of the 15th of June the Greys were unexpectedly
awakened at the village of Denderhautem, to learn that the
enemy was rapidly advancing to surprise and destroy the
scattered fragments of the army in detail. Accordingly,
immediate orders were issued to the various corps to
concentrate in the vicinity of WATERLOO. A rapid march
of fifty miles brought the Scots Greys, on the evening of the

16th, to Quatre Bras, where some of the British troops were surprised by a portion of the French army, under Marshal Ney, and all but cut to pieces. As the eventful morning of the 18th of June dawned, the British army, having completed its concentration, was drawn up in all the magnificence of battle array, and anxiously waited the arrival of their allies. The Prussians, however, had in the interim been attacked by Napoleon himself at Ligny, and nearly overthrown.

In the battle of Waterloo, the Greys occupied a position in rear of the left centre. It was late in the day when the Earl of Uxbridge brought the orders for that fatal and memorable charge, the result of which had such an effect on the battle. It must have been a splendid sight to have seen these gallant regiments (the Greys, Royals, and Inniskillings) "hurl them on the foe;" and it must have been nobly done, since it specially attracted the attention of the great Napoleon—(particularly referring to the Greys)—and drew forth from him those ever-memorable words: "These are splendid horsemen, but in less than half-an-hour I must cut them to pieces;" and therewith he did all that human mind could devise, or human might achieve, to fulfil his boast, and annihilate these brave soldiers. Despite a dreadful carnage, and the resoluteness with which the successive columns of the French sustained the dreadful fight, they could not prevail against our Gaelic infantry, nor dismay the firmness of the British square, far less withstand the shock of our gallant cavalry—they were broken; and amidst the terrible confusion which ensued, Sergeant Ewart, of the Greys, succeeded in capturing the eagle

and colour of the Forty-fifth French regiment — a trophy
which graced the day, and the eagle is a proud emblem on
the regimental guidon. The Ninety-second Highlanders, reduced to 200 men, had long maintained a terrible conflict
with a column of 2000 of the enemy. At length the Greys,
charging a second time—but with sadly diminished numbers
—came to the assistance of their countrymen, and, together,
nearly annihilated the French. At the grand charge, where
the famous and hitherto invincible Guards of Napoleon were
brought forward for a last effort, the remnant of the Greys,
kept in reserve, awaited the repulse of that dread column,
when, a third time charging, they completed the ruin of their
brave foemen. The loss to the regiment was upwards of 200
men. After the battle, they continued the pursuit of the
enemy to the very gates of Paris; and, with other cavalry,
contributed to prevent Napoleon re-forming or re-organising
his still formidable legions. On the abdication of that mighty
chief, the Greys returned to England in 1816. Thus, in three
days, was the fate of an empire, nay, of the world, decided by
British valour and Prussian firmness.

Passing over a long interval of peace—nearly forty years,
during which nothing of sufficient importance transpired
to call the Greys to take the field—we arrive at the time
(1854) of the Crimean war, when Russian ambition, seeking
to overwhelm Turkey in her weakness, was unexpectedly
met and arrested in her unrighteous aggression, by France
and Britain, on the plains of the Crimea. The Greys, as
an after instalment of the British army, were sent out in the

"Himalaya," and landed in September—a few days after the battle of the Alma. With the Fourth (Royal Irish) and the Fifth (Princess Charlotte of Wales's) Dragoon Guards; and the First (Royals) and Sixth (Inniskilling) Dragoons, they formed the heavy cavalry brigade, under Brigadier-General the Hon. James Scarlett, now Adjutant-General to the Forces and K.C.B. At the action of Balaklava, fought on the 25th of October, and which was almost entirely a cavalry one—the Ninety-third Highlanders being the only infantry regiment actively engaged, and bearing the word on their colours— the Scots Greys, with their old comrades, the Inniskillings, fully sustained the ancient and heroic character of the regiment. Numbering together about 750 men, they charged fearlessly upon a body of 3500 of the very choicest Russian cavalry, defended, moreover, by several batteries; and, breaking the first line, had already pierced the column through, when they were aided in the completion of the victory by the Fourth and Fifth Dragoon Guards. Notwithstanding the desperate and unequal contest, the loss on the side of the Greys was very small. In less than five minutes the splendid array of Russian cavalry was broken and put to flight by about 1400 of the British cavalry. This splendid achievement may be considered as the only important event in which our cavalry assumed a prominent part. The severity of the weather and the prevalence of disease all but destroyed the Greys and their no less gallant comrades, and left our country to lament that so very few of that heroic brigade were spared to return and receive the thanks of a grateful people. Two

years afterwards, peace restored the remnant of the regiment
to its native land.

In closing our brief record of the Second Regiment of
Royal North British Dragoons, we cannot help remarking on
the almost unbroken success and splendid trophies which have
crowned their arms. Scarcely in a single instance was the
regiment broken or necessitated to retreat for its own sake;
only once did a standard fall into the hands of the enemy,
although in its several campaigns the regiment has been
always actively engaged. The reader must feel that we have
great reason to be proud of our countrymen—and that it is
an honest pride we indulge in—when sustained by such an
unprecedented series of triumphs as it has been our pleasure
to record. There is not a heart in Scotland which does not
beat with affectionate sympathy and respect for the "Scots
Greys;" and be they Englishmen or Irishmen who join the
regiment, we feel sure they do so with a generous spirit of
emulation, and ungrudgingly unite with us in doing honour to
our countrymen, who early won a good name for the regiment
by brave deeds—no idle tale, but recorded in the most prominent page of the world's history.

"THE GUARDS."

CHAPTER IV.

"Star of the brave! whose beam hath shed
Such glory o'er the quick and dead;
Their radiant and adored deceit!
Which millions rushed in arms to greet:
Wild meteor of immortal birth!
Why rise in Heaven to set on Earth?"

INTRODUCTION—EARLY HISTORY—THE RESTORATION—TIMES
OF THE STUARTS—THE REVOLUTION—1660–1688.

THE very name of "*Guards*" inspires the idea of all that is
militarily splendid and excellent, great and glorious, noble and
brave, faithful and loyal; and awakens in our minds a host
of most interesting and exciting recollections. Guards are
peculiarly a monarchical and despotic institution, having no
real existence in a Republic or similar form of government.
We would esteem this force as a chosen band of faithful, stalwart, and splendidly-equipped soldiers, specially charged with
the defence of the throne, and calculated, by their imposing

array, to add lustre and dignity to the Crown. Apart from
this holiday display, the history of Guards is pre-eminently
distinguished by the most splendid achievements of heroism
and devotion. Their firmness and fidelity have alike rebuked
the arrogance of the nobles who insulted, and stilled the
turbulence of the people who challenged, the prerogative of
the Crown. Nay, more, when the avalanche of revolution,
descending, overthrew the tottering throne, having enjoyed
the smile, unshaken, the Guards encountered the frowning of
fortune; whilst fond memory bids us trace the footprints of
their greatness.

But the great Napoleon had a truer conception of what
such a corps ought to be, in the constitution of his Imperial
Guard, which at one time amounted to upwards of 100,000
of the best troops in the world. Selected not merely for
fidelity or display, each one was a veteran, who, passing
through the fires of battle and inured to war, had won by his
valour the right to a place in the ranks of "the Brave." No
wonder that Europe trembled when the bearskin of the Guard
was recognised amongst the number of her foes; no marvel
that the charm of invincibility should so long be enjoyed by
this phalanx of warriors, and the halo of victory rest upon
their brows.

Romance presents no scene more deeply touching than is
recorded in the page of history, when, amid the crumbling ruins
of his colossal empire—under the eye and directed by the
transcendent genius of their beloved chief, which never on
any occasion shone forth more conspicuously—the shattered

remnant of the French Guards, faithful amid the faithless,
with unmurmuring constancy and heroic devotion, withstood,
all but alone, the attack of allied Europe; dealing out the
same terrible blows as of old, which, were it possible, must
have rescued their country from the countless hosts which
already desecrated her plains. But the closing scene was
postponed for an after year, when France once more marshalled around the Guard, and Napoleon cast the fatal die for
empire or ruin. What Austria, Russia, Prussia, nay, banded
Europe, had failed to do, our British soldiers achieved. The
spell was broken, as the Guard was overthrown. Noble and
brave, ever commanding our respect in their life, they were
doubly so in their death. We cannot help according this
tribute to so brave a foe. Nay, we feel honoured as, regarding
their grave on the plains of Waterloo, we shed a tear for the
worthy representative of the Guard; and, lingering beside
the relics of "the mighty dead," we catch the meaning of their
watchword—

"THE GUARD DIES, BUT NEVER SURRENDERS."

Guards claim to be of a very ancient origin. Perhaps the
earliest record of such a force is to be found in the Bible,
where—in times of the tyranny of Saul, first king of Israel,
1093 B.C.—we read "the goodliest of the young men" (1 Sam.
viii. 11–16; xiv. 52) "were chosen" for himself, and "their
hearts touched" (1 Sam. x. 26), so that "they followed him"
as a guard. Notwithstanding this ill-omened inauguration,
Guards have been perpetuated, and embraced in the military

institutions of the several States which successively attained
the dominion of the known world, especially where victorious
ambition induced them to reject the simplicity of the Republic and adopt the glitter and the pomp of Imperialism.
In despotic monarchies, princes have generally selected their
Guards from foreigners, as less likely to be affected by the
political struggles which from time to time agitated the nation
and threatened the security of the throne. The Guard thus
selected frequently included exiles of rank—of noble, nay,
royal blood. To the Protestant refugees, which the persecu-
tions of the Church of Rome had expatriated, the Guard presented a very general, an honourable, and a secure retreat.
These, as well as the chivalrous and adventurous spirit of
Scotsmen, are foremost amongst the many causes which have
led our countrymen to enlist as the Guard in nearly every
State in Europe.

Coming nearer home, and more immediately to our text,
we find, in England, that Henry VII., in 1485, raised a body-
guard of 50 men, afterwards increased to 200, and styled it
the "Yeomen of the Guard." In 1550, Edward VI. added a
corps of Horse Guards; whilst, in Scotland, at a very early
period, "the Archers of the Guard" surrounded and upheld
the Sovereign.

The Guards of the present British army, comprised in three
regiments—the first of which containing three, and the others
two battalions each—were raised about the year of the Restoration, 1660. The union, and consequent intermixture of the
peoples of the two, nay, of the three nations, has so assimi-

lated the composition of our regiments, that, whatever may
have been their origin, it is exceedingly difficult now to discover aught of the ancient landmarks—national or county—
which once characterised them. Still, it is our business, in the
present undertaking, to trace these originals, and do justice to
the land, whichever it be, that, in earlier years, contributed its
mite to lay the foundation of the present renown of our army.

From the intimate way in which our Guards have always
been associated in duty and a brilliant career of honour, we
have preferred briefly to sketch their history together, rather
than separately and severally. In such a narrative as we have
entered upon, it is scarcely possible to avoid repetition, many
of the regiments having seen the same service. It must
therefore be admitted as a necessary evil; we only trust the
good old story of our nation's glory will not suffer by being
twice told.

The Coldstream, or Second Regiment of Guards—which,
although second in the Army List, is nevertheless the senior—
was raised by General Monk (afterwards Duke of Albemarle)
about the year 1650. They were principally formed from
Fenwick's and Hesellrigg's Regiments, and took their name
from their having proceeded from Coldstream on their famous
march to restore the "Merry Monarch!" Born during a time
of war, they were early initiated into its bloody toils. They
formed part of the army of General Monk, which, in name
of Oliver Cromwell, subdued and occupied Scotland. With
the Scottish army, they marched into England in 1660, were
quartered in London, and there effectually helped to maintain

peace between the factions of the Parliament and army, which
then struggled for the dominion of the State—vacant by the
death of the Protectorate. Ultimately, the intrigue of General
Monk effected the present deliverance of the country from
the disorders which distracted Government, by the restoration
of the monarchy in the person of Charles II. On the disbandment of the army, Charles, grateful for the good offices
of Monk, retained his—the Coldstream—regiment in his own
service. The alarm attending the insurrection of Venner, in
1660—a fanatic preacher, who was ultimately overpowered,
and his followers, about thirty in number, nearly all slain—
presented a favourable opportunity, which the King was not
slow to improve, for insisting upon Parliament granting him
leave to raise money to maintain an additional military force
for his own and the nation's safeguard. The result was the
formation of a chosen body of troops, chiefly composed of
Jacobite gentlemen who had shared with him the vicissitudes
of exile, and so constituted the First, or Grenadier Guards,
under Colonel Russell. Two years later, 1662, the resistance
which the unreasonable demands of the King upon the Scottish Presbyterians stirred up, induced the formation in Scotland, amongst other troops, of a regiment of Scots Foot Guards
—the Scots Fusilier, or Third Regiment of Guards—the command being conferred on the Earl of Linlithgow.

Whilst a small body of the Guards were hotly engaged on
the shores of Africa, heroically defending against the Moors
the fortress of Tangier—the profitless dowry of the Queen of
Charles II.—the main body of the Grenadiers and Coldstreams,

or, as they were then called, the First and Second Regiments of Guards, were employed at home sustaining the tottering throne of the monarch. Failing to profit by the lessons which a recent adversity were so well fitted to teach, Charles, like the rest of his unhappy race, devoted to his own indulgence, plunged heedlessly into all the excesses of folly and passion. Casting aside or neglecting the cares of his kingdom, so far at least as they interfered with his own gratification, he consigned to creatures of his pleasure, to the bigotry of fawning Jesuits, or the blind fanaticism of a cruel brother (the Duke of York) the interests, the business, and the duties of royalty. Amid such dissoluteness and misrule, the Guards, whilst fulfilling their duty, must ofttimes have been forced to witness the dark intrigues of a licentious court; nay, more, they were frequently called to obey officers who had obtained commissions from their having ministered discreditably to the passionate appetites of superiors, or as being the fruit of some unhallowed intercourse. Their duty, too, required they should guard not merely the Sovereign of a great nation, but his *seraglio*—the abandoned crowd who, dishonouring themselves, dishonoured their sex, preyed upon the honour of the nation, with undisguised effrontery daily glittered in finery, and disgraced the palaces of royalty by their presence. Gladly might the brave and honourable soldier welcome a respite from such irksome duties and the influences of such evil examples on the field of battle; but these were times of comparative peace. It was not until Charles had sunk into the grave, the victim of his own indulgence, and his brother, the Duke of York,

had ascended the throne as James II., that the peace was
disturbed—and then but for a moment—by the pretensions
and rebellion of Monmouth, speedily terminated by the battle
of Sedgemoor, in 1685. During the reign of James II., who
departed not from the evil ways of his brother, but added injustice and cruelty to the lengthy catalogue of royal iniquities,
only one incident would we notice as belonging to the history
of the Coldstreams, and as emphatically declaring how far
even these stood apart from the sins of the age. James had
committed to the Tower the Archbishop of Canterbury and
other six bishops, who dared respectfully to remonstrate with
the King on behalf of their Protestant brethren, injured by
the pretensions of the Roman Catholics. Faithful to their
duty, the Coldstreams nevertheless received these martyrs to
their ancient faith with every token of respect and reverence.
From the heart of many a soldier ascended the prayer, and
from his eye dropped the dewy tear, as he guarded the gloomy
dungeons of their prison.

At length, when the cup of royal iniquity was full to over-
flowing, when the follies and cruelties of the race of Stuart
had alienated the affections of an otherwise loyal people, then
the oppressed, called to arms, with one voice drove the last
and worst representative of that unfortunate family from the
throne. Then, even then, when all else failed him, even his
own children—the Duke of Grafton, Colonel of the Grenadier
Guards, deserting—the Guards, the Coldstreams, remained
faithful, and with their Colonel, Lord Craven (appointed on
the death of Monk, in 1670), at their head, refused to give

place to the stranger. Nor did they forsake the unhappy prince, or for a moment belie their allegiance to him, until his pusillanimous flight had rendered their services no longer of advantage to him. Then only did they make their peace with the new Sovereign—William, Prince of Orange. Respecting their constancy to the fallen monarch, and recognising the Guards to be men of worth, the Prince—now the King—retained their services, nor hesitated to confide his own person to their keeping, as the faithful body-guard of a constitutional throne.

Aware that an officer, well versed in military histories, and to whose kindness we are largely indebted for much valuable information embraced in this compilation, is now preparing the annals of the Guards, in separate volumes, we forbear saying more of the Grenadiers and Coldstreams, esteeming the history of the Scots Fusilier Guards sufficient for the purposes of our present undertaking, as being the one regiment of the three undoubtedly Scottish.

CHAPTER V.

" Caledonians, brave and bold!
Heroes, never bought or sold!
Sons of sires, who died of old
To gild a martial story!"

SCOTS FUSILIER GUARDS—SCOTTISH CIVIL WARS—REVOLUTION.

WHILST the Grenadiers and Coldstreams were unwilling witnesses to the *profligacy* and *lewdness* of the Court, the Scots Foot Guards, since their establishment in 1661, were more especially the witnesses of its *cruelties*. The inquisition established by Royal Commission, and presided over by the then Duke of York, rioted in the shedding of the blood of "the faithful," and with merciless cruelty persecuted and tortured our Covenanting forefathers. In 1679, the Scots Foot Guards were called to make their first essay in arms in the defence of Glasgow. Their firm front, as they withstood the army of the Covenanters, may be said to have stemmed the torrent of rebellion, and saved the Government and the royal cause from the ruin which threatened it. At the battle of Bothwell Bridge they were charged with the attack upon the bridge, which, although desperately defended, they ultimately carried. This single achievement was victory; the terror, the panic it inspired in the still formidable army of the Covenanters, led to a disorderly flight, even before the royal troops could be brought across the river and formed in line of attack.

The Scots Foot Guards continued to be deeply involved in the strifes of these unhappy times. Towards the close of their sojourn in Scotland, 200 of the regiment, under Captain Streighton, associated with a portion of the Scots Greys, were employed in taking summary and merciless vengeance upon Macdonald of Keppoch and his unfortunate clan, because of their recent raid upon the Macintosh. Immediately thereafter, the imminent danger to the Crown, caused by the threatened irruption of the Prince of Orange, which was so soon to overthrow the existing dynasty, induced James to draw together to London the whole reliable forces of the kingdom. Accordingly the Scots Foot Guards, under their colonel, Lieutenant-General Douglas, marched with the Scottish army southward. Arriving in London towards the close of October, the regiment, 1251 strong, was quartered in the vicinity of Holborn. Advanced with the royal army, the Scots Foot Guards were stationed at Reading. Here, becoming tainted with the general disaffection then prevalent, a battalion deserted to the Prince of Orange. The events in the sequel, bringing about the dissolution of the authority of the King, and the establishment of the House of Orange under William and Mary, speedily reunited the battalions of the regiment under the new authority, and it is hereafter to be regarded as the Scots Fusilier, or Third Regiment of Guards.

The title of Scots Fusilier Guards was conferred on them as late as the 22d April, 1831.

The ambitious views of Louis XIV.—"*Le Grand Monarque*"—of France were for the moment paralysed, as he found himself outdone in his calculations by the unexpected turn of events in England—the overthrow of the Stuarts and the splendid triumphs of the House of Orange. Nettled by these disappointments, he readily entertained the schemes of James, not so much that he desired the restoration of that imbecile monarch—even although, as hitherto, enjoying the shadow of independent power, he should continue the tool of the Jesuits of France—but rather that he might find a favourable pretext to trouble the House of Orange, whom he had been long accustomed to regard as his natural and mortal foe. He aspired, moreover, to unite the Netherlands—the hereditary dominion of the Stadtholder—to France, perchance to reduce these sea-girt isles of ours to acknowledge his authority and become an appanage of his Crown. Whilst James—encouraged by the fair promises of Louis—laboured to fan into flame the discontents of the English Jacobites, the Scottish Clans, and the Irish Papists, Louis prepared formidable armaments by sea and land, with which he speedily assailed the Netherlands. Meanwhile, aided by the natural reaction which generally follows the outburst of strong feelings, James succeeded but too well in his malignant purpose; in Scotland, by the rebellion of the Highland Clans, under Viscount Dundee, and in Ireland, by the rebellion of Irish Papists, under Tyrconnell. It required all the firmness and ability of William to meet this formidable coalition, which threatened his dominions at home and abroad; but the King, who could point to times in his eventful history when, with far less promise of a successful issue, he had overthrown more powerful foes—sustained now, too, by the veteran experience of Schomberg and the rising genius of Marlborough—promptly prepared to uphold his new-gotten and extensive authority as the Champion of the Protestant cause, a title which he had long enjoyed, and a faith which, despite the wrathful persecution of kings, he had owned and protected.

For a time, in Scotland, victory seemed indecisive, but after the death of Dundee at Killiecrankie, the cause of James, languishing for a while, was at length abandoned as hopeless by the Clans, and in 1691 the rebellion terminated by their submission. In Ireland, the success of James was complete, with the exception of Londonderry and Enniskillen, which, being resolutely and gloriously defended as the last bulwarks of Irish Protestantism, still held out. Even the arrival of Schomberg, in 1689, at the head of a considerable number of newly-raised regiments of English and French Huguenots, aided by a Dutch force, failed to do more than awe the rebels. In the following year William himself joined the army, with large supplies, and by his presence revived the spirit of his troops—now increased to 36,000. A battalion of the Scots Foot Guards at the same time recruiting the royal army, led by their colonel, General Douglas, were present at the battle of the Boyne, where they materially contributed to the overthrow of the Irish rebels. They were

also present with the army, under Ginkel, which ultimately
dispersed the troops of the malcontents, driving James from
the throne of Ireland, and so united the island once more
to the British Empire.

While these events were taking place at home, Marlborough had been sent in command of a British contingent,
which comprised, with other troops, a battalion of the Scots
Foot Guards and one of the Coldstream Guards, to act
with the Dutch and German allies, under Prince Waldeck,
against the French in the Netherlands. It is interesting
to note this, as being the first effort in arms of the Scots
Foot Guards upon a foreign shore and against a foreign foe.
In the first action of the campaign, fought at Walcourt, our
Guards were present, but occupied no very important post,
the brunt of the battle having been sustained by the Coldstreams, under Colonel Talmash, the Sixteenth Regiment of
Foot and the First Regiment of Royal Scots, under Colonel
Hodges. Although forming a part of the Scottish brigade, the
regiment, indeed the army, achieved nothing of importance
until 1692, when King William, having effectually secured
peace at home, placed himself at the head of his forces, infusing
by his presence new energy and life into the war. Notwithstanding the enthusiasm which pervaded the troops when
William assumed the command, they could make no impression upon the French army, directed by the abilities of the
Duc de Luxembourg. On the contrary, the allies were
doomed to suffer severe defeats at Steenkirk in 1692, and
Lauden in 1693. In the latter, Corporal Trim, in Sterne's

renowned "Tristram Shandy," is represented to have been wounded whilst serving with his master, the kindly-hearted Uncle Toby, in Leven's regiment, now the Twenty-fifth King's Own Borderers. The after campaigns are unmarked by any decisive event. The death of Luxembourg, and the incapacity of his successor—Villeroy—enabled the confederates somewhat to retrieve the disasters of the past. Soon the almost impregnable fortress of Namur—bravely defended by Marshal Bouffleurs, and as bravely assailed by our troops—was, after a fearful carnage, lost to France. In 1697, weary of a war which had been fraught with no decided success on either side, the peace of Ryswick put an end for the present to a further waste of blood and treasure.

The Guards, returning to England, enjoyed but for a short space a respite from active service. France having for a moment tasted the sweets of victory, having largely recruited her armies, thirsted for more blood, longed for new worlds to conquer; whilst her ambitious lord, grasping, through minions of his house, the vacant throne of Spain, once more roused the allied wrath of Europe. During the previous reign our country had groaned under a shameful vassalage to France. The gold of the crafty Louis had outweighed the feeble sense of honour which yet lived and lurked amid the corrupt Court of James. But the accession of William to the throne put an end to these traitorous traffickings for the independency of the land. The new rule and healthier administration of the House of Orange dispelled the night of slavery, revived the drooping spirit of liberty,

and restored the nation to its true manhood. Even now did
she begin to assume that position of first importance among
the continental powers which she has never ceased honourably
to retain. Her alliance was anxiously courted, and her enmity
dreaded by all. With becoming majesty her ministers may
be said to have presided in the councils of the nations. With
terrible might she threw the weight of her sword into the
scale as an arbiter—the defender of the right.

In 1701 and 1702 the British army was being assembled
in the Netherlands, and posted in the vicinity of Breda—
the Guards forming an important part of the force. Meanwhile the Dutch and German auxiliaries were drawing
together their several contingents. Difficulties arose amongst
the confederates as to the officer who should assume the
chief command. Happily, however, these were at length
overcome. The Earl of Athlone, as the senior, waving his
claim, the command of the allied army was conferred on
Marlborough, who, in the campaigns which were about to
open, should win laurels of a mighty fame. From the great
number of strong fortresses which studded the plains of the
Netherlands and guarded the frontier, the campaigns were,
in consequence, largely made up of perplexing manœuvres
and sieges. It is, however, worthy of notice that in each
year the might and energy of the combatants were concentrated into one great fight, rather than a succession of minor
engagements. The character of the country, no doubt, helped
to this mode of warfare. Thus we record, in succession, the
great battles of Blenheim, in 1704; Ramilies, in 1706; Oude-

narde, in 1708; Malplaquet, in 1709. It is unnecessary to
detail the marchings and counter-marchings of the Guards as
they waited upon the several sieges; sufficient be it to say,
they did "the State some service." At Nimeguen, with
the First Royals, they rendered essential service in repelling
an unexpected attack of an immensely superior French force,
who had hoped to surprise and proudly capture the allied
chiefs in the midst of their deliberations. In 1703 the strongholds of Huy and Limburg capitulated to the allies. During
this campaign the Guards were brigaded with the Fifteenth,
Twenty-third, and Twenty-fourth Regiments under General
Withers. But the succeeding year was destined to witness
a far more magnificent achievement—the sudden and rapid
transference of the British army from the plains of the
Netherlands to the valley of the Danube: a movement which,
affording timely succour, and graced by the triumphs of
Schellenberg and Blenheim, restored the sinking fortunes of
the Imperial arms, and proved the deliverance of Germany.
Associated with the First Royals, the Twenty-third Regiment,
with detachments from other corps, the Guards sustained a
terrible fight and suffered a severe loss in storming the heights
of Schellenberg. Their valour on this occasion was most
conspicuous. The furious and repeated assaults of their gallant foe entailed frequent repulses; still their firmness was
unconquerable; again and again they returned to the attack,
until their perseverance was at length crowned with complete
success in the utter rout of the enemy. But this defeat on
the part of the French and Bavarians was only the prelude to

a more terrible disaster. The allied army of Germans, Dutch, Prussians, and British, driving the enemy before them, at length halted in the neighbourhood of Blenheim, where the French and Bavarians, largely recruited and strongly posted, under Marshals Tallard and Marsin, had resolved to try the issue of battle. In the action which followed, the Guards had six officers killed and wounded. After the siege and surrender of Landau, which immediately followed this victory, the Guards returned with the army to the Netherlands, where, in the succeeding campaigns, they were hotly engaged, forcing the enemy's lines at Helixem, and more especially at the great pitched contests of Ramilies, Oudenarde, and Malplaquet. In 1712 the peace of Utrecht once more restored them to their native land.

Meanwhile the Spanish Peninsula was the scene of a con- flict, although conducted on a less gigantic scale, embittered by the personal presence of the rival sovereigns—Philip of Bourbon and Charles of Austria. France having espoused the cause of Philip—which was really the cause of the people— had so vigorously pressed the allies, that notwithstanding the presence of a British force, they could hardly maintain a footing in the Peninsula for themselves, or for Charles as claimant to the throne. The war is remarkable as developing the military abilities of two most illustrious soldiers who successively directed the French armies—the Duke of Berwick and the Duc de Vendôme. In 1704 Gibraltar had been captured by a party of British sailors. A portion of the Guards garrisoned the fortress, and heroically withstood all

the efforts of the Spaniards to recover it. In the following
year the British fleet arrived, and forced Marshal Tessé to
raise the siege, in consequence of which the Guards were
withdrawn to form a part of the expedition under the Earl
of Peterborough, which landed in Catalonia and captured
Barcelona. Soon, however, this transient success was dissipated by the return of the French and Spanish armies, who
in turn besieged the British. After enduring many privations,
and making a gallant defence, the besieged were relieved in
the eleventh hour by the presence of a British squadron with
reinforcements. But this temporary aid only served, by
elevating the hopes of the garrison, to induce a more serious
disaster, in the utter rout of the allies at the battle of
Almanaza which shortly followed, and virtually gave the
kingdom to the House of Bourbon. Urged by Marlborough,
the British Government were roused to prosecute the war
with greater vigour in Spain than hitherto, as being a diversion of the utmost importance to the allied operations in the
Netherlands, Germany, and Italy. Accordingly, in 1709 two
formidable armies were sent out, one to act in Portugal, under
Lord Galway, and the other in Spain, under Generals Staremberg and Stanhope. The latter of these included a battalion
of the Scots Fusilier Guards. Advancing upon Madrid, everything seemed to promise success to their enterprise—the
speedy downfall of the Bourbon dynasty, and the establishment of the House of Austria upon the throne. Their advance
was distinguished by the victory of Saragossa, in which the
British captured thirty standards and colours. The French

General retiring, waited his opportunity, when, with recruited ranks, and the popular opinion on his side, he returned and forced the British, under Staremberg and Stanhope, to make a precipitate retreat, in course of which General Stanhope, at the head of 6000 troops, including the Scots Fusilier Guards, was overtaken at Birhuega by a superior force of the enemy. The British for two days heroically defended themselves, but were ultimately forced to surrender.   General Staremberg, however, somewhat repaired the disaster by defeating the enemy in the battle of Villa Viciosa with great slaughter, and thus secured for his wearied yet gallant troops a safe retreat.

In 1715 the Scots Fusilier Guards were placed in garrison in Portsmouth and Plymouth. Notwithstanding the rebellious in Scotland of 1715 and 1719 the regiment continued to be peacefully employed in the south. In 1722 the colonelcy was conferred on General St Clair.

CHAPTER VI.

"Heroes!—for instant sacrifice prepared;
Yet filled with ardour and on triumph bent
'Mid direst shocks of mortal accident—
To you who fell, and you whom slaughter spared
To guard the fallen, and consummate the event,
Your country rears this sacred monument."

WAR OF THE AUSTRIAN SUCCESSION—SEVEN YEARS' WAR—
AMERICAN INDEPENDENCE—FRENCH REVOLUTION—CRIMEA
—ANTICIPATED RUPTURE WITH THE UNITED STATES—
1742–1862.

THE family feuds which at this time divided the House of
Austria once more kindled the flames of continental war.
In support of the Austrians, George II. sent a British army
into the Netherlands. Assuming himself the command of
the allies, he prepared to combat, on this ancient battle-
field, the confederacy of France, Prussia, and Bavaria. With
the army, the present Scots Fusilier Guards landed in Holland
in 1742, under the Earl of Dunmore. They were present at
the battle of Dettingen in 1743, where the French were
signally defeated. In the following year Marshal Wade
assumed the command of the allies. Nothing of importance
was undertaken until 1745, when the Duke of Cumberland
was appointed to the command; the Guards were at this

period brigaded with the Forty-second Royal Highlanders, (then making their first campaign as the Forty-third Regiment, or "Black Watch," which latter title has recently been confirmed to them.) At the battle of Fontenoy, fought for the relief of Tournay, this brigade was charged with the attack upon the village of Veson. Here the French, strongly entrenched, made a gallant defence, but were forced to yield to the fierce onset of such a chosen body of troops. The ill success of the Dutch auxiliaries in other parts of the field, and the last and desperate charge of Marshal Saxe at the head of the French Guards, with the Irish and Scottish brigades in the French service, led on by the young Chevalier, speedily changed the fortunes of the day, compelled the allies to retreat, and our brave Guards reluctantly to relinquish the important post their valour had won.

Meantime, Prince Charles Edward having landed in Scotland, set up the standard of rebellion, and summoned the tumultuous and fierce array of the clans to do battle for his pretensions to the throne. The war on the Continent having occasioned the withdrawal of a large body of the regular army, the rebels succeeded in driving before them the few troops which had been left at home. Their progress southward into England promised the speedy downfall of the House of Brunswick, and the restoration of that of Stuart. The timely return of the major part of the army, including the Scots Fusilier Guards, from Holland, at this juncture, arrested the advance of the rebels upon London, and occasioned their precipitate retreat into Scotland. A strong force of the king's troops, including a portion of the Guards, advanced in pursuit of the prince, whilst the remainder, grouped in positions in and around London, prepared to defend the country from the threatened descent of the French. The bloody defeat of Culloden, as it utterly ruined the rebel army, so it terminated the war, by the dispersion or submission of the clans and the flight of the prince.

> Culloden's moor! a darker scene
> Of civil strife thy sons have seen,
> When for an exiled Prince ye bled,
> Now mourn alas! your "mighty dead,"
> The brave o' bonnie Scotland.

Peace having been restored at home, the Scots Fusilier Guards, with other regiments, returned to Holland in 1747, where the French, in their absence, had made considerable progress. The only event of importance which occurred in the campaign was the battle of Val, in which the immense superiority of the French compelled the retreat of the British, under the Duke of Cumberland. In 1748 peace was concluded at Aix-la-Chapelle.

Disputes arising as to the boundary line of the British and French colonies, and neither party accepting a peaceful solution, war was declared in 1756. Whilst the reputation of the British arms was being gloriously sustained on the distant continent of America and in Lower Germany, the Guards were engaged in frequent descents upon the French coast. At St Cas they specially distinguished themselves. The peace of 1763 secured to our colonists the quiet possession of the fruits of their own industry against the cupidity of the French. Scarcely had this result been attained when difficulties arose with the colonists themselves, by their refusal to be taxed by the home government without an equivalent representation. Our armies were accordingly recalled in 1775 to the American continent, whilst the colonists, preparing for a vigorous defence, allied themselves with their late enemies, the French. The Scots Fusilier Guards formed a part of the British expedition, and under Clinton, Howe, and Cornwallis, upheld their ancient reputation for discipline and valour in the fresh and difficult warfare to which, in the desolate wilds of the New World, they were called. This unfortunate war, fraught with disastrous results, and waged with great fury and bitter hate on both sides, was concluded in 1783, and secured the independence of the colonists, who formed themselves into a Republic, under the designation of the United States.

In 1782 the Duke of Argyll had been promoted to the colonelcy of the Scots Fusilier Guards.

France, too long enslaved but now suddenly emancipated from the galling tyranny of "the privileged orders," writhing under all the miseries of Revolution, had ruined every vestige of righteous government, and consigned the nation to the more cruel bondage of a despot mob. At length these evil influences were incarnated in the demon rule of the "Reign of Terror." Bankrupt in every sense, to feed the starving crowd who daily clamoured for bread, proved a task too hard for the wretched creatures who had been elevated to power through the blood of their predecessors, and who called themselves the Government, whilst the whim of the people continued them in favour. As they were but the Government of a day, so they cared little for the consequences beyond their own time. To maintain their popularity, and if possible avert the fate which ever threatened them from the blind fury and unbridled passion of the mob, they gladly entered upon a universal crusade against the governments and liberties of neighbouring nations, hoping thereby to direct the merciless wrath of the people into this new channel, and so save themselves. Soon the ranks of the armies were recruited by a fierce and undisciplined multitude. But the very magnitude of these armaments proved their ruin, and but for the spasmodic efforts of the Revolutionary tyrants in the national defence, which achieved marvels, the Revolution must have been crushed at this early stage. A small British force, including the Coldstream and Scots Fusilier Guards, was sent over to the Netherlands, under the Duke of York, who vainly endeavoured to stem the torrent of aggression in that direction. Equally fruitless were the attempts of the British Cabinet to patch up an alliance amongst the nations, so as effectually to unite them in defending the liberties of Europe. Although the victory of Lincelles graced our arms, still, alone, our troops could not hope for success against the immense armaments that continued to emerge from France. The British were therefore compelled to recede before the advancing tide, and postpone "the day of reckoning."

Amongst the many ruthless and reckless, yet bold and able

men which the Revolution produced, none claims such a space
in history, none so suited his times, none was so equal to the
crisis, as Napoleon Bonaparte. His brilliant achievements in
Italy under the Consulate had already taken the public mind
by storm, when in 1801 he invaded Egypt, crossed the sterile
desert, overthrew the feeble cohorts of the Sultan, and
threatened to add Syria to the empire of the French. At
Acre his legions were for the first time arrested by the firmness of British valour. In 1801 a British army, including
the present Coldstream and Scots Fusilier Guards, was sent to
Egypt, under Sir Ralph Abercromby, to expel the invader.
Thirsting for some new field of conquest to feed his ambition,
Napoleon had returned to France, leaving General Menou to
make good the defence. The defeats of Mandora and Alexandria effectually broke the already sinking spirit of the
French, and resulted in their abandonment of Egypt. In
consideration of their efforts in this service, the Coldstream
and Scots Fusilier Guards have been allowed the distinction
of "the Sphinx," with the word "EGYPT."

The cloud which for a moment dimmed the lustre of his
arms, as this province was wrested from his sway, was soon
dispelled in the glories that elsewhere crowned his efforts,
especially in Spain, which, by the foulest perfidy, he had
virtually made a portion of his vast empire. Frequent
expeditions had been contemplated—some had sailed, two at
least had landed on the shores of the Peninsula—still nothing
decisive had been accomplished towards aiding the Spanish
and Portuguese in the expulsion of the French. In 1809,

however, a powerful British force under Sir Arthur Wellesley, afterwards "the Great Duke," was sent out, including the Coldstream and Scots Fusilier Guards. It is unnecessary at present to follow them throughout the glories of the war, as we shall have occasion to do so in after chapters; enough for our purpose to mention the battles of Talavera (1809) and Barrosa (1811), in which they specially distinguished themselves.

Having delivered Spain, Sir Arthur Wellesley, now Lord Wellington, advanced into France, and sorely pressed the retiring foe. It needed all the ability of Marshal Soult to hold together the shattered remnant of his broken and dispirited army. With masterly tact and skill he preserved a seeming order in his retreat, so as to save the army from the ignominy of a flight. Meanwhile, France having exhausted her resources, her people became tired of the yoke of the Emperor, who, whilst fortune smiled upon his arms, had been to them a very god, but now that the spell of victory was broken, was revealed in truer colours as the ambitious yet mighty despot. Martial glory, as the ruling passion of the nation, had bewitched the people, and received in ready sacrifice the best blood of the land. Long, too long, had the power of Napoleon, like a dark shadow, rested upon one-half of the known world, whilst the empty vanity of unhappy France was charmed by delusive visions of victory. The times were sadly changed. With a melancholy joy Europe had witnessed the utter ruin of the splendid and countless host which the fiat of the mighty chief had pressed into his service. Buried beneath the snows

of a Russian winter—hurled in confusion back upon his own
land—

"The might of the Gentile, unsmote by the sword,
Hath melted like snow in the glance of the Lord."

This appalling catastrophe, combined with British successes in the Peninsula, had revived the spirit of the
nations, allied them in a holy crusade, and marshalled the
might of Europe in array to crush the tyrant. One by one,
they wrested from his sway the kingdoms he had engulfed,
and which groaned beneath a cruel bondage. Step by step,
their hosts converged, as the tide of war rolled, towards
France. All but alone, with his brave and devoted Guard
driven to bay, he made a desperate but unavailing stand on
the plains of France. In vain he addressed the patriotism of
the people; already the fountain had been dried up by his
incessant wars and the unremitting demands he had made
upon the blood and treasure of the land. Surrendering, at
length, the hopeless contest, abdicating the throne, he passed
into honourable exile in Elba.

Ambition, still the tempter, assailing, soon prevailed.
Eluding the vigilance of the British fleet, he succeeded in
escaping into France, accompanied by a few of his old Guard,
who had shared his exile. The mind of the people, which for
more than twenty years had lived amid a wild delirium of
excitement, still lingering upon the threshold of the mighty
past, had not yet learned to submit to the more benignant rule
of peace. The army, unwisely disbanded, or despoiled of those
symbols of glory which their valour had so nobly won—tro-

phies which, to a soldier, must ever be dear as life itself—
were being consumed by the ennui of idleness, longed for new
employment. Hence the return of Napoleon paralyzed resistance as recalling the military glory of the Empire; awakening
new hopes, promising revenge for the past, employment for
the present, and glory for the future, it stirred within the
bosom of the soldier and the lower classes of the people a
reverence and adoration, almost amounting to idolatry.
Rapidly advancing from stage to stage, as on a triumphal
march, Napoleon found himself once more at Paris—hailed
Emperor—it is true, doubted by the better classes of the
people, but worshipped by the army. His desperate efforts
soon enabled him to take the field, at the head of a powerful
and well-appointed army, with which he proposed to meet in
detail, and so destroy, his numerous and returning enemies.
Unfortunately for him, he chose the Netherlands to be the
scene, and Britain and Prussia the objects, of his first, and, as
the result proved, his last attack. For a moment a gleam of
sunshine shone upon his path, as he attained the victory of
Ligny, over the Prussians under Marshal Blucher. Luring
him to destruction, this flash of success was only the precursor
to the dread thunder of Waterloo. Alarmed by the disastrous intelligence of the Prussian defeat and the rapid advance
of the French, Wellington, who commanded the British and
other auxiliaries, quickly concentrated his army near the village of Waterloo. But ere he could accomplish this, Marshal
Ney, at the head of the second French division, had surprised
and fallen upon, with great fury, the British, as they advanced

upon Quatre Bras, on the same day that Ligny was won.
The action was honourably sustained by a few British
Regiments, especially the Twenty-eighth, and the Forty-second,
Seventy-ninth and Ninety-second Highland Regiments. The
heroic stand made by these gave time for the arrival of other
corps, including the Guards—the Scots Fusilier Guards—who
succeeded, after a desperate struggle, in effectually checking
the progress of the French Marshal, and thus depriving him
of a most favourable opportunity of cutting to pieces in detail
our army. Two days later, on the 18th of June, the Duke
had successfully accomplished the concentration of his forces,
which, drawn up in battle array at Waterloo, waited the arrival
of the Prussians, to begin the fight. But Napoleon, perceiving
his advantage in the absence of such an important succour,
rushed eagerly to battle, put forth every effort to achieve
victory, ere Blucher, impeded by the disorders of recent
defeat, could afford any assistance. The Scots Fusilier Guards,
with the Grenadiers and Coldstreams, were stationed in the
chateau and grounds of Hougomont, where they were soon
fiercely assailed by the French, who repeatedly forcing the
gateway, drove the British into the house. Again and again
the enemy were repulsed, but still anew they returned to the
assault. The combat was resolutely maintained, and it was
not until the close of this eventful day, when the French,
repulsed at every point, and gradually relaxing their efforts,
were ultimately driven from the field, that our Guards found
a release from the incessant toils of the fight. The victory
achieved by the British was now completed by the Prussians,

who continued the pursuit—a pursuit which may be said only
to have ceased at the gates of Paris, when, Napoleon abdicating, the war was terminated by the restoration of the old
Monarchy.

From Mr Carter's interesting work on "The Medals of
the British Army," we, by permission, quote the following
refutation in regard to an alleged sum of £500 having
been accorded to a Waterloo veteran :—" A statement has
frequently appeared in the newspapers, which was repeated
after the decease of General Sir James Macdonell, G.C.B.,
on the 15th of May, 1857, that five hundred pounds had
been bequeathed to the bravest man in the British army,
and that the two executors called upon the late Duke of
Wellington, to give him a cheque for the money. As the
story went, the Duke proposed that it should be given to Sir
James for the defence of Hougomont, and that upon the
money being tendered to him, he at first declined to receive
it, but that ultimately he shared it with Sergeant-Major
Fraser of the 3d Foot Guards, now the Scots Fusilier Guards.

" Having recently seen this statement again in print while
these pages were in preparation, and Sir James Macdonell
having about ten years ago mentioned to me that he had
never received the money, I made further inquiries, from
which I ascertained that Sergeant-Major Ralph Fraser is now
a bedesman in Westminster Abbey. Considering that the
above legacy might possibly have been since received, I called
upon the sergeant-major, who lives at 18 West Street, Pimlico,
and is now in his 79th year, in order to ascertain the fact, and

found that it had not. This gallant and intelligent veteran is
in the full possession of his faculties, and, in addition to his
having aided in closing the gate at Hougomont, can look with
becoming pride on his having shared in the following services:
—He was enlisted in the 3d Foot Guards in 1799, and was
embarked for Egypt in 1801. In the landing at Aboukir
Bay, on the 8th of March of that year, the boat in which
Corporal Fraser was contained sixty persons, officers included;
all except fifteen were destroyed by the resistance of the
enemy. He was present at the battles of the 13th and 21st
March; and in the expedition to Hanover, 1805; bombardment of Copenhagen, 1807; and from 1809 to 1814 in the
Peninsula, being present at the capture of Oporto, battles of
Talavera, Busaco, Fuentes d'Onor (wounded in the leg and
thigh), sieges of Ciudad Rodrigo, Burgos (again wounded in
the leg), Badajoz, and St Sebastian; battles of Salamanca,
Vittoria, passage of the Nivelle and Nive. He received, in
addition to the Waterloo medal, that for the Peninsular war,
with bars for Egypt, Talavera, Busaco, Fuentes d'Onor, Ciudad
Rodrigo, Salamanca, Vittoria, Nivelle, and Nive. Sergeant-
Major Fraser was discharged in December, 1818."

This account, doubtless, may be traced to the following
circumstance mentioned by Colonel Siborne in his valuable
History of the Waterloo Campaign :—"Early in August of
that year, and while the Anglo-allied army was at Paris, the
Duke of Wellington received a letter from the Rev. Mr
Norcross, rector of Framlingham, in Suffolk, expressing his
wish to confer a pension of ten pounds a year, for life, on

some Waterloo soldier, to be named by his Grace. The Duke
requested Sir John Byng (the late Lord Stafford) to choose
a man from the second brigade of Guards, which had so
highly distinguished itself in the defence of Hougomont.
Out of numerous instances of good conduct evinced by several
individuals of each battalion, Sergeant James Graham, of the
light company of the Coldstreams, was selected to receive the
proffered annuity, as notified in brigade orders of the 9th
of August, 1815. This was paid to him during two years,
at the expiration of which period it ceased, in consequence
of the bankruptcy of the benevolent donor."

From the heroic character of the battle, our people have
been prevailed on to credit many incidents, which, savouring
of the romantic, suited their tastes, have been accepted as
truisms, but which facts fail to corroborate. "One very
prevailing idea that Wellington gave out the words, 'Up,
Guards, and at them!' is not borne out by fact, for it was
afterwards ascertained from the Duke himself that he did not;
and another, the meeting of his Grace and Marshal Blucher at
La Belle Alliance, after the battle, is equally apocryphal.
This, however, is to be one of the designs of the House of
Lords, and will therefore be handed down to posterity as
a fact." For nearly forty years the Scots Fusilier Guards had
been retained at home, in or around London.

In 1853, the storm which had been long gathering in the
north—presaging wrath to Liberty and to Man—at length
burst forth, and descending with rapacious might upon the
dominions of the Turkish Sultan, threatened to overwhelm in

utter ruin the crumbling remnant of the empire of Constantine. The impatient covetousness of the Czar of Russia had put forth the hand of the spoiler, intending to appropriate the realms of the Sultan, and make Constantinople the southern gate of his colossal empire. Justly alarmed at the already gigantic power of Russia, which promised further to enlarge itself at the expense of the feebler Powers around, France and Britain took up arms, and threw the weight of their potent influence into the contest on behalf of the oppressed Turks, whose single arm had hitherto proved equal to the struggle. Accordingly, France, Turkey, and Britain, ultimately aided by Sardinia, entered the lists of war, to sustain the liberty of Europe against the despotism of the North, adopting as their watchword the memorable words of Lord John Russell, "May God defend the right."

The first battalion of the Scots Fusilier Guards, brigaded with a battalion of the Grenadiers, and another of the Coldstreams, were embarked for the scene of action, which ultimately proved to be the Crimea. They sailed from Portsmouth, in H.M.S. the "Simoom;" and passing successively from Malta, Gallipoli, and Varna, arrived at length in the Crimea. The brigade of Guards, and that of the Highlanders, consisting of the Forty-second, Seventy-ninth, and Ninety-third, under their favourite chieftain, Sir Colin Campbell, were closely allied in all the dangers and glories of the war in the First Infantry division, commanded by his Royal Highness the Duke of Cambridge. The long peace which had preceded the outbreak of hostilities, and the cry for

"greater public economy," which it had induced from a people
long accustomed to look only at the arithmetic of pounds,
shillings, and pence, in such vital questions, had in consequence brought all that magnificent machinery of war,
possessed by our country, to a standstill.   It followed, as
a necessary result, when our Cabinet failed to achieve a
peaceful solution of the matters at issue, as had been fondly
anticipated, and we were unexpectedly called to a declaration
of war, it was found impossible at once to set in motion the
vast machinery of war, which had so long been "laid up in
ordinary."   Hence our gallant troops were doomed to pay the
penalty of our ill-judged economy, and endure many and sore
privations—privations which were the more keenly felt, inasmuch as they were to be endured, amid the snows of a
Crimean winter, by men, too, whose previous life had been
comparatively one of comfort, in no way calculated to fit
the soldier to encounter the pitiless horrors and fatigues of
war.   Disease and want, like armed men, entered the camp,
closely followed by their master, the grim King of Terrors—
Death ; and thus we have been called to lament, with a truly
bitter sorrow, the loss of our brave countrymen, who, alike in
the hospital as in the battle-field, displayed all the grand and
noble qualities of the soldier and the virtues of the true man.
The conduct of the Guards in their first engagement at the
battle of the Alma is described by Marshal St Arnaud as altogether " superb."   Lieutenants Lindsay and Thistlethwayte,
were especially distinguished for their heroic defence of
the colours of the Scots Fusilier Guards.   At the battle of

Inkermann, the Guards, having driven the Russians out of a battery, named the Sandbag Battery, of which they had early possessed themselves, sustained with desperate gallantry the impetuous assaults of the enemy, and, although forced for a moment to give way, were soon again enabled to retrieve themselves, and maintain possession of the battery, around which and for which they so bravely contended. Although stunned by these repeated disasters in the field, yet with that "dogged obstinacy," which has characterised the Russians, conceiving themselves secure behind the battlements of Sebastopol, they still held out. Strengthened in the idea of impregnability, from the fact that this vast citadel of Southern Russia had already withstood six successive bombardments, defied the combined efforts of the Allies by sea and land, and yet no sensible impression had been made, or aught of decided success attained by the besiegers, they hoped that what their valour could not achieve in the battle-field, the snows of winter or the stroke of the pestilence would effect—the destruction of our armies, and their consequent deliverance. The successive fall of the Mamelon, the Malakoff, and the Redan, dispelled this illusion, and prudence, rightly esteemed the better part of valour, induced a timely evacuation ere our Highland Brigade returned to the assault. Sebastopol no longer defensible, the enemy sued for peace, which was granted, and this stronghold of tyranny, dismantled and abandoned, was assumed to be converted into a haven for fishermen and traders, rather than the mighty arsenal, whence had so long issued the formidable fleets which had inspired terror among weaker and neighbouring states—at least so the treaty required. Meanwhile our gallant Guards, returning to England, were welcomed by a grateful country.

It is only now, when the audacious impudence of "Brother Jonathan" had dared to insult our time-honoured flag—

"Which braved a thousand years the battle and the breeze,"

and thought to bully us out of the glorious charter which has conferred upon us the "dominion of the seas," that our Scots Fusilier Guards were once more called to prepare for action; and, having gone across the Atlantic as the van of our army, anxiously waited the signal to avenge, if need be, such unprovoked insult and aggression. Happily our firm demeanour has effectually quelled the storm, and impressed wiser and more wholesome measures, whereby peace has hitherto been continued.

One sentence only shall express our feelings, as we look back upon the history of our *Scots Fusilier Guards*, which we have here attempted to sketch—Every man has nobly done his duty.

THE FIRST ROYAL REGIMENT OF FOOT:

OR,

ROYAL SCOTS.

CHAPTER VIII.

Heroes, in your ancestral line,
Hallow the shades of "Auld Langsyne;"
Men who in their country's story
Shine brightly on the page of glory,
        Noo sleep in bonnie Scotland.

ANCIENT HISTORY—882–1660.

As we approach the history of this venerable regiment we
cannot help feeling all those sentiments of reverence and
respect which are the becoming tribute to an honoured old
age—a history which well nigh embraces, as it awakens,

"The stirring memories of a *thousand years*."

Consistent with the bold and adventurous spirit of the
Scotsman, we find him pushing his fortune in almost every
land under the sun; with a brave and manly heart going
down to the battle of life; blessing, by his industry and enterprise, many a clime wherein he has settled, and so climbing

the loftiest pinnacles of greatness; or, by "diligence in business," earning the kingdom of a merchant prince. Of all the
many and varied departments of life in which the Scotsman
has been distinguished, he is most pre-eminent in the honourable profession of a soldier. Driven from his beloved country
by the cruel tyrannies which from time to time oppressed her,
or exiled by the hard necessities of a pinching poverty—
wandering in many lands, the Scotsman nevertheless gratefully retains the recollection of his fatherland, and, in spirit,
returns with fondness to the endeared associations of home—

"The bonnie blithe blink o' his ain fireside."

Such is the ruling passion which lives in his soul. "Home,
sweet home," exerting a hallowed, chastening influence upon
his daily life, has nerved the soldier's arm, and, by its magic
charm, awakened the energies of the man. As a "guiding
star," it has pointed out the path of honour—like a "ministering angel," its soothing influence has at other times calmed
the troubled sea of life, and, though it be but for a moment,
has given something of peace to the weary, as it is intended
to be a foretaste of the blessedness—

"A something *here* of heaven above."

Already volumes have been written on the martial achievements of the Scottish nation, and we are fully impressed with
the magnitude of our undertaking when, in these brief pages,
we propose to illustrate the heroic tale of our ancient glory.
Nowhere is there a more perfect representative of our exiles

who have been soldiers, amongst "the bravest of the brave,"
in many lands, than is afforded us in our present sketch of the
First or Royal Scots Regiment of Foot. Many and conflict-
ing have been the accounts given of their early history. Some
have imagined the present regiment to be the representative
of the Archers of the Scottish Guard, which, in the days of
Bruce, had been associated with Royalty and the defence of
the Scottish throne; others have given their origin to the
Scottish Guard, which had for many years been the Body
Guard of the French kings; but the most complete and
authentic account, derived from many sources, is that given
by Richard Cannon, Esq. of the Adjutant General's Office,
in the admirable Historical Records of the Royals, wherein
the origin of the regiment is traced to the ingathering
of our exiles, who had hitherto served with great credit as
soldiers, nay as Royal Guards, in the armies of France, Denmark, Sweden, and the States of Holland, to be formed into
one, the present regiment of First Royal Scots Foot. As early
as the year 882 A.D. Charles III., king of France, had selected
from among the exiles a body of Scottish gentlemen, conspicuous for their fidelity and valour, who enjoyed his special
favour, and were incorporated as a Royal Guard. During the
Crusades these followed Louis IX. into Egypt. They were of
infinite value to France, at a time when the disastrous battle of
Agincourt, fought in 1415, had prostrated her power, and all
but reduced her proud and haughty people to be the vassals
and subjects of triumphant England. The Scots Guards were
retained in the service of Charles VII., and a few years later

were joined by a body of 7000 of their countrymen under the
Earl of Buchan, whose abilities as an officer and valour as a
soldier won for him the thanks of a grateful country, who at
the same time conferred the highest compliment and most
splendid military distinction it was in their power to award,
in creating him Constable of France. The Scottish army
in France was subsequently largely increased by farther
instalments of adventurous exiles from " the fatherland,"
These helped to break the yoke of England upon the Continent, and specially distinguished themselves at the battles
of Baugé, 1421, Crevan, 1423, and Verneuille, 1424: so much
so, that Charles, appreciating their worth, selected from their
ranks, first in 1422, a corps of Scots Gendarmes, and thereafter, in 1440, a corps of Scots Guards. On the fair plains
of Italy, so cruelly desolated by the rude hand of war, and so
long the favourite battle-field of princes, whom the poet fitly
styles

" Ambition's honoured fools"—

was afforded the scene where, during the wars of Francis I., our
Scottish Guards, by brilliant exploits, earned a great renown.
The story of their fidelity and devotion is written in their
blood, and illustrated in the fatal defeat of Pavia, 1524, where,
in defence of their master, the chivalric Sovereign of France,
whose exclamation of, " We have lost all, save honour," has
become a household word,—they nearly all perished, and
honourably rest in "a soldier's grave." The relics of this
old Scots Guard returning to France, remained the nucleus,

the root, upon which was formed and ingrafted a new corps
of Scots Guardsmen, whose character and history have been
aptly described by Sir Walter Scott in "Quentin Durward;"
whilst in his "Legend of Montrose" we trace the yearnings
of the mighty soul of the patriot, conjuring into life, by
the magic of his pen and his rare gifts, the story of our
exiled brave, represented in the gallant veteran of Gustavus
Adolphus, "Dugald Dalgetty." The martial qualities and
gallant bearing of our countrymen had attracted the notice
of Gustavus Adolphus, the warlike King of Sweden, and induced him to invite to his standard our adventurous soldiers,
who, under so renowned a leader, were destined to add new
lustre to our military annals. On no occasion did the Scots
respond more heartily, or muster so strongly in the foreign
service of any country, as in the present instance. The army
of this "Lion of the North" at one time comprised eighteen
British regiments, of whom *thirteen* were Scottish; moreover,
his principal officers were Scotsmen.

In the marvellous feats of arms which distinguish the
masterly campaigns of Gustavus, our countrymen had ever a
prominent place.   Having humbled the pride of Poland,
and crippled the power of Russia by successive defeats, on the
restoration of peace, Gustavus, declaring himself the champion
of the Protestants, turned his arms against the formidable
coalition of the Roman Catholic princes of Germany, headed
by the Emperor. The campaign of 1620 proved unfortunate,
by the total defeat of the Protestant army at Prague, their
consequent retreat, and ultimate disbandment in Holland—

" O sacred Truth! thy triumph ceased a while,
And Hope, thy sister, ceased with thee to smile."

Undaunted by these disasters, Gustavus refused to quit the
field, although, for the present, he changed the theatre of war
into Pomerania. From the wreck of the Protestant army, he
carefully selected a chosen body of his favourite Scotsmen,
which, in 1625, he constituted a regiment, conferring the command on Sir John Hepburn. In the war with Poland which
ensued, the Scots enjoyed, as their gallant demeanour in every
instance well merited, the unbounded confidence of the King.
Subsequently, the King of Denmark sent two Scots regiments,
which had been in his service, to aid the Swedish monarch;
and, in 1628, he further received the very welcome reinforcement of 9000 Scots and English. The following incident,
occurring about this time, serves to illustrate the cordial relationship subsisting between this renowned prince and our
adventurous countrymen:—" In a partial action between the
advance-guards, a few miles from Thorn, Gustavus's hat was
knocked off in a personal encounter with one of the enemy's
officers named Sirot, who afterwards wore the hat without
knowing to whom it belonged. On the succeeding day, two
prisoners (one a Scots officer named Hume) seeing Sirot
wearing the King, their master's, hat, wept exceedingly, and
with exclamations of sorrow, desired to be informed if the
King was dead. Sirot, being thus made acquainted with the
quality of his antagonist in the preceding day's skirmish,
related the manner in which he became possessed of the hat,
upon which they recovered a little from their anxiety and

surprise." The success of the Swedish arms at length achieved
a favourable peace, which enabled the King, espousing the
cause of the persecuted Reformers of Germany, once more to
try the issues of war with the Imperialists, and so, if possible,
redeem the disasters of a former campaign. At this period
no fewer than 10,000 Scots and English exiles were in the
Swedish army, and the King had just concluded a treaty
with the Marquis of Hamilton, who had undertaken to enlist
an additional force of 8000 in these Isles.

Next in seniority to the old Scots regiment of Hepburn is
that of Monro, who has written an interesting account of the
achievements of our countrymen in these wars. This last
narrowly escaped an untimely end—a watery grave—having
been shipwrecked near the enemy's fortress of Rugenwald, on
their passage to Pomerania. Lurking in concealment among
the brushwood on the shore during the day, Monro's soldiers at
nightfall boldly assaulted the defences of the enemy, and, by
this unexpected attack, succeeded in capturing the fortress,
where, by great efforts, they maintained themselves against a
vastly superior foe until the arrival of Hepburn's Scots Regiment relieved them. These two regiments, along with other
two Scots regiments—those of Stargate and Lumsdell—were at
this time brigaded together, and styled the *Green Brigade*, so
celebrated in the military history of the period. In 1631, at
the siege of Frankfort, this bold brigade accomplished one of
the most daring feats of arms upon record; where—charged
with the assault upon this all but impregnable fortress, defended by the best troops of the empire—they undauntedly

entered the breach, and—despite the repeated attacks of
the foe, especially of an Irish regiment, who, amongst the
bravest defenders of the place, twice repulsed the assailants,
and fought with the greatest heroism until nearly all were
either killed or wounded—they, by their valour, effected a
lodgment within the walls. Furiously charged by the splendid cavalry of the Imperial cuirassiers, our Green Brigade
resolutely maintained the ground they had won. The trophies
of this conquest were immense. The Green Brigade, after
having aided in the reduction of the many strongholds of
Germany, had penetrated with the army into the very heart
of the empire, where they were destined to play a very conspicuous part in the memorable and momentous battle of
Leipsic. On this occasion, kept in reserve, the Green Brigade
was only brought into action at the eleventh hour, when the
ignoble and cowardly flight of the Saxons, who had been impressed into the Swedish army, rendered the position of
the army perilously critical. Then our brave Scots, sustained on either flank by Swedish horse, advanced, speedily
checked the progress of the enemy, retrieved what the Saxons
had lost, and throwing the enemy into confusion, changed the
fortunes of the day. The Imperialists, no longer able to withstand the repeated and impetuous attacks of our Scottish
brigade, and charged by the Swedish horse, who completed
their ruin, broke and fled. Thus their mighty army, lately
so confident of victory, which a momentary success had
promised, was utterly cut to pieces or dispersed. A variety
of sieges and minor engagements followed this great battle, in

nearly all of which the Swedes and Scots proved triumphant.
Yet, notwithstanding these series of successes, and the several
and sore defeats of the enemy, the position of Gustavus was
becoming daily, by every new advance, more critical; away
from his arsenals, whilst the enemy, within his own territory,
had ample resources at hand with which to repair defeat, and
thus was becoming hourly more formidable. At Oxenford,
the heroic monarch had only an army of 10,000 men around
him, whilst the Duke of Lorraine was at hand with a well-
equipped force of full 50,000. Still, such was the terror
inspired by the marvellous deeds and the known resolution of
this little band of veterans, that, although the enemy was
in the midst of many advantages, he durst not venture
an attack, and feared to arrest the King in his career of
conquest.

Bavaria had now become the scene of the contest. Soon
that important kingdom was over-run, and—with Munich,
its gorgeous capital—surrendered to the northern army. The
death of Gustavus Adolphus, at the fatal battle of Lutzen,
ruined the hopes of his gallant little army, now sadly reduced
in numbers. The Green Brigade was not present on this
disastrous day. By a process of transfer, not at all uncommon
in those times, the remnant of Swedes and Scots were taken
into the pay of France, and, under the Duke of Saxe-Weimar,
laboured to maintain the cause of the Protestant princes,
which had, for ends of her own, been adopted as the cause of
France. Colonel Hepburn, some time previously, had, by permission of the King of Sweden, returned to Scotland with the

Marquis of Hamilton. His parting with his countrymen in his own regiment is thus quaintly described by Monro:—"The separation was like the separation which death makes betwixt friends and the soul of man, being sorry that those who had lived so long together in amity and friendship, also in mutual dangers, in weal and in woe, the splendour of our former mirth was overshadowed with a cloud of grief and sorrows, which dissolved in mutual tears."

Returning to France in 1633, Hepburn was appointed colonel to a new regiment of Scotsmen. By a combination of events, he at length met with his old regiment in the same army, and the relics of the Old Scots Brigade. These were subsequently merged into one large regiment, whose history is hereafter one with that of France, and whose representative is now the *First Royal Scots Regiment of Foot.* By this union, which occurred in 1635, the regiment so constituted attained the extraordinary strength of 8316 officers and men. In the following year they had to lament the loss of their gallant Colonel, who was killed at the siege of Saverne: he "died extremely regretted in the army and by the Court of France." He was succeeded in the command by Lieut.-Colonel Sir James Hepburn, who survived his illustrious relative only one year. Lord James Douglas, son of William, Marquis of Douglas, was promoted to the vacant Colonelcy, and thereafter the regiment is known as "Douglas's Regiment." In the service of Louis XIII. of France, the regiment had entered upon a new theatre of action in the Netherlands, destined to combat the Spaniards, who then were esteemed to form as soldiers the finest infantry in

the world. Against this redoubtable foe our Scotsmen conducted themselves with credit, being present at the siege of St
Omer, the captures of Renty, Catelet, and at Hesden, under
the eye of the monarch himself. During the minority and
reign of Louis XIV., known as "Louis le Grand," the regiment
was destined to share the glories of a splendid series of
triumphs, successively won by the illustrious chiefs that then
commanded the armies of France. In 1643, led by Louis le
Bourbon, afterwards Prince of Condé, a leader possessed of all
the heroic qualities of the good soldier, and at the same time
graced by all the rarer virtues of the true man—under him
the regiment served with great distinction in the Netherlands
and Italy. Nine years later, when the factions of "the Court"
and "the Parliament" had stirred up among the people a civil
war, we find the Douglas Regiment, with characteristic
loyalty, on the side of "the Court," serving their royal master
under that great adept in the art of war, Marshal Turenne,
whose abilities sustained the sinking State; and although
opposed to that justly celebrated soldier, the Prince of Condé,
at length, out-manœuvring the foe, accomplished the salvation
of "the Court," and, by an honourable peace, secured their
restoration to power. Meanwhile a somewhat analogous civil
strife in England had wholly overturned the old monarchy of
the Stuarts, and inaugurated a new order of things in the
Commonwealth, under Oliver Cromwell, the Protector. Charles
II., and his royal brother, the Duke of York, afterwards James
II., as the surviving heads of their ancient, unfortunate, and
infatuated house, had sought and found an asylum at the

French Court. In those times of war, employment was readily found in the French armies for their many adherents, who had been driven into exile with them. They were formed into several regiments, who bore an honourable part in the contest then raging between France and the allied might of Spain and Austria. In 1656, the fickle Louis, deserting his old friends, the royalists of England, concluded an alliance with the more powerful Cromwell—the exiles, in consequence, changing sides, threw the weight of their arms and influence, or such as they might still be said to retain, into the scale with Spain. Many of the British royalist regiments, hitherto in the service of France, on the command of Charles, exchanged with their prince, into the service of their late foe, now their friend. Louis, who could ill afford such a serious desertion of troops, which had hitherto proved themselves to be the flower of his army, had taken the precaution to remove, into the interior, the older Scots regiments, and amongst others, that of Douglas, which he had justly learned to value very highly, lest they might be induced to follow their royalist brethren.

In 1661, immediately after the Restoration, Charles II., with a view to strengthen his unstable position on the British Throne, strove to establish an army, and Louis being then at peace, and, moreover, on good terms with our King, the regiment of Douglas was called home to these isles, where it has since been generally known as the *First or the Royal Regiment of Foot*, although for a time it was popularly styled the "*Royal Scots.*"

CHAPTER IX.

. . . . . "He lifts on high
The dauntless brow and spirit-speaking eye,
Hails in his heart the triumphs yet to come,
And hears thy stormy music in the drum!"

FRENCH CAMPAIGNS—TANGIER—CIVIL WARS—CONTINENTAL
WARS—1660–1757.

THE regiment, now commanded by Lord George Douglas, afterwards the Earl of Dumbarton, returned to France in 1662, where it was largely recruited by the incorporation of General Rutherford's (Earl of Teviot) regiment of Scots Guards, and another old Scots regiment, also known as a "Douglas Regiment," from its colonel, Lord James Douglas. The muster-roll thus presented a force of more than 2500 men and officers, embraced in twenty-three companies. In 1666, it was recalled to suppress a threatened rebellion in Ireland; but soon returning, with other British troops, was engaged in the wars with Holland and the German Empire. Under the great Turenne they acquired new glory. After his death, in 1675, the foe advanced upon Treves, where the French troops —dispirited by the loss of their favourite chief, and discouraged by the retreat which had since been forced upon them, when his great name was no longer present to infuse courage in the evil hour and inspire a wholesome terror in the

ranks of the enemy—mutinying, insisted that their commander, Marshal de Crequi, should deliver up the fortress to
the enemy. But the regiment of Douglas, with characteristic
fidelity, sustained the gallant Marshal in his resolution to
exhaust every means of defence before submitting to the dire
necessity of surrender. Although the issues of the siege were
disastrous, despite the desperate valour which defended the
city—which at length capitulated—still our countrymen,
although prisoners liberated on condition that they should
not again serve in the war for three months, preserved
that priceless jewel, their *honour*, which, out of the fiery trial,
shone forth only the more conspicuously, both to friend and
foe. Their conduct on this occasion received the thanks of the
King. For a little while, about this period, the regiment was
privileged to serve under another of France's great captains—
the Marshal Luxembourg. In 1678 the regiment was finally
recalled from the French service, and shortly thereafter sent
out to reinforce the garrison of Tangier, in Africa, the profitless marriage dowry of the Princess Catherina of Portugal,
who had become the Queen of Charles II. This earliest of our
foreign possessions had involved the nation in an expensive
and cruel war, which it was very difficult adequately to sustain in those days, when the transport-service was one of
imminent cost and danger; and moreover, news travelling
slowly, we could not, as in the present instance, learn the
straitened circumstances of our armies abroad, so as to afford
that prompt assistance which they urgently needed. Assailed
fiercely by the Moors, who evinced great bravery and resolu-

tion, the contest proved one of uncommon severity, requiring
every effort of our garrison to maintain even their own. We
extract the following announcement of the arrival of the
Douglas, or, as it was then called, Dumbarton's Regiment, on
this new and distant scene of conflict, from Ross' "Tangier's
Rescue:"—"After this landed the valorous Major Hackett
with the renowned regiment of the Earl of Dumbarton; all of
them men of approved valour, fame having echoed the sound
of their glorious actions and achievements in France and other
nations; having left behind them a report of their glorious
victories wherever they came; every place witnessing and
giving large testimony of their renown: so that the arrival of
this illustrious regiment more and more increased the resolu-
tions and united the courage of the inhabitants, and added
confidence to their valour." Also, as further interesting, we
record, from the same author, the stirring address which the
Lieut.-Governor, Sir Palmes Fairborne, is reported to have
made to Dumbarton's Scots on the eve of battle:—"Countrymen and fellow-soldiers, let not your approved valour and
fame in foreign nations be derogated at this time, neither
degenerate from your ancient and former glory abroad; and
as you are looked upon here to be brave and experienced
soldiers (constant and successive victories having attended
your conquering swords hitherto), do not come short of the
great hopes we have in you, and the propitious procedures we
expect from you at this time. For the glory of your nation,
if you cannot surpass, you may imitate the bravest, and be
emulous of their praises and renown."

The excessive cost of maintaining this distant and profitless possession at length induced King Charles to abandon it; accordingly the troops were withdrawn and the fortress destroyed. The " Royal Scots" landed at Gravesend in 1683. Nothing of importance falls to be narrated during the interval of peace which followed—the first, and until our day almost the only, rest which this veteran regiment has been permitted to enjoy at home. The accession of the Duke of York, as James II., to the throne, on the death of his brother Charles, awakened the well-grounded alarm of the Protestants, stirred up discontents, which were quickened into rebellion by the landing of the Marquis of Argyll in the West Highlands, and of a powerful rival—the Duke of Monmouth—in the South of England. Favoured by a considerable rising of the people, and encouraged by the fair promises of many of the old Puritan nobility and gentry—who undertook to join his standard with their followers, enamoured more of the cause speciously set forth upon his banner—"*Fear none but God*"—than of the man, Monmouth had advanced at the head of a considerable force to Bridgewater. His vacillating policy ruined his cause, as it gave time for the assembling of the King's forces, under the Earl of Feversham and Lord Churchill, afterwards so celebrated as the Duke of Marlborough. Amongst these forces were five companies of the " Royal Scots." At the battle of Sedgemoor which ensued, the rebels, deeming to surprise the royal camp in the night, suddenly descended in great force, but, arrested by a ditch immediately in front of the position occupied by the companies of our "Royal Scots,"

which attempting to cross, they were so hotly received,
although they fought with great fury, that they were driven
back in confusion, and ultimately dispersed or destroyed by
the royal cavalry in the morning. Thus the glory of the fight
belongs chiefly to our countrymen, whose firmness proved the
salvation of the royal army, and, in the end, the destruction
of the rebels and the overthrow of their cause—completed in
the after execution of their leaders, the Duke of Monmouth in
England, and his fellow-conspirator, the Marquis of Argyll, in
Scotland. So highly did James esteem the services of the
"Royal Scots" on this perilous occasion, that, by special war-
rant, he ordered that the sum of £397 should be distributed
among the wounded of the regiment. Sergeant Weems was
particularly distinguished in the action, and received accordingly a gratuity of "Forty pounds for good service in the
action of Sedgemoor, in firing the great guns against the
rebels."

When the Revolution of 1688 promised the downfall of
the house of Stuart, whose power had been so long built upon
the suppressed liberty of the people, the exclusion of James
II.—the degenerate representative of an ancient and once
beloved race—from the throne, as the minion of the Papacy and
the dawn of a better state of things, under the more healthy
rule of the Prince of Orange, the champion of Protestantism,
as monarch of these realms, it might have been deemed ex-
cusable had our "Royal Scots," from their antecedents on
behalf of the Protestant cause, sided with the Prince. The
result, however, was far otherwise, and affords us another

splendid illustration of the firm fidelity of the soldier in the sterling devotion of this regiment. The "Royal Scots" had been James's favourite regiment, and well they merited that monarch's trust. Whilst other troops exhibited a shameful defection, the "Royal Scots," with unshaken constancy, adhered to the desperate fortunes of their infatuated King. Nor when all else had submitted, save Claverhouse's Dragoons, and resistance had been rendered fruitless by the pusillanimous flight of James, did they see it their duty to exchange into the service of the new Sovereign. The term "mutiny" is wrongly applied when given to express their conduct on this trying occasion. By lenient measures the 500 men and officers who had refused to tender their submission were at length induced to make their peace with the new king, who, appreciating their ancient name for valour, could admire their unshaken fidelity to one who was even forsaken by his own children; and therefore gladly retained the regiment to grace our military annals. Their conduct was at the same time most exemplary in those days of military license and excess; faithfully they remained at the post of duty, when other regiments, breaking from their ranks, shamefully disgraced themselves by the riot and disorder they everywhere committed. The Earl of Dumbarton, following King James into France, the vacant colonelcy was conferred on one of the oldest, ablest, and most distinguished officers of the age—the veteran Marshal Frederick de Schomberg.

The arrival of the dethroned James at the Court of France, whilst it awakened mingled feelings of commiseration and

contempt in the mind of the crafty Louis, the bitterness of
disappointed ambition roused a spirit of revenge, and was to
be regarded as the signal for war.   Accordingly, a powerful army was advanced towards the frontier, ostensibly to
co-operate in the cause of the exiled monarch, but really to
take advantage of the absence of the Stadtholder, for the
annexation, by way of compensation for his increased power
elsewhere, of his continental dominions in Holland.   To divide
attention, and direct the efforts of William away from his own
more immediate designs, the French King, by paltry succours,
helped to bolster up James in his ricketty Irish kingdom.   To
meet this combined assault, William, whilst himself was present
with his army in the reduction of Ireland, sent the Earl of
Marlborough with a British army, including the "Royals," to
co-operate with the Dutch in the defence of their fatherland.
In 1692 he joined the allied army, and himself assumed the
command.   In an attempt to surprise the powerful fortress of
Mons, Sir Robert Douglas, who, on the death of the Duke de
Schomberg at the battle of the Boyne, had been promoted to
the colonelcy of the "Royals," was taken prisoner by the French
cavalry.   Released, on payment of the regulated ransom, he
was reserved for a sadder but more glorious fate at the battle
of Steenkirk, where he fell at the head of his regiment, gallantly
fighting for and defending the colours he had rescued from the
foe.   General Cannon writes:—"Sir Robert Douglas, seeing the
colour on the other side of the hedge, leaped through a gap,
slew the French officer who bore the colour, and cast it over
the hedge to his own men; but this act of gallantry cost him

his life, a French marksman having shot him dead on the spot
while in the act of repassing the hedge." The able dispositions
of the French commander, the Marshal de Luxembourg, sustained by the valour of his troops, compelled the retreat of the
Allied army. Still pressed by the French at Neer-Landen,
notwithstanding the most desperate resistance of our Infantry,
especially the Royals, and Second, or Queen's Royals, our
army continued to retire. These disasters were somewhat
redeemed by the successes of subsequent campaigns, crowned
in the siege and fall of Namur, a powerful fortress, long
and bravely defended by Marshal Boufflers. The peace of
Ryswick, subscribed in 1697, put an end to the war, and our
army in consequence returned home.

During the war of the Spanish Succession, which commenced in 1701, the Royals were destined to play an important part. They were present under the great Marlborough at the several victories of Schellenberg, Blenheim,
Ramilies, Oudenarde, Wynendale, and Malplaquet, which,
distinguishing the war, we have elsewhere already alluded
to. In many of these battles their gallant colonel, Lord
George Hamilton, Earl of Orkney, who had succeeded Sir
Robert Douglas, was present, and led the regiment to the fight.
Their conduct at Wynendale was specially remarkable, where,
in defence of a large and important train of stores, etc., a
British front of 8000 men resisted the combined and repeated
efforts of 22,000 French to capture the stores and treasure.
The war was terminated by the peace of Utrecht, in 1713.

During the thirty succeeding years the regiment was

employed garrisoning various towns, etc., at home, except in
1742, when the second battalion was sent to do duty in the
West Indies.   In the following year, disputes arising as to the
Austrian Succession, and our country inclining to the side of
Maria Theresa, Queen of Hungary, whilst France, on the other
hand, had, for political reasons, espoused the cause of its old
ally, the Elector of Bavaria, an appeal was made to arms.
A British force, under our own chivalric King, George II.,
had already appeared in Germany, and achieved the signal
victory of Dettingen, when the Royals joined the army in
time to share the disasters of Fontenoy.   The rebellion of
Prince Charles Edward subsequently occasioned their recall.
Whilst the first battalion remained in camp under Marshal
Wade, in the south of England, prepared to defend our shores
from the threatened invasion and co-operation of France, the
second battalion, stationed at York, proceeded in pursuit of
the rebels, who, after having penetrated to Derby, finding that
the expected aid from England was not realised, returned to
Scotland, where, joined by a body of recruits, they undertook
the siege of Stirling Castle.   In this they were interrupted by
the advance of the King's army, towards Falkirk, under Lieut.-
General Hawley.   Encountering the enemy in the vicinity, a
sanguinary battle ensued, but devoid of any decisive result,
both parties claiming the victory.   Whilst some of the King's
troops were broken by the combined assaults of the elements
and the enemy, the Royals stood fast.   The dissensions
which had but lately prevailed to distract the counsels of the
rebels had been hushed by the preponderating eminence of a

coming struggle, and the promise of plunder as the reward of
victory. Now that the excitement of battle had ceased, the
Royal army retired, and the hopes of booty disappointed, those
evil feelings, more fatal than the sword, burst forth with
renewed virulence, to ruin the interests of the Jacobites,
occasioning the retreat of their broken-hearted Prince, with a
diminished, and disspirited, yet brave and faithful army.
Meanwhile the King's forces, greatly strengthened by the
arrival of fresh troops, a second time advanced upon the
enemy. Led by the Duke of Cumberland, the advance soon
assumed the character of a pursuit. At length the rebels,
overtaken and driven to bay, made a stand in the neighbourhood of Inverness, on Culloden Moor, where, notwithstanding
the fiery valour of the clans, they sustained a total defeat,
and were never afterwards able to rally.

> " For a field of the dead rushes red on my sight ;
> And the clans of Culloden are scattered in fight.
> They rally, they bleed, for their kingdom and crown ;
> Woe, woe, to the riders that trample them down !
>
> 'Tis finish'd. Their thunders are hushed on the moors !
> Culloden is lost, and my country deplores.
>
> Culloden that reeks with the blood of the brave."

Their Prince—

> " Like a limb from his country cast bleeding and torn,"

for long lurked a wandering fugitive amongst our Western
Islands, until, through many dangers, he effected his escape to

France. The Duke of Cumberland, visiting with a cruel revenge the rebellious clans, nay, in some cases, with barbarous
heedlessness, mingling the innocent with the guilty in a common ruin, tarnished the lustre of his success, and left behind
a most unenviable memory in these northern provinces.

The Rebellion being thus at an end, several of the regiments
which had been withdrawn from the Continent for its suppression now returned, whilst the first battalion of the
Royals was employed in several descents upon the French
coast with various success. At L'Orient the attempt proved
fruitless; but at Quiberon, sustained by the Forty-second
Royal Highlanders, the destruction of the enemy's arsenal,
stores, and shipping, was attained. Subsequently the battalion
joined the British army in the Netherlands, and, in 1747,
was greatly distinguished in the heroic defence of Fort Sand-
berg. The attack on the part of the French, was made late
in the evening, with more than their wonted impetuosity.
The Dutch garrison, unable to withstand the shock, was signally routed, and the conquest seemed complete, when the progress of the enemy was unexpectedly arrested by the Royals,
who, with unflinching obstinacy, maintained the conflict, which
proved of the most sanguinary and desperate character. The
horrors of the fight were deepened by the sable pall of night.
"The morning light had already dawned upon this scene
of conflict and carnage,—between three and four hundred
officers and men of the Royals were *hors de combat;* yet the
survivors,—though standing amidst the dying and the dead,
and being unable to take one step without treading on a killed

or wounded man,—maintained their ground with resolution, and continued to pour their fatal volleys upon their opponents, who had sustained an equal or greater loss, until five o'clock, when the Royals were relieved by the Highlanders; and the French, dismayed by the sanguinary tenacity of the defence, retreated." Ultimately the fort, rendered untenable, was abandoned. In 1749, the peace of Aix-la-Chapelle put an end to the war, when the battalion returning home, was stationed in Ireland.

CHAPTER X.

"For pleas of right let statesmen vex their head,
Battle's my business, and my guerdon bread;
And with the sworded Switzer I can say,
'The best of causes is the best of pay.'"

AMERICAN WARS—WEST INDIES—FRENCH REVOLUTION—
1755–1804.

THE ancient rivalries subsisting between Britain and France,
and which had begotten so many fierce and sanguinary wars
upon the European continent, were now about to be displayed
with even a more exceeding bitterness among the colonists of
the two nations in the New World of America. Disputes arising
as to the boundary line of what they severally claimed as their
territory, the *might* of France assumed to decide the *right*.
To maintain and defend British interests, an army, comprising
the second battalion of the Royals, and the two newly-raised
regiments of Fraser's and Montgomery's Highlanders, was
sent across the Atlantic in 1757. The first attack of this
expedition was made upon the French island of Cape Breton,
which, with its capital, Louisburg, was speedily reduced. In
the following year the Royals were engaged upon the American
continent in a series of actions around the shores of Lake
Champlain, which resulted in the capture of the strong forts

of Ticonderago, Crown Point, and ultimately the Isle aux
Noix. Several of the Indian tribes taking advantage of our
apparent embarrassments at this period, instigated by, and in
some cases allied with, the French, threw off the British yoke,
strove to recover their fatherland, or were encouraged, by hope
of plunder, to assail our colonial settlements. Against the
most powerful of these foes—the Cherokees—a few companies
of the Royals, with Montgomery's Highlanders and other
corps, were detached from the army, and proceeded to
South Carolina. After repeated incursions into the country
of the Cherokees, in which the foe was rarely seen, or
when the Indian army of sable warriors did appear, our
troops achieved an easy and ofttimes a bloodless victory. Still
was our advance characterised by cruel and uncalled-for
severities, and marked by the melancholy spectacle of burning
villages, in which lay "the little all" of these poor creatures.
Unable to withstand our onset, with ruined homesteads, and
threatened with all the miseries of want, their necessities impelled the Cherokees to sue for peace, which was readily
granted.

The conquest of French Canada having been completed in
the surrender of Montreal, several detachments of the Royals
were employed in various expeditions against the French West
Indian Islands, especially Dominica and Martinique, in which
our efforts were successful. But the crowning achievement of
these expeditions was the capture of the Havannah from the
Spaniards, with immense spoil, on the 30th July, 1762. Meanwhile two companies of the Royals, which had remained on the

American continent, contributed by their gallantry to repulse
a new attempt of the French to recover their lost footing in
these provinces.

In 1763 the second battalion returning home, the regiment was afterwards employed garrisoning our Mediterranean
possessions, Minorca and Gibraltar. During the American
Rebellion a secret treaty having been discovered between the
rebels and Holland, France and Spain, promising aid to, and
otherwise abetting the colonists in their rebellion, the Royals,
with other troops, in 1781, were sent out to assail the West
Indian possessions of these several States. Having possessed
themselves of the island of St Christopher, they were here
attacked by a powerful French expeditionary force which had
landed from the fleet for the recovery of the island. Stationed
on Brimstone Hill with scarce 500 men, without the adequate
matériel to make good the defence, these brave men nevertheless resisted for nearly a month the repeated assaults of 8000
French, aided by a powerful artillery, which played continually
and effectually upon the crumbling defences and the worn-out
defenders. It was not until every means of resistance had
been destroyed, and every hope of relief exhausted, that our
gallant Royals were compelled to surrender.

In 1782, both battalions were at home, and the Duke of
Argyll having been removed to the Colonelcy of the Third,
or Scots Foot Guards, the Colonelcy of the First Royal Regiment, or Royal Scots, was conferred upon Lord Adam Gordon.

Britain, ever recognised as the guardian of true liberty,
had viewed, with mingled feelings of horror, pity, and alarm,

the crimes which alike stained and inaugurated the French
Revolution. Our Government, unhappily, mistaking the real
nature and critical importance of the contest, granted a
feeble and tardy aid to the few remaining friends of order,
chiefly represented in the Royalists, who still struggled for
existence in France. Had these succours been commensurate
with the ability of the nation, and afforded promptly and
liberally, France might have been saved from many of those
dire calamities which, like the judgments of Heaven, gathering
in her political horizon, were so soon to visit her in the fury of
the tempest, to cast a blight upon her people and a curse upon
her fair plains. Europe, moreover, might have escaped the
military tyranny of Napoleon, with all its accompanying evils.
Toulon, the principal station for the French Navy on the shores
of the Mediterranean, possessed of large arsenals and extensive
dockyards, and strongly fortified—its citizens had hitherto regarded with aversion the excesses of blood and rapine in which
the Revolutionists had indulged, and fully sensible of the evils
which must arise from the rule of the democracy, resolved to
declare for the restoration of the old monarchy. In the im-
pending contest in which they were soon involved by their
resistance to the iron will of the Committee of Public Salvation, who then assumed to rule France, they invoked,
and not altogether in vain, the aid of the constitutional
Governments around. Accordingly, a mixed force of British,
Spaniards, and Italians, was thrown into the city for its
defence. The second battalion of the Royals formed part
of the British contingent on this occasion. Lieutenant-

General O'Hara commanding, with 12,000 men, for awhile succeeded in making good the defence, and had well nigh baffled the utmost efforts of the besiegers, who, under General Dugommier, had assembled an army of nearly 40,000 Revolutionists. But the appearance of a young officer in the ranks of the enemy speedily changed the aspect of affairs. As chief of the artillery, by a series of bold and judicious movements, effecting the reduction of the city, he early displayed that aptness for military combination which revealed the genius of Napoleon Bonaparte. Dugommier, writing to the Convention, said—"Reward and promote that young man, for, if you are ungrateful towards him, he will raise himself alone." The following incident, narrated by Sir Archibald Alison, Bart., in his interesting account of the siege, introduces us to another of those great military chiefs who were so soon to glitter in the firmament of the Empire: "Napoleon asked him what he could do for him. 'Everything,' replied the young private, blushing with emotion, and touching his left shoulder with his hand—'you can turn this worsted into an epaulet.' A few days after, Napoleon sent for the same soldier to order him to reconnoitre in the enemy's trenches, and recommended that he should disguise himself, for fear of his being discovered. 'Never,' replied he. 'Do you take me for a spy? I will go in my uniform, though I should never return.' And, in effect, he set out instantly, dressed as he was, and had the good fortune to come back unhurt. Napoleon immediately recommended him for promotion, and never lost sight of his courageous secretary. He was Junot, afterwards Marshal of France, and Duke of Abrantes." Notwithstanding the utmost bravery on the part of the defenders, and of the Royals in particular, the fortress had become no longer tenable from the alarming successes of the enemy. Accordingly, on the night of the 19th December, 1794, the army, with as many of the citizens as could be crowded into the fleet, were embarked, all that might be useful to the foe was destroyed or committed to the flames, and the city abandoned. The scene which ensued is one of the most touchingly interesting and afflicting in the dark story of the Revolution, especially when considered in the light of the cruel fate which awaited the unfortunates who could not find room in the fleet, and who, left behind, must meet the merciless wrath of the Parisian demagogues. Alison thus pictures the sad episode:—

"No words can do justice to the horrors of the scene which ensued, when the last columns of the allied troops commenced their embarkation. Cries, screams, and lamentations arose in every quarter; the frantic clamour, heard even across the harbour, announced to the soldiers in the Republican camp that the last hope of the Royalists was giving way. The sad remnant of those who had favoured the royal cause, and who had neglected to go off in the first embarkation, came flying to the beach, and invoked, with tears and prayers, the aid of their British friends. Mothers, clasping their babes to their bosoms, helpless children, and decrepid old men, might be seen stretching their hands towards the harbour, shuddering at every sound behind them, and even rushing into the waves to escape the less merciful death which awaited them from their

countrymen. Some had the generosity to throw themselves
into the sea, to save, by their self-sacrifice, the lives of their
parents, in danger of being swamped in the boats. Vast
numbers perished from falling into the sea, or by the swamp-
ing of boats, into which multitudes crowded, loaded with their
most valuable effects, or bearing their parents or children
on their shoulders. Such as could seize upon boats, rushed
into them with frantic vehemence, pushed from the beach
without oars, and directed their unsteady and dangerous
course towards their former protectors. The scene resembled
those mournful catastrophes recorded by the historians of
antiquity, when the inhabitants of whole cities in Asia Minor
or Greece fled to the sea at the approach of their enemies, and
steered away by the light of their burning habitations. Sir
Sidney Smith, with a degree of humanity worthy of his high
character, suspended his retreat till not a single individual
who claimed his assistance remained on the strand, though the
total number borne away amounted to fourteen thousand eight
hundred and seventy-seven."

The Royals were shortly after engaged in a successful
descent upon the island of Corsica. Associated with the Fifty-
first Foot, under the command of our gallant countryman, the
future hero of Corunna, Lieutenant-Colonel Moore, they were
largely instrumental in the reduction of the island, which soon
after acknowledged the British sway. The fortified town of
Calvi, refusing to submit, was besieged, captured, and garrisoned by the Royals, where they remained until removed to
the island of Elba, in 1796—Corsica being abandoned. In

1797 the corps was stationed at Cascaes, in Portugal, and in the following year returned to England.

Meanwhile the disorders which prevailed in France had induced a spirit of rebellion amongst the coloured population of her most valuable colony—the island of St Domingo— which, bursting forth in 1793, resulted in the establishment of the Black Empire of Hayti. The French colonists having no faith in, or doubting the ability to help of their home Government, had solicited the protection of Britain. Accordingly a British force, including the first battalion of the Royals from Jamaica (where for the past three years it had been stationed), was sent to their assistance. The expedition proved one of extreme difficulty and exceeding danger, and is replete with interesting incidents. On every occasion the good conduct of the Royals was most conspicuous, especially so in the defence of Fort Bizzeton, where Lieutenant Clunes, with 120 men, repulsed 2000 of the enemy. Major-General Sir Adam Williamson, in his despatch, stated—"Captain Grant and his two Lieutenants, Clunes, of the Royals, and Hamilton, of the Twenty-second Regiment, merit every attention that can be shown them. They were all three severely wounded early in the attack, but tied up their wounds, and continued to defend their posts. It has been a very gallant defence, and does them great honour." But the sword was not the only or the worst enemy our brave countrymen had to encounter in this sultry and unhealthy clime. A malignant fever, invading the quarters of our men, slew in two months about 640. The remains of the battalion returned home in 1797.

Scarcely had our gallant Royals recruited their ranks,
when the sound of war called them to win new glories on the
field.   In 1799 the second battalion, brigaded with the
Ninety-second Gordon Highlanders, formed part of the British
army, which, under that famous chieftain, Sir Ralph Abercromby, landed in the Netherlands, and strove to expel the
French.   The triumph of " Egmont-op-Zee " illustrated " the
gallantry of these brave troops," which " cannot have been
surpassed by any former instance of British valour."   The
Dutch, for whom these efforts had been made, unheeding to
be *free*, were at length abandoned to their own infatuation,
in which they soon experienced those bitter fruits which
sprang from the military despotism of Napoleon to curse the
land.   On the withdrawal of the army, the second battalion
was successfully employed in several descents upon the coast
of Portugal.   In brigade with their old comrades of the
Ninety-second, and two battalions of the Fifty-fourth Foot,
they were included in the British army which, landing at
Aboukir, from one victory to another, vanquished the boasted
" Invincibles" of Napoleon's grand " Army of the East," and
were at length hailed as the deliverers of Egypt—having
driven out the French.   Whilst these desirable ends were being
accomplished upon the African continent, the first battalion
of the Royals, having embarked for the West Indies, was
reaping a harvest of glory in the reduction of the enemy's
possessions in that quarter of the world.   The most illustrious
of these conquests was that of "St Lucia," which, inscribed
upon the colours of the regiment, remains to perpetuate the
record of these brave deeds.

CHAPTER XI.

" His signal deeds and prowess high
Demand no pompous eulogy,—
Ye saw his deeds!
Why should their praise in verse be sung?
The name, that dwells on every tongue,
No minstrel needs."

FRENCH REVOLUTION—CANADA—THE CRIMEA—INDIA—
CHINA—1804–1862.

THE gigantic proportions which the war in 1804 had
assumed, the imminence of the danger which threatened ourselves from the overgrown power of Napoleon, and his still
unsatisfied ambition, had thoroughly roused our Government more completely to arm our people, and occasioned
the raising of many new corps. Aware of the favour in
which our Royal Regiment was held by the people, from the
ancient renown it had acquired, the Government, taking
advantage of this good name, speedily raised and attached
thereto a third and fourth battalion. Returning from the
West Indies, where, for a short time, it had been engaged
in capturing the French and Dutch possessions, the second
battalion embarked for the East Indies, where, for upwards of
five-and-twenty years—returning home in 1831—it remained
actively on duty. Meanwhile, the third battalion, sharing
the glories, was doomed to endure the disasters of the Spanish

campaigns of 1808–9, under that gallant leader, Sir John
Moore—glories which had their consummation in the victory
of Corunna. On this occasion the Royals were brigaded with
our countrymen of the Twenty-sixth Cameronians. The
army, returning to England, was shortly thereafter employed
in a new attempt to expel the French from the Netherlands. In this unfortunate effort, known as the Walcheren
Expedition, our third battalion had a part. But the day of
better things was now about to dawn, when these repeated
disasters should be redeemed, and the eclipse of the world's
liberty be dissipated, through the triumphs which, rewarding
the heroic endurance and persevering valour of our soldiers,
should crown our arms. Trained by adversity, our troops
had learned how to conquer. Under Sir Arthur Wellesley,
the third battalion was, with the British army, which, from
"Busaco" to the "Nive," trod the path of uninterrupted
victory, baffling successively the splendid efforts with which
the genius of Massena, Marmont, Jourdan, and Soult, strove
to preserve for their master the provinces of the Peninsula.
Every attempt to arrest the onward march of British valour
signally failed, entailing upon the foe a series of fatal defeats,
until at length the Peninsula, delivered from the yoke of the
tyrant, our army, in triumph, entered the French territory.
At the siege of St Sebastian our Royals very specially distinguished themselves, and although suffering a loss of more
than 500 men in the several assaults, nothing could quench
the dauntless spirit which twice stirred them to enter the
deadly breach; but the second time with most splendid

success, when, overcoming every obstacle, this famous and
gallantly defended fortress was captured.

"At a Scots corporation dinner, held in London on the
4th of May, 1811, on the health of the Duke of Kent,
the father of our beloved Queen, then Colonel of the Royal
Regiment, being drunk, his Royal Highness rose to return
thanks, and, in the course of his speech, said:—'My
royal brother has been pleased to praise the regiment in
which I have been employed, and have had the honour to
command, and I too can bear testimony to the spirit and
gallantry of the Scottish soldiers. From the earliest days,
when I commenced my military life, it was always my
utmost aim to arrive at the command of a Scots regiment,
and to bring that regiment into action would have been the
greatest glory I could have attained, as I am well convinced
the officers and men would have justified my most sanguine
expectations; their courage, perseverance, and activity, being
undoubtedly such as may always be relied on; and they are
always able and willing to do their duty, if not more than
their duty.' His Royal Highness took great interest in the
welfare of the regiment; and he this year presented, by the
hands of Lieutenant-Colonel M'Leod, a gold medal to Serjeant
Manns of the regiment for the very meritorious manner in
which he had educated upwards of 800 soldiers and soldiers'
children." His Royal Highness was the first to establish
regimental schools,—a rich blessing, which will be ever associated with his memory, conferring as they have done such
priceless benefits upon the army.

When all Europe had combined in a sacred crusade against the despotic rule of Napoleon, the fourth battalion of the Royals was selected to form part of a British force which should act with the Swedo-German army advancing from Pomerania, under Bernadotte, upon France. Thus, at the interval of nearly 300 years, did our Royal Scots revisit the scenes of their early glory; and, under the same Swedish banner, led on by the successor of Gustavus Adolphus, once more do battle for the cause of truth. No doubt, their souls roused within them, their arms must have been nerved, by the "stirring memories" of "auld langsyne." The march of this battalion through Germany, when called to join the army of Lieutenant-General Sir Thomas Graham, afterwards Lord Lynedoch, in the Netherlands, about to attempt the reduction of the strong fortress of Bergen-op-Zoom, is marked by the extreme severity of the weather, which entailed sufferings of the most fatal kind upon our brave soldiers—upwards of 120 men being lost in the snow. To the survivors a darker and a sadder fate was near, whilst these trials served to school them to meet it with the heroic fortitude of the soldier. In the subsequent attack upon Bergen-op-Zoom the several companies of the battalion had struggled with determined yet unavailing valour to dislodge the French. Our troops could not prevail, as they could not destroy the strong natural defences of the place. They suffered a most serious loss from an unseen foe, who visited their temerity with a fatal fire from their powerful and numerous batteries. At length, overwhelmed and encompassed by foemen, and entangled amongst destructive batteries which vomited forth death upon our devoted Royals, they were compelled to surrender, having previously sunk the colours of the regiment in the river Zoom. Peace being accomplished by the abdication of Napoleon, the sword of war was for a moment sheathed. Alas! that it should have been but for a moment. Soon the dream of a fancied security was disturbed, as the captive of Elba once more appearing, the Emperor, idolised by the great army, forged thunder-bolts of vengeance with which he threatened to annihilate his many foes. Happily, his ambitious career was speedily terminated, and Europe thereby saved the repetition of the bloody tragedy of protracted war, so lately and so fondly believed to be closed. The sudden irruption of the French army into the Netherlands was met by the bravery of the British and Prussians, and its progress for ever arrested by the total defeat of Waterloo. In this campaign the third battalion of the Royals was honoured to hold a conspicuous part; especially at Quatre Bras, where it was the first to check the advance of Marshal Ney, and sustain with great credit the brunt of his impetuous and repeated attacks. The following splendid testimony has been recorded to its valour:—"The third battalion of the Royal Scots distinguished itself in a particular manner. Being removed from the centre of the Fifth Division, it charged and routed a column of the enemy. It was then formed in a square to receive the cavalry, and though repeated attacks were made, not the slightest impression was produced. Wherever the

lancers and cuirassiers presented themselves, they found a
stern and undismayed front, which they vainly endeavoured
to penetrate."

It was not alone upon the continent of Europe that the
dire effects of Napoleon's sway were felt and regretted, but
wherever the foot of civilisation had left its impress. Nor
was it only the pulse of true liberty that beat quickly and
faintly beneath the evil rule of his tyrant spirit, but commerce, by iniquitous decrees, lay groaning in chains, or eked
out but a sorry existence. The intention of these ill-advised
decrees was the destruction of the maritime and commercial
might of Britain. Our Government sought to retaliate upon
France the evils their imperial monarch had striven to inflict upon us, by barbarous enactments of a kindred character. Thus, between the two, the avenues of trade were
all but hedged up—the channels of commercial intercourse
dried up. America had hitherto grown rich upon the pover-
ties which war had entailed upon the continental nations;
and hence, when her merchants found their trade at an end,
or, at all events, amounting to a thing of peril, her Government resented such decrees as a personal attack. Retaining
an old grudge arising out of the nature of recent events, and,
moreover, regarding Britain as the chief offender, having
within herself alone the power to set at defiance the attempts
of Napoleon, without adding a new evil to cure the old
iniquity, America declared war against us, and her armies
forthwith proceeded to take possession of Canada. To arrest
the progress of the enemy in this quarter, the first bat-

talion of the Royals was ordered from the West Indies to
Canada. Although the forces engaged on either side were
trifling in numbers when compared with the vast armaments
which were then contending in Europe, still the contest was
no less sanguinary and bitter, and equally developed the
sterling qualities of our Royal Scots. Arrived in Canada in
1813, the battalion was present with credit at the successful
attacks upon Sackett's Harbour, Sodius, Niagara, Black Rock,
and Buffalo; but it was not until 1814, that the preponder-
ance of numbers on the side of the Americans rendering the
contest more unequal, and when victory did not always smile
on our arms—it was then we gather more striking evidence of
the gallant demeanour of the Royals. At Longwood a
superior force of Americans prevailed, and the battalion was
reluctantly withdrawn, having suffered severely, principally in
officers. At Chippewa 6000 Americans assailed a force of
1500 British, including 500 of the Royals. Although repulsed
in the action which ensued, the General Order reports: "It
was impossible for men to have done more, or to have
sustained with greater courage the heavy and destructive fire
with which the enemy, from his great superiority in numbers,
was enabled to oppose them." The Royals only yielded when
upwards of 300 of their number had been disabled—sufficient
proof of the fierceness of the conflict, and the desperate valour
which sustained it. But a more deadly encounter—though
happily a more successful one—took place at Lundy's Lane,
where 5000 Americans were opposed to 2800 British, including
at first only three, latterly ten, companies of the Royals. We

cannot do better than quote the description of the battle from
Mr Cannon's invaluable Records: "About nine in the evening
there was an intermission of firing; but the Americans renewed
the attack soon afterwards with fresh troops, and a fierce
conflict of musketry and artillery followed in the dark. The
Americans charged up the hill; the British gunners were
bayoneted while in the act of loading, and the guns were in
the possession of the enemy for a few moments; but the
troops in the centre, where the three companies of the Royal
Scots were fighting, soon drove back the Americans, and
retook the guns. The storm of battle still raged along the
heights; the muzzles of the British and American artillery
were within a few yards of each other, and the fight was kept
up with a sanguinary obstinacy seldom witnessed. In limber-
ing up the guns, at one period an American six-pounder was
put by mistake on a British limber, and a British six-pounder
on an American limber. At one moment the Americans had
the advantage; at the next the shout of victory rose from the
British ranks; and about midnight the enemy retreated." The
troops were thanked for their distinguished bravery in general
orders on the following day; and "the admirable steadiness of
the Royal Scots, under Lieut.-Colonel Gordon, at several very
critical points and movements," claimed Lieut.-General Drum-
mond's particular notice. On this occasion the Royal Scots
had to mourn the loss of many brave officers and gallant men,
nearly 160 being killed, wounded, or prisoners. The siege
and capture of Fort Erie is distinguished not merely for the
gallantry of our Royals, but possesses, moreover, a melancholy

interest, from the lamentable catastrophe—the explosion of a mine—which destroyed many of our brave soldiers, who, struggling on, had effected a footing in the breach.

It is interesting to note, about this period, the several battalions of this ancient regiment, fighting our battles in so many different corners of the world at the same time, and each contributing to the national glory and their own marvellous fame. In 1814 the positions of the battalions were as follows:—

First Battalion,	...	...	Canada.
Second Battalion,	...	...	India.
Third Battalion,	...	...	Spain and France.
Fourth Battalion,	...	...	Germany and Holland.

The war was brought to a termination in 1815, after the memorable battle of Waterloo, wherein the third battalion of the Royal Scots immortalised itself, when, peace being concluded, the Royals returned home, and the third and fourth battalions were disbanded.

Passing over a long interval of comparative peace which succeeded, like the calm, the storm that but lately raged, we have only time in our present sketch to note that the Royals formed part of the British army in the Crimea. The Crimean campaign gained for them the several distinctions of the "Alma," "Inkermann," and "Sevastopol."

On the alarm occasioned by the recent Indian Mutiny, in 1857, the first battalion of the Royals was sent out to reinforce our army, destined to suppress the Sepoy Revolt. Afterwards the second battalion formed part of the Chinese

Expedition, which, chastising the perfidy of the boasted "Celestials," reduced the "Taku forts," and occupied Pekin.

We close our narrative of the First Royal Regiment, or Royal Scots, with these lines from an old military ditty, the favourite apostrophe of that distinguished veteran and representative of our old Scots brigade in the Swedish service— Sir Dugald Dalgetty, the illustrious hero represented by Sir Walter Scott in his "Legend of Montrose." Thus he sang when waiting in the guard-room of Inverary Castle:—

> "When the cannons are roaring, lads, and the colours are flying,
> The lads that seek honour must never fear dying:
> Then stout cavaliers let us toil our brave trade in,
> And fight for the Gospel and the bold King of Sweden."

THE TWENTY-FIRST FOOT,

OR,

ROYAL NORTH BRITISH FUSILIERS.

CHAPTER XII.

"The warrior boy to the field hath gone,
And left his home behind him;
His father's sword he hath girded on—
In the ranks of death you'll find him."

ORIGIN—EARLY SERVICES—CIVIL WARS—WARS OF THE SPANISH
SUCCESSION—WARS OF THE AUSTRIAN SUCCESSION—1678–1748.

SUCCESS is too commonly esteemed, by a short-sighted public, to be the criterion of excellence. It remains, however, to each of us, an exercise of faith and duty to confute this popular fallacy, inasmuch as it has wronged, foully wronged, many a brave heart who, battling with several and powerful foes, struggling manfully, yet desperately, for the very life, has as yet failed to rise beyond the surface; and hence the man bowed down by adversity, as yet unrewarded by a better success—regarded as nothing beyond the common—this deceit-ful, false world cannot recognise the heroic soul in the martyr to circumstances. Thus it is that the gallant regiment, whose history we are now about to narrate, is in danger of being done injustice to, since its history is not always garnished with splendid success, nor its path to honour strewn with the glittering distinctions of victory, nor its heroism illustrated by a long series of triumphs, which gild many a page of our national history.

This regiment claims an origin co-eval with that of the Scots Greys and Scots Foot Guards. It was regimented and commanded by Charles, Earl of Mar, at a time when the rampant bigotry of the King—oppressing the consciences of the people, had exiled many of the bravest and best, or driven them to desperate measures—induced them to draw together for defence of their liberty and lives. Such was the state of things in Scotland in 1678 when our Fusiliers were raised to hunt down our covenanting forefathers, who, for conscience sake, branded as heretics, endured the cruel ban of the Church of Rome; who, "not ashamed to own their Lord," freely resigned life and property for His sake. The history of the regiment is one with that of the Scots Greys and Scots Foot Guards, already in our previous chapters alluded to, where it may almost be traced page by page; it is therefore needless for us to repeat the incidents which marked their early history. They were present at the battle of Bothwell Bridge, where the Covenanters were signally defeated, and were afterwards engaged in repressing the Rebellion of Argyll in 1685. At length the day of retribution arrived, when the voice of the people declared the sovereignty of the House of Stuart to

be an intolerant burden no longer to be submitted to,—by a
general rising decreed its overthrow, and by an almost universal welcome hailed the advent of a better state of things
under the healthier government of the House of Orange.
Amid these changes our Fusiliers remained faithful to James
II. Having marched into England with a strength of 744
men, under Colonel Buchan, they were stationed in the Tower
Hamlets. The flight of the King rendering all resistance to
the advancing forces of William futile and needless, the
regiment submitted to the victorious party of William and
Mary. Removed to Oxfordshire, the command was conferred on
Colonel O'Farrell. Colonel Buchan, adhering to the fallen fortunes of James, followed him into exile. His name has acquired
a melancholy interest as the chief who, a few years later, after
the death of Dundee at Killiecrankie, headed the rebel forces
in a vain attempt to restore the dominion of the Stuarts.
Subsequently, in 1689, the regiment embarked at Gravesend
for Flanders, where, under Marlborough, it formed part of
the British division which, with the Dutch, strove to check
the aggressions of the French. In the early part of the
campaign they were associated with their countrymen of the
Third, or Scots Foot Guards, and the First, or Royal Scots
Regiment, besides other British troops. These shared the
glory of the victory of Walcourt, where an attack of the
French under D'Humières was repulsed. In 1690 the ill
success of the allied general, Prince Waldeck, yielded to the
enemy many and important advantages, especially in the
disastrous battle of Fleurus. In the following year the Scots

brigade was further augmented by the addition of the regiments of Mackay and Ramsay, known to fame as the Old Scots Brigade in the Dutch service, or as the Ninety-Fourth in later times in the British service. To these were added the Earl of Angus's regiment of Cameronians, now the Twenty-sixth, and subsequently the Earl of Leven's regiment of King's Own Borderers, the present Twenty-fifth. The arrival of King William, who in person assumed the command, as it set at rest the national jealousies which hitherto prevailed among the troops, and hushed the petty contests for precedence on the part of their leaders, infused at the same time new life and vigour into the movements of the Allies. In a vain attempt to surprise the fortress of Mons, Colonel Sir Robert Douglas of the Royals, and Colonel O'Farrell of our Fusiliers, were taken prisoners by the French, but released on payment of the customary ransom. Both were destined for very different fates. The former, as narrated in a previous chapter, fell, gallantly fighting at the head of his regiment, at the battle of Steenkirk; the latter, surviving that bloody day, was reserved to be the unlucky commander who surrendered the fortress of Deinse, garrisoned by his regiment, to the enemy without striking a blow in its defence. This denial of the courage of our Fusiliers under his command, who, with able hands and ready hearts, might have successfully challenged the attempts of a numerous foe—whilst they were delivered over to be prisoners of war—justly received the severe censure of the King; and, tried by court martial, Brigadier-General O'Farrell was cashiered, and his command conferred on Colonel Robert Mackay. Meanwhile, three years previously, the battle of Steenkirk had been fought, and the superior numbers of the French, directed by the ability of the Duke de Luxembourg, had triumphed, notwithstanding the desperate valour of the British. Our Fusiliers, with the Royals, formed part of the advanced guard of our army, and fiercely assailed the French, who, strongly posted behind a series of thick hedges, poured in a deadly fire into our ranks. Successively they were driven from their strong position, but only to take a new position, equally defensible, behind a second hedge. A third and a fourth position was assumed and bravely defended, yet nothing could withstand the onset of our troops. Every obstacle was overcome, and victory was within our grasp, when disasters in other parts of the field compelled the abandonment of all these hard-earned advantages. D'Auvergne says: "Our vanguard behaved in this engagement to such wonder and admiration, that though they received the charge of several battalions of the enemy, one after the other, yet they made them retreat almost to their very camp;" and the *London Gazette* records: "The bravery of our men was extraordinary, and admired by all; ten battalions of ours having engaged above thirty of the French at one time." At the battle of Landen in 1693, brigaded with the Twenty-fifth, the Twenty-sixth, and the regiments of the Old Scots Brigade, separated from the army by the prevailing efforts of the French, they most heroically maintained themselves, until overwhelming numbers compelled them to retire. With

difficulty they effected their retreat, without disorder, by
fording the river Gheet, and so succeeded in rejoining the
main army. The ignominious surrender of Deinse, and the
consequent dismissal of Colonel O'Farrell, occurring in 1695,
have been already alluded to. Nothing of importance falls to
be recorded in the history of our Fusiliers during the
remainder of the war, which was terminated in 1697 by the
peace of Ryswick. Returning to Scotland, the rest they
enjoyed was but of short duration. Once again the rude
blast of war lashed into fury the ambition of princes. Would
that princes acted out the words of the ballad writer—

> "Oh, were I Queen of France, or still better, Pope of Rome,
> I would have no fighting men abroad, or weeping maids at home.
> All the world should be at peace, or if kings would show their might,
> I'd have those that make the quarrels be the only ones to fight."

Unhappily, it is not so, and perhaps, however beautiful the
idea, it is better it should be otherwise. In 1702 the war of
the Spanish Succession broke out, which was destined to
witness the splendid successes of a renowned soldier—the
Duke of Marlborough. Brigaded with the second battalion
of the Royals, the Tenth, the Sixteenth, and the Twenty-sixth
regiments, our Fusiliers were present at the siege of Huy, and,
detached from the army, took part in the enterprise which
resulted in the capture of Limburg. But these events, however glorious, sink into insignificance when compared with
the marvellous achievements which shed a flood of glory upon
our national history, as recorded in the memorable year of
1704. Then the plains of Germany for the first time owned

the tread not of a mere band of island adventurers, as in the
ancient days of our veteran Royals, but now these plains
resounded with the martial tramp of a British army. In the
attack upon the heights of Schellenberg our Fusiliers bore an
honourable part, but that was but the prelude to the grander
victory of Blenheim, wherein the confederate might of France
and Bavaria succumbed before the allied arms of Britain and
Germany. But this signal triumph was not accomplished
save by the most desperate bravery. "Brigadier-General
Row, (Colonel of the Royal North British Fusiliers,) who
charged on foot at the head of his own regiment with
unparalleled intrepidity, assaulted the village of Blenheim,
advancing to the very muzzles of the enemy's muskets, and
some of the officers exchanged thrusts of swords through the
palisades : but the avenues of the village were found strongly
fortified, and defended by a force of superior numbers.
Brigadier-General Row led the North British Fusiliers up to
the palisades before he gave the word 'Fire,' and the next
moment he fell mortally wounded : Lieutenant-Colonel Dalyel
and Major Campbell, being on the spot, stepped forward to
raise their colonel, and were both instantly pierced by musket-
balls ; the soldiers, exasperated at seeing the three field-officers
of the regiment fall, made a gallant effort to force their way
into the village, but this was found impossible, and the regiment
was ordered to retire. The moment the soldiers faced about,
thirteen squadrons of French cavalry galloped forward to charge
them, and one of the colours of the regiment was captured by
the enemy ; but the French horsemen were repulsed by the

fire of a brigade of Hessians, and the colour was recovered."
A second assault failed likewise, so resolute was the defence
of the enemy, but a third attempt, with additional forces, was
crowned with success; the French being driven out of the
village with great loss. There is no more treasured illustration of the worth of our British soldiers than is recorded in
this famous battle, and no more distinguished honour than
belongs to the regiments who have won a title, by their
presence and brave deeds on the occasion, to share its glory
or bear upon their colours the proud and envied word
"Blenheim." But this mode of commemorating battles was
not adopted until a later period,—MINDEN, borne by the
Twenty-fifth King's Own Borderers, and other corps,—
being the earliest instance of a battle thus emblazoned.*
Throughout the remaining years of the war, graced by
the victories of Ramilies, Oudenarde, and Malplaquet, and
the capture of many of the strong fortresses of the Netherlands, our Fusiliers maintained their character for bravery
and steadiness, proving themselves in every way worthy
the honours their valour had hitherto won. During this
period they were successively commanded by Viscount Mor-
daunt, Brigadier-General De Lalo—a distinguished French
Protestant officer, who fell whilst gallantly leading his regiment at the battle of Malplaquet—Major-General Meredith,
and the Earl of Orrery. Peace at length terminated the
struggle, and our heroes returned home in 1714. Shortly
afterwards a rebellion broke out in Scotland, under the

* Vide "Curiosities of War," page 225.

Earl of Mar, son of the Earl of Mar who first commanded our Fusiliers. Supported largely by the clans, presenting a formidable array, he advanced into the Lowlands, proclaiming the Pretender—the son of James II.—to be the rightful sovereign. His vacillating policy—notwithstanding the uncertain issues of the battle of Sheriffmuir, where the royal troops, including our Fusiliers, led by the Duke of Argyle, encountered the rebels—ruined the cause he had assumed to maintain: so that when the Pretender joined his partizans, he found them reduced to such desperate straits, that whilst prudence counselled, cowardice sought the earliest opportunity to effect an escape, leaving his friends to suffer alone the vengeance of the Government. The clans dispersing or submitting, the rebellion died out in 1716.

In 1743 the war of the Austrian Succession once more stirred up the wrathful passions of man, and plunged the European continent into all the horrors of war. The combatants were much the same as on previous occasions—France and Bavaria pitted against Austria and Britain. The Scots Greys, the Third or Scots Foot Guards, (first battalion,) the First or Royal Scots, (first battalion,) the Twenty-first or Royal North British Fusiliers, the Twenty-fifth or King's Own Borderers, and the Forty-second or Royal Highlanders, formed the Scottish regiments embraced in the British army. Under the eye of their chivalric monarch, George II., who in person commanded, our Fusiliers were greatly distinguished by their good conduct, especially at the victory of Dettingen. Subsequently, under Marshal Wade, the regiment was with the

army which penetrated into France in 1744. In the following
year, under the Duke of Cumberland, present at the disastrous
battle of Fontenoy, the regiment lost 285 officers and men.
The valour of our troops, and the successes they had achieved,
were negatived, and the battle lost, by the failure of the Dutch
in other parts of the field. So severe had been the losses of
our Fusiliers on this occasion, that, for the sake of being
recruited, the regiment was removed from the army to garrison
Ostend, where, assailed by a very superior French force, it
was compelled to surrender. At this crisis in our country's
history, the King of France, aiding and abetting the Jacobites, succeeded but too well in inciting the clans to rebellion
under Prince Charles Edward. These troubles at home
occasioned the recall of the major part of the British army,
and amongst others, our Fusiliers, who, advancing from
Edinburgh, were engaged in the pursuit and ultimate overthrow of the rebels at Culloden. Thereafter returning to the
continent, the regiment was engaged at the unavailing battle
of Val in 1747, which led to the peace of Aix-la-Chapelle.

CHAPTER XIII.

" Ye sons of the strong, when that dawning shall break,
Need the harp of the aged remind you to wake?
That dawn never beam'd on your forefathers' eye,
But it roused each high chieftain to vanquish or die."

AMERICA—FRENCH REVOLUTION—WEST INDIES—NEW ORLEANS
—CRIMEA—1748–1862.

RESTLESS like the ocean, anew the spirit of ambition, the thirst
for conquest, awakened the flames of war between these ancient
rivals—France and Britain. In those days, when standing
armies were dreaded by a people ever jealous of the prerogative
of the Crown, with whom, moreover, there still lingered the
bitter experience of the past, or the lively, yet painful, recollection of the tyranny of the Stuarts—in those days our army
was limited. Hence, when war broke out, we find the whole
force of the kingdom called into action, or embarked on foreign
service, leaving to militia and volunteers the defence of "our
hearths and homes"—just as it should ever be. In such
circumstances, in 1761 our Fusiliers were engaged in a
desperate descent upon the French island of Belleisle, situated
in the Bay of Biscay. The natural and artificial defences of
the island had almost defeated the object of the expedition;
and when, after much searching and toil, a landing had been

effected, the dangers to be encountered required the utmost
steadiness and perseverance to be overcome. The French
made a resolute defence, and only surrendered when their
position had become no longer tenable, and no promise of
relief seemed at hand. Afterwards stationed in England, the
regiment in 1765 was sent out for the occupation of West
Florida in America, whence, in 1770, it was removed to
Quebec. It had been commanded by the Earl of Panmure,
who, in 1738 succeeded the Duke of Argyle in the colonelcy,
and in 1770 he was in turn succeeded by Major-General
the Hon. Alexander Mackay. In 1772 our Fusiliers returned
to England; soon, however, to be recalled to the American
States, to take an active part in the unnatural war which
had arisen out of vexing disputes on the all-important question of taxation between the Home and Colonial Governments. Accordingly, in 1776 the regiment was sent out for
the relief of Quebec, then besieged by the Americans. The
timely arrival of such welcome reinforcements, strengthening
and encouraging the garrison, produced an opposite feeling of
weakness and dejection in the ranks of the besiegers, so as to
induce the American General to raise the siege and retire. In
his retreat he was pursued and harassed by the British troops.
In the following year, the Twenty-first, as we shall hence-
forth call them, was employed reducing the American forts,
especially Ticonderago, which studded the shores of Lake
Champlain. Ultimately the regiment formed part of an
unfortunate expedition under Lieut.-General Burgoyne, who,
encouraged by previous successes, was tempted to advance

into the enemy's territory, away from his own resources, where
—notwithstanding the repeated defeats, especially at Still-
water, with which our troops visited the temerity of the foe,
and the heroism with which they conquered all obstacles and
endured many sufferings from the pinchings of want, reduced
to about 3500 fighting men, and surrounded by an American
army of fully 16,000—the Twenty-first, with the relics of the
other regiments included in the expedition, were under the
painful necessity of laying down their arms, and surrendering
themselves prisoners of war. This untoward event terminated
for the present the active service of the Twenty-first. The
battalion, on being released, returned to Britain, where it
remained on home duty until 1789, when, embarking for
America, it was employed for nearly four years in that
country.

The French Revolution having, by a flood of evil influences,
submerged well nigh every vestige of living righteousness,
war, with all its horrors, had been accepted as the dire alternative which, with its fiery deluge, should purge the political
world of the cankering iniquities which hitherto fattened
upon the miseries a tyrant democracy had inflicted upon
civilisation. Unable to cope with the vast armaments which
the revolutionary energy of France had brought into being
and sent forth to convert Christendom to its own dogmas of
"Equality, Fraternity, and Liberty," and whilst these overran
the Netherlands and other adjacent countries, our Government
directed the efforts of its arms against the French West
Indian Islands, the natives and lower classes of which,

becoming infected by the republican fever, had assumed to
be free, and in token thereof adopted the tri-colour cockade,
whilst the Royalists, who, as proprietors and capitalists,
had everything to lose, invoked the friendly aid of Britain.
Accordingly, the Twenty-first, proceeding from Canada to the
West Indies with the army under Major-General Bruce, took
part in the first attempt upon the island of Martinique in
1793, which failed. A second attempt in 1794, under General
Sir Charles Grey, was more successful, the Republicans being
overthrown. This desirable result was speedily followed by
the reduction of the islands of St Lucia and Guadaloupe, in
the capture of both of which the Twenty-first was honourably
distinguished. Our possession of Guadaloupe was not long to
be enjoyed. A powerful French fleet from Europe, with a
considerable body of troops on board, arrived and succeeded
but too well in resuscitating the republican interests, and at
length prevailing, the few British defenders, numbering only
125, were forced to surrender to overwhelming odds. In the
fall of Fort Matilda, which terminated our dominion in the
island, the Twenty-first met with another heavy disaster,
which, with the ravages of the yellow fever, had so reduced
the effective strength of the regiment, that in 1796 it was
sent home to recruit, where it soon attained a strength of 800
men, by volunteers from the Scots Fencible Regiments.

Whilst stationed at Enniskillen, the good conduct of the
regiment won for our Fusiliers the esteem of the inhabitants,
whose good-will could not fail to be appreciated as a record
of no small importance, considering the excellent regiments,

which, bearing the name of "Inniskilling," have ever done
honour by their gallantry to British valour. These good
impressions were deepened, and the deserved esteem of our
Fusiliers greatly increased, by the firm attitude maintained
by the regiment during the Dublin riots of 23d July, 1803.
On this trying occasion, stationed in the Irish metropolis, the
determined front of the Twenty-first, under Major Robertson, (Lieut.-Colonel Brown having been murdered by the
rioters whilst proceeding to join his regiment,) succeeded
in overawing and reducing to obedience the refractory mob
whose discontents had assumed the dangerous character of
a fierce insurrection, and whose malignity towards Government had avenged itself in the barbarous murder of the Lord
Chief Justice, Viscount Kilwarden. The good conduct of the
regiment was rewarded with the public thanks, whilst Lieutenant Douglas and the Adjutant (Brady), as specially distinguished for activity and judgment, were each presented
with a valuable gift of plate.

The vastly increasing power and menacing attitude
assumed by Napoleon had roused the latent energies of the
nation, and in the exigencies of the times, induced one of
those most splendid efforts of true patriotism of which only
a free nation like our own is capable of producing. The
people as one man rose to arms, and practically illustrated
the fervid eloquence of the immortal Pitt, when, with a
soul pregnant with devotion to his country, he exclaimed
—"Were an enemy on our shores, I *never* would lay
down my arms. *Never! never! never!*" whilst the muse

of Campbell summoned the charms of language to aid the
sacred cause:—

> "Rise, fellow-men! Our country yet remains!
> By that dread name we wave the sword on high,
> And swear for her to live, with her to die!"

Amongst the many means adopted to secure an effectual
national defence, the increase of our army was deservedly the
chief. From the youth of the counties of Renfrew and Ayr a
second battalion was raised for our Fusiliers in December
1804; but it was not until 1806 called to an active part in
the terrible contest which then shook Europe to its base. The
defence of Sicily for the legitimate sovereignty of Naples, to
which the Twenty-first was called, although a duty but of
minor importance when compared with the mighty events
which were being enacted on the vaster theatre of Europe,
still the result, redundant with glory, served to give hope to
liberty when the threatened night of tyranny had elsewhere
descended to cloud the nationalities of Christendom; whilst
our British soldiers, if aught dare aspire to the title, proved
themselves to be the real "*invincibles*"—when all else had
been borne down by the legions of France, they alone remained
unconquered. Under Major-General Alexander Mackenzie
Fraser, the first battalion was engaged in the expedition to
Egypt against the Turks; who, in an evil hour, when French
power seemed omnipotent, and French influences in consequence triumphed, had been pressed into the service of the
Emperor, against their better judgment and truer interests.

A single campaign successfully terminated the war, when our first battalion returned to Sicily.

In 1809, with the expedition under Sir John Stuart, the Twenty-first attacked and captured from Murat, vicegerent of Napoleon, styled King of Naples, the islands Ischia and Procida, containing immense material of war. An attack upon the castle of Scylla in Calabria failed, and an attempt to defend the town of Valmi resulted in serious loss to our gallant Fusiliers—no fewer than 80 officers and men falling into the hands of the enemy. Imbued, like his great master, with an insatiate appetite for conquest, and a restless ambition, Murat vehemently longed for an opportunity to expel the British from Sicily, and so unite that valuable island to his new kingdom. Having concentrated a powerful army, and prepared an immense flotilla of gunboats and transports on the shores of Calabria, he, on a dark night in September, 1810, attempted a descent. As the morning dawned it revealed the enemy to the British, and so interrupted their further transport and landing. Those who had come over in the night were so fiercely assailed by the Twenty-first and other regiments, that, with the sea behind and a powerful enemy around, without the prospect of relief or any chance of escape, the French surrendered. The ill success of this well-concerted expedition, induced Murat to abandon for the present the idea of extending his territory beyond the mainland. But our troops were not always thus successful. In 1812 the grenadiers of the Twenty-first sustained a severe disaster as part of the British expedition which failed in an attempted

descent upon the Spanish coast at Alicante. In the expiring
agonies of "the empire of Napoleon," our Fusiliers, although
not seriously exposed to the stern shock of battle, yet helped
materially, by their presence in Italy, and their advance from
Leghorn to Genoa, to drive out the relics of the French "army
of Italy," and so restore freedom to the oppressed who peopled
those lovely plains. At Genoa the regiment encountered the
enemy and prevailed.

Meanwhile our Government, concentrating the whole
energies of the nation, and labouring to hold together the
discordant materials which composed the Grand Alliance,
strove, by one gigantic, persevering effort, to crush out the
usurped dominion of France—the empire—to dethrone the
tyrant, and liberate Europe. Accordingly, a British force
had been sent to the Netherlands, including the second
battalion of the Twenty-first. It took part in the unfortunate attack upon Bergen-op-Zoom, where, miscalculating the
strength and resolution of the enemy, who was strongly posted
in a vast citadel of powerful works, the battalion suffered
severely; encompassed by a numerous foe, many were taken
prisoners. The abdication of Napoleon having conferred
peace upon Europe, the second battalion returned with the
army to Britain, whilst the first battalion was embarked for
service in the West Indies.

The innate pride of the Yankee being hurt by our sovereignty of the seas, determined to dispute our generally acknowledged title thereto. America in consequence became involved
in war with us. To chasten them for repeated insults which

they sought to heap upon our flag, a British expedition, including the first battalion of the Twenty-first, with the Twenty-ninth and Sixty-second regiments, landed in the Bay of Chesapeake. Advancing up the river Patuxent to Upper Marlborough, our army destroyed a numerous fleet of gunboats which had molested our commercial interests in these waters. Within sixteen miles of Washington, the troops, encouraged by the promise of so rich a prize, ventured still further to advance. Encountering and defeating the American army at Bladensburg, they entered Washington in triumph. The Twenty-first, as the van of the British, was the first to set foot in this haughty metropolis of the New World. By the hard decrees of war, not only the arsenals, but much of that which claimed, as public edifices, etc., to beautify and ornament this splendid city, were given over to destruction; and having thus avenged the indignities of the past, our army retired to the fleet at St Benedict. An expedition was afterwards undertaken against Baltimore; but, although success crowned our arms whenever or wherever the enemy encountered our soldiers on any thing like equal terms, especially in the action which ensued at Godly Wood, still was it impossible for such a handful of brave men, amidst increasing difficulties and numerous enemies, to do more; and hence, when our troops had drawn near to Baltimore, they found that opulent and populous city so strongly defended by an American army of 15,000, and deprived, moreover, by circumstances of the assistance of the fleet, it was considered impossible to prosecute the attack with any prospect of success. Retiring, therefore, our army embarked, well satisfied with the results their valour had already achieved. This battalion of the Fusiliers was stationed at Jamaica for a time, until a new expedition was set on foot. The prize in view was the reduction of the great maritime city of New Orleans, situated below the level of the Mississippi which flows by to the sea. The Americans, learn-ing wisdom from the past, and appreciating the value and importance of this city, had laboured to strengthen its means of defence, by the construction of vast and formidable entrenchments which shielded it effectually from assault on the land side. To make good these defences, a powerful army of 12,000 men was thrown into the city, commanded by an able officer—General Jackson. The Britishers who dared to assail such a powerfully defended city did not exceed 6000 men, comprising the Fourth, the Seventh, the first battalion of the Twenty-first, the Forty-third, the Forty-fourth, the Eighty-fifth, the Ninety-third Highlanders, and the Ninety-fifth or Rifle Brigade, with a body of seamen from the fleet. Notwithstanding the disparity in numbers, all might have gone well in the assault, but for the culpable negligence of those in charge, who had forgotten to bring up the scaling-ladders, and ere they could be brought up, our men, unprotected from the deadly discharge of the enemy's numerous artillery, helpless to defend themselves, were mowed down like grass; and yet their front, though sadly contracted by the loss of upwards of 2000 men, remained firm as ever. Sir Edward Pakenham, the British commander, and his generals of division, Gibbs and Keane, had fallen. Major-General Gibbs died of his

wounds, but Major-General Keane became afterwards Lord
Keane. These sore disasters negatived Colonel Thornton's success against the battery on the right, and rendered retreat an
absolute necessity, which was ably conducted by Major-
General Sir John Lambert, although in presence of a vastly
superior and victorious enemy. The relics of this gallant
little army, who had dared to assail such strength and numbers,
were embarked in the fleet on the 27th January, 1815. The
total loss of the Twenty-first on this occasion was 451 officers
and men, which serves to show how dreadful was the carnage
throughout, and how desperate the valour that sustained it
without once flinching from duty. Ere peace was concluded,
which happened shortly thereafter, the expedition succeeded
in the capture of Fort Bowyer, near Mobile.

After such severe service, having returned home and
been somewhat recruited by drafts from the second battalion,
although too late to share the glories of the Waterloo campaign, the battalion was sent to the Netherlands, and thence,
advancing into France, formed part of the "army of occupation" which remained in that kingdom until peace had not
merely been restored but secured. In 1816 the second battalion
was disbanded at Stirling; and a year later, the first battalion,
returning home, was variously stationed in England. In 1819
the regiment was sent on foreign service to the West Indies,
where it was successively stationed in Barbadoes, Tobago,
Demerara, St Vincent, and Grenada. Whilst in Demerara a
rebellion of the negroes occurred. The good conduct of the
regiment in suppressing the revolt elicited the commendation

of the King; the Duke of York, commander-in-chief; Sir Henry
Ward, K.C.B., commanding in these islands; and the Court of
Policy of the colony. These were accompanied by more
substantial rewards. "The Court of Policy voted, as a special
and permanent mark of the high estimation in which the
inhabitants of the colony held the services of Lieut.-Colonel
Leahy, the officers, and soldiers, 'Five Hundred Guineas to be
laid out in the purchase of Plate for the regimental mess,' and
Two Hundred Guineas for the purchase of a sword for Lieut.-
Colonel Leahy; also Fifty Guineas for the purchase of a sword
for Lieutenant Brady, who commanded a detachment at
Mahaica, and whose cool, steady, and intrepid conduct, aided
by the courage and discipline of his men, gave an early and
effectual check to the progress of revolt in that quarter."
Returning home in 1828, the regiment was honoured in doing
duty at Windsor Castle, the residence of royalty. In these
times of comparative peace little of interest falls to be narrated.
We find the regiment employed in various garrisons throughout the kingdom, until, in 1832 and 1833, it was sent out in
charge of convicts to New South Wales, and stationed in the
colonies of Australia and Van Diemen's Land. In 1839 it
was removed to the East Indies, and was stationed successively at Chuiswiah, Calcutta, Dinapore, Kamptee, Agra, Cawnpore, and Calcutta, returning to England in 1848.

In 1854 Russian aggressions had so stirred the nations in
defence of the right, that Turkey in her weakness found ready
sympathisers. Foremost of these, France and England, side
by side, had sent forth powerful armaments, which, landing

upon the Crimean peninsula, created a helpful, and, as the
long-expected result proved, a successful diversion in favour
of the oppressed empire of the Sultan. Amongst the brave,
composing the 26,800 British, that landed at Old Fort, were
our gallant Fusiliers, the Twenty-first. In the Fourth
Division, brigaded with the Twentieth, Fifty-seventh, and
Sixty-eighth, they were present in reserve at the Alma, and
in action at Inkermann. It is needless to repeat the details
of the war, seeing especially we must take occasion so frequently to recur to incidents connected with it; besides, the
general events must be still so fresh in the memories of most
of our readers as to need no repetition here. Enough be it
to say of the conduct of the Twenty-first Royal North British
Fusiliers, that it displayed the same excellence as of old.
Since the return of the regiment to the beloved shores of Old
England, it has enjoyed the peace which its own gallantry had
well contributed to achieve.

As the glory of the sun shining through a humid atmo-
sphere is even more resplendent and more to be admired in the
heaven-bespangled, many-coloured robe of the rainbow than
when he appears in the full strength of noon-day, so valour—
true, genuine valour, the valour of our gallant Twenty-first—
is the more illustrious and meritorious that it is to be found
emerging from amid many vicissitudes and adversities. It is
usually the bravest of the brave that fall. Alas! that so many
who gave fair promise to ornament and illustrate the British
soldier as the hero, should have fallen—buds nipped by the
frost of death. Let it be borne very encouragingly in mind,

that adversity is the furnace wherein the gold of true valour is purified—is the schoolmaster which teaches how to win prosperity. The greatest glory which rests upon the departed genius of Sir John Moore, is that which pictures him in adversity in retreat—his lion spirit unsubdued, his towering abilities shining forth. And so, in closing our record, we would do justice, not merely to valour gilded by brilliant victories, but especially testify to true valour incarnated in the man—the hero ever *struggling*, not always *winning*, yet always *worthy*, the reward.

THE TWENTY-FIFTH FOOT.

KING'S OWN BORDERERS,

OR,

EDINBURGH REGIMENT.

CHAPTER XIV.

"Many a banner spread, flutters above your head,
Many a crest that is famous in story;
Mount and make ready, then, sons of the mountain glen,
Fight for your king and the old Scottish glory.
March, march, forward in order,
A' the blue bonnets are over the border."

ORIGIN — KILLIECRANKIE — IRELAND — NETHERLANDS —
SHERIFFMUIR — NETHERLANDS — CULLODEN — 1688—1755.

It is recorded of Sir Walter Scott that he claimed descent from one of the most distinguished families of "the land-louping gentry" of the Scottish border. The title, "King's Own Borderers," borne by the Twenty-fifth, would induce the belief that the regiment had sprung from the same source; and however much we may excuse the military license of the times, or the marauding propensities of our border country-men, and extol their martial achievements, so prolific with romantic incident and chivalric feats of daring, we cannot but question the respectability of such a parentage.

"She's o'er the border, and awa' wi' Jock o' Hazeldean."

Happily the Twenty-fifth owns a much more recent connection with the Scottish border, when the feuds which had disgraced earlier years, by the wrongs and cruelties they occasioned, were healed, and the failings of the past are forgotten amid the excellencies and the glories of the present. The regiment was raised in the City of Edinburgh by the Earl of Leven, in 1688, from among the noblemen and gentlemen who had come over from the Continent as the adherents of William, Prince of Orange. The advent of the House of Orange, apart from the religious and political liberty it conferred and assumed to guarantee, had been further hailed by an emancipated people as restoring to the bosom of their dear native land, and to the home of their fathers, those "lost and brave," who, for conscience' sake, had endured a long and painful exile. Consistent with that fidelity which has ever been a conspicuous jewel in Scottish character, once that the Reformed faith found an entrance and an abiding-place in the heart of the Scotsman, nor priest, nor king, nor pope could drive it out, quench the light of truth, or shake the steadfastness of the Covenanter. Hence the number of Scottish exiles was very many, and, in consequence, the return of the refugees was an event of no common interest in the Scottish metropolis, diffusing a very general joy throughout the land. Their first duty fulfilled of thanks and gratitude to God for their deliverance, their next duty to their country impelled them to tender the service of their swords to the king. Accordingly, their offer being accepted, the embodiment of the Twenty-fifth King's Own Borderers was the result, which in four hours attained a strength of near a thousand men. Whilst the Scottish estates hesitated to acknowledge the sovereignty of William and Mary, and the Duke of Gordon held possession of the Castle of Edinburgh for King James, the Twenty-fifth was quartered in the Parliament House. But it was not until Viscount Dundee, descending into the Lowlands at the head of the disaffected clans, seriously disturbing the peace of the land, that the regiment was called into action. Advancing with the royal army to Killiecrankie, the Borderers bore a conspicuous and honourable part in the contest which ensued. Major-General Mackay, in his despatch to the Duke of Hamilton, stated, "There was no regiment or troop with me but behaved like the vilest cowards in nature, except Hastings' and Lord Leven's, whom I must praise at such a degree, as I cannot but blame others." The regiments thus commended were the present Thirteenth and Twenty-fifth Foot. Although borne back by the impetuosity of the Highlanders, and although the day was lost to the king, still the result—especially the death of Dundee—proved the ruin of the Jacobites—the beginning of the end, each successive struggle which convulsed the nation more effectually serving to destroy the hopes of the House of Stuart.

In 1691 the regiment embarked for Ireland, and was present, with much credit, at the sieges of Ballymore, Athlone,

Galway, and Limerick, and at the battle of Aughrim. These
several successes having accomplished the deliverance of that
island from the yoke of James, the regiment with other troops
was sent to England, whence it embarked with the British
army for the Netherlands, to check the progress of the French.
Under the command of King William, the allies made a determined stand at Steenkirk and again at Landen, but on both
occasions failed to make any decided impression upon the
masses of the enemy commanded by Marshal de Luxembourg,
who continued to advance in spite of the most gallant opposition. At the siege of Namur, by the explosion of a mine, the
regiment lost twenty officers and 500 men. The gallant
conduct of the allies at this celebrated siege is thus eulogised:

> The British were esteemed most bold;
> The Bavarians most firm; and
> The Brandenburghers most successful;

whilst the French, out of a garrison originally 15,000 strong,
had lost in the defence about two-thirds of their number.
The engineering skill of these great masters of the art—
Coehorn and Vauban, exerted to the utmost on their respective sides—has preserved no more magnificent testimony to
their several abilities than is found recorded in the assault
and defence. The resolution and ability of Marshal Boufflers,
the French Governor, in so gloriously maintaining the defence,
is not to be overlooked, but merited a better success. Sterne's
facetious story of "Tristram Shandy"—how questionable so-
ever its discretion in our times, yet replete with much that

is beautiful, quaint, and true—has borrowed from the ranks of our Borderers its most noted and popular characters, "Uncle Toby," who was wounded in the groin at this siege of Namur, and his faithful body-servant, "Corporal Trim," who, two years previously, had been wounded at the battle of Landen; both, by the pen of the author, being life pictures of the veterans of Chelsea. It was during this war that the bayonet, which had been invented by the French, instead of being fixed *inside* the muzzle of the musket, was first used by the French fixed round the *outside* of the muzzle, thus enabling the soldier to charge and deliver fire promptly. Grose, in his "Military Antiquities," thus records the introduction of this improvement:—

"In an engagement, during one of the campaigns of King William III. in Flanders, there were three French regiments whose bayonets were made to fix after the present fashion (1690), a contrivance then unknown in the British army; one of them advanced with fixed bayonets against Leven's (now the Twenty-fifth) regiment, when Lieutenant-Colonel Maxwell, who commanded it, ordered his men to 'screw bayonets' into their muzzles, thinking the enemy meant to decide the affair point to point; but to his great surprise, when they came within a proper distance, the French threw in a heavy fire, which for a moment staggered his men, who nevertheless recovered themselves, charged, and drove the enemy out of the line."

On the peace of Ryswick being concluded in 1697, our Borderers, returning home, were quartered in the disturbed districts of the North of Scotland. Nothing of importance

falls to be narrated of the regiment until the Rebellion of
the Earl of Mar, in 1715, called it to take the field. It
was present at the unfortunate battle of Sheriffmuir. The
desertion of the Hon. Captain Arthur Elphinstone to the
rebel army, however it might have been regretted as casting a
shadow over the loyalty of the Twenty-fifth, that doubt has
been dispelled, and the lie contradicted, by the exemplary
fidelity of the regiment on all occasions. Captain Elphinstone, as Lord Balmarino, in 1746, paid the penalty of his
error by his execution on Tower Hill.

During the Spanish War of 1719, the regiment was engaged in a successful expedition against various towns on the
north-western sea-board of the Peninsula. For several years
thereafter it was variously stationed in Ireland, and, in 1727,
removed to Gibraltar, where, with other corps, it successfully
defended that important fortress against every attempt of the
Spaniards to reduce and regain it. The war of the Austrian
Succession, which began in 1742, occasioning the assembling of
a British and allied army in the Netherlands, our Borderers
were sent thither to reinforce the troops which had already
won the bloody victory of Dettingen. The regiment shared
the glories and sustained the dangers of Fontenoy, which
elicited from Marshal Saxe, the conquering general, the following graphic and generous testimony to the worth of the
foe he had overthrown :—

"I question much whether there are many of our generals
who dare undertake to pass a plain with a body of infantry
before a numerous cavalry, and flatter himself that he could hold

his ground for several hours, with fifteen or twenty battalions in the middle of an army, as did the English at Fontenoy, without any change being made to shake them, or make them throw away their fire. This is what we have all seen, but self-love makes us unwilling to speak of it, because we are well aware of its being beyond our imitation."

Taking advantage of the disasters which had crowded upon the allied arms in the Netherlands, Prince Charles Edward had stirred up a formidable Rebellion in Scotland, chiefly among the Highland clans, in favour of his pretensions, as the representative of the House of Stuart, to the British throne. This untoward event occasioned the recall of many regiments from the Continent, and required those left behind to confine themselves to the defence of strongly-fortified lines. The Twenty-fifth was one of those that returned. With the Twenty-first Royal North British Fusiliers, it formed the rear guard of the Royal army, advancing in pursuit of the rebels into Scotland. Too late to take any part in the battle of Falkirk, the regiment was stationed in Edinburgh, until the Duke of Cumberland arriving, gave the signal for an immediate advance upon the enemy, then prosecuting the siege of Stirling. Interrupted in their enterprise by the near approach of the Royal army, the rebels retreated precipitately, until, hemmed in, they made a last and fatal stand on Culloden Moor, where they were utterly routed with great slaughter. The most distinguished service performed by a detachment of 300 men of the Twenty-fifth is thus graphically described in the biography of General Melville:—

"The second detachment, consisting of 300 men, commanded by Sir Andrew Agnew, Lieutenant-Colonel of the Royal North British Fusiliers, was sent by the route of Dunkeld, through the Pass of Killiecrankie, to take post in Blair Castle, the seat of James, Duke of Athole—a very faithful subject of his Majesty. The garrison was frittered away in small detachments, for the purpose of intercepting traitorous correspondence. Early on the morning of the 17th March, the rebels, in a considerable body, surprised and made prisoners of several of the outposts, and by break of day closely invested the castle on all sides, firing upon the out-picquet, which retired with some difficulty, bringing with it some horses belonging to the officers, and a small quantity of provisions. Blair Castle was a very high, irregular building, the walls of great thickness—having what was called *Cumming's Tower* projecting from the west end of the front of the house, which faces the north. Adjoining the east gable of the old castle, a square new building had been begun, but only carried up a few feet above the beams fixed for the first floor. The great door in the staircase having been barricaded, and a small guard placed at it, the garrison was mustered and found to consist of about 270 rank and file, having only nineteen rounds of ammunition per man. The men were immediately posted throughout the castle in the manner best adapted for its defence, with instructions not to fire unless actually attacked. For the protection of the new, unfinished building before mentioned, to which the only communication from the castle was by ten or twelve steps of a ladder, from a door in

the east end; a platform of loose boards was hastily laid on
the joists, and Ensign Robert Melville (afterwards General
Melville) of the Twenty-fifth regiment, with 25 men, was
posted on it, who was not relieved during the whole of the
blockade, which ended 1st April.   On the 17th March, a
little after noon, Lord George Murray, a general to the Pretender, wrote a summons of surrender to Sir Andrew Agnew,
which he could not find a Highlander to deliver, on account of
the well-known outrageousness of Sir Andrew's temper, but a
pretty girl, who was acquainted with the garrison, undertook
the task, but could hardly find an officer to receive it, for the
reason before mentioned; however, after much entreaty, one
was bold enough to convey the summons, when Sir Andrew,
in so loud a voice, that he was heard distinctly by the girl
outside the castle, desired him to be gone, and tell Lord
George that the ground would, before long, be too hot for him
to stand upon, and any future messenger would be hanged or
shot if sent upon such an errand.   Lord George took the hint,
sent no other messenger, but endeavoured to reduce the castle
by famine, knowing it was short of provisions.   The rebels
had two field-pieces, from which they fired hot shot upon the
castle, with so little effect that, though some stuck in the roof,
they fell out before the house took fire, and were lifted off
the floors by an iron ladle, which was found in the Duke's
kitchen, and deposited in the cellars in tubs of wine, as water
could not be spared.   The King's troops, in dread of being
starved, endeavoured to apprise the Earl of Craufurd at Dunkeld of the state in which they were placed, but they were so

closely hemmed in, that, with great difficulty, the Duke's gar-
dener, a loyal man, stole out during the ninth night of the
blockade and rode off through the enemy, fired at from several
places by the Highlanders, from whom he escaped, having
fallen from his horse, and gone on foot to Dunkeld and
apprised the Earl, which was not known for some time; in
the meantime, the garrison had great faith in the good luck
of Sir Andrew, concerning whom many strange stories were
told—such as, that he never was wounded nor sick, nor in any
battle wherein the English were not victorious; therefore, they
were the less surprised when, at break of day on the 1st of
April, not a single Highlander could be seen—Lord George
having taken the alarm and decamped, to avoid encountering
the Earl of Cranfurd from Dunkeld. On the morning of the
2d, an officer arrived and announced that the Earl was within
an hour's march of the castle with a force of cavalry, when Sir
Andrew drew up his men to receive his Lordship, and after
the usual compliments, thus addressed him—'My Lord, I am
glad to see you; but, by all that is good, you have been very
dilatory, and we can give you nothing to eat.' To which his
Lordship jocosely replied, with his usual good humour, 'I
assure you, Sir Andrew, I made all the haste I could, and I
hope you and your officers will dine with me to-day;' which
they accordingly did, in the summer-house of the Duke's garden, where they had a plentiful meal and good wines. The
Earl made so favourable a report of the conduct of Sir Andrew
and the garrison of Blair Castle, that the Duke of Cumberland
thanked them, in public orders, for their *steady and gallant*

defence, and the gallant commandant was promoted to the command of a regiment of marines (late Joffries'). A Highland pony, belonging to Captain Wentworth of the Fourth foot, which had been seventeen days (without food) in a dungeon of the castle, being still alive, was recovered by care and proper treatment, and became in excellent condition."

Having thus effectually suppressed the Rebellion, the Twenty-fifth, and most of the other regiments, returned to the Netherlands. Defeated at the battle of Roucoux, the allies were on the point of falling into confusion, when Houghton's British brigade, composed of the Eighth, Thirteenth, and Twenty-fifth, arriving from Maestricht, immediately formed as the rear guard, their steady valour effectually withstanding every attempt of the enemy to break in upon our line of retreat. In the sanguinary battle of Val, our Borderers bore a more prominent part with equal credit. This disastrous war terminated in 1747, with the unsuccessful defence of Bergen-op-Zoom, which was ultimately taken by the French. The regiment encountered a variety of misadventures on its passage home. One transport, containing six and a-half companies, being shipwrecked on the French coast, yet all escaping to land, were kindly treated by their recent foes. The regiment, at length reaching England, was removed to and variously quartered throughout Ireland.

CHAPTER XV.

"He's brave as brave can be;
He wad rather fa' than flee;
But his life is dear to me,
    Send him hame, send him hame.

" Your love ne'er learnt to flee,
But he fell in Germanie,
Fighting brave for loyalty,
    Mournfu' dame, mournfu' dame."

GERMANY—MARINE SERVICE—WEST INDIES—EGYPT—WEST
INDIES—GIBRALTAR—1755–1802.

In 1755 the encroachments of France awakened a new war, in which our Borderers were employed in several generally successful expeditions against the fortified towns and arsenals on the coast of France, especially the Isle of Oleron, St Maloes, and Cherbourg. A few years later, with the Twelfth, the Twentieth, the Twenty-third, the Thirty-seventh, and Fifty-first Foot, the Horse Guards, the First and Third Dragoon Guards, the Second, Sixth, and Tenth Dragoons, they formed the British army, which, advancing from the north of Germany, allied with the Germans and other auxiliaries, latterly served under the command of Prince Ferdinand of Brunswick. Encountering at first severe reverses, they were at length rewarded by the victory of Minden. "This was the first occasion on which the British troops took aim by placing

the butt of the firelock against the shoulder, and viewing
the object along the barrel, when firing at the enemy, in
which mode they had been instructed during the preceding
peace. On former occasions, the firelock was brought up
breast-high, and discharged towards the enemy a good deal
at random; because it was considered a degradation to take
aim according to the present custom. And in this year the
cavalry adopted the trumpet, in place of the side-drum and
hautbois." Throughout the war, the regiment suffered very
severely, its loss at the battle of Campen alone amounting to
two-thirds of its number. In the Regimental Records, which
afford a most interesting and ably-written account of the
many "brave deeds" of the regiment, as well as a comprehensive, yet most accurate, record of the wars in which it was
concerned, and to which we are largely indebted, it is recorded: "1760, December 9, died, in the 34th year of his
age, of the wounds he had received in the battle of Campen,
Henry Reydell Dawnay, Viscount Down, Baron Dawnay of
Cowick, county York, M.P. for that county, Colonel in the
army, and Lieutenant-Colonel commanding the Edinburgh
Regiment, greatly regretted and lamented by every officer
and soldier of the corps, and by all his companions in arms.
His Lordship commanded the regiment in the battle of Minden." Notwithstanding the great superiority of the enemy,
ably commanded by the Marshal Duke de Broglio, the allies,
by the most heroic efforts, not merely held their own, but frequently repulsed the enemy, especially at the battle of Kirch
Denkern, or Fellinghausen, where the French were defeated

with great slaughter. "Hitherto, punishments in the British army were, to a certain extent, discretionary with commanding officers of corps, and inflicted by means of switches, generally willows; but during the present year, regimental courts-martial, consisting generally of a captain and four subalterns, were instituted, and punishment with a cat-of-nine-tails introduced."

At length, in 1763, peace was restored. The Twenty-fifth, returning to England, whilst stationed at Newcastle, buried, with military honours, the shreds of the colours which they had so honourably fought under at the battles of Fontenoy, Culloden, Roucoux, Val, Minden, Warbourg, Campen, Fellinghausen, and Wilhelmsthal. Having replaced the losses they had suffered in the recent war, and having enjoyed for several years peaceful and pleasant quarters at home, our Borderers, in 1768, embarked in H.M.S. "Dorsetshire," 70 guns, for Minorca, where they discharged the duties of the garrison for some time with the Third, Eleventh, Thirteenth, and Sixty-seventh regiments.

The magistrates of Edinburgh having denied a recruiting party from the regiment the ancient privilege, conferred upon it by the city in token of its good conduct at Killiecrankie, of marching at all times through the streets and beating up for recruits, the ire of the Duke of Richmond, whose brother, Lord George Lennox, then commanded the regiment, was so stirred by this indignity, that he applied for leave to have the title of the regiment changed, and, in accordance therewith, it was for a while known as the Sussex Regiment—Sussex being the county where the Lennox family held extensive estates.

About this period France and Spain, at war with Great Britain, coveting the possession of Gibraltar, had laid siege to that powerful fortress. It was no easy thing in those days, when our navy was comparatively in its infancy, to cope with the armaments of such powerful neighbours—powerful alike on land and water, and whose combined fleets had hitherto "swept the seas." To throw in reinforcements, and re-victual Gibraltar, was in consequence a hazardous undertaking; nevertheless the British fleet, under Lord Howe, not only successfully accomplished it in spite of the immediate presence of the Spanish fleet, but signally defeated the foe off Cape St. Vincent. The Twenty-fifth and Twenty-ninth regiments were on this occasion thrown into the garrison, where they helped in the successful defence of the fortress, baffling the most gigantic efforts of the enemy to reduce it.

The Twenty-fifth was ordered home in 1792, where it arrived at a time when our country was in great peril from internal enemies—the discontents which the fair promises of the French Revolution had excited, and which proved such a lamentable delusion, had their effects even amongst "our sober selves," begetting a progeny of evils which threatened to shipwreck our good ship—the Constitution. Happily, the abilities of our Administration brought the vessel of the State in safety through the storm. Meanwhile France had declared war against us, and the tempest, which had been imminent, descended with terrible fury. Our fleet, which was then wofully inefficient, was put into commission; but, for lack of marines, detachments from various regiments, amongst others the Second (Queen's), the Twenty-fifth (Borderers), the Twenty-ninth, and Sixty-ninth, were allotted to this service. In this new capacity a portion of the Twenty-fifth was engaged in the several land actions which are recorded in the fruitless defence of Toulon and conquest of Corsica. Although this new duty was at first attended with many disagreeables, it in the end proved a most profitable service to our soldiers, who soon became reconciled to the change. The spoil got on the sea by repeated captures far exceeded aught that might have been expected on shore. On one occasion the "St George" and "Egmont," with detachments of the Twenty-fifth on board as marines, captured the French privateer "General Dumourier," with a Spanish prize in tow, the "St Jago"—treasure-ship containing about one million sterling. Under Lord Howe this amphibious regiment was present to share the glories of the fight which almost annihilated the French fleet off Brest. At length, in 1794, the corps of marines having been strengthened, the regiment was relieved and returned to its native element—the land. Still we shall find that its adventures, as well as misadventures, throughout these records manifest a strong predilection for the sea—perhaps not of choice, but certainly of necessity. The loyalty of the regiment whilst serving as marines was most conspicuous during the mutiny which, in 1797, threatened very disastrous results.

In 1795, the regiment was sent to the West Indies; and whilst stationed in Grenada, rendered most important service were employed in defending Granada from the incursions of numerous hordes of brigands who infested it. The heroic defence of Pilot Hill by the Twenty-fifth, under Major Wright, is one of the most gallant actions to be found in the records of our army. Reduced by disease and the sword to about 130 officers and privates, these brave men refused to yield, well knowing, moreover, the ferocious character of the enemy with whom they had to deal. At length, exhausted and without the means to sustain life or longer maintain the post, they determined to break through the enemy, which they successfully accomplished, joining the few British that yet remained in St George's, the capital, where they were hailed by the inhabitants as the saviours of the island: the ladies, in token of their appreciation of such valour, wore ribands round their waists—inscribed, "Wright for ever;" whilst the following address was presented to the relics of the regiment:—"The inhabitants of this island congratulate Major Wright of the Twenty-fifth regiment, and his gallant little garrison of Pilot Hill, on their safe arrival in St George; and assure him that it was with the most lively sensation of joy they beheld the landing of a handful of brave men, whom, a few hours before, they considered as devoted to the relentless cruelty of a savage and ferocious enemy; and impressed with a high sense of their meritorious exertions in defence of that post, and the well-conducted retreat upon the evacuation of it under the most desperate circumstances, request his and their acceptance of this tribute of their approbation and thanks, so justly due to such bravery and conduct."

The arrival of reinforcements enabled the British once more to take the field, recovering the posts which lack of numbers had compelled them hitherto to abandon; and in the end, the brigands, defeated, were dispersed, or craved, by submission, the clemency of the Government.

Meanwhile the detachments which had been called in from the marine service on board the " St George," the "Egmont," the " Gibraltar," the "Monarch," the "Stately," and the "Re-union," with a number of recruits obtained chiefly from among the Dutch sailors, who had become prisoners of war, were enrolled as a second battalion. Encamped with the army assembled on Shirley Common, this battalion was, in 1795, moved to the coast, and embarked on board the "Boddington" and the "Belfast." The fleet, containing the army, which amounted to nearly 26,000 fighting men, consisted of about 300 sail. A variety of accidents arose to detain the expedition, and ultimately caught in a tempest, the vast armament was broken or dispersed. In the confusion which ensued, the "Boddington," with part of the Twenty-fifth on board, her officers having opened the sealed orders, and found the West Indies to be the destination of the expedition, encountering many perils, at length reached Barbadoes in safety; whilst the "Belfast," with the remainder of the regiment, was captured by a French corvette, the "Decius," twenty-four guns. The unfortunate prisoners were treated most cruelly, and the more so that a conspiracy to rise upon their captors had been divulged by one of the Dutchmen who had re-cently joined the regiment. Landed at St Martin's, they

were afterwards removed to the common gaol at Guadaloupe,
during the passage to which the men of the regiment rose
against and overpowered the crew of one of the transports,
and succeeded in escaping to the British island of Grenada,
where they joined their comrades of the first battalion who
still survived. The officers remaining prisoners were inhumanly treated, and only released by exchange, after enduring for ten months the miseries of confinement on board the
prison hulk "Albion"—a vessel captured from the British.
On their passage to rejoin the regiment which had returned
home, calling at the island of St Christopher, they had the
satisfaction of witnessing the captain and crew of the
"Decius" in irons as prisoners. Unhappily this "chapter of
accidents" had not yet ended. On the homeward voyage
the transports, under convoy of the "Ariadne" frigate, encountered so severe a tempest that several foundered—the
frigate was under the necessity of throwing her guns over-
board; the "Bee" transport, shifting her ballast, was cast on
her beam ends, and was only saved by a marvel of mercy—
saved from the storm, to become the prey of a French privateer. Landed as prisoners in France, the officers were sent
on their parole into Brittany, until regularly exchanged.
On returning, the survivors rejoined the relics of the regiment in Plymouth lines in 1797. Whilst in garrison here,
along with the Second and Twenty-ninth Foot, and the Down
Militia, the regiment was exposed to the villany of an evil-
disposed and disaffected class—revolutionary incendiaries—
the creatures of an iniquitous delusion, in whose soul the God-

like emotion of patriotism had been stifled, and who appeared
the specious friends yet certain foes of virtue. Armed with
all the seductive attractions of the licentious liberty they
preached, they therewith hoped to ruin our ancient constitution, and set up in its stead the lying, fatal dogmas of democracy. To accomplish this end, they strove to destroy the
bulwarks of our strength as a nation by the seduction of
our soldiers and sailors. In the presence of other grievances,
and the absence of immediate redress, these incendiaries had
succeeded but too well in imposing upon the navy, and exciting a dangerous mutiny, to which we have already referred,
as illustrating the fidelity of the Twenty-fifth, who served as
marines, and who could not be induced to forsake their duty
to their country, nor stain the honour of the regiment by any
defection. We now turn to record the fidelity of the regiment as equally creditable in the army; and we have
pleasure in adding the following as a testimony of the
loyalty which animated our Borderers. This interesting docu-
ment—the production of the Non-Commissioned Officers of
the regiment—affords us an earnest of their anxiety to detect
and bring to punishment the incendiaries who had dared to
sap the allegiance of the soldier :—

"*Nemo me impune lacessit.* The subscribing Non-Commissioned Officers of H.M. Twenty-fifth regiment of foot, find,
with great regret, that attempts have been made by base and
infamous persons to alienate some of the soldiers of this garrison
from their duty to their King and country, by circulating in-

flammatory papers and hand-bills containing the grossest false-
hood and misrepresentation, thereby insulting the character of
the British soldier. In order to bring the incendiaries to the
punishment they so justly deserve, we hereby offer a reward
of ten guineas (to be paid on conviction) to the person or
persons who will inform upon, secure, or deliver over to any
of the subscribers, the author, printer, or distributor of papers
or hand-bills criminal to the military establishment and laws
of the country, or for information against any such person
found guilty of bribing with money, or of holding out any
false allurements to any soldier in this district tending to
injure the good order and discipline of the army; which
reward of ten guineas is raised and subscribed by us for this
purpose, and will immediately be paid on conviction of any
such offenders. God save the King!

> "Signed by the whole of the Non-Commissioned
> Officers of the Regiment."

Stationed in Jersey in 1798, on returning to England the
regiment formed part of the army encamped on Barham
Downs and Shirley Common, until embraced in the unfortunate expedition which, in 1799, under the Duke of York, occasioned the loss of so much British blood and treasure in a
vain attempt to deliver Holland from the thraldom of France.
Notwithstanding the glory obtained in the battle of Egmont-
op-Zee, little practical good resulted. The Dutch seemed dis-
inclined to help themselves, and the French were in such force,
whilst our expedition was so inadequate to do more than hold

its own, that retreat and the ultimate abandonment of the enterprise ensued as a necessary consequence. On the return of the
army, the Twenty-fifth was encamped on Shirley Common,
where the troops assembled were, in 1800, reviewed by the
King, who afterwards engaged in a sham fight with the Duke
of York, and is represented as having beaten him. Shortly
thereafter an expedition sailed under Sir Ralph Abercromby
for Spain, but ill success there led that chief ultimately to
direct his efforts for the expulsion of the French from Egypt.
Here he fell gloriously, at the battle of Alexandria, in the
arms of victory. The Twenty-fifth joined the army towards
the close of the campaign. The surrender of the French
having completed the deliverance of Egypt, the army returned
in part to England, whence, in 1807, the Twenty-fifth was
sent out to the West Indies, where, in 1809, it shared in the
capture of the French island of Martinique.

" In the year 1813, while Lieut.-Colonel Light commanded
the first battalion, Twenty-fifth Foot, in the island of Guadaloupe, happening to dine with the Governor, he was riding home
to the barracks, distant about one mile from the Governor's
house, in a violent thunderstorm with heavy rain. A vivid
flash of lightning coming very close to his horse, the animal
took fright, and suddenly sprang over a precipice of fifty-four
feet deep, which lay about five yards from the road on the
right, into a river swelled considerably by the rain. The
horse was killed by the fall, but Lieut.-Colonel Light swam
on shore, with very little injury, and walked home to his
barracks, a quarter of a mile distant from the place.

"Lord George Henry Lennox, son to Charles, second Duke of Richmond, and father of Charles, fourth Duke of Richmond, was colonel of the Twenty-fifth Regiment from 22d December, 1762, to 22d March, 1805 (the day of his death), a space of forty-two years and three months. His lordship was particularly attached to the regiment; so much so, that, notwithstanding his great interest—being a personal friend of the King (George III.)—his lordship was understood to have declined being removed to any other corps, although it was at the time alleged and believed that he had frequently the offer of a cavalry regiment. Lord George Henry Lennox was truly a father to the corps—never sparing any expense in its equipments, and never failing to use all his interest in promoting the officers to every vacancy which occurred in the corps; and his lordship has been known, in anticipation of a failure in this respect with the Commander-in-chief, to have solicited and succeeded with His Majesty in preventing promotion in passing out of the regiment"—and in the word "Minden" being allowed to be borne on its colours and appointments.

Having been engaged in nearly all the actions which, one by one, reduced the French West Indian Islands and placed them under British rule, the regiment returned to England in 1816, whilst the second battalion was about the same time disbanded or merged in the first battalion. After doing duty in various garrisons in Ireland for nearly ten years, the regiment, in 1825, once more was sent out to the West Indies.

Since its return to Great Britain it has remained on home service, excepting now, when, again increased to two battalions, the first is stationed at Gibraltar, whilst the second, garrisoning Edinburgh Castle, revels in the pleasing associations of "auld langsyne."

THE TWENTY-SIXTH FOOT;

OR,

CAMERONIANS.

CHAPTER XVI.

"The Martyr's Hill's forsaken,
In simmer's dusk sae calm,
There's nae gath'ring now, lassie,
To sing the e'ening psalm;
But the martyr's grave will rise, lassie,
Aboon the warrior's cairn;
And the martyr soun' will sleep, lassie,
Aneath the waving fern."

ORIGIN AND EARLY HISTORY—DUNKELD—1689–1691.

THE bigotry which at various times in our world's history
has lighted the fires of persecution, has always proved itself
impotent to make men righteous or unrighteous. Rather
has it entailed a curse upon the tyrant whilst inflicting a
woe upon the people who groaned beneath his rule. The
freedom which the accession of the House of Orange conferred upon every rank of society, and every phase of be-

lief, established the sovereignty of William and Mary, not merely over the heads of the people, but in the love and loyalty of their hearts. We have already alluded to the origin of the Twenty-fifth as expressive of these sentiments, and we now turn to the history of the Twenty-sixth, or Cameronians, as furnishing another exponent of the gratitude and loyalty of the emancipated Covenanters. The origin of this famous regiment—well worthy, by the lustre of its deeds, of the pen of a Macaulay to record—has elicited from that great national historian the following graphic account, which, as well for the sake of variety as its own excellence, we are here tempted to quote:—

"The Covenanters of the West were in general unwilling to enlist. They were assuredly not wanting in courage; and they hated Dundee with deadly hatred. In their part of the country the memory of his cruelty was still fresh. Every village had its own tale of blood. The greyheaded father was missed in one dwelling, the hopeful stripling in another. It was remembered but too well how the dragoons had stalked into the peasant's cottage, cursing and damning him, themselves, and each other at every second word, pushing from the ingle nook his grandmother of eighty, and thrusting their hands into the bosom of his daughter of sixteen; how the adjuration had been tendered to him; how he had folded his arms and said 'God's will be done;' how the colonel had called for a file with loaded muskets; and how in three minutes the goodman of the house had been wallowing in a pool of blood at his own door. The seat of the martyr was still vacant at the fire-side; and every child could point out his grave still green amidst the heath. When the people of this region called their oppressor a servant of the devil, they were not speaking figuratively. They believed that between the bad man and the bad angel there was a close alliance on definite terms; that Dundee had bound himself to do the work of hell on earth, and that, for high purposes, hell was permitted to protect its slave till the measure of his guilt should be full. But intensely as these men abhorred Dundee, most of them had a scruple about drawing the sword for William. A great meeting was held in the parish church of Douglas; and the question was propounded, whether, at a time when war was in the land, and when an Irish invasion was expected, it were not a duty to take arms? The debate was sharp and tumultuous. The orators on one side adjured their brethren not to incur the curse denounced against the inhabitants of Meroz, who came not to the help of the Lord against the mighty. The orators on the other side thundered against sinful associations. There were malignants in William's army: Mackay's own orthodoxy was problematical: to take military service with such comrades, and under such a general, would be a sinful association. At length, after much wrangling, and amidst great confusion, a vote was taken; and the majority pronounced that to take military service would be a sinful association. There was, however, a large minority; and, from among the members of this minority, the Earl of Angus was able to raise a body of infantry, which is still, after the lapse of more than a hundred and sixty years, known

by the name of the Cameronian Regiment. The first Lieut.-
Colonel was Cleland, that implacable avenger of blood who
had driven Dundee from the Convention. There was no small
difficulty in filling the ranks, for many west country Whigs,
who did not think it absolutely sinful to enlist, stood out for
terms subversive of all military discipline. Some would not
serve under any colonel, major, captain, serjeant, or corporal
who was not ready to sign the Covenant. Others insisted
that, if it should be found absolutely necessary to appoint any
officer who had taken the tests imposed in the late reign, he
should at least qualify himself for command by publicly con-
fessing his sin at the head of the regiment. Most of the
enthusiasts who had proposed these conditions were induced
by dexterous management to abate much of their demands.
Yet the new regiment had a very peculiar character. The
soldiers were all rigid Puritans. One of their first acts was to
petition the Parliament that all drunkenness, licentiousness,
and profaneness might be severely punished. Their own conduct must have been exemplary: for the worst crime which
the most austere bigotry could impute to them was that of
huzzaing on the King's birth-day. It was originally intended
that with the military organisation of the corps should be
interwoven the organisation of a Presbyterian congregation.
Each company was to furnish an elder; and the elders were,
with the chaplain, to form an ecclesiastical court for the
suppression of immorality and heresy. Elders, however, were
not appointed; but a noted hill preacher, Alexander Shields,
was called to the office of chaplain. It is not easy to conceive

that fanaticism can be heated to a higher temperature than that which is indicated by the writings of Shields. According to him, it should seem to be the first duty of a Christian ruler to persecute to the death every heterodox subject, and the first duty of a Christian subject to poinard a heterodox ruler. Yet there was then in Scotland an enthusiasm compared with which the enthusiasm even of this man was lukewarm. The extreme Covenanters protested against his defection as vehemently as he had protested against the Black Indulgence and the oath of supremacy, and pronounced every man who entered Angus's regiment guilty of a wicked confederacy with malignants."

Immediately after its formation, the regiment, which was raised to a strength of near 1000 men in a few hours, marched and was stationed in Edinburgh, where it served to keep under the rebellious schemes of many a hot-headed Jacobite. Although Dundee appeared the natural enemy of such a regiment, still it had not the satisfaction of being present at Killiecrankie, where that great chieftain fell in what may be well considered the greatest victory of his life. The disasters of the fight, and the apparent ruin of the Royal cause, called for immediate succour being sent to Major-General Mackay; but the blunders of those in power at Edinburgh, distrusting Mackay, and, like too many councils, essaying to be generals as well as statesmen, very nigh consigned our Cameronians to a cruel fate. Advancing into the heart of the disaffected districts, and stationed at Dunkeld, the regiment—but for its dauntless spirit and heroic endurance, and the incapacity of General Cannon, who had succeeded Dundee in the command of the rebels—would have been utterly cut to pieces. The result of the conflict was most glorious, early displaying the mettle of this gallant regiment. Lord Macaulay thus summons the rich elegance and might of language to describe the scene:—

"The Cameronian regiment was sent to garrison Dunkeld. Of this arrangement Mackay altogether disapproved. He knew that at Dunkeld these troops would be near the enemy; that they would be far from all assistance; that they would be in an open town; that they would be surrounded by a hostile population; that they were very imperfectly disciplined, though doubtless brave and zealous; that they were regarded by the whole Jacobite party throughout Scotland with peculiar malevolence; and that in all probability some great effort would be made to disgrace and destroy them.

"The General's opinion was disregarded; and the Cameronians occupied the post assigned to them. It soon appeared that his forebodings were just. The inhabitants of the country round Dunkeld furnished Cannon with intelligence, and urged him to make a bold push. The peasantry of Athol, impatient for spoil, came in great numbers to swell his army. The regiment hourly expected to be attacked, and became discontented and turbulent. The men, intrepid, indeed, both from constitution and enthusiasm, but not yet broken to habits of military submission, expostulated with Cleland, who commanded them. They had, they imagined, been recklessly, if not perfidiously, sent to certain destruction.

They were protected by no ramparts: they had a very scanty stock of ammunition: they were hemmed in by enemies. An officer might mount and gallop beyond reach of danger in an hour: but the private soldier must stay and be butchered. ' Neither I,' said Cleland, ' nor any of my officers will, in any extremity, abandon you. Bring out my horse, all our horses: they shall be shot dead.' These words produced a complete change of feeling. The men answered that the horses should not be shot, that they wanted no pledge from their brave Colonel except his word, and that they would run the last hazard with him. They kept their promise well. The Puritan blood was now thoroughly up; and what that blood was when it was up had been proved on many fields of battle.

" That night the regiment passed under arms. On the morning of the following day, the twenty-first of August, all the hills round Dunkeld were alive with bonnets and plaids. Cannon's army was much larger than that which Dundee had commanded, and was accompanied by more than a thousand horses laden with baggage. Both the horses and baggage were probably part of the booty of Killiecrankie. The whole number of Highlanders was estimated by those who saw them at from four to five thousand men. They came furiously on. The outposts of the Cameronians were speedily driven in. The assailants came pouring on every side into the streets. The church, however, held out obstinately. But the greater part of the regiment made its stand behind a wall which surrounded a house belonging to the Marquess of Athole. This wall, which had two or three days before been hastily repaired with timber and loose stones, the soldiers defended desperately with musket, pike, and halbert. Their bullets were soon spent; but some of the men were employed in cutting lead from the roof of the Marquess's house and shaping it into slugs. Meanwhile all the neighbouring houses were crowded from top to bottom with Highlanders, who kept up a galling fire from the windows. Cleland, while encouraging his men, was shot dead. The command devolved on Major Henderson. In another minute Henderson fell pierced with three mortal wounds. His place was supplied by Captain Munro, and the contest went on with undiminished fury. A party of the Cameronians sallied forth, set fire to the houses from which the fatal shots had come, and turned the keys in the doors. In one single dwelling sixteen of the enemy were burnt alive. Those who were in the fight described it as a terrible initiation for recruits. Half the town was blazing; and with the incessant roar of the guns were mingled the piercing shrieks of wretches perishing in the flames. The struggle lasted four hours. By that time the Cameronians were reduced nearly to their last flask of powder: but their spirit never flagged. 'The enemy will soon carry the wall. Be it so. We will retreat into the house: we will defend it to the last; and, if they force their way into it, we will burn it over their heads and our own.' But, while they were revolving these desperate projects, they observed that the fury of the assault slackened. Soon the Highlanders began to fall back: disorder visibly spread among them; and whole bands began to march off to the

hills. It was in vain that their general ordered them to
return to the attack. Perseverance was not one of their
military virtues. The Cameronians meanwhile, with shouts
of defiance, invited Amalek and Moab to come back and to
try another chance with the chosen people. But these
exhortations had as little effect as those of Cannon. In a
short time the whole Gaelic army was in full retreat towards
Blair. Then the drums struck up: the victorious Puritans
threw their caps into the air, raised, with one voice, a psalm
of triumph and thanksgiving, and waved their colours, colours
which were on that day unfurled for the first time in the
face of an enemy, but which have since been proudly borne
in every quarter of the world, and which are now embellished
with the 'Sphinx' and the 'Dragon,' emblems of brave actions
achieved in Egypt and in China."

"The Cameronians had good reason to be joyful and
thankful; for they had finished the war." The loss of the
regiment did not exceed 70 men, whilst the rebels lost 300:
but the death of their brave Commander, Colonel Cleland,
was a source of great regret to the Cameronians. This
desperate resistance, insignificant in itself, so cooled the
fiery zeal of the clans, that, melting away like snow, General
Cannon was compelled to retreat, and, soon without an
army, to submit.

CHAPTER XVII.

"Farewell! ye dear partners of peril, farewell!
Tho' buried ye lie in one wide bloody grave,
Your deeds shall ennoble the place where ye fell,
And your names be enroll'd with the sons of the brave."

1691–1862 — THE NETHERLANDS—REBELLION, 1715—AMERICA—
EGYPT—CORUNNA—WALCHEREN—INDIA—CHINA—CANADA.

IN 1691 the regiment joined the British army then serving
in Flanders against the French, and, by its steady valour,
fully maintained its character at the battle of Steenkirk and
the siege of Namur. So highly did the King appreciate its
worth, that, when peace induced the Government to disband
many regiments, he retained the Cameronians in his own pay,
on the establishment of the Dutch Estates.

The arrogant pretensions of the House of Bourbon to the
vacant throne of Spain, in opposition to the claims of the
House of Hapsburg, re-kindled the flames of war, and bade
France and Austria, as the principals, seconded by Bavaria
and Britain, engage in mortal combat. Of the British
army sent to Holland in consequence, the Twenty-sixth
formed a part. In 1703, brigaded with the Tenth, the
Sixteenth, the Twenty-first, and the second battalion of the
First Royal Scots, it served with great distinction in the army

of Marlborough at Donawerth, and specially at the battle of
Blenheim, where, suffering severely, it had to lament the loss
of nineteen officers. At the battle of Ramilies, in 1706,
the regiment, after being much exposed throughout the
fight, was engaged in the pursuit of the beaten foe until
midnight. It further shared the sanguinary glories of
Malplaquet ere the war was terminated by the peace of
Utrecht in 1713. Soon after its return home, the infatuation
of the Jacobites, whose licentious habits could not brook to
be bridled by the austere yet healthier *morale* which presided in the Protestant Court of the House of Hanover—
longing for the restoration of that of Stuart as likely to
afford freer scope for the indulgence of their own evil appetites
—organised a conspiracy, which brought forth the rebellion
of 1715. The Earl of Mar, an imbecile chief and ungrateful minion of the Court, essayed to be its leader in Scotland, whilst Sir John Foster and other cavaliers vainly
strove simultaneously to arouse the malignant Jacobitism
which slumbered in the northern counties of England. To
meet the few who had dared to challenge the existing
sovereignty, and under Foster were advancing southward
through Lancashire in hopes of being reinforced by other
malcontents, a body of royal troops was hastily collected,
chiefly cavalry—the Twenty-sixth being the only infantry
regiment. Without order, a distinct plan of action, or any
definite understanding as to a leader, the enemy, who had
taken possession of, and proposed to hold Preston against the
assault of the Royalist army, was easily broken, dispersed, and

their cause utterly ruined. During this unfortunate rebellion, which occasioned the effusion of much blood, Colonel Blackader—who had accompanied the Twenty-sixth in its continental campaigns, where he was ever distinguished among "the bravest of the brave," and whose ably-written records have bequeathed to our day much that is valuable in the thread of Scottish military history, and interesting in the annals of the Cameronian regiment—at this period commanded the Glasgow Volunteers. The rebellion being suppressed, the regiment was placed upon the Irish establishment, garrisoning various posts in the emerald isle until the year 1727, when it was removed to reinforce the troops which then defended the important fortress of Gibraltar, baffling the most stupendous efforts of the Spaniards to reduce it. Eleven years later it was sent to Minorca, and thence returned home in 1754. This long absence on foreign service was succeeded by an interval of quietude at home, so far at least as the service of our Cameronians was concerned. In 1775, the unhappy conflict began which bereft us of a valuable colony, and severed us from those who ought to have been one with us as brethren. Like the Northern States of America *now*, so we *then*, in the pride of our own self-righteous will which had been challenged, supposed to enforce legislation by the sword. Hence a British army, including the Twenty-sixth, was sent out to America. Although at first the progress of our arms was graced with many successes, still the end proved most disastrous. The Colonists, sorely schooled in adversity, learned, through many defeats, how to conquer, the more so when the shining abilities of Washington appearing, directed their native valour and commanded their confidence as well as their obedience. Shortly after the capture of St John's, a detachment of the regiment having been embarked in a vessel for secret service, the expedition, discovered by the enemy, was pursued and captured. When escape was seen to be impossible, and resistance hopeless, to prevent the colours falling into the hands of the foe, they were wound round a cannon shot and sunk in the river; and thus, however severe the dispensation which befel themselves in being made prisoners of war, the regiment was spared the aggravated pain of seeing the colours it had followed to so many glorious successes— the epitome of a soldier's honour—becoming now, in the hands of the enemy, the record of its present misfortune. Subsequently the regiment was engaged with the army, under Lieut.-General Sir Henry Clinton, during the campaigns of 1777–78.

Returning home from Halifax, in 1800, the transport, containing one company of the regiment, under command of Captain Campbell, was captured by the French privateer "Grande Decidée." With the British army under Sir Ralph Abercromby—which achieved the deliverance of Egypt—the Cameronians won a title by distinguished service, to include "Egypt" among the records of its bravery. Meanwhile, the necessities of the state were such that, the Government resolving to strengthen the army, a second battalion was raised and grafted upon the good old stock of the Twenty-sixth. In these times of war little rest could be expected.

To the brave, the patriot, it was peculiarly a time of action, not mere idle alarm. Our country rejoiced in the security which was ensured by an army, of which our Cameronians were so honoured a representative. Our sovereigns benignantly smiled upon and proudly felt themselves happy when they regarded the ranks of these our gallant defenders, nor feared invasion so long as they possessed the allegiance of such soldiers. Grieving that so large a kingdom as that of Spain should have fallen a prey to the rapacious perfidy of Napoleon, and sympathising with the patriotic efforts which a spirited people were then putting forth to be free, our Government had recognised in that peninsula, with its extensive sea-board, a fair theatre for action, and as the result proved, a vulnerable point where Europe might strike a fatal blow at the absorbing dominion of France. Following up these ideas, and in answer to the earnest petitions for help from the people themselves, who gathered together into patriotic bands, yet dared to struggle against the tyranny which enslaved and ruined all who owned its supremacy, our Government, in 1808, sent out a British army under Sir John Moore, which, co-operating with the natives and the British army of Portugal, it was vainly hoped should expel the enemy. The Twenty-sixth regiment, included in this expedition, was doomed to share its cruel disappointments, yet earn a title to the glory which must ever rest upon the memory of the soldiers of Corunna. With the native daring of his race, Sir John Moore advanced with 25,000 men into the very heart of Spain, and only retreated when the expected aid from the Spaniards had been dissipated by their defeat and ruin, and when Napoleon in person, at the head of an army of 300,000 men, threatened to overwhelm his little phalanx of British. Then, but not till then, he undertook that masterly retreat which achieved the salvation of his brave troops, and in the end loaded himself with honour, as closing a life of worth, he won the laurel crown, and

"Like a soldier fell"

in the arms of victory.   Lieut.-General Hope thus fitly records the irreparable loss sustained in the death of Sir John Moore:—

"I need not expatiate on the loss which the army and his country have sustained by the death of Sir John Moore. His fall has deprived me of a valuable friend, to whom long experience of his worth had sincerely attached me. But it is chiefly on public grounds that I must lament the blow. It will be the conversation of every one who loved or respected his manly character, that after conducting the army through an arduous retreat with consummate firmness, he has terminated a career of distinguished honour, by a death that has given the enemy additional reason to respect the name of a British soldier. Like the immortal Wolfe, he is snatched from his country at an early period of a life spent in her service; like Wolfe, his last moments were gilded by the prospect of success, and cheered by the acclamation of victory; like Wolfe, also, his memory will for ever remain

sacred in that country which he sincerely loved, and which he
had so faithfully served."

The brunt of the action fell upon the Fourth, the Forty-
second, the Fiftieth, the Eighty-first regiments, a portion of
the brigade of the Guards, and the Twenty-sixth regiment.
We are left to regret that the Twenty-sixth had not afterwards
an opportunity to avenge the death of its commander upon the
French—not again being seriously engaged in the desolating
wars of the time, which deluged the Continent with blood ere
a lasting peace had been attained by the triumph of Waterloo.
This blank in the active history of the regiment may be
accounted for from the fact that, after its return to England,
serving with the army in the Walcheren expedition, it
suffered so severely in that unfortunate campaign, that only
ninety effective men returned to represent it. Nevertheless,
in 1811, recruited, it was embarked for Portugal, and in the
following year removed to Gibraltar, where the fatigues of
military duty pressed so severely upon the raw lads who then
constituted the regiment, that sickness appearing, fated many
of those brave youth, who feared not man, to faint and fail in
the presence of this unseen and unrelenting foe.

On the return of peace the second battalion was reduced.
In 1826 the regiment was sent to India, where it served successively in the presidencies of Madras and Bengal.

If the sword, the pestilence, or the famine should slay
each their thousands, the vice of intemperance, the crying
iniquity of our land, has slain its tens of thousands. The
throne, the senate, the pulpit, and the press, alike deplore

its ravages; and although differing as to the remedy to be
applied, professedly all declare a crusade against this social
hydra. Exalted, not alone by our own might, or our own
goodness, but by the blessing of God resting upon these,
Britain may well be regarded as the lighthouse, divinely
lighted, shedding abroad upon the tumultuous waste of sin
and ignorance around the saving light of truth and righteousness. Strange inconsistency! notwithstanding all this, our
merchants sacrifice honour at the shrine of gold, and amass
wealth by becoming the moral degenerators of others who
have the sublime virtue—which we lack—to expel by enact-
ment the drug which would ruin, by the passion it excites, an
intellectual nation. In defiance of these enactments, and
despite our fair professions, we regret to think Britain should
afford countenance to the opium traffic, and lend the might
of her arms to maintain it, although involving a breach of the
law of China, and inflicting upon the Chinese a moral wrong.
Happy are we to know that there were not a few amongst us
who had the courage to repudiate the action of Government
in this matter, and at length awakening our people to the
iniquity, so impressed our rulers as to induce a better policy.
But for the supreme vanity and duplicity of the Chinese, war
might have been averted. Their obnoxious impudence, and
the insults they strove to heap upon us, necessitated the
vindication of our honour, and occasioned the landing of a
British force to chastise their folly and protect British property. Accordingly, in 1840, the Twenty-sixth, with the
Eighteenth and Forty-ninth regiments, and other Indian

troops, embarked from Madras, and, arriving in China, accomplished a landing on the island of Chusan. Excepting in some few cases where the Chinese did behave themselves like men in the defence of their country, our soldiers victoriously marched upon the cities of Shanghae and Chin-Keang-foo, which fell an easy triumph to their daring. The campaigns afford little to interest us in their record: we are, therefore, content to say the arduous services of our troops were rewarded, and, with the Eighteenth, Forty-ninth, Fifty-fifth, and Ninety-eighth regiments, our Cameronians won the distinction of the "Dragon." Returning to Calcutta in 1843, the Twenty-sixth proceeded thence to England, and in 1850 garrisoned Gibraltar. In 1853 the regiment embarked for Canada, and was stationed at Montreal, afterwards, re-embarking, removed to Bermuda, whence, in 1859, it once more returned to the beloved shores of our native land. Restored to Scotland in 1861, garrisoning Edinburgh Castle, the regiment was welcomed amongst us with every expression of the highest veneration and heartfelt interest as the representative of the Cameronians, whose prompt loyalty and patriotism, more than a hundred and seventy years ago, wrested that same castle from the dominion of the Stuart, and helped to give that liberty of faith which we now so abundantly enjoy.

CHAPTER XVIII.

"Think on Scotia's ancient heroes,
Think on foreign foes repell'd,
Think on glorious Bruce and Wallace,
Wha the proud usurpers quell'd."

LIFE GUARDS—SEVENTH HUSSARS—SEVENTEENTH LIGHT DRAGOONS—SEVENTIETH FOOT.

NOT to exceed the limits we prescribed in setting out, we are reluctantly compelled, in fulfilling our promise, to group into a single brief chapter a variety of records incidental to our history.

LIFE GUARDS.

It is only fitting to note, that two troops of Scots Life Guards, raised in Scotland shortly after the Restoration, and engaged with the Scots Greys and Claverhouse's Scots Horse in putting down Presbyterianism by the sword, were at the Revolution included in the splendid cavalry of the Life Guards, which have since been retained in waiting upon the sovereign—their magnificent equipment and martial appearance, lending dignity to the pageant of Royalty. Their excellence as soldiers has been proved in the memorable victory of "Waterloo."

THE SEVENTH HUSSARS—"QUEEN'S OWN."

Viscount Dundee's regiment of Scots Dragoons, or, as familiarly known in Scottish song, "the bonnets o' Bonnie

Dundee," refusing to enter the service of William and Mary upon the involuntary abdication and flight of James II., retiring into Scotland, becoming partners in the treason and rebellion of their fiery leader, involved in his ruin, was lost to the country. As if to replace this regiment, which had thus fallen to pieces, the King, in 1690, raised a new cavalry corps in Scotland, known as Cunningham's Dragoons. It shares much of the history, and participates largely in the honours, which we have already attempted to describe as belonging to the "Scots Greys." The regiment was disbanded in 1713; but, two years later, re-formed from three companies of the Scots Greys, two companies of the Royal Dragoons, and one newly raised. As the "Seventh Queen's Own Hussars," it has never since ceased to sustain its early reputation for steadiness and valour—the tokens of which, emblazoned upon its colours and appointments, are comprised in these two words: "Peninsula" and "Waterloo."

SEVENTEENTH LIGHT DRAGOONS.

Whilst France and Britain fiercely contended as to the extent of their dominions in the American continent, where each might well be supposed to have enough and to spare, Lord Aberdour, in 1759, raised a regiment of cavalry in Scotland. Light dragoons had just then been introduced into the service, and proved a most valuable arm thereof. We have failed to discover precisely in what services this corps was employed, but are inclined to think, with the Fifteenth Light Dragoons, the Inniskilling, and Scots Greys, it must have served in Germany, under the Duke of Brunswick, during the Seven Years' War. It was disbanded in 1763.

The Seventeenth Lancers, inheriting the martial ardour of this old regiment, have more than sustained the credit of the "Seventeenth"—bearing upon its colours and appointments "The Alma," "Balaklava," "Inkermann," and "Sevastopol"—and has gained a mightier fame as one of the five regiments who formed the Light Cavalry Brigade under the Earl of Cardigan in his memorable charge during the Crimean war, fitly styled, from its fatal glory—"The Death's Ride."

THE SEVENTIETH FOOT, OR SURREY REGIMENT.

The disputes arising in 1758 between France and Britain as to the boundary line of their American colonies failing to be amicably adjusted, war was accepted as the stern arbiter. To meet the emergency, our army was increased, and the—

Second Battalion of the	3d	Foot constituted the	61st	Regiment.
"	4th	"	62d	"
"	8th	"	63d	"
"	11th	"	64th	"
"	12th	"	65th	"
"	19th	"	66th	"
"	20th	"	67th	"
"	23d	"	68th	"
"	24th	"	69th	"
"	31st	"	70th	"
"	32d	"	71st	"
"	33d	"	72d	"
"	34th	"	73d	"
"	36th	"	74th	"
"	37th	"	75th	"

Thus the Seventieth was born out of the second battalion of the Thirty-first English Regiment, (raised about the year 1702, during the reign of Queen Anne, and for some time serving as marines in the fleet). Shortly after its formation, being stationed in Scotland, and largely recruited in Glasgow, the Seventieth was styled, in consequence of its interest in that city and its light grey facings, the "Glasgow Greys." Ten years later the facings were changed to black. In 1782, probably in compliment to its colonel, it became the "Surrey Regiment." From some unaccountable reason, in 1812 it was restored to somewhat of its original character as the "Glasgow Lowland Regiment;" and again in 1823, likely for recruiting purposes, it was re-christened the "Surrey"—which designation it still retains. Although stationed in British America during the war which raged amid the wilds of the New World, we do not find it fortunate enough to be engaged. Indeed, the captures of the islands of Martinique in 1794, and Guadaloupe in 1810, seem to be the only trophies which it has been honoured to attain. No doubt its ranks contained the same brave spirits as have everywhere and always sustained the credit of the British soldier—yet have these been destined to reap in quietude a glory by good conduct no less meritorious, although apparently less lustrous, than that which is acquired amid the carnage of the battle-field—consecrated in "the stormy music of the drum," and proclaimed in the shrill sound of the trumpet.

THE SEVENTY-THIRD FOOT:

ORIGINALLY

SECOND BATTALION

OF THE

FORTY-SECOND ROYAL HIGHLANDERS.

CHAPTER XIX.

" Then our sodgers were drest in their kilts and short hose,
Wi' their bonnets and belts which their dress did compose,
And a bag of oatmeal on their backs to make brose.
O! the kail brose o' auld Scotland,
And O the Scottish kail brose."

1780–1862 — CAPE OF GOOD HOPE — INDIA — MANGALORE —
SERINGAPATAM — NEW SOUTH WALES — GERMANY — WATERLOO
— CAPE OF GOOD HOPE.

THE immense and increasing territory which circumstances
had placed under British protection, and in the end consigned
to our possession in India, occasioned a considerable increase
of our army in order to maintain these new gotten provinces
against the incursions of neighbouring and powerful tribes.

Thus, in 1780, a second battalion was raised for the Forty-second Royal Highlanders, which was ultimately constituted independently the Seventy-third regiment. The battalion was embodied at Perth, under Lord John Murray as Colonel, and Macleod, of Macleod, as Lieut.-Colonel. Amongst its early officers, Lieutenant Oswald was distinguished as the subject of a strange speculation which at this time so tickled the brilliant imaginings of our "literati," as to call forth from the pen of a learned doctor an elaborate disquisition, intended to prove that Napeolon the Great was none else than Lieutenant Oswald, who, imbibing republican ideas, had passed over to France, and by a chain of circumstances been elevated from the command of a republican regiment to be the great captain and ruler of France. Such marvellous transformations were by no means uncommon in the then disordered state of French society. Virtue as well as vice was ofttimes the idol for a time, to be exalted and adored. But the life and adventures of Lieutenant Oswald, however notorious, did not attain such a grand ideal. With his two sons, he fell fighting at the head of his regiment in La Vendee in 1793.

Scarce had the battalion been completed ere it was shipped for foreign service. Intended to prosecute an attack upon the colony of the Cape of Good Hope, the aim of the expedition was frustrated by the promptitude of Admiral Suffein, who commanded the French fleet, and arriving first at the colony, prevented a landing being successfully effected. The expedition thus interrupted sailed for India, in the passage making a valuable capture of richly laden Dutch Indiamen.

In the division of the spoil arising, after much disputing, the
soldiers shared. One hundred and twenty officers and men
of the regiment fell a prey to the scurvy and fever on the
voyage, which, from the ignorance and incapacity of the com-
manders of the transports, was protracted to twelve months.
The "Myrtle," without maps or charts, separated from the
fleet in a tempest, was only saved by the cool resolution of
Captain Dalyell, who, amid many perils, succeeded in navigat-
ing the vessel to St Helena, and so rescuing many valuable
lives who otherwise would probably have been lost. Arrived at
Madras, the battalion was immediately advanced into the
interior, where the critical position of British affairs, assailed
by the numerous black legions of Hyder Ali and his son
Tippoo Saib, aided by a French force under General Lally,
rendered the presence of every bayonet of importance. The
utmost efforts of Lieut.-Colonel Thomas Frederick Mackenzie
Humberston could only muster a British force of 2500 men,
of whom 2200 were Sepoys. Nevertheless, with these he
advanced to check the progress of the enemy, who had an
army of 10,000 cavalry and 14,000 infantry. Notwithstanding this immense superiority in numbers on the part of the
enemy, nothing could daunt our troops: bravely they held
their own, defying the most desperate attempts of the foe
to drive them back. The general order thus records the
action that ensued: "This little army, attacked on ground
not nearly fortified, by very superior numbers, skilfully disposed and regularly led on; they had nothing to depend on
but their native valour, their discipline, and the conduct of

the officers. These were nobly exerted, and the event has been answerable. The intrepidity with which Major Campbell and the Highlanders repeatedly charged the enemy was most honourable to their character."

More effectually to strike at the power of the Sultan by cutting him off from the source whence he had hitherto drawn his supplies, a considerable force was ordered to assemble in the Bombay Presidency, and, under Brigadier-General Matthews, assail Beddinore. To join this army the battalion was embarked and sailed for Bombay, whence, advancing into the country, it effected a junction with the army near Cundapore. The Highlanders were particularly distinguished in the attack and capture of a series of forts which impeded the march, and especially so in the taking of a strong fortress which lay in the way, named, because of its strength, Hyder Gurr. The enemy was so impressed by the spirit evinced in these assaults, that, dreading a further attack, they evacuated Beddinore without an attempt to defend it, which was immediately occupied by the British in January, 1783. This battalion was not of the army which soon after was surrendered to the enemy by General Matthews, who foolishly deemed himself too weak to withstand the imposing force which had surrounded him in Beddinore.

The conduct of Major Campbell, who commanded this battalion in the defence of Mangalore, stands forth in brilliant contrast to the errors which led General Matthews to surrender an equally brave army into the cruel hands of the Mysore tyrant. With 250 Highlanders and 1500 Sepoys, Major

Campbell, although assailed by an army of 100,000 men, aided by a powerful artillery, defended Mangalore for nine months. Throughout the siege the defenders behaved with the most heroic constancy and gallantry, although experiencing the pinchings of famine, and exposed to the most cruel disappointments. Even the Sepoys, emulating the Highlanders, so distinguished themselves, that, in compliment to their bravery, our countrymen dubbed one of their regiments their own third battalion. Truly it was a new and strange thing to have within the Royal Highland Regiment a cohort of "brave blacks;" yet it displays a generous sentiment which reflects honour upon the regiment. Three times did a British squadron enter the bay, having on board stores and reinforcements, yet as often did this needed and expected aid retire without helping these perishing, exhausted brave—out of respect to the armistice of a faithless foe, which for a time existed and apparently terminated the siege. Their perfidy in one instance, scorning the sacredness of treaties, exploded a mine, which blew into the air the flag of truce then waving from the British ramparts. Reduced to the last extremities, shut up to a dark despair, indignant for the seeming neglect of friends, and dreading the relentless wrath of the enemy, the brave garrison accepted the only hope of life which yet remained, by surrender; and, be it said to the honour of the Indian character—with the generosity which becomes the conquering soldier in the presence of a brave yet vanquished foe—the terms imposed were such as enabled the exhausted remnant of the garrison to retire with all the honours of war. Scarce 500 effective men could be mustered to march out of the fortress, and these so feeble as to be hardly able to bear the weight of their muskets. Colonel Fullarton, in his interesting volume upon British India, thus writes: " Colonel Campbell has made a defence which has seldom been equalled and never surpassed." The memorial of this service is still borne alone upon the colours and appointments of the Seventy-third. So redundant with honour had been the services of this second battalion of the Forty-second Royal Highlanders, that when the army, in 1786, was being reduced, by the disbanding of second battalions, the representations of the officers of the regiment were so favourably received by the Government, that this battalion was retained as an independent corps, under the command of Sir George Osborn, Bart., thereafter known as the Seventy-third Regiment. In the division of Major-General Robert Abercromby, the regiment joined the army of Lord Cornwallis, which, in 1792, advanced upon Seringapatam; the attack was only arrested by the proposals of a treaty of peace. In the brigade of Lieutenant-Colonel David Baird, the Seventy-third was engaged in the reduction of the French colony of Pondicherry, and, in 1795, in the army of Major-General James Stuart, assailed and occupied the valuable island of Ceylon. At length the arm of vengeance —vengeance for the murdered brave who had fallen victims to the cruelty of Hyder Ali in the pestilential dungeons of Seringapatam—so often threatened, yet always averted, descended to consume the guilty city and destroy its merciless ruler. Seringapatam fell before the arms of our troops, including the Seventy-third Regiment, in 1799. The history of the regiment at this period is associated with the early achievements of the "Great Duke," then the Honourable Colonel Arthur Wellesley.

Returning home in 1805, the regiment proceeded to Scotland to recruit, and in 1809, despoiled of its Highland character, laid aside "the garb of old Gaul" and the designation it had hitherto enjoyed. Increased by the addition of a second battalion, the first battalion was sent to New South Wales; whilst the second, remaining at home, was, in 1813, employed as the solitary representative of the British army in the north of Germany.

The Annual Register gives the following account of the battle of Gorde, where it fought with honour:—"After landing at Stralsund, and assisting in completing the works of that town, Lieutenant-Colonel Harris, with the Seventy-third, was detached into the interior of the country, to feel for the enemy, and also to get into communication with Lieutenant-General Count Wallmoden, which dangerous service he successfully effected, though he had with great care and caution to creep with his small force between the large *corps d'armée* of Davoust and other French Generals at that time stationed in Pomerania, Mecklenburg, and Hanover. Having joined Count Wallmoden, the Seventy-third contributed greatly to the victory that General gained over the French on the plains of Gorde, in Hanover, where Lieutenant-Colonel Harris, at the head of his battalion, declining any aid, and at the moment when the German hussars had been routed, charged up a

steep hill, took a battery of French artillery, and unfurling
the British colours, at once spread terror amongst that gallant
enemy which feared no others; a panic struck them, and they
fled."

This battalion was also hotly engaged at the desperate
conflict of Quatre Bras, and the decisive victory of Waterloo,
in 1815. In the Kaffir Wars, which desolated South Africa
from 1846–47, and 1850–53, the Seventy-third bore an important part. It was also present in India during the recent
Sepoy Mutiny. Having abandoned its national character
since 1809, it does not fall within the scope of this work
further to follow the narrative of those achievements that
have never failed worthily to sustain the excellence which—
whilst our own—belonged to it. We are sure that, whoever
they be that now represent the Seventy-third, the perusal
of this imperfect sketch will not make them ashamed of its
Highland origin, but rather incite them to emulate those brave
deeds, the glory of which they are privileged to inherit.

THE SEVENTY-FIFTH FOOT:

ORIGINALLY

HIGHLANDERS.

CHAPTER XX.

" Courage! Nothing e'er withstood
Freemen fighting for their good;
Armed with all their fathers' fame,
They will win and wear a name
That shall go to endless glory,
Like the gods of old Greek story;
Raised to heaven and heavenly worth,
For the good they gave to earth."

1787–1862—INDIA—CAPE OF GOOD HOPE—INDIAN MUTINY.

In General Stuart's admirable and interesting annals of the
Highland Regiments, the brief record of the Seventy-fifth
Highlanders is introduced by a series of wholesome counsels
as to military administration, gathered from his own large
experience and wide field of diligent inquiry, from which we
shall quote a few extracts, as being useful and helpful to our
history. It seems that this regiment, raised by Colonel
Robert Abercromby in 1787 from among his tenantry around

Stirling, and the veterans who, in earlier life, had served under
him in the army as a light brigade, had been subjected to
an unusually strict system of discipline, which had operated
prejudicially upon the corps. The system adopted "was formed
on the old Prussian model; fear was the great principle of
action; consequently, it became the first object of the soldiers
to escape detection, more than to avoid crimes." This system,
when enforced, "was carried into effect by one of the captains
who commanded in the absence of the field-officers. He was
an able and intelligent officer; but he had been educated in a
school in which he had imbibed ideas of correctness which
required no small strength of mind to enforce, and which,
when enforced with severity, tended to break the spirit of the
soldiers to a degree which no perfection in movement can
ever compensate. When applied to the British soldier in particular, this system has frequently frustrated its own purpose."
Brotherly-kindness and charity—patience and forbearance—
are virtues which should not be banished, but rather be
exercised, as thoroughly consistent with the best military
institutions. A considerate attention to the wants, nay, the
very weaknesses of the soldier, is likely to accomplish more for
good discipline than the stern frigidity of mere military
despotism. It was in the camp that the iron will of Napoleon,
unbending, achieved a charmed omnipotence over his soldiers,
and by a single simple, pithy sentence fired them with that
ardour and devotion which made Europe tremble beneath the
tread of his invincible legions. The charm was only broken
when the vastness of his dominion had scattered the old

soldiers of the empire, and the feeble conscript failed to sustain the veteran remnant of "The Guard," the more especially at a time when disasters, quickly crowding upon his arms, and bereft of the invincibility which had hitherto been inseparable to his presence, no power remained to animate the soul of the recruit, rudely torn from his home and pressed into the fatal vortex of the dying army. The marvellous sway of this great captain over the hearts as well as the wills of his soldiers teaches many useful lessons, and illustrates what General Stuart so well observes:—"When a soldier's honour is in such little consideration that disgraceful punishments are applied to trifling faults, it will soon be thought not worth preserving." We must have a degree of faith equally in the honour as well as the loyalty of our soldiers, to help them to a cheerful and not a Russian stolidness in the discharge of duty. In the case of the Seventy-fifth "the necessity of this severe discipline was not proved by the results, when the regiment passed under the command of another officer. The system was then softened and relaxed, and much of the necessity of punishment ceased; the men became more quiet and regular, and in every respect better soldiers. A soldier sees his rights respected, and while he performs his duty, he is certain of being well treated, well fed, well clothed, and regularly paid; he is, consequently, contented in his mind and moral in his habits."

At length released from the terrors under which, for eighteen months, the corps had been trained, it embarked for India, where, with other King's regiments, chiefly High-

land, and the British native troops, it was present with great
credit at the several attacks upon Seringapatam, which, in
1799, terminated in the capture of that capital. Subsequently
the Seventy-fifth was engaged with the army under Lord Lake in
the campaigns of Upper India. It was one of the five British
regiments which, in 1805, were so disastrously repulsed in an
attempt upon the strong fortress of Bhurtpore. Returning
to England in 1806, like the Seventy-third, the regiment was
shortly thereafter shorn of its dignity as a Highland corps,
not a hundred Highlanders remaining in its ranks.

We cannot but lament the circumstances which have
bereaved us of an interest in so many regiments once
representatives of our Old Highland Brigade. Believing
our "Scottish Rights Association" to sympathise with us
in these regrets, and believing it to be composed of men
truly in earnest, we commend, to their most serious consideration—not merely as a theme for eloquent disquisition,
but as a field for action—the revival and preservation, in
their original integrity, of the old Scottish and Highland
regiments. By suggesting some better mode of recruiting
and stirring up our countrymen to rally round the national
colours of those regiments, which still in name belong to us,
they may be prevented from still farther degenerating, and
sharing a similar fate as those who have already been
lopped from the parent stem—lost to our nationality, lost
because of our own apathy, lost in the great sea of British
valour. A very interesting cotemporary work, giving "An
Account of the Scottish Regiments," published by Mr Nimmo

of Edinburgh, and compiled by an official well versant in
these matters, is now before us, and shows how the tide of
professed improvement, encroaching in this utilitarian age, is
likely soon to obliterate the ancient landmarks. Wave after
wave of civilisation has broken upon the shore of privilege
and custom, hallowed by a venerable age, and, by assimilation,
would sweep away the time-honoured characteristics which
distinguish our Scottish soldiers and people.

The Seventy-fifth regiment served with distinction at the
Cape of Good Hope during the Kaffir War of 1835, which
threatened to wrest that valuable colony from us. It is also
distinguished for its heroic efforts before Delhi during the
Indian Mutiny, where Lieutenant Wadeson and Private
Patrick Green won the Victoria Cross.* With the Royal
Tiger emblazoned upon its colours—a distinction gained on
the same sultry plains for previous service in India, conferred
in July, 1807—it increased its merited reputation by driving
the enemy before it, at the point of the bayonet, and effecting
the capture of all his guns. The conduct of the little army
which achieved the fall of Delhi is thus eulogised by the Governor-General:—"Before a single soldier, of the many thousands
who are hastening from England to uphold the supremacy of
the British power, has set foot on these shores, the rebel force,
where it was strongest and most united, and where it had the

* For these and many other details, the Author is indebted to the "*Medals of
the British Army*," by Mr Carter, who has therein endeavoured to individualise the
several regiments, and to show the particular deeds, not only of the corps, but also
of the officers and men.

command of unbounded military appliances, has been destroyed or scattered by an army collected within the limits
of the North-western Provinces and the Punjab alone.

"The work has been done before the support of those
battalions, which have been collected in Bengal from the forces
of the Queen in China, and in Her Majesty's eastern colonies,
could reach Major-General Wilson's army; and it is by the
courage and endurance of that gallant army alone; by the
skill, sound judgment, and steady resolution of its brave
commander; and by the aid of some native chiefs, true to
their allegiance, that, under the blessing of God, the head
of rebellion has been crushed, and the cause of loyalty,
humanity, and rightful authority vindicated."

THE NINETIETH FOOT;

OR,

PERTHSHIRE VOLUNTEERS.

CHAPTER XXI.

" He, in the firmament of honour, stands
Like a star, fixed, not moved with any thunder
Of popular applause, or sudden lightning
Of self-opinion; he hath saved his country,
And thinks 'twas but his duty."

1794–1862—GIBRALTAR—MINORCA—EGYPT—WEST INDIES—
CRIMEA—INDIAN MUTINY.

FROM the wilds of Perthshire have hailed many of the best
and bravest soldiers, whose deeds grace our military annals,
and whose lives have been the embodiment of all that truly
ennobles character and makes the man. Of these there is
none perhaps more justly celebrated than Thomas Graham,
Lord Lynedoch, whose abilities early marked him to be the
leader of the patriotism of his native county, which, in
1794, found its expression in the enrolment of the Nine-

tieth Regiment of Foot, or Perthshire Volunteers. Shortly after its formation, the corps was included in the army under Lord Moira; and in 1795, from the Isle Dieu, proceeded to reinforce the garrison of Gibraltar. With the Twenty-eighth, the Forty-second, and the Fifty-eighth regiments, the Ninetieth formed the force which, under Lieutenant-General Sir Charles Stuart, in 1798, assailed and captured the island of Minorca from the Spaniards. A more important service, and more serious encounter with the enemy, awaited the arms of the Ninetieth, as part of the expedition of Sir Ralph Abercromby, which, in 1801, was destined to drive the French out of Egypt. Commanded by Lieutenant-Colonel Hill, afterwards Viscount Hill, it was brigaded with the Eighth, the Thirteenth, and the Eighteenth regiments. At this period the regiment wore helmets, giving it the appearance of a body of dismounted cavalry. At Mandora, believing it to be such, and supposing, in consequence, that being thus out of its own element, the regiment should lack the wonted steadiness of British infantry, the French cavalry charged fiercely and repeatedly upon the Ninetieth, yet always fruitlessly. The phalanx of our Perthshire men remained firm, whilst many a saddle was emptied by its murderous fire. It was on this occasion that Sir Ralph Abercromby, separated from his staff, having his horse shot under him, was on the point of being captured, when a soldier of the Ninetieth afforded such prompt assistance, and by heroically exposing his own life in defence of his commander, accomplished his rescue. At the same battle, Colonel Hill, who, as the associate of Wellington, afterwards shared the glory of the

Peninsular campaigns, had his life saved by the fortunate circumstance of the helmet he wore. "A musket ball struck it on the brass rim with such force, that he was thrown from his horse to the ground, and the brass completely indented. Without this safeguard, the ball would have passed through his head." The conspicuous bravery of the Nintieth and Ninety-second regiments on this occasion was rewarded by the honourable distinction of "Mandora," in addition to the "Sphinx" and "Egypt," borne by other corps engaged in the expedition.

Whilst the British were accomplishing glorious results on the plains of Spain, the Ninetieth was employed, in 1809–10, with the Seventh, Eighth, Thirteenth, Fifteenth, Twenty-third, Twenty-fifth (flank companies), Sixtieth, Sixty-third, and First West Indian Regiments, in the reduction of the valuable island of Martinique. This success was soon afterwards followed by the capture of Guadaloupe, in which the Ninetieth bore a conspicuous part. The five and thirty years which intervene betwixt this and the next active service in which the regiment was engaged, although a blank so far as mere fighting is concerned, displayed in its soldiers excellences not less to be admired than those which manifest a mere physical might or brute courage. From the "Account of the Scottish Regiments"—to which we have already referred—we find that in 1812 the composition of the regiment in its several battalions was as follows:—English, 1097; Scots, 535; Irish, 486; Foreigners, 24. Total, 2144.

In 1846 the Kaffirs of South Africa attempted to recover

their ancient territory from British dominion, and accompanied these attempts with a series of predatory incursions upon our settlements, especially in the neighbourhood of Graham's Town. It became necessary, for the defence of the colony, to assemble a British army of some strength. Ere this could be accomplished, much valuable property became the prey of these savages, and many lives were sacrificed on the altar of their vengeance. At first the disparity in numbers was very great—so great as to preclude a decisive result in our favour—the whole British force scarcely amounting to 700 men, whilst the enemy possessed 60,000 sable warriors. Moreover, the peculiarity of the warfare in "the bush" served somewhat to advantage the foe, and negative the superiority we might otherwise enjoy, from troops better armed and disciplined. The assembled British, augmented by reinforcements from home, comprised, besides Royal Artillery and Engineers, the Seventh Dragoon Guards, the Sixth, Twenty-seventh, Forty-fifth, Seventy-third, Ninetieth, and Ninety-first regiments, the first battalion of the Rifle Brigade, and the Cape Mounted Riflemen. This army, advancing in two divisions, after undergoing the most harassing service, exposed continually to the attack of an unseen and treacherous enemy, at length so hunted down the guerilla bands which infested the country, that the Kaffirs were glad to purchase peace by the surrender, as hostages, of their chief Sandilli, together with his brother and eighty of his principal followers. "During this long and protracted desultory warfare great fatigue and exertions had been undergone with the characteristic heroism of the British soldier; and the humanity and forbearance displayed by him towards the fickle, treacherous, and revengeful enemy, were as conspicuous as his bravery."

The Ninetieth joined the "army of the Crimea" before Sebastopol early in December, 1854, and served during that fatal winter when so many brave men fell the victims of disease, induced by the hardships to which they were exposed, and which so abundantly displayed the unmurmuring firmness of the British soldier, so graciously cheered by the sympathy of our beloved Queen, who thus beautifully expressing her feelings, has unwittingly rewarded the heroic endurance of our soldiers, by conferring, in these words, a well-merited tribute to their bravery, which must ever be treasured by our country:—

"Would you tell Mrs Herbert that I begged she would let me see frequently the accounts she receives from Miss Nightingale or Mrs Bracebridge, as I hear no details of the wounded, though I see so many from officers, etc., about the battlefield, and naturally the former must interest me more than any one. Let Mrs Herbert also know that I wish Miss Nightingale and the ladies would tell these poor noble wounded and sick men that no one takes a warmer interest, or feels more for their sufferings, or admires their courage and heroism *more* than their Queen. Day and night she thinks of her beloved troops; so does the Prince. Beg Mrs Herbert to communicate these my words to those ladies, as I know that our sympathy is much valued by these noble fellows. VICTORIA."

It was during the third bombardment of Sebastopol, and in the assault and defence of the fortifications known as the Quarries, that the Ninetieth first seriously encountered the Russians. In this attack, which took place on the 7th June, 1855, the regiment was gallantly led by Lieut.-Colonel Robert Campbell, who fell severely wounded. Belonging to the Light Division, it afterwards formed part of the assailing force which so heroically yet unsuccessfully attempted to carry the powerful defences of the Redan. Fearing the result of a second assault, sustained by the same impetuous valour, and incited by the resolve to wipe out the seeming stain of the previous repulse, the Russians declining the contest, beat a timely retreat, evacuating that portion of the fortifications deemed no longer tenable, and by a series of masterly movements successfully effecting an escape to the other side of the harbour, from whence the Governor negotiated the surrender of the entire city. These good tidings, received with joy by all classes at home, elicited from the Throne the following expression of our nation's gratitude to the heroes of the "Crimean Army:"—

"The Queen has received with deep emotion the welcome intelligence of the fall of Sebastopol. Penetrated with profound gratitude to the Almighty, who has vouchsafed this triumph to the allied army, Her Majesty has commanded me to express to yourself, and through you to her army, the pride with which she regards this fresh instance of their heroism. The Queen congratulates her troops on the triumphant issue of their protracted siege, and thanks them for the cheerfulness and fortitude with which they have encountered its toils, and the valour which has led to its termination. The Queen deeply laments that this success is not without its alloy, in the heavy losses that have been sustained; and while she rejoices in the victory, Her Majesty deeply sympathizes with the noble sufferers in their country's cause."

It remains for us now simply to record the memorable services of the Ninetieth in that dark period of our country's history—the Indian Mutiny. Brigaded with our Highlanders, "Havelock's Seventy-eighth—the Saints," the regiment was advanced, under Generals Outram and Havelock, for the relief of Lucknow. Whilst guarding the baggage near the Alumbagh, the Ninetieth was fiercely attacked by a strong column of the rebel cavalry, and it was only after a desperate fight and much loss that the mutineers were repulsed and dispersed. The further relief of Lucknow being accomplished by Sir Colin Campbell, now Lord Clyde, the regiment was thereafter engaged with the Forty-second and Fifty-third storming the position of the mutineers at the Martinière. The numerous acts of individual bravery which marked the conduct of so many of our Perthshire Volunteers have received, as the reward of distinguished merit, the decoration of the "Victoria Cross;" whilst Perthshire may well indulge a becoming pride as she reviews the famous achievements of her soldier sons.

> "Courage, therefore, brother-men,
> Cry 'God!' and to the fight again."

THE NINETY-FIRST FOOT:

OR,

ARGYLLSHIRE, ORIGINALLY HIGHLANDERS.

CHAPTER XXII.

"The Campbells they are a' in arms,
Their loyal faith and truth to show,
With banners rattling in the wind;
The Campbells are coming, O-ho, O-ho!"

1794–1862—CAPE OF GOOD HOPE—PENINSULA—CORUNNA—SHIP-
WRECK—KAFFIR WARS—INDIAN MUTINY.

To the cursory reader of Scottish history it appears somewhat strange that a chief such as the Duke of Argyll, who,
of first importance amongst our Scottish nobility, possessed
of so vast a territory, and exercising an almost regal power—
notwithstanding the military character of his family, and the
many officers of celebrity who have sprung from among his
vassals—should have comparatively failed to induce his
tenantry, so famed for bravery in our national wars, to
assume, as a body of soldiers distinctively belonging to the

clan of Campbell, that prominence in our army to which
their ancient renown entitles them. This may be explained
in the fact that the natives of Argyllshire have always manifested a strong predilection for the navy rather than the
army, probably arising from the almost insular position of the
county, and the sea-faring life of so many of its people. The
Ninety-first, at first numbered the Ninety-eighth, which now
remains the only, and, in our day, ill-defined representative
of the martial renown of the Campbells, was raised by Lieut.-
Colonel Duncan Campbell of Lochnell, and embodied at
Stirling in 1794. It was almost immediately thereafter
embarked for service at the Cape of Good Hope, where it
remained until that colony was restored to the Dutch in
1801. The severe and constant drain which had drafted
from the scanty population of our Highlands and Lowlands
whole regiments of recruits, had so exhausted the military
resources of our country that, in 1809, it was found impossible to maintain all the numerous Gaelic corps which then
existed in their original national integrity and completeness.
Hence the Seventy-third, Seventy-fifth, Ninety-first, and the
old Ninety-fourth (Scots Brigade), were of necessity doomed
to lay aside the Highland costume, and, to a great extent,
abandon their Scottish character. This regiment was present in the brigade of Brigadier-General Craufurd in reserve
at the battles of Roleia and Vimiera in 1808, which seemed
to foreshadow the triumphs of after years. It was also with
the army of Sir John Moore in his disastrous retreat, terminated so gloriously in the victory of Corunna, the lustre of

which was only dimmed by the death of the hero, who fell
whilst yet achieving it, and whose decease Marshal Soult,
with a true soldier spirit, alike with ourselves lamented.
Chivalrously he paid the last tribute of military respect to
the departed brave, by firing the funeral salute, and raising
a monument over the grave of his fallen foe. The generous
behaviour of Marshal Soult, notwithstanding his after faults,
must ever command our admiration, and remain a record of
his own nobleness—the tribute of the friend of the brave;
and justified the ovation he received at the hands of the
British public, when he visited our shores as the ambassador
of Louis Philippe.

For a moment the success of the French seemed complete,
and the sway of Napoleon universal; whilst the British army
appeared, as had been often threatened, "driven into the sea."
But the British meantime returning to England, the chasms
which want, fatigue, and the sword had occasioned in the
recent retreat, were speedily filled up, and now our army
only waited the opportunity when, returning to the Peninsula,
it should avenge the past and deliver the oppressed. Soon,
under Lieutenant-General Sir Arthur Wellesley, landed at
Lisbon, it began that victorious career which, by a perpetual series of successes, advanced the tide of war through
Spain, and, at length entering France, helped materially to
overthrow the dominion which the Empire had usurped.
Although the Ninety-first claims an interest in the actions of
the "Peninsula," it was not until the British army was about
entering France that its connection therewith led to con-

spicuous service—the memorials of which are still borne upon
the colours and appointments of the regiment in these words:
the "Pyrenees," the "Nive," the "Nivelle," "Orthes," and
"Toulouse."

From these scenes of stirring and thrilling interest, we
turn to record a signal instance of heroism which, occurring
nearer our own time, presents an illustrious example of
the qualities which brightly distinguish the British soldier
far more truly than even the triumphs of the battle-field.
We give the incident as inscribed by order of the Duke of
Wellington in the Records of the Regiment, who declared " he
had never read anything so satisfactory," that is, in its compilation, and the marvellous obedience to orders and fidelity
to duty it serves as a report to show :—

"The reserve battalion of the Ninety-first Regiment
arrived in Table Bay on the 25th of August, 1842, under the
command of Lieut.-Colonel Lindsay.

"On the 27th of August the command of the battalion
and of the detachments embarked on board the 'Abercrombie
Robinson' transport, devolved on Captain Bertie Gordon of
the Ninety-first Regiment, Lieut.-Colonel Lindsay and Major
Ducat having landed on that day at Cape Town.

"The situation of the transport was considered a dangerous
one from her size (being 1430 tons), and from the insufficient
depth of water in which she had brought up. The port-
captain, who boarded her on the evening of the 25th, advised
the captain to take up another berth on the following day.
This was impossible, for the wind blew strong into the bay

from the quarter which is so much dreaded there, and had continued to increase in violence during the 26th, 27th, and 28th August.

"At eleven o'clock P.M., on the night of the 27th, it was blowing a strong gale, and the sea was rolling heavily into the bay. The ship was pitching much, and she began to feel the ground; but she rode by two anchors, and much cable had been veered out the night before.

" Captain Gordon made such arrangements as he could, in warning the officers, the sergeant-major, and orderly non-commissioned officers to be in readiness.

"From sunset on the 27th the gale had continued to increase, until at length it blew a tremendous hurricane; and at a little after three A.M., on the morning of the 28th, the starboard cable snapped in two; the other cable parted in two or three minutes afterwards, and away went the ship before the storm, her hull striking, with heavy crashes, against the ground as she drove towards the beach, three miles distant, under her lee.

"About this time the fury of the gale, which had never lessened, was rendered more terrible by one of the most awful storms of thunder and lightning that had ever been witnessed in Table Bay. While the force of the wind and sea was driving the ship into shoaler water, she rolled incessantly; and heaved over so much with the back-set of the surf, that to the possibility of her going to pieces before daylight, was added the probability of settling down to windward, when the decks must have inevitably filled, and every one of the seven hundred souls on board must have perished.

"While in this position the heavy seas broke over her side and poured down the hatchways. The decks were opening in every direction, and the strong framework of the hull seemed compressed together, starting the beams from their places. The ship had been driven with her starboard-bow towards the beach, exposing her stern to the sea, which rushed through the stern ports and tore up the cabin floors of the orlop-deck.

"The thunder and lightning ceased towards morning, and the ship seemed to have worked a bed for herself in the sand, for the terrible rolling had greatly diminished, and there then arose the hope that all on board would get safe ashore.

"At daybreak (about seven o'clock), it was just possible to distinguish some people on the beach opposite to the wreck. Owing to the fear of the masts, spars, and rigging falling, as well as to keep as much top-weight as possible off the ship's decks, the troops had been kept below, but were now allowed to come on deck in small numbers.

"An attempt was made to send a rope ashore; and one of the best swimmers, a Krooman, volunteered the trial with a rope round his body; but the back-set of the surf was too much for him. A line tied to a spar never got beyond the ship's bows, and one fired from a cannon also failed. One of the cutters was then carefully lowered on the lee-side of the ship, and her crew succeeded in reaching the shore with a hauling line. Two large surf-boats were shortly afterwards conveyed in waggons to the place where the ship was stranded,

and the following orders were given by Captain Gordon for
the disembarkation of the troops, viz.:—

"1st. The women and children to disembark (of these
there were about seventy). 2d. The sick to disembark after
the women and children. 3d. The disembarkation of the
troops to take place by the companies of the Ninety-first drawing lots; the detachments of the Twenty-seventh Regiment
and of the Cape Mounted Riflemen taking the precedence.
4th. The men to fall in on the upper deck, fully armed and
accoutred, carrying their knapsacks and great-coats. 5th.
Each officer to be allowed to take a carpet-bag or small port-
manteau.

"The disembarkation of the women and children and of the
sick occupied from half-past eight until ten o'clock A.M. The
detachments of the Twenty-seventh Regiment and of the Cape
Mounted Riflemen followed. That of the Ninety-first was
arranged by the wings drawing lots, and then the companies
of each wing.

"At half-past ten A.M., one of the surf-boats which had
been employed up to this time in taking the people off the
wreck, was required to assist in saving the lives of those on
board the 'Waterloo' convict ship, which was in still more
imminent peril, about a quarter of a mile from the 'Abercrombie Robinson.'

"Having now but one boat to disembark four hundred
and fifty men, and the wind and sea, which had subsided a
little since daylight, beginning again to rise, together with the
captain's apprehension that she might go to pieces before

sunset—which (however unfounded, as was afterwards proved,) powerfully influenced Captain Gordon's arrangements—it became necessary to abandon the men's knapsacks, as they not only filled a greater space in the surf-boats than could be spared, but took a long time to hand down the ship's side. The knapsacks had been brought on deck, but were now, for these reasons, sent below again, and stowed away in the women's standing-berths.

"The officers were likewise informed that they would not be allowed to take more than each could carry on his arm. The disembarkation of the six companies went on regularly, but slowly, from eleven A.M. until half-past three P.M.; there being but one boat, which could only hold thirty men at a time. At half-past three P.M., the last boat-load left the ship's side. It contained those of the ship's officers and crew who had remained to the last; the sergeant-major of the reserve battalion Ninety-first; one or two non-commissioned officers, who had requested permission to remain; Captain Gordon, Ninety-first Regiment; and Lieutenant Black, R.N., agent of transports. This officer had dined at Government House the night before, but came on board the wreck with one of the first surf-boats that reached it on the following morning.

"Nearly seven hundred souls completed their disembarkation after a night of great peril, and through a raging surf, without the occurrence of a single casualty. Among them were many women and children, and several sick men, of whom two were supposed to be dying.

"Although it had been deemed prudent to abandon the

men's knapsacks and the officers' baggage, the reserve battalion
of the Ninety-first Regiment went down the side of that
shattered wreck, fully armed and accoutred, and, with the
exception of their knapsacks, ready for instant service. It
would be difficult to praise sufficiently the steady discipline of
that young and newly-formed battalion, thus severely tested
during nearly seventeen hours of danger; above eight of which
were hours of darkness and imminent peril. That discipline
failed not, when the apparent hopelessness of our situation
might have led to scenes of confusion and crime. The double
guards and sentries which had at first been posted over the
wine and spirit stores, were found unnecessary, and they were
ultimately left to the ordinary protection of single sentries.

"Although the ship was straining in every timber, and
the heavy seas were making a fair breach over us, the companies of that young battalion fell in on the weather-side of
the wreck, as their lots were drawn, and waited for their turn
to muster at the lee-gangway; and so perfect was their confidence, their patience, and their gallantry, that although
another vessel was going to pieces within a quarter of a mile
of us, and a crowd of soldiers, sailors, and convicts were
perishing before their eyes, not a murmur arose from their
ranks when Captain Gordon directed that the lot should not
be applied to the detachments of the Twenty-seventh Regiment
and Cape Mounted Riflemen, but that the Ninety-first should
yield to them the precedence in disembarking from the wreck.

"The officers of the Ninety-first Regiment who disembarked
with the battalion were Captains Gordon and Ward, Lieutenant

Cahill, Ensigns M'Inroy and Lavers, and Assistant-Surgeon Stubbs. If from among the ranks of men who all behaved so well, it were allowable to particularise any, the names of Acting Sergeant - Major Murphy, Colour - Sergeant Philips, Sergeant Murray, and Corporal Thomas Nugent, deserve this distinction. It was through the first that Captain Gordon communicated his orders, and carried them into execution. Every order he (Sergeant-Major Murphy) received was obeyed, during the confusion of a wreck, with the exactness of a parade-ground. He never left the particular part of the ship where he had been stationed, during the darkness and terror of the night, although a wife and child seemed to claim a portion of his solicitude; and when he received permission to accompany them into the surf-boat, he petitioned to be allowed to remain with Captain Gordon to the last.

"The two sergeants were young lads, barely twenty-two years of age. They had married shortly before the battalion embarked at Kingstown, and their wives (quite girls) were clinging to them for support and comfort when the ship parted from her anchors. The guards were ordered to be doubled, and additional sergeants were posted to each. This brought Sergeants Philips and Murray on duty. Without a murmur they left their wives and joined the guards of the lower deck. Their example of perfect obedience and discipline was eminently useful.

"And, if an officer's name may be mentioned, the conduct of Assistant-Surgeon Stubbs well deserves notice. He was in wretched health; but on the first announcement of danger he repaired to the sick-bay, and never left his charge until they were all safely landed.

"And, though last in this narrative, the beautiful calmness and resignation of the soldiers' wives ought to be ranked among the first of those ingredients of order which contributed to our safety. Confusion, terror, and despair, joined to the wildest shrieks, were fast spreading their dangerous influence from the women's quarter when Captain Gordon first descended among the people on the lower decks. A few words sufficed to quiet them, and from that moment their patience and submission never faltered.

"By half-past three P.M. the bilged and broken wreck was abandoned with all the stores and baggage—public and regimental—to the fast-increasing gale, and to the chances of the approaching night."

The excellent conduct of the Ninety-first throughout the Kaffir Wars of 1846-47, and again in 1850-53, received, with the army, the grateful thanks of the country, conveyed through the Government, in these expressive terms, to Lieutenant-General the Hon. Sir George Cathcart:—" The field of glory opened to them in a Kaffir war and Hottentot rebellion, is possibly not so favourable and exciting as that which regular warfare with an open enemy in the field affords, yet the unremitting exertions called for in hunting well-armed yet skulking savages through the bush, and driving them from their innumerable strongholds, are perhaps more arduous than those required in regular warfare, and call more constantly for individual exertion and intelligence. The British soldier, always cheerfully obedient to the call, well knows that, when he has done his duty, he is sure to obtain the thanks and good opinion of his gracious Queen."

The subsequent foreign service of the Ninety-first has been in the Mediterranean, and in September, 1858, it proceeded overland to India.

THE SCOTS BRIGADE;

OR,

THE OLD NINETY-FOURTH FOOT.

CHAPTER XXIII.

> " When midnight hour is come,
>   The drummer forsakes his tomb,
> And marches, beating his phantom-drum,
>   To and fro through the ghastly gloom.
>
> " He plies the drum-sticks twain,
>   With fleshless fingers pale,
> And beats, and beats again, and again,
>   A long and dreary reveil!
>
> " Like the voice of abysmal waves
>   Resounds its unearthly tone,
> Till the dead old soldiers, long in their graves,
>   Awaken through every zone."

WHEN we regard the battle-fields of earth, and think of the mighty dead who slumber there, apart from feelings of sentimental or real respect for the sacred dust, imagination animates the scene, as Memory, conjuring up from the graves of the past, bids us confront the soldiers who lived, and fought, and have long since died to "gild a martial story." Yet it is

our business, in the present undertaking, to gather from the
mouldering records of a bygone age, the truth, and rescue
from the shades of oblivion that "martial story" which
belongs to the soldiers of Scotland.

The Old Scots Brigade claims an antiquity of nearly 300
years, and only yields in prominence to that of the Royal
Scots, which in previous chapters we have discussed.   The
love of adventure, the hope of gain, and the troubles at home
having variously conspired to expatriate many Scotsmen,
these readily found employment in the armies of the Continent, wherein, conspicuous for fidelity and bravery, their
services were highly appreciated, frequently honoured as a
distinctive, select corps, or as a body of royal guards.   In
the States of Holland, about the year 1568, our countrymen
were included in numerous independent companies of soldiers,
which, in 1572, united into several regiments, constituted one
brigade—the Old Scots Brigade—the strength of which varied
from four to five thousand men.

"The first mention we find of their distinguished behaviour
was at the battle of Reminant, near Mechlin, in the year 1578;
the most bloody part of the action, says Meteren, a Dutch
historian, was sustained by the Scotch, who fought without
armour, and in their shirts, because of the great heat of the
weather.   After an obstinate engagement, the Spaniards, commanded by Don Juan of Austria, were defeated."

Throughout the long and sanguinary wars which ultimately resulted in the deliverance of Holland from the dominion
of Spain, the valiant behaviour of the Scots was very remark-

able, and is honourably recorded in most of the old histories of the period. The brigade was originally commanded by General Balfour, and under him by Colonel Murray and Walter Scott, Lord of Buccleugh. It learned the business of war under those great masters of the art, the Princes Maurice and Frederick Henry of Orange. Its early history is one with that of the present Fifth and Sixth Regiments of the line, which then constituted the English Brigade, long commanded by the noble family of De Vere, afterward the illustrious House of Oxford. "King James VI. of Scotland having invited the States-General to be sponsors to his new-born son, Prince Henry, on the departure of the ambassadors, fifteen hundred Scots were sent over to Holland to augment the brigade."

At the battle of Nieuport, in 1600, the firmness of the Scots Brigade saved the army of Prince Maurice from imminent danger, and contributed largely in attaining the victory gained over the Spanish army of the Archduke Albert of Austria. "After having bravely defended the bridge like good soldiers, they were at length forced to give way, the whole loss having fallen on the Scots, as well on their chiefs and captains as on the common soldiers, insomuch that eight hundred of them remained on the field, amongst whom were eleven captains, and many lieutenants and other officers."

At the siege of Ostend the Scots, by their unflinching steadiness, helped so materially in the defence that the giant efforts of the enemy under the Marquis Spinola, one of the ablest of the Spanish Generals, failed to accomplish its re-

duction by force of arms. A capitulation, honourable alike
to besieger and besieged, was agreed upon; "and the garrison
marched out with arms, ammunition, and baggage, drums
beating, and colours flying, after having held out three years
and three months."

"According to a memorial found in the pocket of an
officer of Spinola's suite, after he was killed, the number
of slain on the side of the Spaniards amounted in all to
seventy-six thousand nine hundred and sixty-one men. The
loss on the part of the States was not less than fifty
thousand. When the remaining garrison, which consisted
of only three thousand men, arrived at Sluice in Flanders,
Prince Maurice received them with the pomp of a triumph;
and both officers and private men were promoted or otherwise
rewarded."

The gallant conduct of Colonel Henderson, who commanded
the brigade in the defence of Bergen-op-Zoom in 1621, is
worthy of note. At the siege of Bois-le-duc in 1629 we find
the brigade composed of three regiments, respectively commanded by Colonels Bruce, Halket, and Scott (Earl of Buccleugh, son of the Lord of Buccleugh previously mentioned).
We do not pretend here to follow the narrative of sieges
and battles in which the brigade was at this period engaged. We shall only further mention that at the siege of
Sas-van-Ghent in 1644, Colonel Erskine, at the head of one of
the Scots regiments, won great renown by his excellent
bravery, being foremost in effecting the passage of the river
Lys; and again, at the siege of Ghent, Colonel Kilpatrick and

another Scots regiment fulfilled a similar mission with equal credit. The peace of Munster, concluded in 1648, gave an honourable issue to the contest in favour of the Dutch, who, for a little while, were permitted to enjoy repose from the horrid turmoil of war.

The British Revolution, which drove Charles II. from the throne of his father and established instead the Protectorate of Cromwell, occasioning his exile—a king without a kingdom or a throne—his Scots partizans, sharing his banishment, greatly recruited the Brigade, where many of them gladly found refuge and honourable employment.

Cromwell, in the plenitude of power, insisted upon the Dutch Estates declaring the exclusion of the House of Orange from the Stadtholdership, thereby hoping to break what appeared to be an antagonistic power to his rule, because of the bond which, by marriage, united the families of Orange and Stuart, imagining, in the blindness of bigotry, thereby to crush out the last remnant of Jacobitism, and extirpate the creed which had inflicted so many and grievous evils upon his country. The effect of this unfortunate exclusion Act was immediately felt throughout the States of Holland in the confusion and distress which it entailed. Taking advantage of these circumstances, and the imbecility of its rulers, the crafty and ambitious monarch of France, Louis XIV., without provocation, and with no other aim than his own aggrandisement, at once invaded Holland with three vast armies, under three of the greatest soldiers of the day—Condé, Turenne, and Luxembourg. With these difficulties and dangers the embarrassments of the State so increased that its feeble rulers in this hour of terror implored the aid of William, Prince of Orange, readily restoring all the rights they had formerly despoiled him of, and conferring upon him the powers of a Dictatorship. The genius of William proved equal to the emergency. At once he set to work, restoring the army to its ancient vigour, and reforming all manner of abuses which had crept into the government.

We are happy to record that, however weak and faulty the Dutch army had become, the Scots Brigade retained its effectiveness, despite the languor of the State, and, in consequence, particularly enjoyed the Prince's confidence on his restoration. It was commanded by Colonels Sir Alexander Colyear (Robertson), Graham, and Mackay, in 1673. United into one British brigade, the three Scots and the three English regiments served together under Thomas Butler, Earl of Ossory, throughout the wars with France. On the death of the Earl of Ossory in 1680, the command was conferred upon Henry Sidney, Earl of Romney.

On the outbreak of Monmouth's Rebellion in England and Argyll's Rebellion in Scotland, King James II. sent for the three Scots regiments, then serving in Holland, which, on being reviewed by the King on their arrival at Gravesend, drew forth the following compliment, expressed in a letter of thanks to the Prince of Orange for his prompt aid—"There cannot be, I am sure, better men than they are; and they do truly look like old regiments, and one cannot be better pleased with them than I am."

Colonel Hugh Mackay, who commanded the brigade on this occasion, was promoted to the rank of Major-General.

On the return of these regiments to Holland, the perfidy and ingratitude of James gradually oused out and revealed his truer character. Rightly esteeming the value of such soldiers to the Prince of Orange, and ever jealous of that Prince's increasing power, he vainly attempted to seduce the brigade and persuade it to exchange into the service of the King of France. He was further extremely mortified to find that, apart from the influence of the Prince, the men declined to serve under the Roman Catholic officer he proposed to appoint. When dangers thickened around himself, he earnestly desired its return; alas, too late! already sickened with his unworthy conduct, the brigade refused to obey.

In the subsequent Revolution the English and Scots brigades were of essential service to the Prince of Orange— "commanded by General Mackay, a Scotsman of noble family, sailed under the red flag."

At the battle of Killiecrankie the Scots Brigade was present, but unable to withstand the furious onset of the Highlanders, betrayed a weakness altogether inconsistent with its previous reputation, being utterly routed and dispersed. It is very remarkable that Viscount Dundee and General Cannon, who commanded the rebels, had both previously served in the Scots Brigade. Afterwards, employed with the Royal army in Ireland, it somewhat redeemed its character by good conduct at the siege of Athlone and the battle of Aghrim, at both which it held the post of peril and of honour with great credit.

Peace having been restored to unhappy Ireland, the brigade was sent to join the British army in Flanders, and at the battle of Steenkirk suffered severely, especially in the death of General Mackay, who finished a career of honour on that bloody field. The retreat of the allied army in 1695 was successfully covered by the Scots under Brigadier Colyear, afterwards Earl of Portmore. On the death of Brigadier Æneas Mackay, at the siege of Namur, the command of the Scots regiments was conferred on Robert Murray of Melgum, afterwards General Count Murray, Commander-in-Chief of the Emperor Joseph's forces in the Netherlands, and acting Governor-General of these provinces. On the Peace of Ryswick in 1697, the Scots Brigade returned with the army to Britain, and was stationed in Scotland until 1698, when it was restored to the service of Holland.

During the Wars of the Succession the Brigade was increased by the addition of three new Scots regiments, and the command conferred on John, Duke of Argyll—the "Great Argyll"—of whom it is well said—

> "Argyll, the State's whole thunder born to wield,
> And shake alike the Council and the Field."

It was hotly engaged in all the great actions of the war, and amongst the fearful carnage of Malplaquet mourned the loss of a brave officer, John, Marquis of Tullibardine, eldest son of the Duke of Athole. On the conclusion of hostilities, in 1713, the three new regiments of the brigade were disbanded. The peace was not again seriously disturbed until 1745, when the outbreak of war occasioned the increase of the brigade by the addition of second battalions, and a new regiment under command of Henry Douglas, Earl of Drumlanrig. The total strength of the brigade at this time rose to about 6000 men. At the battle of Roucoux five battalions of the Scots, forming the extremity of the left infantry wing, covered the retreat of the troops from the villages abandoned in front. "An officer who was present relates that General Colyear's regiment, in which he then served as an Ensign, was drawn up on the ridge of a rising ground, the slope of which was to the rear, so that by retiring a few paces the cannon-balls must have passed over their heads; but it was thought requisite that they should appear in full view of the French, who kept up an incessant fire of their artillery upon them for more than two hours, without ever advancing near enough to engage with small arms. The ardour of British soldiers to charge an enemy by whose fire they saw their comrades fall on every side, may easily be conceived, but was so much restrained by the authority of their officers, that the whole brigade seemed immoveable, except when the frequent breaches which the cannon made in the ranks required to be closed up. The intrepidity and perfect order which those battalions then showed, were greatly extolled ever after by the Prince of Waldeck, and likewise by Baron d'Aylva, a Dutch General of distinguished reputation, who happened to have the command of that part of the army. He had before shown a violent prejudice against the Scots," but their gallantry on that memorable occasion so impressed him, that ever after he regarded the Scots with peculiar favour, and on one occasion in his presence, a certain Prince having observed that the Scottish soldiers were not of such a size as those of some German regiments, the General replied, "I saw the day that they looked taller than any of your grenadiers."

In the defence of Bergen-op-Zoom, two of the Scotch battalions, supported by a Dutch battalion of infantry, made a most determined stand, refusing for a long time to yield ground to the enemy, until superior numbers compelled them to retire. Some idea of the severity of the struggle may be formed from the fact that Colyear's battalion, which had gone into action 660 strong, could only muster 156 men afterwards. It is thus described by an old writer:—"Overpowered by numbers, deserted, and alone, the Scotch assembled in the market-place and attacked the French with such vigour that they drove them from street to street, till fresh reinforcements pouring in compelled them to retreat in their turn, disputing every inch as they retired, and fighting till two-thirds of their number fell on the spot, valiantly bringing their colours with them, which the grenadiers twice recovered from the midst of the French at the point of the bayonet. 'Gentlemen,' said the conquering General to two officers who had been taken prisoners—Lieutenants Travers and Allan Maclean—'had all conducted themselves as you and your brave corps have done, I should not now be master of Bergen-op-Zoom.'"

Succeeding the sunshine of victory, there arose a cloud upon its history which we wish, for the credit of our Government, we could omit to record. Denied the privilege of further recruiting at home, the States of Holland insisted upon the admission of foreigners into its ranks, and thus to a great extent its Scottish character was destroyed. When war broke out and our country needed troops, our Scotsmen repeated the petition that their brigade should be recalled for the service of their own land. The request was refused, whilst regiments were raised in Scotland, and even German auxiliaries enrolled upon the British establishment, rather than do what appears only an act of justice to the soldiers of the Old Scots Brigade. As if further to exasperate the Scots, when war was declared between Britain and Holland, and our brigade thus placed in a cruel dilemma, unheeded, it was surrendered to the enemy, who, almost as prisoners of war, sent it to garrison distant fortresses on the inland frontier. At length recalled by George III. in 1793, it was, in 1795, sent to reinforce the garrison of Gibraltar, and in the following year was removed to the Cape of Good Hope. In 1798 it was transferred to India, where it shared with the Highland regiments the glory of "Seringapatam" in 1799, and the battle of "Argaum" in 1803; the former being afterwards authorised for the colours and appointments.

Returning home in 1808 as the Ninety-fourth regiment, it was actively and creditably engaged in the various actions of Spain and the South of France, and received permission to bear on its colours the words—"Ciudad Rodrigo," "Badajoz," "Salamanca," "Vittoria," "Nivelle," "Orthes," and "Toulouse," and also the inscription of "Peninsula." In the defence of Cadiz it suffered very severely, and amongst its brave was found a heroine—a sergeant's wife, who on this occasion displayed a remarkable degree of cool courage, which is fitly described in Mr Carter's admirable work, "Curiosities of War." The regiment was disbanded at Belfast in 1818. A new regiment, raised six years afterwards, now bears the number of the Ninety-fourth, but as yet has had no opportunity to distinguish itself. We only hope it may emulate, nay, if possible excel, the deeds of the Old Scots Brigade, which so worthily sustained the characteristic valour of the Scot.

THE NINETY-NINTH FOOT;

OR,

LANARKSHIRE.

CHAPTER XXIV.

"How sleep the brave, who sink to rest,
By all their country's wishes blest!
When spring, with dewy fingers cold,
Returns to deck their hallow'd mould,
He there shall dress a sweeter sod,
Than Fancy's feet have ever trod.
By fairy hands their knell is rung,
By forms unseen their dirge is sung;
There Honour comes, a pilgrim gray,
To bless the turf that wraps their clay,
And Freedom shall awhile repair
To dwell, a weeping hermit, there!"

1824–1862—COLONIAL EMPIRE—SOLDIER'S LETTER—CHINA.

HOWEVER deeply interested we may personally feel in Lanarkshire, and however proud we may be of the many gallant
soldiers who have gone forth from us to fight the battles of
our one country, still to the Ninety-ninth the relationship
indicated above exists scarcely but in name. Nay, even as a

Scottish regiment its present composition would belie its seeming nativity. As in the case of many other regiments, so with it, these titles have been mostly attached for purposes of recruiting, and seldom bestowed to record the origin of the corps. Nevertheless, it is looked for as a consequence that the designation thus conferred should serve to stimulate the youth of Lanarkshire, bid them rally round the Ninety-ninth, and thus constituting it their own, immortalise its number by distinguished service in its ranks.

The regiment was raised in 1824, along with the present Ninety-fourth, Ninety-fifth, Ninety-sixth, Ninety-seventh, and Ninety-eighth regiments, at a time when our vast colonial empire demanded an augmentation of our army to ensure its adequate defence. Notwithstanding the anxiety of the Ninety-ninth to be released from the monotony of a passive service, and engage in the more stirring scenes of battle peculiar to the soldier, its brief history displays few events specially calling for notice, having been doomed to quietude, and denied by circumstances an opportunity of distinguishing itself during the Indian or Crimean wars. The following remarkable letter from one of its soldiers, extracted from Mr Carter's interesting volume, the "Curiosities of War," is truly a curiosity:—

"My Lord Duke,—I mean to take the liberty of writing these few lines before your Grace, flying under the protection of your wings, and trusting in your most charitable heart for to grant my request.

"May it please your Grace to reject me not, for the love of the Almighty God, to whom I pray to reward your soul in heaven.

"My Lord Duke, I shall convince you that I am a pt°. soldier in the 99th depôt, at Chatham, a servant to Her Majesty since the 29th of September, 1846; likewise that I was born of poor parents, who were unable to provide any means of education for me but what I scraped by over-hours and industry, till I grew thus eighteen years of age, and was compelled to quit their sight and seek my own fortune.

"I think I am possessed of honesty, docility, faithfulness, high hopes, bold spirit, and obedience towards my superiors. I partly know the Irish language, to which I was brought up, and am deficient of the English language, that is, of not being able of peaking [qy. speaking] it correctly. One of my past days, as I was guiding a horse in a solitary place, unexpectedly I burst into a flow of poetry, which successfully came from my lips by no trouble. From thence I wrote during the following year a lot of poems, some of which, it was given up, being the best composed in the same locality for the last forty years past. However, I did no treason, but all for the amusement of the country.

"My Lord, I mean to shoe a little proof of it in the following lines:—

Once from at home, as I did roam my fortune for to try,
All alone along the road, my courage forcing high;
I said sweet home, both friends and foes, I bid you all good-bye.
From thence I started into Cork and joined the 99th.

This famous corps, which I adore, is brave and full of might,
With fire and sword, would fight the foe, and make their force retire.
Supplied are those with Irish Poet for to compose in rhyme,
I pray to God his grace upon the flaming 99th.

"My Lord, to get an end to this rude letter, my request, and all that I want, is twelve months' leave, for the mere purpose of learning both day and night, where I could accommodate myself according to my pay, at the end of which twelve months I might be fit for promotion in the protection of Her Majesty.

"Your most obedient Servant,

"———— ————"

Public opinion is inclined to regard a war with China as something ridiculous; to smile at the odd equipment of its "Braves," and laugh at the absurd pretensions of its "Celestials." We fancy its hosts, like a summer cloud, as something to be at once dissipated by the first breath of the Western breeze. In this we have deceived ourselves, and on more than one occasion paid the penalty of our folly in the blood of the gallant few, who, overwhelmed by countless numbers, the victims of a matchless perfidy, have fallen as exposed to an almost certain destruction. Alone, as in a nest of hornets, we felt the sting of defeat when we had supposed an easy victory. Our discipline, our bravery, and our superior arms, failed to grasp the success we had imagined was to be had for the mere taking. The truth was revealed when too late; we had underrated the valour of the foe, and too much despised their means of defence; then we learned by a bitter experience that our handful of brave men, in the language of Pitt, " were capable of achieving everything *but impossibilities.*"

The Ninety-ninth was engaged in the recent Chinese war, but only in time to share the concluding glories of the campaign which crowned a severe and harassing contest in the capture of Pekin. The good conduct of the regiment on this occasion amply demonstrated the excellence of the corps—of what honourable service it was capable, and betokened an illustrious history, which may yet render it famous as the Lanarkshire regiment, and fill a larger space in the national records of "*Our Brave.*"

> " Great acts best write themselves in their own stories;
>   They die too basely who outlive their glories."

THE OLD HIGHLAND BRIGADE.

CHAPTER XXV.

" In the garb of old Gaul, with the fire of old Rome,
From the heath-cover'd mountains of Scotia we come,
Where the Romans endeavour'd our country to gain,
But our ancestors fought, and they fought not in vain.
Such is our love of liberty, our country and our laws,
That, like our ancestors of old, we'll stand in freedom's cause,
We'll bravely fight like heroes bold for honour and applause,
And defy the French, with all their art, to alter our laws."

LOUDON'S — MONTGOMERY'S — FRASER'S — KEITH'S — CAMPBELL'S
— DUKE OF GORDON'S — JOHNSTONE'S — FRASER'S — M'DONALD'S.

PASSING through the glens of the Grampians, northwards or
westwards, we are introduced to the sterner grandeur of the
Scottish Highlands. Having briefly viewed the glorious
records of our Lowland regiments, we feel as more immediately in the heart of our subject when, entering upon
its second part, we propose to give an account of our Highland regiments. We think we cannot fairly be challenged for
an undue partiality to the latter, or be thought guilty of
injustice to the former, in yielding the prominence to the
Highlanders, because they retain more of the national characteristics, whilst the Lowlanders, intermingled with others,

have sadly degenerated from the original purity of the Scottish, if indeed they have not already forfeited every claim, beyond the name, to be included in the catalogue of Scottish regiments.

The romantic story of the clans bids us return to the feudal age, when strange but true war revealed itself to be the unwitting civiliser of the ancient world; apparently the harbinger of evil, yet in reality the herald of good—the purifier—the evil out of which, in the mysterious providence of God, blessing should in the end abundantly flow. In the Highlands the memorials of these barbaric times of civil strife among the clans are sadly ample and very evident; scarce a dell but bears traces of the ruin which fire and sword had inflicted; scarce a glen but has its tale of woe; scarce a heath but beneath the cairn gathers to its shaggy bosom the ashes of some warrior chief. But there were also times in our history when the stormy tempest of angry passion was at least for the moment hushed, and the fiery valour of the clans, gathered into one, descended from the Highlands, resistless as the mountain torrent, to do battle for Scottish freedom in the day of Scotland's need. And thus their gallant demeanour upon the field of Bannockburn has waked the muse of Scott to immortalise their fame, as he beautifully tells of our "Scottish Chiefs" in his "Lord of the Isles."

The devoted loyalty of the clans to the unhappy Stuarts has given to their history a melancholy interest, and claims our admiration, because of the dauntless resolution with which they vainly strove to maintain the falling fortunes of that degenerate race, although manifested on the wrong side; furnishing, moreover, a theme for song which has given birth to some of the most touching lyrics of our bards.

Shortly after the battle of Culloden the fighting strength of the various clans was rated by Lord Forbes for the Government as follows:—

Argyle,	3000
Breadalbane,	1000
Lochiel and other Chieftains of the Campbells,	1000
Mackays,	500
Maclachlans,	200
Stewart of Appin,	300
Macdougals,	200
Stewart of Grandtully,	300
Clan Gregor,	700
Duke of Athole,	3000
Farquharsons,	500
Duke of Gordon,	300
Grant of Grant,	850
Macintosh,	800
Macphersons,	400
Frasers,	900
Grant of Glenmorriston,	150
Chisholms,	200
Duke of Perth,	300
Seaforth,	1000
Cromarty, Suatwell, Gairloch, and other Chieftains of the Mackenzies,	1500
Menzies,	300
Munroes,	300
Rosses,	500
Sutherland,	2000
Mackays,	800
Sinclairs,	1100
Macdonald of Slate,	700
Macdonald of Clanronald,	700

Macdonell of Glengary,	500
Macdonell of Keppoch,	300
Macdonald of Glencoe,	130
Robertsons,	200
Camerons,	800
M'Kinnon,	200
Macleod,	700
The Duke of Montrose, Earls of Bute and Moray, Macfarlanes, Colquhouns, M'Neils of Barra, M'Nabs. M'Naughtans, Lamonts, etc., etc.,	5600
	31,930

Government, awakened to the danger which threatened the peace of the country whilst the fiery valour of the clans, unrestrained, ran wild—save for the chieftain who exercised a species of independent sovereignty, not always for the weal of the State—wisely determined to enlist the sympathy of these petty tyrants on its side, and present a more useful and nobler field for the employment and development of that exceeding bravery and martial spirit which have ever characterised the clans, and the efforts of which had, when embraced in the rebel army of the Stuarts, justly caused most serious alarm. "I sought for merit," said the great Chatham, "wherever it was to be found; it is my boast that I was the first minister who looked for it and found it in the mountains of the North. I called it forth, and drew into your service a hardy and intrepid race of men, who, when left by your jealousy, became a prey to the artifice of your enemies, and had gone nigh to have overturned the State. . . . . These men were brought to combat on your side, have served with fidelity, have fought with valour, and conquered for you in every part of the world."

About the year 1740, a variety of companies of Highlanders, known as the "Black Watch," were regimented, and, under the Earl of Crawford, formed the *Royal Forty-second Highlanders*, whose history will be treated in succeeding chapters; meanwhile, we shall shortly enumerate the several corps, since disbanded, which at several periods constituted the Highland Brigade. The oldest of these

LOUDON'S HIGHLANDERS,

was raised by the Earl of Loudon, a nobleman of great influence in the Highlands, in 1745. In its short but eventful career, the regiment served with credit and fidelity during the rebellion of 1745, and afterwards with equal distinction with the allied army in Holland. At the battle of Preston it was unfortunately captured. Having completed its term of service, the regiment was disbanded in 1748.

On the outbreak of the American war, the Government again appealed to the clans to enrol beneath the British banner, and on no occasion with more splendid success. Of the regiments then embarked were

MONTGOMERY'S HIGHLANDERS,

raised in 1757 by Archibald Montgomery, afterwards Earl of Eglinton, and which served with its cotemporary,

FRASER'S HIGHLANDERS,

in America throughout the war. This last was raised, hence

its title, by Sir Simon Fraser, son of Lord Lovat, a chieftain enjoying largely the confidence of the clans, yet dispoiled of his lands and destitute of funds by the misfortunes of the recent rebellion, in which he had figured conspicuously among the Jacobites.

Immediately upon their embodiment, these two regiments were embarked for America at Greenock. Associated in the British army, they were honourably distinguished in the contest which ensued. Their disbandment took place respectively in 1775 and 1763. Hostilities having extended to the continent of Europe, and the Government thoroughly appreciating the value of the Highland soldier, resolved to enrol, in 1759, other two regiments for service in Germany, respectively

The EIGHTY-SEVENTH, or KEITH's HIGHLANDERS; and
The EIGHTY-EIGHTH, or CAMPBELL's HIGHLANDERS.

These so seasonably impressed the enemy with the might of Scottish valour, that it is alleged the French so magnified the numbers of our Highlanders as to imagine our army contained twelve instead of two battalions of kilted warriors. A French officer, lamenting his own little stature and wishing he had been a six-foot grenadier, is reported to have become quite reconciled with himself, "when," as he expresses it, "he had seen the wonders performed by the little mountaineers." One of the journals of the day has this curious account of our Highlanders:—"They are a people totally different in their dress, manners, and temper from the other inhabitants of Great Britain. *They are caught in the mountains when young,* and still run with a surprising degree of swiftness. As they are strangers to fear, they make very good soldiers when disciplined." Accustomed to regard retreat as equivalent to defeat, as something cowardly, it was with great reluctance our mountaineers yielded obedience to such commands.

The EIGHTY-NINTH, or DUKE OF GORDON'S HIGHLANDERS,

was raised by His Grace, upon his extensive estates, in 1759, and was destined for service in India. Also, raised in 1760,

The HUNDRED-AND-FIRST, or JOHNSTONE'S HIGHLANDERS.

These, with other Highland corps, were disbanded on the conclusion of the war in 1763, but not without having won the nation's confidence — deserving well of the country, whose gratitude followed them.

A few years later and a new American war burst forth, intensified in its virulence by its civil character. In the attempts made to suppress the rebellion of the colonists the old Highland brigade, re-assembled, was highly distinguished.

Sir Simon Fraser of Lovat, who had already shown his forwardness in raising the clans in 1757 and ranging them in regiments in defence of the State, now restored to the patrimony which the rebellion of his predecessor had forfeited, was again the first to gather around him a regiment of clansmen, known as

The SEVENTY-FIRST, or FRASER'S HIGHLANDERS.

This corps was engaged in the very hottest of the contest, especially in and around Savannah and Charleston. One only instance, illustrative of the excellence of the regiment, we have space to quote:—At Stone Ferry, assailed by 2000 Americans, Captain Campbell, with 59 men and officers, heroically maintained his post, until only seven soldiers were left standing— the rest being either killed or wounded. To most of the men this was their first encounter with the enemy; "they had not yet learned to retreat," nor had they forgotten what had been always inculcated in their native country, that "to retreat was disgraceful." When Captain Campbell fell, he desired such of his men as were able to make the best of their way to the redoubt, but they refused to obey, as it would bring lasting disgrace upon them all to leave their officers in the field with none to carry them back." The seven men retired carrying their wounded officers with them, and accompanied by those of the soldiers who were able to walk. Fraser's Highlanders closed a brilliant career as part of the unfortunate garrison of Yorktown, who were obliged to capitulate, and so, as prisoners of war, only restored to their liberty and country on the conclusion of the war, when they were disbanded. In this last disaster, Fraser's Highlanders became associated with another body of Highlanders,

The SEVENTY-SIXTH, or M'DONALD'S HIGHLANDERS,

which had been engaged in the war, although at first on a different field.

The SEVENTY-FOURTH, or ARGYLLSHIRE HIGHLANDERS

served at the same period with the British army of the north on the frontiers of Canada. Acting with these were two battalions of Highland emigrants, mostly veterans of the previous war, who, serving in the Highland brigade of that time, had thereafter accepted the bounty of Government and settled in America, known as the

ROYAL HIGHLAND EMIGRANT REGIMENT.

Besides these, the wars of the time induced the formation of the

ATHOLL HIGHLANDERS and ABERDEENSHIRE HIGHLANDERS:

and, when the French Revolution further enveloped the world in the flames of war,

The NINETY-SEVENTH, or STRATHSPEY HIGHLANDERS: and
The HUNDRED-AND-SIXTEENTH, or PERTHSHIRE HIGHLANDERS:

constituted a part of the old Highland Brigade. Without more extended detail or enumeration of the many Highland corps once on our army establishment—now disbanded—esteeming we have sufficiently recorded the story of the old brigade, to enable the reader to feel it worthy his attention, as replete with incidents of heroism and daring scarcely ever surpassed—we come to the consideration of the present Highland Brigade.

THE HIGHLAND BRIGADE.

THE FORTY-SECOND FOOT:

OR,

ROYAL HIGHLANDERS—"BLACK WATCH."

CHAPTER XXVI.

" Awake on your hills, on your islands awake,
Brave sons of the mountain, the frith, and the lake!
'Tis the bugle—but not for the chase is the call;
'Tis the pibroch's shrill summons—but not to the hall.

" 'Tis the summons of heroes for conquest or death,
When the banners are blazing on mountain and heath:
They call to the dirk, the claymore, and the targe,
To the march and the muster, the line and the charge."

"BLACK WATCH"—FONTENOY—REBELLION 1745—AMERICA—
1729–1760.

THIS distinguished regiment has long deservedly enjoyed the
public favour. It is the link which binds us to the Old
Highland Brigade, of which it remains the only and worthy
representative. Mr Cannon, in his Military Records, thus
introduces his account of the regiment by the following

eulogy on the excellence of our Highland soldiers: "The
Highlanders of Scotland have been conspicuous for the possession of every military virtue which adorns the character of
the hero who has adopted the profession of arms. Naturally
patient and brave, and inured to hardship in their youth
in the hilly districts of a northern climate, these warlike
mountaineers have always proved themselves a race of
lion-like champions, valiant in the field, faithful, constant,
generous in the hour of victory, and endued with calm perseverance under trial and disaster." As already noted, the
Government had wisely determined more largely to enlist the
sympathy and good services of the clans on their side; and, in
consequence, had armed a certain proportion of the well-
affected clans—such as the Campbells, the Frasers, the Grants,
and the Munroes—who, formed into independent companies
under the command of their own or other well-known
chieftains, were quartered in the more troubled districts of
the Highlands, where the Jacobite clans of Cameron, Stuart,
M'Intosh, M'Donald, and Murray rendered their presence
necessary for maintaining order and preventing any sudden
rising, as well as for the protection of property in those
lawless times. They were called the "Freicudan Dhu," or
"Black Watch," from the sombre appearance of their tartan
uniform, compared with the scarlet coats of the regular
soldiers. They were mostly composed of the sons of the
landed gentry, as the Government felt that care was necessary,
especially in this their first experiment, in selecting individuals who had something at stake in the common country,

and consequently affording some guarantee for their fidelity.
The success of the experiment was soon abundantly manifest;
and whilst, in 1729, the "Black Watch" consisted only of
six companies, ten years later these were assembled at
Perth, augmented to ten companies, and regimented as the
Highland Regiment, under the Earl of Crawford.   The
original high character of this famous regiment has never
been excelled; no, not even by the Royal Guards.   Nearly
all its members were six feet in height — illustrious for
physical prowess and might — highly connected, as may
be well inferred from the fact that many, when proceeding
to drill, went on horseback, followed by servants bearing
their firelock and uniform.   On one occasion the King,
having heard of the splendid physical appearance of the
men, desired to see a specimen; and accordingly three
were sent up to London.   One of these, Grant of Strath-
spey, died on the way; the other two, M'Gregor and
Campbell, were presented to His Majesty, and, in presence
of the King, the Duke of Cumberland, Marshal Wade, and
other officers, performed the broadsword exercises and
that of the Lochaber axe.   Their dexterity and skill so
pleased His Majesty that he gave each a gratuity of one
guinea — a large sum in those days — imagining he had
appropriately rewarded them; but such was the character of
these men — above want, generally in good circumstances —
that each bestowed his guinea upon the porter at the palace
gate as he passed out.   There is one feature which we
record with more peculiar pleasure, as leaving a mightier

impress of character upon these gallant men, and we quote it in the words of an English historian who was evidently no friend of theirs, yet wondrously surprised, as he relates, "to see these savages, from the officer to the commonest man, at their several meals, first stand up and pull off their bonnets, and then lift up their eyes in the most solemn and devout manner, and mutter something in their own gibberish, by way, I suppose," says he, "of saying grace, as if they had been so many Christians."

The idea that they should only serve in their own country had so strongly possessed the minds of many, that, when marched into England, and learning they were destined for service in the West Indies—a place associated in their minds only as a place of punishment for felons and the like—the regiment mutinied; but by a judicious blending of firmness and lenity on the part of Government, this splendid corps was not only brought to submit, but preserved to win honour for our country, and amply redeem, by brave deeds, the faults which for a moment clouded its early history.

In 1743 the Highlanders joined the British army in Flanders, where their conduct was so exemplary that the Elector Palatine specially thanked our King "for the excellent behaviour of the regiment while in his territories, and for whose sake," he added, "I will always pay a respect and regard to a Scotsman in future." Of their valour, no higher tribute can be paid than to say that at the battle of Fontenoy, where the regiment made its first essay in arms, our Highlanders were placed in brigade with the veterans of the

British Guards. The result proved them to be every way worthy
of the compliment. Truly they presented the choicest troops of
the land, and eminently their success, like a meteor flash,
for a moment lighted up the fortunes of battle and promised
victory. Alas! all in vain; the disasters in other parts of the
field compelled retreat. Marshal Saxe, who commanded the
French on this occasion, with all the generosity which becomes
a soldier, and who could distinguish valour even in a foeman,
said of the Highlanders—"These furies rushed in upon us
with more violence than ever did a sea driven by a tempest."

The rebellion of Prince Charles Edward in 1745 occasioned
the recall of the Forty-second, or, as it was then designated,
the Forty-third, from the Continent, the scene of its early
glory. With the army, the regiment was encamped in the
south of England, prepared to dispute the menaced landing
of a French force upon our coasts, which the rebels hoped
should effect a favourable diversion. Meanwhile, three new
companies which had not as yet joined the regiment,
served in the royal army against the rebels—one company
being taken prisoner at the battle of Prestonpans. The
internal peace of the country being secured by the decisive
victory of Culloden, many of the regiments returned to Flanders; whilst the Highlanders, with 2000 of the Foot Guards
and other troops, attempted a descent upon the French coast,
but failed to accomplish that success which had been anticipated, from the superior strength of the enemy. In the
attack upon port L'Orient, assuming the disguise of Highlanders, a body of French, in a sally, succeeded in approach-

ing the British lines, and had nearly entered them when discovered. They experienced the deadly wrath of our true Highlanders, whose blood was roused because of the indignity offered to the kilts in the foe attempting to deceive our troops thereby. The result proved that it needed more than the tartans to constitute the genuine Highlander—the dauntless native courage being wanting.

Returning home, the regiment was stationed a while in Ireland, until removed to reinforce the army fighting in Flanders, in alliance with the Austrians and Dutch, against the French. Excepting, however, at the siege of Hulst, and covering the embarkation of the army for South Beveland, the regiment was little engaged in these campaigns, being kept in reserve in South Beveland. Returning to Britain in 1749, the Highlanders were variously stationed in Ireland during the following six years. In 1756, the outbreak of hostilities in America between the British and French colonists called for the immediate presence of a British army, of which the Forty-second formed a part. On their arrival, the strangeness of their garb excited the interest of "the Indians, who flocked from all quarters to see the strangers, who, they believed, were of the same extraction as themselves, and therefore received them as brothers." Landed in America, Lord Loudon, as commander-in-chief, hesitated to advance against the enemy until his soldiers had acquired some knowledge of the novel warfare of the bush in which they were to be so much engaged. The enemy, meanwhile, reaped many valuable advantages from the precious moments thus lost through the over-cautiousness and procrastination of the British commander.

In 1758, with the Twenty-seventh, the Forty-fourth, the Forty-sixth, the Fifty-fifth, two battalions of the Sixtieth, and upwards of 9000 provincials, the Forty-second formed the division of our army, under Major-General James Abercromby, which attempted the reduction of the strong fort of Ticonderoga, on Lake Champlain. The obstacles to be overcome, and the strength of the garrison were such, that the utmost and repeated efforts of our soldiers failed to effect its capture. The distinguished bravery of the Forty-second is thus commemorated by an eye-witness:—"With a mixture of esteem, grief, and envy, I consider the great loss and immortal glory acquired by the Scots Highlanders in the late bloody affair. Impatient for orders, they rushed forward to the entrenchments, which many of them actually mounted. They appeared like lions, breaking from their chains. Their intrepidity was rather animated than damped by seeing their comrades fall on every side. I have only to say of them, that they seemed more anxious to revenge the cause of their deceased friends, than careful to avoid the same fate." Their valour was further rewarded by an order to dignify the regiment with the title of the "*Royal*" Highlanders. So desperate was the fight, that the loss of the regiment exceeded 650 men and officers. It was here that the gallant and brave Brigadier-General Viscount Howe, of the Fifty-fifth regiment, met his death: he who had been "the life and soul of the expedition," and was peculiarly the favourite of the soldiers.

In October, 1758, a second battalion was raised at Perth and grafted upon the good old stock of the Royal Highlanders. Soon after its formation, it was embarked for Barbadoes, where it joined the expedition under Major-Generals Hopson and Barrington, which was baffled in an attempt upon the French Island of Martinique. This reverse was, however, somewhat avenged by a more successful attack upon the Island of Guadaloupe, which, after four months' hard fighting and much suffering from the insalubrity of the climate, was surrendered to the British. The defence is remarkable as affording a striking instance of female heroism in the person of Madame Ducharmey, who, arming her negroes when others had retired, refused to yield, resolutely defending the island for some time.

Removed from the West Indies to the continent of America, the second battalion was at length united to the first. These formed part of the expeditionary force, under General Amherst, which, advancing, occupied the strong fortresses of Ticonderago, Crown Point, and Isle aux Noix, successively evacuated by the French. In the campaign of 1760 our Highlanders were with the army which, crossing Lake Ontario, descended the St Lawrence, effected the surrender of Montreal, and in its fall sealed the subjugation of the entire province of Canada.

CHAPTER XXVII.

" For gold the merchant ploughs the main,
    The farmer ploughs the manor;
But glory is the sodger's prize,
    The sodger's wealth is honour.
The brave poor sodger ne'er despise,
    Nor count him as a stranger:
Remember he's his country's stay,
    In day and hour o' danger."

MARTINIQUE—HAVANNAH—BUSHYRUN—ILLINOIS—AMERICAN
REVOLUTION—HALIFAX—CAPE BRETON—1762–1769.

ITS sobriety, abstemious habits, great activity, and capability
of bearing the vicissitudes of the West Indian climate, had commended the selection of the Forty-second as part of an expedition then assembling at Barbadoes for a renewal of the attack
upon the valuable island of Martinique, which, after some severe
fighting, was surrendered, in 1762, by the French governor to
the British commander, Major-General the Honourable Robert
Monckton.   Scarcely had the rude tempest of war subsided in
its wrath, and the genial calm of peace asserted its blessed influence over the nation, ere that tranquillity was again disturbed by
the malignant passions which unhappily prevailed, and launched
our country into antagonism with Spain.   Reinforced by fresh
troops from home—including our Highlanders—the British
army of the West Indies, under the Earl of Albemarle,

embarking, effected a landing on the Spanish island of Cuba, and gloriously captured its wealthy metropolis, acquiring therein prize-money to the enormous extent of three millions sterling. After achieving this very successful result, the regiment, embraced in one battalion, returned to the continent of America, where it was employed in most harassing duty, checking and punishing the depredatory incursions of the Indians, who were ever on the alert to avenge themselves on the white men of the colony, whom they could not help regarding, and not altogether unreasonably, as their spoilers, and hence their natural enemies. At Bushyrun the Forty-second encountered the army of red warriors, and inflicted a severe defeat, which so sorely distressed them, that, tendering their submission, a favourable peace was thereupon secured. Thereafter a party of a hundred men, detached from the regiment, under Captain, afterwards General Sir Thomas Stirling, was engaged in an exploring expedition, journeying 3000 miles in ten months, as far as Fort Charteris on the Illinois; and notwithstanding all the difficulties and dangers encountered in the way, returning to head-quarters safe and sound. At length, after these many faithful and arduous services, the regiment received the order to return home. Enjoying the esteem of the colonists, its departure was most deeply regretted. The regiment reached Cork in October, 1767, and remained on duty in Ireland for about twelve years, whence it was removed to Scotland in 1775, to be recruited. Scarcely had its establishment been completed when the American Revolution, involving our country in a new war, occasioned its recall to that continent. On the eve of its departure from Greenock, the regiment comprised 931 Highlanders, 74 Lowlanders, 5 Englishmen (in the band), 1 Welshman, and 2 Irishmen—ample evidence of its genuine Highland character. In the passage outwards the fleet was separated in a tempest, and a company of the Forty-second, which had been quartered on board the "Oxford" transport, was so unfortunate as to be captured by an American privateer. Retained as prisoners on board the "Oxford," the soldiers succeeded in overpowering the crew, and, assuming the command of the vessel, navigated it to the Bay of Chesapeake, unwittingly to find themselves in the enemy's grasp, who held possession of the bay. As captives, our Highlanders were removed into the interior of the continent, where every attempt was made to seduce them from their allegiance, and tempt them to enter the American service, but, "true to their colours," without avail. Meanwhile, the rest of the regiment had joined the British army in Staten Island, under General the Honourable Sir William Howe.

During the whole course of the war which followed, it may with truth be averred that no one regiment was more constantly employed, serving chiefly with one or other of the flank corps, and that no regiment was more exposed to danger, underwent more fatigue, or suffered more from both.

The events of the war are so much a matter of history, that we forbear to detain the reader with more than a mere enumeration of those in which the Forty-second bore a conspicuous part. Having, through the battle of Brooklyn, achieved the capture of Long Island, landing with the British army on the mainland, the Highlanders were present with distinction at the siege of Fort Washington, the capture of Fort Lee, the re-taking of Trenton, but especially in the affair of Pisquata, where, assailed by overwhelming numbers, the gallantry of the regiment was beyond all compliment. The Forty-second was also present, although in a subordinate position, at the battle of Brandywine, where General Washington was defeated. On the 20th September, 1777, it was detached with the first battalion of Light Infantry and the Forty-fourth regiment, to surprise a strong force of Americans which lay concealed in the recesses of the forest in the neighbourhood of the British camp, purposing to annoy the army and cut off stragglers. The surprise—effected with scarcely any loss—favoured by the darkness of the night, was successful. The enemy, wholly unsuspecting, was utterly dispersed with great slaughter. The regiment was further engaged in the attack upon Billingspoint and the defence of Germanstown.

At length allied with France, the Americans were so helped and encouraged that it became necessary to concentrate the British army, and, in consequence, relinquishing many of their more distant conquests, our troops retired to the sea coast to oppose the threatened debarkation of a French force from their fleet which cruised off the coast. Dispersed by a storm, this armament failed to afford that assistance which had been anticipated, compelling General Sullivan, who commanded an auxiliary army of Americans, to abandon the siege of Nieuport, in Rhode Island, and beat a precipitate retreat to the mainland. Meanwhile, the Forty-second, with the Thirty-third, Forty-sixth, and Sixty-fourth regiments, successfully accomplished the destruction of the arsenals and dockyards of Bedford and Martha's Vineyard. At Stoneypoint and Vereplanks, after a desperate struggle, the persevering efforts of the Royal Highlanders were rewarded with complete success. Under General Sir Henry Clinton, the regiment formed a part of the expedition which undertook and achieved the siege of Charlestown. The increasing force and daring of the enemy, inspired and sustained by the genius of Washington, glorying in the disaster of Yorktown, where a British army was forced to surrender, induced peace, which, concluded in 1782, put an end to further hostilities. The regiment served for a while thereafter in Halifax, and, ere it returned home in 1789, garrisoned the island of Cape Breton. Whilst in Nova Scotia, in 1785, Major-General John Campbell, in presenting a new set of colours to the regiment, thus ably addressed it—an address which, in its excellence, lives to encourage our army, and than which we are convinced no better epitome of a soldier's duty exists:—

"I congratulate you on the service you have done your country, and the honour you have procured yourselves, by protecting your old colours, and defending them from your enemies in different engagements during the late unnatural rebellion.

"From those ragged, but honourable remains, you are now to transfer your allegiance and fidelity to these new National and Regimental Standards of Honour, now consecrated and solemnly dedicated to the service of our King and Country. These colours are committed to your immediate care and protection; and I trust you will, on all occasions, defend them from your enemies, with honour to yourselves and service to your country — with that distinguished and noble bravery which have always characterised the ROYAL HIGHLANDERS in the field of battle.

"With what pleasure, with what peculiar satisfaction—nay, with what pride, would I enumerate the different memorable actions where the regiment distinguished itself. To particularise the whole would exceed the bounds of this address; let me therefore beg your indulgence while I take notice only of a few of them.

"And, first, the conduct of the regiment at the battle of *Fontenoy* was great and glorious! As long as the bravery of the fifteen battalions in that conflict shall grace the historic page, and fill the breast of every Highlander with pleasure and admiration, so long will the superior gallantry of the Forty-second Regiment bear a conspicuous part in the well-fought action of that day, and be recorded in the annals of Fame to the latest posterity!

"I am convinced that it will always be a point of honour with the corps, considered as a collective body, to support and maintain a *national* character!

"For this purpose you should ever remember that, being

a national and reputable corps, your actions as citizens and
civil subjects, as well as your conduct as soldiers, will be
much observed—more than those of any other regiment in
the service. Your good behaviour will be handed down
with honour to posterity, and your faults, if you commit any,
will not only be reported, but magnified, by other corps who
are emulous of your *civil* as well as of your *military* character.
Your decent, sober, and regular behaviour in the different
quarters you have hitherto occupied, has rendered you the
distinguished favourites of their respective inhabitants. For
the sake, then, of your country—for the sake of your own
established character, which must be dearer to you than
every other consideration—do not tarnish your fame by a
subsequent behaviour less manly!

"Do not, I beseech you, my fellow-soldiers, allow your
morals to be corrupted by associating with low, mean, or bad
company. A man is always known by his companions; and
if any one among you should at any time be seen spending
his money in base, worthless company, he ought to be set up
and exposed as an object of regimental contempt!

"To conclude: As you have, as soldiers, displayed sufficient valour in the field by defeating the enemies of your
country, suffer me to recommend to you, as Christians, to use
your best endeavours, now in the time of peace, to overcome
the enemies of your immortal souls! Believe me, my fellow-
soldiers, and be assured, that the faith and virtues of a
Christian add much to the valour, firmness, and fidelity of a
soldier. He, beyond comparison, has the best reason, and

the strongest motive, for doing his duty in scenes of danger, who has nothing to fear, but every thing to hope, in a future existence.

"Ought you not, therefore, to be solicitous to adorn your minds with, at least, the principal and leading Christian virtues, so that if it should be your fate hereafter to fall in the field of battle, your acquaintances and friends will have the joyful consolation of hearing that you leave an unspotted name, and of being assured that you rose from a bed of honour to a crown of immortality."

CHAPTER XXVIII.

"O! to see his tartan trews,
Bonnet blue, and laigh-heel'd shoes,
Philabeg aboon his knee!
That's the lad that I'll gang wi'."

THE HIGHLANDS—FRENCH REVOLUTION—FLANDERS—GERMANY —WEST INDIES—GIBRALTAR—MINORCA—EGYPT—EDIN- BURGH—1789–1803.

THE honourable bearing of the Royal Highlanders throughout the war had been so conspicuous as to win for them the hearty esteem of their countrymen. Hence their return was welcomed by all classes, and their progress northward was little else than a triumphal march. At Glasgow, the joy of the people was unbounded.

Whilst stationed in Scotland, the regiment was called to fulfil a most painful duty, in the suppression of the riots which had arisen in the Highlands from the expulsion of the poorer peasantry from the haunts and homes of "auld lang- syne." From a long and quiet possession, they had come to consider such as their own, and therefore were disposed to resist the right of the legal proprietor, who desired to disencumber his estates of the unproductive poor, and render these lands remunerative, rather than, as hitherto, a barren burden.

To curb the furious passions which the evil genii of the French Revolution had let loose, wherewith to plague Christendom, the might of Britain was called to the rescue. The Forty-second, largely recruited, was accordingly embarked at Hull, and joined the British army fighting under the Duke of York in Flanders. Soon, however, the regiment was recalled, to form part of a meditated enterprise against the French West Indian Islands. This scheme being abandoned for the present, it was engaged in a vain attempt to aid, by a descent on the French coast, the Vendean royalists, who yet dared manfully, but, alas! ineffectually, to struggle against the sanguinary tyranny of the Revolution, for liberty and righteousness. Returning to Flanders, the regiment was doomed to share the retrograde movement which had been necessitated by the overwhelming superiority of the enemy, and the listless indifference, nay, even hate, of the Dutch, whose cause we had assumed to espouse. Retreating through Germany to Bremen, the sufferings of the army were severe, but endured with a fortitude which well commanded the admiration of friend and foe. Never were the capabilities of the Highland soldier more thoroughly tested, and more triumphantly apparent, than in the midst of the fatigues of an incessant warfare, the severities of a bitter winter, and the discouraging prospects of retreat. Under these cruel circumstances, whilst other regiments counted their losses by hundreds, the Forty-second only lost twenty-five men.

Returning to England, the regiment was once more included in the long-contemplated West Indian expedition.

A vast armament had been assembled in 1795, and sailed at first prosperously, only to be dispersed and driven back with heavy loss by a furious tempest which almost immediately arose. A second attempt, promising as favourably, encountered a like catastrophe, but not so fatal. Although dispersed, some of the transports continued the voyage, others returned to port, and some few became the prey of the enemy's privateers. Providence seemed to be adverse to the expedition, or in friendly warning indicated the coming struggle—when hearths and homes, menaced by a relentless, dangerous foe, needed that a large portion of this ill-omened expedition should be retained for the defence of our own shores, and play a more important part in the exciting events of the Revolutionary War. Five companies of the Royal Highlanders were thus detained at home, and soon afterwards removed for service to Gibraltar. The other five companies of the regiment, embarked in the "Middlesex," East Indiaman, battling the tempest, completed the voyage, and rendezvoused at Barbadoes, whence they proceeded, with what remained of the vast armament, against the French island of St Lucia, which, after some sharp fighting, was wrested from the Republicans. In the subsequent attack upon the island of St Vincent, the Highlanders were praised for the "heroic ardour" they always displayed, but especially illustrated in the attack upon the post of New Vigie, on the 10th June, 1796, on which occasion Major-General David Stewart relates the following episode of the wife of a soldier of our Royal Highlanders:—"I directed her husband, who was in my company, to remain behind in charge of the men's knapsacks, which they had thrown off to be light for the advance up the hill. He obeyed his orders; but his wife, believing, I suppose, that she was not included in these injunctions, pushed forward in the assault. When the enemy had been driven from the third redoubt, I was standing giving some directions to the men, and preparing to push on to the fourth and last redoubt, when I found myself tapped on the shoulder, and turning round, I saw my Amazonian friend standing with her clothes tucked up to the knees, and seizing my arm, 'Well done, my Highland lads!' she exclaimed, 'see how the brigands scamper like so many deer!' 'Come,' added she, 'let us drive them from yonder hill.' On inquiry, I found she had been in the hottest fire, cheering and animating the men, and when the action was over, she was as active as any of the surgeons in assisting the wounded."

Allied with the Caribbee Indians, the Republicans, driven from the open plain and the regular strongholds of the island, found a refuge in the woods, where, screened by the luxuriant foliage of the forest, or perched in unassailable positions, they maintained a guerilla warfare, which to our troops proved of the most trying and harassing kind, similar in character to that sustained by our Highlanders in the backwoods during the American war. Mr Cannon, in his valuable official records of the regiment, gives the following description illustrative of the general character of the contest:—

"The out-posts being frequently alarmed by parties of the enemy firing at the sentries in the night, a serjeant and

twelve Highlanders, under Lieutenant David Stewart, penetrated the woods at nine o'clock in the evening, with short
swords to cut their way through the underwood, to discover
the post or camp from whence these nightly alarms came.
After traversing the woods all night, an open spot, with a
sentry, was discovered; this man fired his musket at a dog
which accompanied the soldiers, and then plunged into the
wood, as the serjeant rushed forward to cut him down. The
soldiers were on the edge of a perpendicular precipice of great
depth, at the bottom of which was seen a small valley crowded
with huts, from whence issued swarms of people on hearing
the report of their sentry's musket. Having made this
discovery, the soldiers commenced their journey back; but,
when about half way, they were assailed by a fire of musketry
on both flanks, and in the rear. The Caribbees were expert
climbers; every tree appeared to be manned in an instant;
the wood was in a blaze, but not a man could be seen—the
enemy being concealed by the thick and luxuriant foliage.
As the Highlanders retreated, firing from time to time at the
spot from whence the enemy's fire proceeded, the Caribbees
followed with as much rapidity as if they had sprung from
tree to tree like monkeys. In this manner the retreat was
continued, until the men got clear of the woods."

The reduction of the island being at length completed, the
five companies of the Forty-second were employed in an
ineffectual attack upon Porto Rico. In 1797, from Martinique
the companies returned home, and, on reaching Portsmouth,
presented a clean bill of health—somewhat extraordinary in the

circumstances, yet silently but unmistakeably testifying to the
good conduct of the corps, and the completeness of its economy.
In 1798 the several companies were united at Gibraltar,
whence the regiment proceeded, with other troops, under
Lieut.-General the Honourable Sir Charles Stewart, against
the Spanish island of Minorca, which, with its capital,
Ciudadella, was speedily surrendered, although the defending
force exceeded in number the attacking force; the Spaniards,
by the admirable dispositions of the British, being deceived
as to our actual strength. This achievement was but the
presage to a more glorious enterprise. The ambition of
Napoleon had pictured for himself an Eastern Empire; and to
work out the realisation of his dream, he had transported the
veterans of Italy into Egypt, as the basis of his operations.
Already had the burning sands of the dreary desert wasted
the strength of this "Army of the East," and his conquering
legions been arrested in their triumphal career by the stern
decrees of Nature's God, when our island-might dared to
challenge the boasted "Invincibles" of France. The Forty-
second was included in the expedition which, under Sir Ralph
Abercromby, was so long detained and tossed upon the treacherous waves of the Mediterranean, the slave of a cruel uncer-
tainty as to its destination. At length the fleet cast anchor
in Aboukir Bay, and despite the proud array of horse, foot,
and artillery which lined the beach and manned the hills
environing the bay—each of which contributed its deadliest
thunder to daunt or destroy our gallant army—the British
successfully effected a landing in March, 1801, gained a victory

which, apart from the honour accruing to our arms, served to revive the fainting spirit of Europe, and gave a glimpse of hope to the enthralled who had been crushed by the military tyranny of France.

Passing over the action of Mandora, we arrive at the battle of Alexandria, wherein the valour of the Royal Highlanders, associated with the Twenty-eighth regiment, has never been excelled. Posted amid the ruins of an old Roman palace, and looking down upon the classic memorials of a by-gone age, the Forty-second, on the morning of the 21st March, 1801, awaited with portentous silence the approach of the foe, who, concealed by a thick mist, advanced, purposing to surprise our position. The assault was conducted with the wonted impetuosity of the French, and the defence maintained with characteristic firmness by the British. Amid the confusion of the fight, the uncertain light of the morning, and whilst our troops were hotly engaged at all points, the famed "Invincible Legion" of Napoleon crept silently and unnoticed to the rear of our Highlanders, cutting the wings of the regiment asunder. A desperate and deadly fight ensued, when these redoubtable troops discovered and encountered each other. The French, entering the ruins of the palace, displayed a valour worthy the title they bore, and which, in other circumstances, might have won that better success which such heroic bravery merited as its reward. Exhausted and overpowered, with 650 fallen, the relics of the "Invincibles," of whom there remained but 250, surrendered to our Highlanders. Scarce had the regiment achieved this splendid result, ere it was anew assailed by a fresh and more powerful, but not braver column of the enemy. At length these repeated and resolute attacks of cavalry, infantry, and artillery, broke the array of the Forty-second. To all appearance flight seemed the only refuge, and prudence might have urged the same as being the better part of valour. The French cavalry at this critical moment charged the regiment, deeming an easy conquest at hand, but nothing daunted, grouped into small detached parties, the Highlanders faced about and fearlessly encountered the foe. Sir Ralph Abercromby, witnessing the gallant behaviour of his countrymen in such a crisis, unable to reinforce them with troops, hastened to the spot to encourage, by his presence, these brave men, exclaiming, with patriotic fervour, "My brave Highlanders, remember your country, remember your forefathers!" Thus nerved to resistance, and cheered to know that so beloved a commander beheld with pride and grateful affection their efforts, the result was soon gloriously evident in the retreat, flight, and ruin of the cavalry, who imagined they would have annihilated the broken, bleeding remnant. During the fight, Sir Ralph Abercromby was furiously assailed by two dragoons. "In this unequal conquest he received a blow on the breast; but with the vigour and strength of arm for which he was distinguished, he seized on the sabre of one of those who struggled with him, and forced it out of his hand. At this moment a corporal of the Forty-second, seeing his situation, ran up to his assistance, and shot one of the assailants, on which the other retired.

" The French cavalry charged *en masse*, and overwhelmed the Forty-second; yet, though broken, this gallant corps was not defeated; individually it resisted, and the conduct of each man exalted still more the high character of the regiment."

Towards the close of the battle the Highlanders, having expended their last cartridge, were on the point of being annihilated—although still resolutely resisting with the bayonet —when the French, repulsed everywhere, relaxed their efforts, and gradually retired. The loss of the regiment, in killed and wounded, exceeded 300 men; but the most grievous loss of all, felt by every rank, was the fall and subsequent death of Sir Ralph Abercromby.

It is unnecessary here further to detail the various events which marked the progress of the British arms in Egypt— crowned in the conquest of its two capitals, Cairo and Alexandria, accomplishing the extinction of the French dominion in the land, and for ever dissipating the dream of Napoleon, which had promised an Eastern Empire—an idea early and fondly nurtured, but, like the toy of a child, as quickly cast away when it failed to please, and, by that despot, abandoned when circumstances presented an easier path and more glorious results to his ambition in the crown of France.

On the return of the Royal Highlanders, every compliment was lavished upon the regiment by a grateful country. Whilst at Edinburgh in 1802, Lieutenant-General Vyse, in presenting a new set of colours, thus closed his address to the regiment:—" Remember that the standards which you have this day received are not only revered by an admiring world, as the honourable monuments and trophies of your former heroism, but are likewise regarded by a grateful country as the sacred pledges of that security which, under the protection of heaven, it may expect from your future services.

"May you long, very long, live to enjoy that reputation and those honours which you have so highly and so justly merited; may you long participate and share in all the blessings of that tranquillity and peace which your labours and your arms have restored to your native country; but should the restless ambition of an envious and daring enemy again call you to the field, think then that you behold the spirit of those brave comrades who so nobly, in their country's cause, fell upon the plains of Egypt, hovering round these standards—think that you see the venerable shade of the immortal Abercromby leading you again to action, and pointing to that presumptuous band whose arrogance has been humbled, and whose vanity has been compelled, by your intrepidity and courage, to confess that *no human force has been 'invincible' against British valour*, when directed by wisdom, conducted by discipline, and inspired by virtue."

CHAPTER XXIX.

" When wild war's deadly blast was blawn,
    And gentle peace returning,
And eyes again with pleasure beam'd
    That had been blear'd wi' mourning,
I left the lines and tented field,
    Where lang I'd been a lodger,
My humble knapsack a' my wealth,
    A poor but honest sodger."

THREATENED INVASION—THE PENINSULAR WAR—CORUNNA—
    TOULOUSE—QUATRE BRAS—WATERLOO—CRIMEA—INDIA—
    1803–1862.

THE peace of Amiens in 1803, which for a short period released our army from the bloody toils of war, was but as the
portentous calm presaging the lowering storm, when the waves
of angry passion, lashed into fury, should beat upon the shore
of every continent of the world. The pride of France had been
humbled, and the ambitious schemes of her haughty despot
thwarted by British valour, which, upon the plains of Egypt,
had wrested from veteran legions their boasted "invincibility."
The French navy, moreover, had been swept from the seas
and all but exterminated—there remaining not an armament
in Europe which could dare to dispute the British ocean

sovereignty. Stung by the remembrance of many defeats by sea and land—the painful recollection of which ever and anon haunted and troubled the dreamer of universal empire, begetting

"The vengeance blood alone could quell"—

a spirit of malignity was awakened in the mind of Napoleon. These combined occasioned the concentration of the giant might of his empire upon the western shores of France, purposing therewith to crush, were it possible, the only power which, amidst the general wreck of nations, yet lived to challenge his assumed omnipotence. Vainly he hoped to bridge the channel, or, as he termed it, the "ditch," which divided this beloved land from our natural rival and implacable enemy, France. Loudly he threatened that, with an army of 600,000 men, he would land to desolate our homes, and overwhelm our country in a doom as awful as had hitherto befallen less favoured countries. But apart from the "ditch," which proved an impassable gulf to the mightiest efforts of his power, the patriotism of our people, appreciating the emergency, was equal to the danger, and in 1804 achieved the following magnificent result:—

Army in the British Isles,	129,039
Colonies,	38,050
India,	22,807
Recruiting,	583
Militia in Great Britain,	109,947
	401,046

Regular and Militia,	301,046
Volunteers in Great Britain,	347,000
Total in Great Britain,	648,046
Irish Volunteers,	70,000
Military,	718,046
Navy,	100,000
Grand Total in arms,	818,046

In this vast armament we must include a second battalion raised in 1803, and attached to the Royal Forty-second. In 1805 the first battalion was removed to Gibraltar. Napoleon, disappointed in his favourite scheme of effecting our conquest, suddenly directed his march eastward, launching the thunder-bolts of war with remorseless wrath upon the devoted sovereignties of Germany, yea, piercing, in his aggressions, the gloomy wilds of Russia. By a crooked policy, begetting a matchless perfidy, Napoleon had found further employment for the myriad spoilers who looked to him for prey, in the invasion and appropriation of Spain and Portugal. In this crisis of their country's calamity, the patriots of the Peninsula invoked the friendly aid of Britain, as alone able to help them in the unequal yet protracted struggle for independence they maintained. Ever the champion of the weak and oppressed, Britain descended to the rescue; and in accordance therewith, a British army, under Sir Arthur Wellesley, landed in Portugal in 1808. The first battalion of the Forty-second was ordered to join this expedition from Gibraltar, but reached too late to participate in the glories of Roleia and Vimiera. The

deliverance of Portugal being for the time accomplished, the
Forty-second thereafter joined the army of General Sir John
Moore, which attempted to drive the French from Spain.
Inadequately supported, this gallant chief failed to do more
than penetrate into the interior, occasioning the concentration
of the several French armies to repel him. Unable to cope
with such a vast superiority, retreat was inevitable. Shattered
by the vicissitudes of the war, his army retired to the sea
coast, hotly pursued by a powerful French force under Marshal
Soult. At length halting near Corunna, the British, in defence
of their embarkation, accepted battle from the French, which,
whilst victory crowned our arms, was dearly bought in the
death of Sir John Moore. Brigaded with the Fourth and
Fiftieth regiments, under Major-General Lord William Ben-
tinck, and in the division of Sir David Baird, these regiments
sustained the weight of the attack. Twice on this memorable
day did the Commander-in-Chief address himself to the Highlanders. In the advance to recover the lost village of Elvina,
he uttered these thrilling words, awakening the recollection of
the time when he himself had led them to victory—" Highlanders," he said, "remember Egypt!" And again, when
sorely pressed by the enemy, having expended their whole
ammunition, he thus distinguished them:—

"'My brave Forty-second, join your comrades, ammunition
is coming, and you have your bayonets.' At the well-known
voice of their general, the Highlanders instantly sprang
forward, and closed upon the enemy with bayonets. About
this period Sir David Baird was wounded, and forced to quit

the field, and soon afterwards Sir John Moore was struck to
the ground by a cannon ball.   He was raised up, his eyes
were steadily fixed on the Highlanders, who were contending
manfully with their numerous antagonists, and when he was
assured that the Forty-second were victorious, his countenance
brightened up, he expressed his satisfaction, and was removed
to the rear, where he expired, to the great regret of the officers
and soldiers, who admired and esteemed their excellent commander."

> On dark Corunna's woeful day,
> When Moore's brave spirit passed away,
> Our Highland men, they firmly stood,
>   Nor France's marshalled armies could
>   Break through the men of Scotland.

In this severe fight the loss of the Forty-second exceeded
200 killed and wounded.   In consequence of this victory, the
British were enabled to embark without further molestation
from the enemy.   The regiment arrived in England in 1809.
As soon as sufficiently recruited—brigaded with the Seventy-
ninth and Ninety-second regiments, constituting the Highland
Brigade—it was embarked with the army which attempted to
gain a footing in Flanders; but failed, rather from the evil
effects of the climate, inducing a malignant disease, than the
sword of the enemy.   Of 758 men, which comprised the
battalion, 554 were stricken down or disabled in less than
six weeks.   Meanwhile, the second battalion, which had joined
the army of Lord Wellington in Portugal, suffered severely
from a similar cause whilst stationed on the banks of the

Guadiana River. Commanded by Lieutenant-Colonel Lord Blantyre, this battalion was creditably present in the actions of the Peninsular War, which arrested the progress of the French under Marshal Massena, at Busaco, and finally defied their every effort at the formidable, impregnable lines of Torres Vedras. The battalion won a title to the distinction of "Fuentes d'Onor," by gallantly resisting a charge of French cavalry thereat. It was present at the siege of Ciudad Rodrigo, and, previous to the battle of Salamanca, was joined by the first battalion from England, with whom it was consolidated. A recruiting party was sent home to enrol a new second battalion, afterwards disbanded in 1814.

It is needless here to detain the reader with a record of the military transactions of the war. These words— "Pyrenees," "Nivelle," "Nive," "Orthes," "Toulouse," and "Peninsula"—borne upon the colours and appointments of the regiment, are sufficiently expressive of its gallantry. At the battle of Toulouse, the public despatch refers to the conduct of the Forty-second as "highly distinguished throughout the day;" whilst an officer of the regiment contributes the following account of its dauntless behaviour on the occasion. In the sixth division of our army, and in brigade with the Seventy-ninth and Ninety-first regiments, he says:— "We advanced under a heavy cannonade, and arrived in front of a redoubt, which protected the right of the enemy's position, where we were formed in two lines—the first consisting of some Portuguese regiments, and the reserve of the Highland Brigade.

"Darkening the whole hill, flanked by clouds of cavalry, and covered by the fire of their redoubt, the enemy came down upon us like a torrent; their generals and field-officers riding in front, and waving their hats amidst shouts of the multitude, resembling the roar of an ocean! Our Highlanders, as if actuated by one instinctive impulse, took off their bonnets, and, waving them in the air, returned their greeting with three cheers.

"A death-like silence ensued for some moments, and we could observe a visible pause in the advance of the enemy. At that moment the light company of the Forty-second regiment, by a well-directed fire, brought down some of the French officers of distinction, as they rode in front of their respective corps. The enemy immediately fired a volley into our lines, and advanced upon us amidst a deafening roar of musketry and artillery. Our troops answered their fire only once, and, unappalled by their furious onset, advanced up the hill, and met them at the charge. Upon reaching the summit of the ridge of heights, the redoubt which had covered their advance fell into our possession; but they still retained four others, with their connecting lines of entrenchments, upon the level of the same heights on which we were now established, and into which they had retired.

"Major-General Pack having obtained leave from General Clinton that the Forty-second should have the honour of leading the attack, which it was hoped should drive the French from their strong position, that distinguished officer exultingly gave the word—'The Forty-second will advance.'

We immediately began to form for the charge upon the redoubts, which were about two or three hundred yards distant, and to which we had to pass over some ploughed fields. The grenadiers of the Forty-second regiment, followed by the other companies, led the way, and began to ascend from the road; but no sooner were the feathers of their bonnets seen rising over the embankment, than such a tremendous fire was opened from the redoubts and entrenchments, as in a very short time would have annihilated them. The right wing, therefore, hastily formed into line, and, without waiting for the left, which was ascending by companies from the road, rushed upon the batteries, which vomited forth a most furious and terrific storm of fire, grape-shot, and musketry.

"The redoubts were erected along the side of a road, and defended by broad ditches filled with water. Just before our troops reached the obstruction, however, the enemy deserted them, and fled in all directions, leaving their last line of strongholds in our possession; but they still possessed two fortified houses close by, from which they kept up a galling and destructive fire. Out of about five hundred men, which the Forty-second brought into action, scarcely ninety reached the fatal redoubt from which the enemy had fled.

"As soon as the smoke began to clear away, the enemy made a last attempt to re-take the redoubts, and for this purpose advanced in great force. They were a second time repulsed with great loss, and their whole army was driven into Toulouse, which they evacuated on the 12th of April, 1814."

The peace which crowned these glorious achievements afforded but a brief interval of repose to our army. In the spring of the following year, Europe was startled in her dream of fancied security by the sudden and unexpected return of Napoleon from Elba. In the campaign of Waterloo, which quickly and decisively broke his power, and almost annihilated the military strength of imperial France—with which strong, convulsive effort it hoped to restore its earlier and mightier dominion—the Forty-second claims a most conspicuous place, especially in the action of Quatre Bras, so immediately followed by the grander event of Waterloo. The unexpected and furious attack of Marshal Ney upon the advanced position of the allies at Quatre Bras, gave the French a momentary advantage. Roused to arms, and hurried forward to the scene of conflict, the Highlanders (Forty-second and Ninety-second regiments) were conspicuous for the promptitude with which they mustered and took the field, hastening forward to relieve the gallant few that dared to withstand the impetuous assaults of the French. The good conduct of the Highlanders, whilst quartered in Brussels, had so won the esteem of the citizens, that they are said to have mourned for them as a brother, grieving for their departure—perchance

> "The unreturning brave,—alas!
> Ere evening to be trodden like the grass
> Which now beneath them, but above shall grow
> In its next verdure; when this fiery mass
> Of living valour rolling on the foe,
> And burning with high hope, shall moulder cold and low!

"Last noon beheld them full of lusty life;
Last eve, in beauty's circle proudly gay;
The midnight brought the signal-sound of strife;
The morn the marshalling in arms; the day
Battle's magnificently-stern array!
The thunder-clouds close o'er it, which, when rent,
The earth is cover'd thick with other clay,
Which her own clay shall cover—heap'd and pent,
Rider and horse,—friend, foe,—in one red burial blent!"

One historian speaks of the Forty-second as displaying "unparalleled bravery;" whilst another thus narrates the attack of the Highlanders at Quatre Bras:—" To the Forty-second Highlanders, and Forty-fourth British regiment, which were posted on a reversed slope, and in line, close upon the left of the above road, the advance of French cavalry was so sudden and unexpected, the more so as the Brunswickers had just moved on to the front, that as both these bodies whirled past them to the rear, in such close proximity to each other, they were, for the moment, considered to consist of one mass of allied cavalry. Some of the old soldiers of both regiments were not so easily satisfied on this point, and immediately opened a partial fire obliquely upon the French lancers, which, however, Sir Denis Pack and their own officers endeavoured as much as possible to restrain; but no sooner had the latter succeeded in causing a cessation of the fire, than the lancers, which were the rearmost of the cavalry, wheeled sharply round, and advanced in admirable order directly upon the rear of the two British regiments. The Forty-second Highlanders having, from their position, been the first to recognise them as a part of the enemy's forces, rapidly formed a square; but just as the two flank companies were running in to form the rear face, the lancers had reached the regiment, when a considerable portion of their leading division penetrated the square, carrying along with them, by the impetus of the charge, several men of those two companies, and creating a momentary confusion. The long-tried discipline and steadiness of the Highlanders, however, did not forsake them at this critical juncture; these lancers, instead of effecting the destruction of the square, were themselves fairly hemmed into it, and either bayoneted or taken prisoners, whilst the endangered face, restored as if by magic, successfully repelled all further attempts on the part of the French to complete their expected triumph. Their commanding officer, Lieutenant-Colonel Sir Robert Macara, was killed on this occasion, a lance having pierced through his chin until it reached the brain; and within the brief space of a few minutes, the command of the regiment devolved upon three other officers in succession: Lieutenant-Colonel Dick, who was severely wounded, Brevet-Major Davidson, who was mortally wounded, and Brevet-Major Campbell, who commanded it during the remainder of the campaign." Their subsequent service at Waterloo fully sustained, nay, rather excelled the heroism of previous achievements.

Peace has long reigned over our land, and the after history of the regiment appears, when shorn of a farther warlike character, devoid of interest. We only, therefore, mention that, after serving in various garrisons at home, the regiment was removed in 1826 to Gibraltar, thence in 1832 to Malta, and thereafter, in 1834, to the Ionian Islands. Returning home in 1836, it was welcomed by a grateful public. In 1841 it was again stationed in the Ionian Islands, until removed to Malta in 1843.

In the Crimean war, the Forty-second, with the Seventy-ninth and Ninety-third regiments, shared the dangers and the sufferings through which, as our "Highland Brigade," they gloriously won a deathless renown—as the "Rocks of Gaelic Infantry." The regiment was present at the battle of the Alma, the siege of Sebastopol, and with the expedition against Kertch. Many of its soldiers earned, as the reward of personal courage, the Victoria Cross.

In July, 1857, the Forty-second proceeded to India, to aid in the suppression of the mutiny. It still remains in India, being now stationed at Dugshai, Bengal. It is worthy of remark, that all the Highland regiments were more or less employed in suppressing this terrible outbreak.

In conclusion, these records, if "aught inanimate e'er speaks," speak in silent yet living eloquence to the soul, and more than ever endear to us the soldiers who inherit, and who will not fail to emulate, by their own good conduct and gallant demeanour, the illustrious and glorious career of their predecessors.

THE SEVENTY-FIRST FOOT:

OR,

GLASGOW HIGHLAND LIGHT INFANTRY.

CHAPTER XXX.

"To leave thee behind me my heart is sair pain'd,
But by ease that's inglorious no fame can be gain'd;
And beauty and love's the reward of the brave,
And I maun deserve it before I can crave."

INDIA—GIBRALTAR—CEYLON—1777-1798.

Whilst the American continent was the scene of a sanguinary
and bitter strife, the embers of war were being quickened into
flame in another and far distant province of our vast colonial
empire. In India the usurpation of Hyder Ali had occasioned
the interference of the British, awakening the ill-disguised
hatred of the native race against the grasping policy of the
British, whose cupidity had already appropriated much of
their native land, and whose avarice was only too ready to
embrace any farther opportunity for aggrandisement. The
incendiaries of France had been busy sowing the seeds of

jealousy and distrust of the British rule, which soon produced
its malignant fruits in the cruel and remorseless war that
ensued. Thus encircled and assailed by enemies from so many
quarters at once, our Government, in its dire extremity, called
upon the patriotism of the country to supply the means of
defence. The result was most satisfactory; and in no case did
the appeal receive a more cordial response than amongst our
clansmen, from whence were drawn, in the course of eighteen
months, upwards of 12,500 Highlanders. From the following
list of the regiments raised in 1778 to meet this emergency,
the subject of our present sketch may be selected:—

72d Regiment, or Royal Manchester Volunteers, disbanded in 1783.
73d Highland Regiment, . numbered the 71st Regiment in 1786.
74th Highland Regiment, . . . disbanded in 1784.
75th Prince of Wales' Regiment, . . disbanded in 1783.
76th Highland Regiment, . . . disbanded in 1784.
77th Regiment, or Athole Highlanders, . disbanded in 1783.
78th Highland Regiment, . numbered the 72d Regiment in 1786.
79th Regiment, or Royal Liverpool Volunteers, disbanded in 1784.
80th Regiment, or Royal Edinburgh Volunteers, disbanded in 1784.
81st Highland Regiment, . . . disbanded in 1783.
82d Regiment, ... disbanded in 1784.
83d Regiment, or Royal Glasgow Volunteers, disbanded in 1783.

The Earl of Cromarty and his son, Lord M'Leod, having
been partners in the guilt of rebellion in 1745, were made
partners in the punishment which followed. At length
pardoned, Lord M'Leod was permitted to pass into honourable exile. He found employment in the Swedish army,
where he rose to the rank of Lieutenant-General. Oppor-
tunely venturing to return, he was unexpectedly received

with much favour by the King, and his offer to raise a
Highland regiment on his forfeited estates gladly accepted.
His success was worthy of his zeal; and at Elgin, in 1778,
he appeared at the head of a magnificent corps of 840
Highlanders, 236 Lowlanders, and 34 English and Irish,
which were accordingly regimented as the Seventy-third,
afterwards our Seventy-first Regiment. The success of this
corps induced the formation of a second battalion, which
soon attained its complement. Although styled the "Glasgow Highland Light Infantry," that western metropolis can
boast no legitimate claim to an interest in its formation
beyond the thirty-four English and Irish recruits, who, it is
said, hailed from Glasgow. It acquired the property, at a
later period, when a second battalion was being grafted upon
the parent stem, when many of its citizens enlisting, manifested so strong a predilection in its favour, as induced the
government to confer the present title, and ever since the
Glasgowegians have proudly adopted the Seventy-first as
their own.

Almost immediately on its completion, the first battalion
was embarked for India. Landing at Madras in 1780,
it became the nucleus for the Highland Brigade, which the
subsequent and successive arrival of the Seventy-second,
Seventy-third, Seventy-fourth, Seventy-fifth, and Ninety-
fourth Highland regiments constituted. These earned distinctions for gallant service almost exceptional to themselves. It is worthy of note—eliciting our surprise, yet reflect-
ing infinite credit on our arms—that notwithstanding the insig-

nificance of the British force, opposed to the countless hosts of the Indian chiefs—generally as one to ten—we almost always prevailed. Had the native pride been less rampant, and the Indian chiefs submitted to the superior generalship of the French officers sent out to discipline their troops—wherein was admirable material for good soldiers—the danger to the British would have been greater, and success more exceptional. Fortunately for us, the incapacity of these sable chiefs to command, and their exceeding fear of dictation, lost them many an opportunity, and in the end proved our safety. It is strangely true of the Indian soldier that, in the field, when well led, he behaves with the utmost firmness, whilst, in defence of fortifications or walled towns, he betrays a weakness which altogether belies any favourable impression of his resolution previously formed. Notwithstanding the overwhelming superiority of the enemy who, under Hyder Ali, threatened annihilation to the small force of 4600 men, including the first battalion of the Seventy-third (as we must as yet call the Seventy-first), these, under Major-General Sir Hector Munro, dared to advance into the interior. Meanwhile, a division of 3000 men, under Lieut.-Colonel Baillie, descending from the north, strove to effect a junction with the army of General Munro. The hesitation of the latter, when in presence of the foe, to prosecute his advance, and secure his junction with the former, placed the small force of Colonel Baillie in a position of peril. This opportunity, vigorously improved by Hyder Ali, occasioned its destruction, which, with two companies of the Seventy-third, and other troops under Lieut.-Colonel

Fletcher, had, despite the treachery of the guides, threaded
their way through the jungle, and arrived as a reinforcement
from Major-General Munro, but in reality as so many
more victims who should be engulfed in the fatal ruin so
nigh.   The terrible disaster which ensued, and the calamitous result which yielded so many brave men prisoners into
the cruel, merciless power of Hyder Ali, can never fail to
inspire feelings of the truest sympathy.   With a hundred
thousand men, he descended with the most sanguinary fury
upon this little and devoted column.   Even when the whole
ammunition was, by an unlucky accident, blown into the air
in their very midst, and the British guns silenced, they
remained unconquered.   The converging hosts of the enemy
drew closer around the little band of heroes, and poured in
upon them a deadly fire of artillery and musketry, to which
they could no longer reply.   Reduced to 500 men, "History
cannot produce an instance, for fortitude, and intrepidity, and
desperate resolution, to equal the exploits of this heroic band.
. . . . The mind, in the contemplation of such a scene, and
such a situation as theirs was, is filled at once with admiration,
with astonishment, with horror, and with awe.   To behold
formidable and impenetrable bodies of horse, of infantry, and
of artillery, advancing from all quarters, flashing savage fury,
levelling the numberless instruments of slaughter, and dart-
ing destruction around, was a scene to appal even something
more than the strongest human resolution; but it was beheld
by this little band with the most undaunted and immoveable firmness. . . . .   Like the swelling waves of the ocean,

however, when agitated by a storm, fresh columns incessantly poured in upon them with redoubled fury, which at length brought so many to the ground, and weakened them so considerably, that they were unable longer to withstand the dreadful and tremendous shock; and the field soon presented a horrid picture of the most inhuman cruelties and unexampled carnage." * Happy were those who found on the burning sands of Perambaukam "a soldier's grave;" happy indeed, compared with the cruel fate of the survivors, who, reduced from 4000, scarce mustered 200 prisoners, nearly all of whom were wounded. Colonel Baillie, stripped, wounded in three places, was dragged into the presence of the victor, who exulted over him with the imperious tone of a conqueror. Baillie replied with the true spirit of a soldier, and soon after died. The remainder, cast into the dungeons of Bangalore, scantily fed on unwholesome food, were doomed to endure a miserable imprisonment for three long years. These trials, however, served only to bring out, in brighter effulgence, the characteristics of the Highland hero. "These brave men," says General Stewart, "equally true to their religion and their allegiance, were so warmly attached to their officers (amongst whom was one afterwards destined to win a mighty fame as their gallant leader—Sir David Baird), that they picked out the best part of their own food and secretly reserved it for their officers; thus sacrificing their own lives for that of their officers, as the result proved, for out of 111, only 30 feeble and emaciated men ever

* Narrative of the Military Operations on the Coromandel Coast from 1780 to 1784, by Captain Innes Monro, of the Seventy-third Regiment.

emerged from that almost living tomb." Mrs Grant says in her narrative, "Daily some of their companions dropped before their eyes, and daily they were offered liberty and riches in exchange for this lingering torture, on condition of relinquishing their religion and taking the turban. Yet not one could be prevailed upon to purchase life on these terms. These Highlanders were entirely illiterate; scarcely one of them could have told the name of any particular sect of Christians, and all the idea they had of the Mahommedan religion was, that it was adverse to their own, and to what they had been taught by their fathers; and that, adopting it, they would renounce Him who had died that they might live, and who loved them, and could support them in all their sufferings. The great outlines of their religion, the peculiar tenets which distinguish it from any other, were early and deeply impressed on their minds, and proved sufficient in the hour of trial.

> ' Rise, Muses rise, add all your tuneful breath;
> These must not sleep in darkness and in death.'

"It was not theirs to meet Death in the field of honour; while the mind, wrought up with fervid eagerness, went forth in search of him. They saw his slow approach, and though sunk into languid debility, such as quenches the fire of mere temperament, they never once hesitated at the alternative set before them."

> "Billeted by death, he quarter'd here remained;
> When the last trumpet sounds, he'll rise and march again."

In 1781, in the army of Lieutenant-General Sir Eyre

Coote, the regiment took the field, although sorely weakened by sickness and the sword. After considerable manœuvring on both sides, the two armies confronted each other on the plains of Porto Novo. The British, not amounting to 8000 men, of which the Seventy-third was the only Line regiment, were opposed to a vast host, exceeding 100,000.

Notwithstanding our great inferiority in numbers, the enemy signally failed in every attempt to annihilate, as he imagined, the heroic band who fought beneath the banner of Albion. Discouraged and worn out with these repeated and unavailing assaults, the foe was only too glad to retire and escape from such a vain struggle, where superior numbers could make no impression on bravery and discipline, but only entailed disgrace and defeat. The excellent valour of the regiment on this critical occasion, received the warmest approbation of the Commander-in-chief. Sir Eyre Coote was particularly pleased with the gallantry of one of its pipers, who, amid the hottest of the fire, ceased not to cheer his comrades by the shrill scream of his bag-pipes, which was heard even above the din and roar of battle—so pleased, he exclaimed, " Well done, my brave fellow, you shall have silver pipes when the battle is over," a promise which he most munificently fulfilled. Sir Eyre Coote always retained a warm interest in, strong attachment to, and confidence in the Highland regiments, which he learned to esteem as the flower of the British army. Having followed up this great victory by a series of further minor successes, the army, reinforced by a body of troops from the Bengal Presidency under Colonel Pearse, anew arrived upon the blood-stained plains of Perambaukam, so pregnant with melancholy associations, and which, yet reeking with the gore of the murdered brave, bore memorials of the disaster which had overtaken so many of their comrades but a year previous; stirred by these painful recollections, our army consecrated the spot to avenge thereon the butchery which had so lately bereaved them of their brethren. The foe, too, were inspired for the fight, but by a very different feeling. Superstition bade them believe their gods propitious to the spot, and, as with them, to give over the British as the victims of a new sacrifice. Thus impelled, it may well be inferred that the struggle was severe and bloody, although, as usual, British prowess triumphed.

To relieve the important fortress of Vellore, our army advanced by the Pass of Sholingur, where it encountered the enemy. A protracted and desperate fight ensued, but nothing could withstand the impetuous and persevering assaults of the British, who ultimately drove the enemy before them. In the spring of 1782, the relief of Vellore was a second time accomplished, despite the strenuous efforts of Hyder Ali to prevent it. The after and unsatisfying inactivity of our army permitted a powerful French force, landed from the fleet of Admiral Suffrein, to effect a junction with the Indian army, and these together succeeded in reducing the important strongholds of Permacoil and Cudalore. These successes, energetically followed up by Hyder Ali, threatened our utter destruction, and brought about the battle of Arnee, in which the Seventy-third was conspicuous under the leadership of Lieutenant-Colonel Elphinstone and, more immediately, of Captain the

Honourable James Lindsay. The British, reinforced by the arrival of the Seventy-eighth (now the Seventy-second) regiment, recently arrived from Europe, were in a position to assume the offensive, and having anew provisioned Vellore, undertook the siege of Cudalore, which was only abandoned for lack of the requisite means of attack, thus postponing its fate for another year. So deeply interested was the Commander-in-chief, Sir Eyre Coote, in this undertaking, that, vexed with its miscarriage—esteeming himself inadequately supported by Government in the attempt—grieved and disappointed, he fell a prey to melancholy, which, ere an opportunity to retrieve the present failure had come, the veteran chief had fallen. He was succeeded in the command by Major-General James Stuart, and the army, reinforced by the arrival of the Twenty-third Light Dragoons, the One-hundred-and-first and One-hundred-and-second British regiments, and the Fifteenth regiment of Hanoverian infantry, resumed the siege of Cudalore under more auspicious circumstances. The defence was resolutely maintained by the French under General Bussy. The besiegers so vigorously pressed the enemy that he was at length compelled to withdraw within the fortress. The loss on our side was very severe—the Seventy-third had to mourn a melancholy list of nearly 300 comrades killed or wounded. The news of a treaty of peace having been signed between Great Britain and France, snatched the prize from our troops which we had imagined within our grasp.

In 1786, the numerical title of the regiment was changed

from the Seventy-third to the Seventy-first, as at present, by the reduction, etc., of senior corps.

Nothing of importance falls to be recorded in the course of our narrative till the year 1790, when Tippoo Saib, the son and successor of Hyder Ali, encroaching upon the territory of the Rajah of Travancore, a faithful ally of the British, occasioned our interference, resulting in a renewal of hostilities. In the army of Major-General Medows, the Seventy-first and Seventy-second regiments formed the second or Highland brigade, afterwards increased by the addition of the Seventy-fourth Highlanders from Madras. As we shall have frequent opportunity of following the movements of the brigade in after chapters, we will not here burden our history with a repetition, contenting ourselves with the simple mention of the chief events that ensued. Under General the Earl Cornwallis, the Seventy-first was with the army in the various actions which led to the siege and capture of Bangalore; thence it proceeded with the expedition intended to act against Seringapatam, but which, overcome by the force of circumstances, in the meantime retired, awaiting a more favourable opportunity, when better prepared to accomplish the design. In the interval, the regiment was creditably engaged in the reduction of the strong forts of Nundydroog, Savendroog, etc., which had hitherto hindered our progress. At length, in 1792, the army resumed the enterprise against Seringapatam. This forward movement alarmed Tippoo Saib, who, dreading the fate which awaited his capital, strove to arrest the army by accepting battle. The result proving unfortunate, the enemy were driven within the island on which the city stands, and even here, although very strongly posted, the Mysoreans had become so straitened in their circumstances, and were so pressed by the British, that, suing for peace, the Sultan was only too glad to purchase the safety of his capital and preserve the last remnant of his once mighty dominion by any sacrifice which the conquerors chose to impose. Disappointed of a further triumph, the army retired, laden with the spoil which had ransomed the haughty metropolis and its ambitious prince.

Holland having caught the revolutionary fever which prevailed in 1793, and being allied with France, was involved in the war with Britain, which, arising out of the sins of the Revolution, had already torn from these states nearly their entire colonial dominions. Pondicherry, on the Coromandel coast, had succumbed to our arms; and the valuable island of Ceylon was, in turn, wrested from the Dutch by a British expedition, including the Seventy-first regiment. This was the last achievement of any importance which was attained by the corps in India. In 1798, it received orders to return home; and, after a long voyage, landed in safety at Woolwich.

CHAPTER XXXI.

" Right onward did Clan-Alpine come,
　Above the tide, each broadsword bright
　Was brandishing like beam of light,
　　Each targe was dark below;
　And with the ocean's mighty swing,
　When heaving to the tempest's wing,
　　They hurled them on the foe.
I heard the lance's shivering crash,
As when the whirlwind rends the ash;
I heard the broadsword's deadly clang,
As if an hundred anvils rang!
　But Moray wheeled his rearward rank
　Of horsemen on Clan-Alpine's flank—
　　'My banner-man advance!
I see,' he cried, 'their column shake;
Now, gallants! for your ladies' sake,
　　Upon them with the lance!'
The horsemen dashed among the rout,
　As deer break through the broom;
Their steeds are stout, their swords are out,
　They soon make lightsome room."

GIBRALTAR—CAPE OF GOOD HOPE—BUENOS AYRES—PENINSULA
—FLANDERS—WATERLOO—CANADA—WEST INDIES—1778–1862.

WHILST the first battalion was gallantly combating its
country's foes on the plains of India, a second battalion,
raised in 1778, had, in 1780, embarked for Gibraltar. On the
voyage, the fleet fell in with a valuable Spanish convoy of
Carracca merchantmen, guarded by several ships of war. Sir

George Rodney, the British admiral, having impressed the Seventy-first as marines, assailed the enemy, and soon compelled them to surrender. Arrived off Cape St Vincent, a new and more formidable antagonist awaited the coming of the British. A powerful Spanish fleet, under Admiral Don Juan de Langara, appeared in sight, charged with their destruction. But a very different result was the issue of the collision: out of eleven line-of-battle ships, comprising the enemy, nearly all either perished or were captured. Arrived at Gibraltar, the battalion was engaged in the defence of that important fortress, contributing by its gallantry to beat off the most stupendous efforts of Spain and France combined to reduce it. Successively it witnessed the failure of the tremendous cannonade with which the Spaniards assailed the fortifications, hoping therewith to render these splendid works a heap of ruins, no longer defensible even by British valour. In 1781, the flank companies of the battalion participated in the glory of the sortie which accomplished the destruction of the numerous and powerful batteries and immense magazines of the enemy; and finally, in the following year, it beheld the might of France and Spain discomfited, and itself, surviving the iron tempest of shot and shell with which the enemy proposed to exterminate the garrison, was glorified along with the British troops who dauntlessly maintained the fortress. Ten ponderous battering ships had been prepared and were supposed to achieve marvels in the tremendous artillery of the assault. But alas! how oft is the counsel of the wise mocked and the loftiest designs of man humbled by the God of battles!

Instead of victory, which it was fondly imagined should crown such gigantic efforts of skill, these floating batteries were nearly all utterly destroyed by the red-hot shot used for the purpose by the British. Thus triumphing over the vast efforts of two of the mightiest military powers of the age, our brave garrison received the royal thanks, expressive of the people's gratitude, conveyed through the Secretary of State for War, in these flattering terms:—"I am honoured with His Majesty's commands to assure you, in the strongest terms, that no encouragement shall be wanting to the brave officers and soldiers under your command. His royal approbation of the past will no doubt be a powerful incentive to future exertions; and I have the King's authority to assure you, that every distinguished act of emulation and gallantry, which shall be performed in the course of the siege by any, even of the lowest rank, will meet with ample reward from his gracious protection and favour." Peace at length dawned, and the blockade was in consequence raised in February, 1783. The second battalion, returning home, was disbanded at Stirling in the autumn of the same year.

The first battalion, which had returned from India, had proceeded to Scotland to recruit, but, being unsuccessful, passed over to Ireland in 1800, where it received 600 volunteers from the Scots Fencibles. Afterward, when the peace of Amiens had been transgressed, and a French invasion seemed imminent, the "Army Reserve Act" occasioned the formation of a second battalion at Dumbarton in 1804. Enrolled for a limited time, and restricted to home duty, it was employed in various garrisons in Scotland, Ireland, and South Britain, and was disbanded at Glasgow in December, 1815, on the termination of the war. Meanwhile, the alarm of invasion having passed away, the first battalion, with the Seventy-second and Ninety-third regiments, formed the second or Highland brigade, under Brigadier-General Ronald Crawfurd Ferguson, engrossed in the army of Major-General Sir David Baird, destined to operate against the Dutch colony at the Cape of Good Hope. Having successfully accomplished a landing in Saldanha Bay, conquered at the battle of Blenberg, driven the Dutch army of Lieutenant-General Janssens into the interior, and advanced upon Cape Town, the fruitlessness of further resistance becoming evident, the entire colony was surrendered in 1806. In token of the honour acquired by the regiment in this enterprise, the words "Cape of Good Hope" have been since borne by permission upon its regimental colour. No sooner had this conquest been completed than the Seventy-first was detached, with 200 men of the St Helena regiment—making a total of 1087 rank and file, in an expedition against Buenos Ayres, in South America. Commanded by Brigadier-General William Carr (afterwards Viscount) Beresford, this ill-advised and ill-fated expedition at first met with considerable success—a bloodless landing being effected, and the enemy easily broken and dispersed, all promised to go well. Recovering from their first alarm, and ashamed that such a handful of British should have so easily assumed to be their masters, the citizens, gradually drawing together into a formidable phalanx, resolved to wipe away the disgrace, and achieve their liberty by the

expulsion of the invaders. Driven into the citadel, without
hope of relief, and unable to contend against the hourly increasing enemies that surrounded them and threatened vengeance upon them, the besieged felt themselves compelled
to surrender. Removed as prisoners into the interior
of the country, the battalion was treated leniently, but the
landing of a second expedition at Monte Video, fated to an
issue as unfortunate, occasioned a more rigorous treatment.
Negotiations having brought about an amicable arrangement, the entire British, released, agreed to relinquish all
hostilities against South America. Unarmed and ununiformed,
the battalion reached Cork in 1807, and was immediately
re-equipped, and presented with new colours by Lieutenant-
General Floyd, who thus addressed it:—" Brave Seventy-first,
the world is well acquainted with your gallant conduct at the
capture of Buenos Ayres, in South America, under one of His
Majesty's bravest generals.

"It is well known that you defended your conquest with
the utmost courage, good conduct, and discipline to the last
extremity. When diminished to a handful, hopeless of succour, and destitute of provisions, you were overwhelmed by
multitudes, and reduced by the fortune of war to lose your
liberty and your well-defended colours, but not your honour.
Your honour, Seventy-first regiment, remains unsullied. Your
last act in the field covered you with glory. Your generous
despair, calling upon your General to suffer you to die with
arms in your hands, proceeded from the genuine spirit of
British soldiers. Your behaviour in prosperity—your sufferings

in captivity—and your faithful discharge of your duty to your King and country, are appreciated by all.

"You who now stand on this parade, in defiance of the allurements held out to base desertion, are endeared to the army and to the country, and your conduct will ensure you the esteem of all true soldiers—of all worthy men—and fill every one of you with honest martial pride.

"It has been my good fortune to have witnessed, in a remote part of the world, the early glories and gallant conduct of the Seventy-first regiment in the field; and it is with great satisfaction I meet you again, with replenished ranks, with good arms in your hands, and with stout hearts in your bosoms.

"Look forward, officers and soldiers, to the achievement of new honours and the acquirement of fresh fame!

"Officers! be the friends and guardians of these brave fellows committed to your charge!

"Soldiers! give your confidence to your officers. They have shared with you the chances of war; they have bravely bled along with you; they will always do honour to themselves and you. Preserve your regiment's reputation for valour in the field, and regularity in quarters."

Spain and Portugal having been despoiled of their independence by the perfidious usurpation of France, Britain—allied with the patriots of the Peninsula in the struggle going on for the emancipation of these kingdoms from the thraldom of Napoleon—sent an army to Portugal, which included the first battalion of the Seventy-first, and under the command of Sir

Arthur Wellesley, effected a landing in Mondego Bay in 1808. Through the victories of "Roleia" and "Vimiera," commemorated upon the colours of the regiment, the convention of Cintra was achieved, which expelled the French under Marshal Junot, Duke of Abrantes, from Portugal. At Vimiera, the Grenadier company of the Seventy-first, under Captain Forbes, captured a battery of five guns and a howitzer, which every attempt of the enemy failed to recover. On the same occasion George Clarke, the piper of the regiment, was specially commended for his gallantry in resolutely continuing at his post, although severely wounded, cheering his countrymen by the wild inspiring music of the bag-pipe. Corporal M'Kay, at the same battle, was fortunate enough to receive the sword of the French General Brennier. Advancing upon Madrid, associated in brigade with the Thirty-sixth and Ninety-second regiments, the Seventy-first was ultimately joined to the army of Lieutenant-General Sir John Moore, which had promised to relieve the citizens of that metropolis from the intolerant yoke of France. The corps was with the British army in the disastrous yet glorious retreat, terminated in the victory of Corunna, possessing a melancholy interest from the death of the hero whose genius had accomplished it, and which delivered a British army from a situation of imminent peril.

Embarked, the regiment returned to England, and in 1809—a year to be mournfully remembered, as fatal to the wearing of the kilt in the army—it was ordered to lay aside the Highland garb, and was uniformed as a light infantry

regiment. Every care was in consequence bestowed to promote its efficiency. Strengthened, it was associated with the
Sixty-eighth and Eighty-fifth regiments in the light brigade,
and was ordered to accompany the army in the ill-advised
expedition, which wasted a splendid armament in a vain
attempt to obtain a footing in Flanders. The good conduct
of the regiment was nevertheless most conspicuous in the
various actions of the brief campaign.

Returning to England towards the close of the year, in
the spring of 1810, the first, second, third, fourth, sixth, and
tenth companies were selected to reinforce the army of
Lieutenant-General Viscount Wellington, then fighting in
Portugal. It arrived at a very critical period in the history
of the war, when Marshal Massena, pressing our troops with
overwhelming numbers, they were retreating towards the
impregnable lines of Torres Vedras, defeating the sanguine
hopes of the French general. The Seventy-first, commanded
by Lieutenant-Colonel the Hon. Henry Cadogan, was brigaded
with the Fiftieth and Ninety-second regiments under Major-
General Sir William Erskine. Whilst maintaining these
formidable defences, the following incident is related of
Sir Adam Ferguson, who was so posted with his company
that the French artillery might operate with fatal effect upon
his men, but, for better security, they were ordered to lie
prostrate on the ground. While in this attitude the captain,
kneeling at their head, read aloud the description of the battle,
as introducing our present chapter, and as selected from Sir
Walter Scott's "Lady of the Lake." The little volume had

just come into the camp as a stranger, but was soon welcomed
as a friend. The listening soldiers, charmed with the poet's
tale, only interrupted the reading by an occasional and joyous
huzzah whenever the French shot struck the bank close above
them. Wearied, disappointed, and distressed by ravages of
disease amongst his troops, the French Marshal was constrained in turn to retreat—a retreat which, but for the
unslumbering vigilance of his pursuers, promised to be as
successful as the ability with which it was conducted merited,
worthy the genius of Massena—justly esteemed the right hand
of Napoleon.

In 1811 the regiment was joined by its other companies.
In the action of Fuentes d'Onor it was warmly engaged; repeatedly and powerfully assailed by the enemy, it was all but
overpowered in the defence of the village, when, happily, the
Seventy-fourth and Eighty-Eighth regiments arrived to its
support, and so the post was retained. The corps was afterwards detached as a reinforcement to the army of Marshal
Sir William Beresford, and subsequently, in the army of
Lieutenant-General Rowland (afterwards Viscount) Hill,
was employed in the southern provinces of the Peninsula,
keeping in check the French under Marshal Soult, and otherwise covering the operations of the grand army of Wellington. It helped to disperse and destroy a considerable detachment of the enemy which had been surprised at Arroyo-
del-Molinos. It was more especially commended for the exceeding gallantry it displayed in the capture of Fort Napoleon,
embraced in the action and commemorated in the word

"Almaraz." At the battle of Vittoria it suffered very severely in the loss of nearly 400 men and officers; but the most grievous loss was felt in the death of its Lieutenant-Colonel, the Hon. Henry Cadogan, who largely enjoyed the esteem of the soldiers. He "fell mortally wounded while leading his men to the charge, and being unable to accompany the battalion, requested to be carried to a neighbouring eminence, from which he might take a last farewell of them and the field. In his dying moments he earnestly inquired if the French were beaten; and on being told by an officer of the regiment, who stood by supporting him, that they had given way at all points, he ejaculated, 'God bless my brave countrymen,' and immediately expired." The Marquis of Wellington thus gave effect to his own regrets in the official dispatch communicating his fall:—"In him His Majesty has lost an officer of great zeal and tried gallantry, who had already acquired the respect and regard of the whole profession, and of whom it might be expected, that if he had lived he would have rendered the most important services to his country."

In all the after battles and actions, which resulted in the expulsion of the French from Spain, and their repeated defeats and ultimate rout on their native plains, the Seventy-first bore an honourable part, returning to Britain in 1814, richly laden with a harvest of glory. A short interval of peace soon recruited the "precious remnant" of the regiment, and so restored its strength as enabled it once more to go on foreign service. Ordered to embark for America, it was fortunately detained by tempestuous weather, and so privileged to win laurels on a mightier field. Napoleon having escaped from his honourable exile in Elba, by his presence in France, overturning the ricketty government of the Bourbon, involved that bleeding country in a universal war, since it brought down the combined wrath of Europe, whose allied armies now hastened to arrest and punish the ambitious man who had proved himself so dire a curse to Christendom. Upon the plains of Waterloo the die for empire was cast and lost. In that great battle the Seventy-first had a part, forming with the first battalion of the Fifty-second, and the second and third battalions of the Ninety-fifth, or Rifles—a light infantry brigade which sustained the charge of three regiments of French cavalry: one of cuirassiers, one of grenadiers-à-cheval, and one of lancers. It also withstood the shock of the grand final charge of the Old Imperial Guard, witnessing the discomfiture of these choice troops, so long the citadel of imperial strength, now reeling, broken, dying, dead—of whom, borrowing the words, it may well be said—

"They never feared the face of man."

This great victory having ruined irretrievably the fortunes of Napoleon, the allied army, rapidly advancing, entered Paris a second time, and there dictated the terms of peace. The Seventy-first remained in France as part of the "army of occupation;" and whilst stationed at the village of Rombly in 1816, its soldiers were presented with the Waterloo medals by Colonel Reynell, who thus, addressing the regiment, said:—
"These honourable rewards bestowed by your Sovereign for

your share in the great and glorious exertions of the army of
His Grace the Duke of Wellington upon the field of Waterloo,
when the utmost efforts of the army of France, directed by
Napoleon, reputed to be the first captain of the age, were not
not only paralysed at the moment, but blasted beyond the
power of even a second struggle.

"To have participated in a contest crowned with victory
so decisive, and productive of consequences that have diffused
peace, security, and happiness throughout Europe, may be to
each of you a source of honourable pride, as well as of gratitude to the Omnipotent Arbiter of all human contests, who
preserved you in such peril, and without whose protecting
hand the battle belongs not to the strong, nor the race to the
swift.

"I acknowledge to feel an honest, and, I trust, an excus-
able, exultation, in having had the honour to command you
on that day; and in dispensing these medals, destined to record in your families the share you had in the ever-memorable
battle of Waterloo, it is a peculiar satisfaction to me that I can
present them to those by whom they have been fairly and
honourably earned, and that I can here solemnly declare, that
in the course of that eventful day I did not observe a soldier
of this good regiment whose conduct was not only creditable
to the English nation, but such as his dearest friends could desire. I trust that they will act as powerful talismans, to keep
you, in your future lives, in the paths of honour, sobriety, and
virtue." A year later and Major-General Sir Denis Pack
presented new colours to the regiment, and, alluding to its

services, said:—"Never, indeed, did the character of the corps stand higher; never was the fame of the British arms or the glory of the British empire more pre-eminent than at this moment, an enthusiastic recollection of which the sight of these colours must always inspire."

Returning to England in 1818, the Seventy-first remained on home service until 1824, when it was removed to Canada, and in 1831 was sent to Bermuda, thence restored to its native land in 1834. It returned to Canada in 1838, and in 1842 was included in a first and reserve battalion. Whilst the latter remained in Canada, the former was ordered to the West Indies, thence to Barbadoes, and in 1847 restored to England. In 1853 the first battalion proceeded to the Ionian Islands; and in November, 1854, the reserve battalion, which had recently arrived from Canada, embarked for the Crimea, followed by the first battalion from Corfu. Both battalions were subsequently united on arrival at the seat of war. "SEVASTOPOL" commemorates its service before that place. The regiment was next stationed at Malta, and was sent thence by overland route, in January, 1858, to Bombay, and is now at Sealkote, in the Punjaub.

THE SEVENTY-SECOND FOOT:

OR,

DUKE OF ALBANY'S HIGHLANDERS.

CHAPTER XXXII.

> " We would not die in that man's company,
> That fears his fellowship to die with us.
> .   .   .   .
>   Then shall our names,
> Familiar in their mouths as household words,
> Be in their flowing cups freshly remember'd
> From this day to the ending of the world;
> We few, we happy few, we band of brothers.
> For he to-day that sheds his blood with me,
> Shall be my brother."

ORIGIN—CHANNEL ISLANDS—INDIA—CEYLON—1778–1799.

THE history of the clans presents no more splendid illustration of that devotion which bound the clansman to his chief, and of the happy relationship implied therein, than is afforded in the circumstances attendant upon the origin of the Seventy-second Highlanders. The Earl of Seaforth, chief of the Mackenzie, had, as a leader in the rebellion of 1715, been banished from his country, his title attainted, and his estates forfeited, yet, withal, 400 of his late followers and tenants remitted to him in his exile a large portion of the rents they might have been liable for had he retained the estate. This most generous testimony of respect and practical expression of sympathy to the father was gratefully remembered by the son, and, notwithstanding the changes which, passing over the face of society, had swept away the old institution of clanship, induced the grandson, who, restored by purchase to the family pro- perty, and by his acknowledged loyalty, to the honours of the Earldom of Seaforth, in return for these favours, volunteered to raise a regiment for the Government. His appeal to his clansmen was amply successful. The Mackenzies and Macraes, rallying around him as their chief, gave thereby most hearty and flattering testimony to their own loyalty to the King, and unimpaired attachment to the family of Seaforth, which had so long and worthily presided over them. Accordingly, 1130 men were assembled and enrolled in the regiment—then known as the Seventy-eighth—at Elgin, in 1778. Marched to Edin- burgh, it was thence removed to the Channel Islands, where its firm attitude, remarkable in such young soldiers, so won the confidence of the islanders, and encouraged the militia, as, together with our Highlanders, enabled them successfully to resist an attempted debarkation of French troops on the island of Jersey.

A sister regiment to the Seventy-first, the Seventy-second (Seventy-eighth) was ordered to follow it to India in 1781, in fulfilment of the original purpose for which both corps had been raised. The transport service of those times was miserably inefficient, especially when compared with the leviathan ships and floating palaces—the Scotias, Persias, and Great Easterns—which in our day are, by a patriotic public, ever at the command of our Government for any sudden emergency. A voyage in a troop-ship eighty years ago ofttimes consumed more of life than the battle-field; was more fatal than the dreaded pestilence which lurked in the swamps of the Indies; nay, in some cases was as cruel in its miseries as the horrors of the Black Hole of Calcutta. The passage of the Seventy-second Highlanders to India proved to be such. Two hundred and forty-seven men perished on the voyage, which was protracted to nearly ten months; and when the regiment did arrive at Madras, only 369 men were mustered as fit for duty. One transport having parted from the fleet in a gale, was placed in imminent peril, being destitute of charts, and her commander utterly unfit for his position, having hitherto trusted to keep his vessel in the track of the fleet. By the wise precautions of Sir Eyre Coote, although the requirements of the service were urgent and entailed an immediate advance, the Seventy-second regiment was not immediately hurried into action, but time was allowed it to recruit its strength. In consequence of these measures, the regiment was soon able to appear in the field with upwards of 600 men.

Hyder Ali, who, by usurpation, had arisen from being a mere soldier of fortune to be the dreaded tyrant of the Mysore, allied with France and Holland, threatened to expel the British from the Indian continent.

" 'Tis true that we are in great danger,
    The greater, therefore, should our courage be."

These words of wisdom, from the glowing pen of Shak-
spere, worthy his mighty soul, bespeaking in every lineament
the true undaunted spirit of a son of Albion, were acted out
to the letter in the bold advance of the British against this
formidable coalition.   Our army, under Major-General Stuart,
comprised the Seventy-third (afterwards the Seventy-first),
the Seventy-eighth (afterwards the Seventy-second), and the
One-hundred-and-first regiments, with a considerable body of
native troops and Hanoverians.   The strong fortress of Cudalore was the first to challenge the assault.   Defended by a
veteran garrison of French, under General Bussy, it needed
the utmost gallantry of our Highlanders—"the ardour and
intrepidity giving presage of the renown they afterwards
acquired"—to force the enemy's lines, and ultimately compel
him to relinquish the external defences of the place and
retire more immediately within the fortress.   Amongst the
prisoners was Colonel the Chevalier de Dumas, conspicuous as
"the bravest of the brave," also "a wounded young serjeant of
very interesting appearance and manners, who was treated
with much kindness by Lieutenant-Colonel Wagenheim, commanding the detachment of Hanoverians.   Many years afterwards, when the French army entered Hanover, General Wagenheim attended the levée of General Bernadotte, who referred to the circumstance at Cudalore in 1783, and added—
'I am the individual, who, when a young serjeant, received
kindness from you in India.'"   The death of Hyder Ali, and

the withdrawal of France, occasioned the breaking up of this
formidable league against the British power in India, and for
a moment the sun of peace smiled upon our war-worn
soldiers.

The new Sultan of the Mysore, as capricious as his father and
predecessor, broke off the negotiations which had promised a
continued and favourable peace. In consequence, the Seventy-
eighth (Seventy-second) advanced, with the army under
Colonel Fullerton, against the almost impregnable fortress of
Palghautcherry, which was won mainly by the daring of the
Honourable Captain Maitland and a company of the regiment,
who, taking advantage of a violent storm, when the enemy,
seeking shelter from the pitiless rain, had left unguarded the
covered way, and thereby affording an opportunity which,
improved by Captain Maitland and his company, gave such
a footing within the walls as terrified the defenders into
a speedy surrender. This success was followed by the fall
of Coimbatore, and might probably have been crowned in the
capture of Seringapatam, had not peace interfered, postponing
the fate of the capital for ten years.

In 1790, the unprovoked aggressions of Tippoo Saib, the
ambitious Sultan of the Mysore, upon the Rajah of Travancore, an ally of the British, occasioned the renewal of the war.
Still associated in a common glory with their brethren of the
Seventy-third (Seventy-first) Highlanders, the Seventy-eighth
(Seventy-second) advanced with the army under Major-General Medows, which, obtaining possession unopposed of Coimbatore and capturing Dindigal, proceeded against the powerful

fortress of Palghautcherry, which, notwithstanding Tippoo
Saib's utmost efforts to relieve it, was surrendered to the flank
companies of the two Highland regiments, under Lieutenant-
Colonel Stuart.

Aware of his own inferiority in the field, the Sultan
dared not hazard a battle, but omitted no opportunity to
harass and annoy our army wherever superior knowledge of
the country, position, or overwhelming numbers gave him the
advantage. The arrival of Colonel Maxwell's reinforcements
from the Bengal Presidency occasioned the addition of the
Seventy-fourth regiment to the Highland brigade; and, on
General the Earl Cornwallis assuming the command in 1791,
he approved this arrangement by retaining in one brigade
the Seventy-first, Seventy-second, and Seventy-fourth Highlanders.

Out-manœuvred by the British commander, an entrance was
obtained through an unguarded defile into the enemy's territory. The siege of Bangalore was the immediate result, which,
despite its powerful fortifications and the menacing attitude of
the Mysore army, which anxiously strove to relieve it, was
gallantly won by storm in March, 1791. Having witnessed
the fall of this chief city of his empire, the Sultan precipitately
retreated, closely pursued by the Highland brigade. The
British army thereafter advanced against Seringapatam.
Alarmed for the safety of his capital, Tippoo ventured to try
the fate of battle. Defeated, he failed to arrest our progress,
all seemed lost, when unfortunate circumstances interposed on
his behalf, and a second time rescued the doomed city from

our grasp. Several minor enterprises beguiled the time ere
the march upon Seringapatam might be resumed. Savendroog was successfully stormed, and the strong fort of Outra-
Durgum was captured, chiefly through the heroic ardour of
two companies of the Seventy-second, who, having possessed
themselves of the town, pursued the fugitives to the rock upon
which the fort stood. We quote from Lieutenant Campbell's
Journal:—"Lieutenant M'Innes, senior officer of the two
Seventy-second companies, applied to Captain Scott for liberty
to follow the fugitives up the rock, saying he should be in
time to enter the first gateway with them. The Captain
thought the enterprise impracticable. The soldiers of M'Innes's
company heard the request made, and not doubting of consent
being given, had rushed towards the first wall, and were
followed by M'Innes. The gate was shut: but Lieutenant
M'Pherson arrived with the pioneers and ladders, which were
instantly applied, and our people were within the wall, as
quick as thought, when the gate was unbolted and the two
companies entered. The enemy, astonished at so unexpected
an attempt, retreated with precipitation. M'Innes advanced
to the second wall, the men forced open the gate with their
shoulders, and not a moment was lost in pushing forward for
the third wall; but the road, leading between two rocks, was
so narrow that only two could advance abreast; the pathway
was, in consequence, soon choked up, and those who carried
the ladders were unable to proceed; at the same time, the
enemy commenced throwing huge stones in numbers upon the
assailants, who commenced a sharp fire of musketry, and

Lieutenant-Colonel Stuart, who had observed from a distance
this astonishing enterprise, sent orders for the grenadiers not
to attempt anything further. Lieutenant M'Pherson forced
his way through the crowd, causing the ladders to be handed
over the soldiers' heads, from one to another, and before the
colonel's orders could be delivered, the gallant Highlanders
were crowding over the third gateway. The enemy fled on
all hands; the foremost of our men pursued them closely, and
gained the two last walls (there were five walls to escalade)
without opposition. The garrison escaped by the south-east
side of the fort, over rocks and precipices of immense depth
and ruggedness, where many must have lost their lives. By
one o'clock, our two companies were in possession of every
part of the fort, and M'Innes had planted the colours on the
highest pinnacle, without the loss of a single man. The Kile-
dar and two of his people were taken alive. Colonel Stuart
declared the business to be brilliant and successful, beyond his
most sanguine hopes."

In 1792, the advance upon Seringapatam was renewed.
In the glorious events of the siege, the Seventy-second bore
a most conspicuous part, and largely contributed to the attain-
ment of the victory which destroyed the power of the Sultan,
and made him a suppliant for peace.

Scarcely had one enemy been overcome, ere a new one
appeared—the French, hurled into fatal antagonism with us
because of the unhappy avowal of sentiments subversive of
good order. Accordingly, in 1793, the Seventy-second was
engaged in the siege of Pondicherry — the principal Indian

colony of France; which fell into our hands rather from a mutiny among its defenders than our own efforts. It is related by Lieutenant Campbell, that "the moment the piper began to play, the fire from the enemy slackened, and soon after almost entirely ceased. The French all got upon the works, and seemed astonished at hearing the bag-pipe." The Dutch having allied themselves with the French, paid the penalty of their folly in the loss of many of their most valuable colonies, conquered by the British. Ceylon, the principal, perhaps the most valuable of them, was in consequence assailed by our Indian army, including the Seventy-second regiment, which, capturing Trincomalee, Batticaloe, Manaar, and Colombo, reduced the island under British dominion. This was the closing achievement, for the present, of the regiment in India. Returning from Ceylon to Pondicherry, thence removed to Madras in 1798, it was ordered home, and landed at Gravesend. These many and distinguished services are commemorated in the word "Hindoostan," now borne by Royal authority upon its colours and appointments.

CHAPTER XXXIII.

"Then glory, my Jeanie, maun plead my excuse;
Since honour commands me, how can I refuse?
Without it, I ne'er can have merit for thee,
And losing thy favour I'd better not be.
I gae, then, my lass, to win glory and fame,
And if I should chance to come gloriously hame,
I'll bring a heart to thee with love running o'er,
And then I'll leave thee and Lochaber no more."

CAPE OF GOOD HOPE—MAURITIUS—INDIA—CAPE OF GOOD HOPE
—1799–1862.

THE regiment returned to Europe at a very critical period in
our national history, when the rampant passions of revolution,
as yet untamed by adversity, imperiously taxed the nations
in their maintenance. It had no sooner arrived than it was
sent to Scotland to recruit, and thence, in 1801, to Ireland.
From the number of new regiments called into being at this
period to meet the necessities of the times, recruiting went on
but slowly. The respite from the dire calamity of war which
the Peace of Amiens afforded, occasioned a reduction in the
establishment of the Seventy-second. The resumption of
hostilities in 1803, not only called for an immediate augmentation of its strength, but occasioned the addition of a second
battalion, which was employed in various home garrisons,
especially in Ireland, throughout the war, until disbanded in
1816. The immediate peril from a French invasion having

passed away, the Seventy-second was ordered to join a secret expedition under Lieut.-General Sir Eyre Coote, K.B., but was ultimately included in the force under Major-General Sir David Baird, which sailed in 1805, and after viewing the beauties of Madeira, and landing for a few days' refreshment at San Salvador in the Brazils, steered for the coast of Africa, when the object of the expedition was disclosed by an attack upon the Dutch colony at the Cape of Good Hope. In addition to its old comrades of the Seventy-first, the Seventy-second was associated with the Ninety-third Regiment in the Highland Brigade of the army. On the morning of the 6th January, 1806, the British effected a landing in Lospard's Bay, despite the efforts of the Dutch to prevent it. The Highlanders in the van drove the enemy before them, and on attaining the summit of the Blue Mountains, beheld the Batavian army awaiting battle on the other side. The position of the enemy was well chosen, and maintained with determined bravery. The fate of the battle was only decided in our favour when the Highland Brigade was brought forward, and "Brigadier-General Ferguson gave the word 'Charge.' A loud British shout instantly rent the air, and the heroic Highlanders closed with bayonets upon their numerous adversaries, who instantly fled in dismay, pursued across the deep sands by the victorious Highland Brigade." As the army advanced towards Cape Town, the Dutch retired. The conduct of Lieutenant M'Arthur and thirty men of the regiment in the capture of Hout's Bay, was conspicuous for the gallantry it evinced. These repeated disasters convinced the Dutch of the hopelessness of resistance against troops accustomed to conquer. Accordingly, negotiations were entered into which resulted in the surrender of the colony to the British.

In 1809 the Seventy-second was ordered to discontinue wearing the Highland costume, in consequence of the difficulty experienced in gaining recruits. A year later the regiment was selected to co-operate with troops from India in an attack upon the valuable French colony of the Mauritius. The Indian army arriving off the island first, the Governor determined to maintain the defence to the last extremity, but the timely arrival of the Seventy-second so discouraged him, that, abandoning the idea of resistance, he at once surrendered. The corps remained in garrison at Port Louis until the outbreak of a new war in America in 1814 occasioned its withdrawal. It accordingly embarked for that continent, but was detained at the Cape of Good Hope, where, after a brief service, it was ordered to India, arriving at Calcutta in 1815. The Rajah of Nepaul having, however, made his peace with the British, the necessity for its service in that portion of the world no longer existed, hence it returned to the Cape of Good Hope, calling on the passage at the Mauritius. Stationed at Algoa Bay, it was thence directed to occupy a chain of posts along the banks of the Great Fish River, charged with the protection of the colonists from the numerous predatory incursions of the Kaffirs. This proved an arduous and dangerous duty; the soldiers being constantly exposed to a surprise from the swarms of unseen enemies that ever lurked in the bush around their camp. On one occasion, in

1819, a Dutch farmer, robbed of his cattle by the Kaffirs, sought the interference of the military for the recovery of his property and the punishment of the thieves. Accompanied by a body of armed farmers, a detachment of the Seventy-second, under Captain Gethin, overtook the thieves. The little party of soldiers was instantly enveloped and cruelly butchered by a host of enemies, whilst the cowardly farmers witnessed the destruction of their friends without venturing to afford the slightest assistance. Captain Gethin was a distinguished soldier, and like a brave man "fighting fell," pierced with thirty-two wounds. The Seventy-second continued efficiently to discharge this harassing duty until relieved by the Sixth Regiment in 1821, when it returned home. It was successively stationed at Portsmouth, Fort Cumberland, Plymouth, and Woolwich. In 1823 it was removed to the Channel Islands of Jersey and Guernsey.

Although the service of the Seventy-second, hitherto confined to "Hindoostan" and the "Cape of Good Hope," recorded upon its colours and appointments, and embracing in these, actions which had been comparatively lost sight of in the multitude of grander events transacted on the battle-fields of Europe, still, the true heroism of these, to be just, must convince us that the achievements of the Seventy-second are "second to none," and well deserving the splendid compliment at this period conferred upon the regiment by His Grace the Duke of York and *Albany*, the Commander-in-Chief. It was permitted, in reward of its valour, to wear its present designation—

DUKE OF ALBANY'S OWN HIGHLANDERS.

At the same time it received a further compliment, in the restoration of the Highland costume, with the difference of *trews* instead of *kilts*.

Returning to England from the Channel Islands in 1824, it thence proceeded to re-visit dear old Scotland.

"Home of my fathers, my heart clings to thee."

Whilst stationed in Edinburgh, the lady of Lieut.-General Sir John Hope (colonel of the Seventy-second), presented new colours to the regiment. In 1825 it was sent to Ireland, and stationed successively in Belfast, Londonderry, and Dublin. Thence it proceeded to England; and whilst garrisoning the Tower of London, was reviewed, with the First Life Guards, the Royal Horse Guards, and four battalions of Foot Guards, by the Duke of Wellington, in presence of Don Miguel of Portugal. In proof of its efficiency, as worthy to be so associated with our choicest troops, we quote the words of General Lord Hill, when (the same year) he inspected the regiment at Canterbury:—

"That although it had been his lot to see and serve with most of the regiments in the service, he felt he should not be doing full justice to the Seventy-second Highlanders, if he did not express his particular approbation of every thing connected with them, and add, he had never before seen a regiment their equal in movements, in appearance, and in steadiness under arms."

Having acquired these public honours and Royal favours, the Seventy-second was once more ordered to the Cape of Good Hope, to arrest and punish the aggressions of the Kaffirs, who continued to prey upon the industry of our colonists, and had become a hinderance, by the terror they inspired, to the progress of the colony. At length the expulsion from the colony of a vagrant chief, Macomo, who had abused the British protection, stirred the animosity of earlier years, which, encouraged by our lenity, unmasked itself in a desolating irruption, especially evident in and around Graham's Town, which fell an easy prey to the rapacious fury of the enemy. To avenge the innocent blood thus shed, and retaliate the ruin that had been entailed, the Seventy-second advanced with other troops into Kaffirland, inflicting a severe but just chastisement for the atrocities that had been committed; taking, moreover, such pledges from the foe as it was fondly hoped should secure protection and peace for the future. Having apparently subdued the spirit of lawless aggression, and restored confidence in the colonists by a residence of nearly ten years amongst them, the regiment returned home, and landed at Plymouth in 1840.

Whilst stationed at Windsor in 1841, it was destined anew to receive a signal mark of Royal favour—its new colours being presented by the Duke of Wellington, in the quadrangle of the palace, and in presence of Her Majesty the Queen, Prince Albert, and the King of Prussia. In presenting these colours, the Duke of Wellington thus addressed the soldiers:—

"I have long known the Seventy-second Highland Regiment.

Half-a-century has now nearly elapsed since I had the pleasure of serving in the same army with them in the plains of Hindoostan; since that period they have been engaged in the conquest of some of the most valuable colonies of the British Crown; and latterly, in performing most distinguished services at the Cape of Good Hope. Fourteen years out of the last sixteen they have spent on Foreign service; and with only eighteen months at home for their re-formation and their re-disciplining, appear in their present high state of regularity and order. . . . . . I have made it my business to inquire particularly, and am rejoiced to find that the Seventy-second have always commanded that respect and regard, wherever they have been stationed, to which their high state of discipline and good order so justly entitle them. You will, I am sure, always recollect the circumstances under which these colours are now given into your charge; having been consecrated by one of the highest dignitaries of the Church, in the presence of Her Majesty, who now looks down upon you, and of her Royal Visitor; and I give them into your charge, confident that at all times, under all circumstances, whether at home or abroad, and in all privations, you will rally round them, and protect them to the utmost of your power."

After a variety of home services, the regiment was removed, in 1844, to Gibraltar, and thence, in 1848, to the West Indies. Leaving the West Indies for North America in July, 1851, it returned home in October, 1854. Proceeding to Malta in January, 1855, and thence, in May following, to the Crimea, it there gained " SEVASTOPOL " for the regimental colours.

Returning to England at the peace, the Seventy-second remained at home until August, 1857, when the corps embarked for Bombay on the breaking out of the Indian mutiny, and served with distinction in Central India, under Sir Hugh Rose, especially in the storming of the strongly-fortified town of Awah, being thereafter associated with the Seventy-first Highland Light Infantry in the campaign.

The regiment is still serving in the Bombay Presidency.

SEVENTY - FOURTH HIGHLANDERS.

CHAPTER XXXIV.

> " This homage to the chief who drew his sword
> At the command of duty; kept it bright
> Through perilous days; and soon as Victory smiled
> Laid it, unsullied, in the lap of Peace."

INDIA—SERINGAPATAM—ASSAYE—1787–1806.

THE proximity of two such formidable rivals as France and Britain, notwithstanding the friendly intervention of the Channel, has occasioned on both sides thereof an almost perpetual series of alarms, jealousies, and feuds, too often resulting in wars of the most stupendous magnitude, generally involving in their toils the other kingdoms of Europe. It is of one such crisis we write, when France, politically meddling with the affairs of Holland, excited the suspicions of our Government, and occasioned the combined interference of Britain and Prussia, to preserve, no doubt, the *"balance of power."* Contemplating an appeal to arms, each prepared for the expected struggle. France and Holland possessing a large colonial empire in India, and both having a rival and antagonistic interest in the politics of that country to the

new-born power of Britain, each marked that far-off land
as an important theatre of strife. Hence, our legislature
determined to strengthen our forces in that quarter of the
British world by the addition of four new regiments, ordered
to be raised in 1787. Two of these, the Seventy-fourth and
Seventy-fifth,* were raised amongst the Highlanders of Scotland; and the others, the Seventy-sixth and Seventy-seventh,
in England, or generally throughout the kingdom. No sooner
were these completed—nay, in the case of the Seventy-fourth,
before being completed—than they were shipped off for
immediate service in India; whilst the question of their
maintenance was installed in Parliament as a subject of bitter
wrangling between the home Government and the East India
Company, affording a theme for the genius of Pitt to work
upon, and in the end to triumph, in the passing of the
"Declaratory Bill," which saddled the East India Company
with the expense. This Bill was afterwards confirmed by
Acts passed in 1791, and again in 1793.

Of these regiments, thus raised, the Seventy-fourth claims
our present attention. It was assembled at Glasgow under
command of Major-General Sir Archibald Campbell, K.B.,
and was largely composed of Argyleshire Highlanders—the
Campbells and their kin. To meet the urgent demand for
reinforcements, every soldier as yet available for duty was at
once forwarded to India, followed by a second instalment
of six companies, which completed the regiment, in 1789.

* The Seventy-fifth has just received the Royal permission to be styled the
Seventy-fifth, or "Stirlingshire" Regiment.

Landed at Madras with an effective strength of 750 men, the Seventy-fourth, brigaded with the Seventy-first and Seventy-second Highlanders, joined the army of Major-General Medows in 1790. The Earl Cornwallis assuming the command, advanced upon Bangalore, which was taken by storm; thereafter the regiment was with the Highland Brigade in the fruitless expedition against Seringapatam. Detached during the winter for service in the Baramhal district, the Seventy-fourth was very conspicuous for its spirited but ineffectual attempt to storm Penagra, an almost impregnable hill fort, which was only saved by the natural obstacles that defended it, and defied the most desperate efforts of our Highlanders to surmount. In 1792 the siege of Seringapatam was once more undertaken, and considerable progress had been achieved, when the intervention of peace disappointed our army of the anticipated prize.

Brigaded with the Seventy-second and Seventy-third Highland regiments, the Seventy-fourth was engaged in the operations which brought about the surrender of the French settlement of Pondicherry. The garrison, in consequence, became prisoners of war, but the officers released on parole were hospitably entertained by the captors. Amid these hospitalities, an incident occurred which displays in bold relief the generous gallantry of the officers of the Seventy-fourth. With the French officers they were present in the theatre, when the former, in love with the new-born ideas of republicanism, in course of the evening vehemently called for the revolutionary air "Ca Ira." This was objected to by the

British; and from the uproar of words, a serious disturbance arose to break in upon the harmony, and bewilder and terrify the orchestra. Happily, the senior officer of the Seventy-fourth, stepping upon the stage, obtained silence, and addressing the audience in a firm but conciliatory manner, stated that the British officers had agreed not to insist upon their objections, but were prepared to sacrifice their feelings on the subject, seeing such might gratify their French friends and the ladies who had seconded the request. No sooner had the air been played, amid the acclamations of the French, than the same officer asked the audience to uncover to the National Anthem—"God save the King." Rebuked by this generous forbearance, and heartily ashamed of their rudeness in so insisting upon their own gratification, the French felt themselves outdone in gallantry, and only too glad of an opportunity to repair the discord they had bred, granted a ready consent; and the Royal Anthem was only the more vociferously welcomed that it had been forestalled by the revolutionary ditty "Ca Ira." Ever afterwards the utmost cordiality subsisted between the representatives of the two nations.

In 1798, when the war with France required a great financial effort adequately to sustain it on our part, and when the patriotism of the public liberally and voluntarily contributed to the national funds for the purpose, the men of the Seventy-fourth voted eight days' pay; the non-commissioned officers a half-month's pay; and the commissioned officers a full month's pay, towards the vigorous prosecution of the war—"a war unprovoked on our part, and justified by the noblest of motives: the preservation of our invaluable constitution."

In 1799, with the army of Lieutenant-General Harris, the Seventy-fourth advanced against Seringapatam, which ultimately fell a conquest to our arms. The distinguished service of the regiment on this occasion is recorded in the word "Seringapatam" borne upon its colours. Subsequently it was engaged against the Polygars; and in 1801 was removed to Bombay to replace the troops drawn from that Presidency for service in Egypt. Under Major-General the Hon. Arthur Wellesley, in the invasion of the Mahratta states, the regiment was most conspicuous for its fortitude in enduring many severe privations, and refusing withal to petition or complain when grievances remained unredressed. The capture of the strong fortress of Ahmednuggur, was but the prelude to the exceeding glory so soon destined to grace the records of the Seventy-fourth in the victory of Assaye.

On the 23d September, 1803, the British army, not exceeding 5000 men, of which the Nineteenth Dragoons and the Seventy-fourth and Seventy-eighth Highlanders were the only King's regiments, came up with the combined hosts of Scindiah and the Rajah of Berar, amounting together to 40,000 well-disciplined and excellent troops. Undaunted by this formidable superiority, Major-General the Hon. Arthur Wellesley at once ordered the attack, which undertaken with spirit and upheld with heroic gallantry, soon overcame the resolution and desperate defence of the enemy. The Seventy-fourth, posted on the right of the second line, prematurely

SEVENTY-FOURTH HIGHLANDERS.

advancing against the village of Assaye, became exposed to a
terrific tempest of shot and shell; and, moreover, charged by
a powerful body of horse when somewhat confused by the
fatal effects of the artillery, was almost annihilated. True to
its duty, and borne forward by an unconquerable perseverance,
the Seventy-fourth struggled on, carried and maintained the
post, although at a fearful sacrifice of human life, upwards of
400 men and officers being *hors-de-combat*. Of its officers,
the only one escaping scatheless was Quarter-Master James
Grant, who seeing so many of his comrades fall, although by
office a non-combatant, resolved to share with his brethren the
dangers and the glory of the fight, and, accordingly, joining in
the terrible *mêlée* of the battle, resolutely fought till its close,
miraculously surviving the disasters of so severe and fatal a
strife. The Major-General thus writes: "Our loss is great,
but the action, I believe, was the most severe that ever was
fought in this country, and, I believe, such a quantity of
cannon and such advantages have seldom been gained, by any
single victory, in any part of the world."

On this occasion the valour of the regiment was rewarded
by the exceptional permission to carry a third colour, bearing thereon the "Elephant" and "Assaye," specially commemorative of the unparalleled glory of the day. The
inconvenience of a third colour has since brought about its
disallowance as other than an honorary distinction to be borne
only when on peaceful parade.

The severe losses of the regiment at the battle of Assaye
required it should be released from active duty for a time, to

allow these losses to be repaired, and the wounded to recover and resume their posts. However, in November of the same year we find it in the field with the army on the plains of Argaum, burning to avenge, by a new victory, the death of friends sacrificed at Assaye. Major-General Wellesley, in his official despatch, particularly commends the perseverance, steadiness, and bravery of the Seventy-fourth and Seventy-eighth Highlanders as materially helping to the triumph of Argaum. A variety of minor actions closed the campaign, crowned by the submission of the enemy.

Thereafter selected by the Commander-in-Chief, the regiment was detached with other troops, under his own command, which marching sixty miles in twenty hours, destroyed a camp of freebooters, which, quartered at Perinda, had been the pest and terror of the neighbourhood.

In 1804, the regiment was stationed with the Seventy-eighth and some native troops for protective purposes in the territory of the Peishwah, until the war with Holkar anew occasioned it to undertake more active service. In the capture of Gaulnah, the Seventy-fourth was called upon to supply volunteers for the forlorn hope. Such was the spirit of the corps, that the whole regiment spontaneously offered itself.

After sixteen years' service in India, during which it was almost always engaged with an enemy—earning therefrom the name it afterwards gloriously upheld as the "fighting regiment" —the gallant remnant was ordered to return home, and, in consequence, embarking at Madras in September, 1805, landed at Portsmouth in February, 1806.

CHAPTER XXXV.

" Upon his brow shame is ashamed to sit;
For 'tis a throne where honour may be crowned
Sole monarch of the universal earth."

PENINSULA—AMERICA—WEST INDIES—CANADA—"THE WRECK
OF THE BIRKENHEAD"—1806—1852.

As soon as the Seventy-fourth had returned, the business
of recruiting occupied the earnest attention of its officers.
Removed to Scotland for this purpose, it failed to complete its
establishment, and, in consequence, was transferred to Ireland
to receive its complement by volunteers from the militia. In
1810 it received orders to prepare for foreign service; and,
accordingly, embarked from Cork for Portugal, under Lieut.-
Colonel the Honourable Robert De Poer Trench, with a total
strength of 730 effectives. Arrived in the Tagus and disembarked, it was advanced to Visen. Its junction with the
allied army of Lord Wellington was hailed with delight by
that chief, who ever felt a warm interest in its history, as the
"Assaye regiment" whose heroes had won for him his first
great victory. Complimenting Colonel Trench, he said: " If
the Seventy-fourth would behave in that country as they had
done in India, he ought to be proud to command such a
regiment." Included in the third or well-known "Fighting
Division" of Major-General Picton, the Seventy-fourth was

brigaded with the first battalion of the Forty-fifth, the Eighty-
eighth, and three companies of the fifth battalion of the
Sixtieth Regiment. From the concentrated and overwhelming
military might of Napoleon, Marshal Massena was detached at
the head of 75,000 veterans, styled the "Army of Portugal,"
charged with the destruction of the British who had dared
to dispute the claims of his master to the dominion of the
Peninsula. In presence of such a superior foe, as regards numbers, Wellington resolved on retreat; and, accordingly, with-
drawing to his own defences, induced the enemy to draw off
in pursuit. Taking advantage of every position which by
natural or artificial strength afforded an opportunity to check
or impede the pursuit of the French, Lord Wellington frequently severely punished the temerity of the foe. Thus, in
the battle of Busaco, where the Seventy-fourth for awhile
withstood the attack of an entire French column, until sustained by the Ninth and Thirty-eighth regiments, it drove the
enemy down the hill.

Finally arrested by the formidable lines of Torres Vedras,
the French, vainly endeavouring to blockade the position,
fatally suffered from disease and want, whilst our troops
enjoyed every comfort in abundance and in safety within the
entrenchments. Convinced of the futility of any attempt to
surmount the defences of the position, Marshal Massena was
constrained in turn to retreat, closely pursued along the banks
of the Mondego by the British. With the third division, in
the van of the army, the Seventy-fourth was almost incessantly
engaged driving the enemy from post to post. For the relief

of Almeida, Marshal Massena, considerably reinforced, once
more ventured to advance. Encountering the light companies
of the first, third, and fifth divisions, and the second battalion
of the Eighty-third Regiment, in occupation of the village of
Fuentes d'Onor, the French laboured to expel them. Reinforced by the Twenty-fourth, Seventy-first, and Seventy-
ninth regiments, and ultimately supported by the Forty-fifth,
Seventy-fourth, and Eighty-eighth regiments, the whole of the
enemy's sixth corps was routed and driven from the village
it had at first won. Interrupted in the siege of Badajoz by the
approach of the combined armies of Marmont and Soult, the
British temporarily retired. A similar diversion by the army
of Marshal Marmont in favour of Ciudad Rodrigo, in like
manner disturbed its blockade. Whilst quartered in this
vicinity, the third division of our army, threatened by an
attack from a very powerful corps of French, which, taking
advantage of the immediate presence of Marshal Marmont,
had undertaken a sortie from the fortress, retreated. Under
command of General Montbrun, the enemy so severely pressed
the British division, that, in retiring, the Seventy-fourth
became separated from the rest, and was generally believed to
have been captured. A long detour, under the friendly shield
of night, enabled the regiment to escape the danger and rejoin
the division in its camp at Guinaldo. Overjoyed in their
safe return, Major-General Picton uttered these memorable
words, expressive of his faith in the valour of our Highlanders,
saying, "he thought he must have heard more firing before
the Seventy-fourth could be taken."

On the retirement of the French, returning to the duties of the siege, the regiment, on the 19th of January, was included in the storming party which, despite the most strenuous resistance of the foe, won Ciudad Rodrigo. This achievement was immediately followed by the re-investment of Badajoz; a fortress esteemed impregnable, the more so as it was defended by some of the choicest troops of France. The progress had been so satisfactory, and the breaches in the ramparts deemed so far practicable, that by the 6th April, 1812, the assault was ordered, and the Herculean duty of storming the defences of the castle committed to the third division; accomplished, nevertheless, after "a combat so furiously fought, so terribly won, so dreadful in all its circumstances, that posterity can scarcely be expected to credit the tale." Lieutenant Alexander Grant of the Seventy-fourth, leading the advance, entered the castle, but fell in the moment of victory. "Foremost in the escalade was John M'Lauchlan, the regimental piper, who, the instant he mounted the castle wall, began playing on his pipes the regimental quick step, 'The Campbells are coming,' at the head of the advance along the ramparts, as coolly as if on a common parade, until his music was stopped by a shot through the bag; he was afterwards seen by an officer of the regiment seated on a gun-carriage, quietly repairing the damage, regardless of the shot flying about him, and presently recommenced his animating tune." Although the other assaults were not so successful, still the triumph of the third and fifth divisions at their several points of attack so turned the defences of the place,

that resistance appearing hopeless, the fortress was surrendered.

Various manœuvres at length brought about the battle of
Salamanca, where the French, under Marshal Marmont, were
totally defeated, driven "as it were before a mighty wind
without help or stay." The brunt of the action was sustained
by the French division of General Thomières, originally 7000
strong, but which, notwithstanding the most splendid illustration of heroism, was utterly cut to pieces or dispersed. In this
great battle the third division figured conspicuously. Lord
Londonderry writes: "The attack of the third division was
not only the most spirited, but the most perfect thing of the
kind that modern times have witnessed. Regardless alike of
a charge of cavalry and of the murderous fire which the
enemy's batteries opened, on went these fearless warriors,
horse and foot, without check or pause, until they won the
ridge, and then the infantry giving their volley, and the
cavalry falling on sword in hand, the French were pierced,
broken, and discomfited. So close, indeed, was the struggle,
that in several instances the British colours were seen waving
over the heads of the enemy's battalions;" whilst the advance
in unbroken line of the Seventy-fourth, for upwards of three
miles, testified to its efficiency, and drew forth the plaudits
of Major-General Pakenham, then commanding the division,
who vehemently exclaimed, "Beautifully done, Seventy-fourth!
beautiful, Seventy-fourth!"

The glorious results immediately flowing from this great
victory, were crowned in the capitulation and occupation of

Madrid. Whilst stationed in the capital, the gaieties of which agreeably relieved the hardships of the camp, our officers at the same time beheld the splendid misery the tyrant-extortionating rule of France had entailed upon the citizens, many of whom, once great and opulent, now reduced to abject beggary, gratefully accepted the assistance of their deliverers. In these deeds of charity the officers of the Seventy-fourth were not wanting, but, with those of the Forty-fifth, daily fed about two hundred of the starving grandees.

Meanwhile, the converging of the various French armies of the Peninsula for the relief of Burgos, once more necessitated the retreat of the British, who, evacuating Madrid, retired towards Portugal, and finally halted, going into winter quarters, behind the Agueda. The spring of 1813 found the British army largely recruited, and with new energy prepared to resume the offensive—to begin that victorious march which stayed not until the heights of Toulouse owned the triumphs of the British flag.

At the great battle of Vittoria, which may be said to have broken the last remnant of French power in Spain, the third division was most severely engaged; and the gallantry of the Seventy-fourth was anew conspicuous in its successful attack upon the village of Arinez, whence it drove out the enemy. In the after advance, over a rugged country, in pursuit of the retiring columns of the foe, the unbroken line of the Seventy-fourth attracted general attention, and its admirable order was highly commended. In the grand attack which completed the ruin of the French, the third division, being foremost, was assailed by a fiery storm of artillery and musketry, which made fearful chasms in its ranks. At length the success of the fourth division from another quarter compelled the enemy to abandon his strong position, and soon converted the retreat into a disorderly flight. Marshal Soult was afterwards sent to command the army in the Peninsula, as " Lieutenant of the Emperor," and never was his genius more conspicuous. His master-mind came to the rescue; he re-organised the broken remnant of the once mighty host, and, largely reinforced, once more advanced, thereby inspiring new confidence in his troops, and casting a momentary gleam of hope athwart the lowering horizon which presaged the storm steadily moving vengefully towards devoted France. The hope thus excited was speedily dissipated, and every effort failed to retrieve the disastrous consequences of Vittoria. Driven successively across the " Pyrenees," the " Nive," and the " Nivelle," he found a refuge and a rest for his dispirited and wearied troops within the fortress of Bayonne. At "Orthes" and "Toulouse" Wellington required a great exercise of his own abilities as a chief to overthrow the dogged resolution of his great antagonist, who, equal to the crisis, by prodigies of skill, strove to avert the dissolution of his master's empire. In all these closing actions of the war, the Seventy-fourth, in the "fighting" third division, more than creditably maintained its part, returning home in 1815 crowned with glory.

Ireland became thereafter the scene of its more peaceful service. Whilst stationed at Fermoy in 1818, new colours were presented to the regiment; and the shreds of the old ones—which had been so victoriously borne in the battles of the Peninsula—burnt to ashes, had their sacred dust treasured up in the lid of a gold sarcophagus snuff-box, inlaid with part of the wood of the colour-staves, and bearing the following inscription:—"This box, composed of the old standards of the Seventy-fourth regiment, was formed as a tribute of respect to the memory of those who fell, and of esteem for those who survived the many glorious and arduous services on which they were always victoriously carried, during a period of sixteen years, in India, the Peninsula, and France. They were presented to the regiment at Wallajahbad in 1802; and the shattered remains were burned at Fermoy on the 6th of April, 1818."

Having thus disposed of this venerable memorial of its early renown, the regiment embarked at Cork for Halifax, Nova Scotia. Its service in America and Bermuda in 1825, and again in 1828, affords nothing of importance to detain the reader. Returning to Ireland in 1830, it was employed in various garrisons in that country until, ordered on foreign service, it sailed for the West Indies in 1834. Thence, in 1841, it was removed to Canada, returning to England in 1845. By desire of the officers, the Seventy-fourth was restored to its original dignity as a Highland corps, having the trews instead of the kilt; and in 1846 re-visited Scotland for a brief period, whence it proceeded to Ireland, where, associated with the Seventy-fifth and Eighty-eighth regiments, and other troops, it was encamped in the vicinity of Thurles

and Ballingarry, to overawe the rebellious, and repress the
foolish attempt at insurrection which, stirred by idle demagogues, had excited the people during the famine of 1848.
This military demonstration proved sufficient to suppress,
without blood, these ill-advised seditions.

One event remains to be recorded in our present sketch,
ere we close the brief summary; one event which alone is
all-sufficient to glorify the Seventy-fourth, although casting a
melancholy interest over its history, yet enshrining the memory
of its brave as *heroic*; one event which, although belonging in
common to the records of the Seventy-third and Ninety-first,
as well as other regiments, deserves its place here out of
respect to the lost and gallant officer commanding; one event
which sheds a brighter lustre, as it reveals in truer character
the qualities of the British soldier, than the exciting and
sanguinary achievements of the battle-field; one event which
wakes the soul to truest sympathy, and bids the heart bleed at
the recitation of the narrative.

> " —— The youthful and the brave,
>   With their beauty and renown,
> To the hollow chambers of the wave
>   In darkness have gone down."

One event which has bidden a gush of grief for the lost and
brave from the noble-minded of every clime. Such was the
wreck of the "Birkenhead." This vessel, one of the finest in Her
Majesty's service, with a living freight of 632 souls, including
14 officers and 458 soldiers, draughts from various regiments,
reinforcements from home on their way to join their comrades

fighting in Kaffirland, reaching Simon's Bay, had sailed thence for Algoa Bay on the evening of the 25th February, 1852.

> "Ah no!—an earthly freight she bears,
> Of joys and sorrows, hopes and fears;
> And lonely as she seems to be,
> Thus left by herself on the moonlight sea,
> In loneliness that rolls,
> She hath a constant company
> In sleep, or waking revelry—
> Five hundred human souls!"

Striving to quicken the voyage by shortening the passage, the commandant hugged the shore too closely off Cape Danger, and in doing so the vessel struck upon a sunken rock whilst steaming at the rate of eight miles an hour. So tremendous was the shock, that, although the night was clear and the sea calm, the stately ship was in a moment a broken wreck. The catastrophe occurred three miles from land, and six hours after starting. Yet all save the vessel might have been saved, but for the unfortunate command to back the engines, which had the effect, instead of easing the vessel, to dash her amidships upon the rocks, precipitating her fate; so that, in little more than half-an-hour, breaking in two, she went down, with 9 officers and 349 men, besides fully 80 of the crew. Whilst these so truly brave men were engulfed the prey of the insatiate sea, *the weak and helpless—the women and children, were all saved,* but only by such a noble sacrifice. The heart sickens as we contemplate so dreadful a scene, thus pathetically and feelingly narrated in the *New York Express:*—

"The steamer struck on a hidden rock, stove a plank at

the bows, and went to the bottom, we believe, in half-an-hour's time. There was a regiment of troops on board. As soon as the alarm was given, and it became apparent that the ship's fate was sealed, the roll of the drum called the soldiers to arms on the upper deck. That call was promptly obeyed, though every gallant heart there knew that it was his death summons. There they stood as if in battle array—a motionless mass of brave men—men who were men indeed. The ship every moment was going down and down—but there were no traitors, no deserters, no cravens there! The women and children were got into the boats, and were all, or nearly all, saved. There were no boats for the troops—but there was no panic, no blanched, pale, quivering lips among them! . . . . Men like these never perish; their bodies may be given to the fishes of the sea, but their memories are, as they ought to be—immortal!"

These, records the *Spectator*—"the very men whom we shrank from when we met them wearing flying ribbons in their battered hats, reeling through the streets—were the same who went down in the 'Birkenhead'—as which of us can feel sure that he would have had nerve to do?—in their ranks, shoulder to shoulder, standing at ease, watching the sharks that were waiting for them in the waves—at the simple suggestion of their officers that the women and children filled the boats, and must be saved first. No saint ever died more simply; no martyr ever died more voluntarily; no hero ever died more firmly; no victim ever met his fate in a more generous spirit of self-immolation."

Bravest of the brave, Lieut.-Colonel Seton of the Seventy-fourth, displayed in his conduct, as commander of the troops, a nobleness, a true courage, a self-sacrificing devotion, worthy of his country, and which bespeaks the *man* — the *hero;* and than which history or biography can furnish no brighter or more illustrious example. It is indeed a pity so brave a spirit should have fallen; and it shames the living—

> " That instinct
> Which makes the honour'd memory of the dead
> A trust with all the living—"

that no suitable memorial marks his fall, save the common tablet of a common grief for a common loss which stands in the corridor of Chelsea Hospital, bearing the following inscription :—

"This monument is erected by command of Her Majesty Queen Victoria, to record the heroic constancy and unbroken discipline shown by Lieutenant-Colonel Seton, Seventy-fourth Highlanders, and the troops embarked under his command, on board the 'Birkenhead,' when that vessel was wrecked off the Cape of Good Hope, on the 26th February, 1852, and to preserve the memory of the officers, non-commissioned officers, and men, who perished on that occasion, The names were as follows:—

" Lieut.-Colonel A. Seton, 74th Highlanders, Commanding the Troops.
   Cornet Rolt, Serjeant Straw, and three Privates, 12th Lancers.
   Ensign Boylan, Corporal M'Manus, and thirty-four Privates, 2d
      Queen's Regiment.
   Ensign Metford and forty-seven Privates, 6th Royals.

Fifty-five Privates, 12th Regiment.

Serjeant Hicks, Corporals Harrison and Cousins, and twenty-six Privates, 43d Light Infantry.

Three Privates, 45th Regiment.

Corporal Curtis and twenty-nine Privates, 60th Rifles.

Lieutenants Robinson and Booth, and fifty-four Privates, 73d Regiment.

Ensign Russell, Corporals Mathison and William Laird, and forty-six Privates, 74th Highlanders.

Serjeant Butler, Corporals Webber and Smith, and forty-one Privates, 91st Regiment.

Staff-Surgeon Laing.

Staff-Assistant-Surgeon Robertson."

> "Yet more! the billows and the depths have more!
> High hearts and brave are gather'd to thy breast!
> They hear not now the booming waters roar—
> The battle-thunders will not break their rest.
> Keep thy red gold and gems, thou stormy grave!
>   Give back the true and brave!"

In the last and most sanguinary war with the Kaffirs of South Africa, which desolated that valuable colony between 1850 and 1853, the Seventy-fourth was engaged, and fully sustained its illustrious character. The enemy, sensible of his weakness, avoided meeting our army in the field, and maintained a harassing series of skirmishes in the bush, which proved most annoying and destructive.

It is remarkable that, in the course of our sketch, we should so frequently have been pleasingly impressed with the duty of recording the heroism of the officers of the regiment; and, commanded by such distinguished chiefs, it is no wonder the corps, moulded in their image, should fitly follow the good and glorious examples which have rendered the Seventy-fourth

so signally known to fame. In the African campaign, its
commanding officers are mournfully conspicuous as amongst
the lost and brave. Whilst employed in the operations
against the Waterkloof Post in November, 1851, Lieutenant-
Colonel Fordyce was killed.

"At the moment he was hit, he was giving directions to a
company of his own well-loved corps, which was skirmishing
in the bush, and the position of which he wished to alter a
little. Whilst raising his arm to indicate the ground he
alluded to, a huge Hottentot stepped rapidly from a thick
clump close by, and delivered the fatal shot; observing, with
characteristic cunning, the irreparable mischief he had done,
he screeched out, in hellish accents, '*Johnny, bring stretcher,*'
and, turning on his heel, dived into the clump again before
the infuriated Seventy-fourth could wreak their vengeance
upon him.

"Simultaneously they madly rushed on, and, in their too
eager haste to renew the carnage, they rendered themselves an
easy prey to their savage foe, who struck down Lieutenants
Carey and Gordon, and many brave men, before they observed
the necessity of rallying, when the sad work of carnage was
amply avenged. Such, however, was the number of the
wounded, that a waggon had to be sent from the hill to the
spot to carry off the sufferers to their bivouac.

"Fordyce lived a quarter of an hour after receiving his
death-wound. The ball had passed through his abdomen;
and, as he was borne away in the consciousness of approaching
death, he was just able to utter, in faint accents, the words—

'*Take care of my poor regiment*—I AM READY,' when he passed placidly away. Such was the end of this brave soldier. In life, straightforward, thoughtful, a friend to the poor and needy, and a truly Christian man; so in death he was calm, resigned, noble, and mindful of his duty both to God and man. His latest expression showed that, while he committed his regiment to the care of those whose duty it was, his uppermost thoughts lay in the final work of meeting his Maker. Such was Fordyce, beloved and respected by all who had the good fortune to know him!"

The regiment left the Cape for India in November, 1853, and has since continued in the Madras establishment. During the Indian Mutiny, a detachment of the Seventy-fourth, in the autumn of 1857, formed part of a moveable column under Brigadier Whitlock, on field service in the Kurnool district; and, in November, 1858, the head quarters composed a portion of a moveable column, under Brigadier Spottiswoode, in the Nizam country. The regiment is now stationed at Bellary.

THE SEVENTY-EIGHTH HIGHLANDERS;

or,

ROSS-SHIRE BUFFS.

CHAPTER XXXVI.

"Rouse, rouse, ye kilted warriors!
Rouse, ye heroes of the north!
Rouse and join your chieftain's banners,—
'Tis your prince that leads you forth.

"See the northern clans advancing!
See Glengary and Lochiel!
See the brandish'd broad-swords glancing!
Highland hearts are true as steel."

CHANNEL ISLANDS—FLANDERS—CAPE OF GOOD HOPE—INDIA—
BATAVIA—1793–1817.

ALREADY had the noble lords of Seaforth stood forth foremost
in the breach where British liberty, involved in our glorious
constitution, was assailed by aggressive and vindictive foes;
already had the beloved chieftains of the Mackenzie bidden
their clansmen rally around the state, which a few years earlier
(1715) they had sworn to overthrow; already had the regiment

they thus contributed, the Seventy-second, illumined the page
of history by the stirring narrative of its brilliant achievements,
and, honoured by a grateful people, returned to its native
land, to rest for a time upon the laurels won on the far-distant
plains of India. Sprung from this race of heroes, as the new-
begotten and second representative of this distinguished
family in our army, the Seventy-eighth has strong claims
upon our interest and sympathy—an interest and sympathy
which have been quickened into a warm affection, finding
an echo in the soul of the brave and noble of every land.
Appreciating the gallantry of its services at Lucknow in behalf
of suffering valour and murdered innocence, we hail it with
feelings of national gratitude as the "Saviour of India."

Whilst the horrid cruelties perpetrated by the demagogues
of Paris excited the commiseration of beholding Europe for an
unfortunate and misguided people, the victims of their own
folly, it at the same time inspired feelings of fear among the
terror-stricken tyrants of the Continent, and palsied the might
of their councils. A momentary irresolution seized the British
Cabinet, until the energy and eloquence of Pitt awakened the
Government to its true duty. The charm which spell-bound
other states, failed to ravish us of our freedom. Thoroughly
aroused from the fatal lethargy into which the nation was
being lulled by false ideas of "liberty, equality, and fraternity"
—rightly interpreted, lust, rapine, and murder—it assumed a
sounder policy, befitting its dignity. Buckling on its armour,
Britain fearlessly challenged this giant iniquity to trespass
upon the sacred soil of our chartered and constitutional

liberty. Impelled by a stern necessity, our country laid aside
the beloved garb of peace, and assumed the dread panoply of
war, as our "meteor flag" was unfurled—

> "The flag which braved a thousand years
> The battle and the breeze."

Fleet after fleet forsook the tranquil bosom of the harbour
where hitherto they had nestled, and struggling with the
stormy billows of the sea, begirt our island home with those
"wooden walls" which, defended by our "hearts of oak," have
so long been our pride, and deemed impregnable; whilst
regiment after regiment mustered on the beach, daring the foe
to set foot upon these hallowed shores.

In such times the noble lord of Seaforth a second time
drew his father's sword, and with the valour and loyalty of
his house swelling in his breast, called on his clansmen yet
remaining to follow him. Foremost, in the very van of this
army of patriots, was thus marshalled the gallant subject of
our sketch—the Seventy-eighth Highlanders.

Assembled and embodied at Fort George on the 10th July,
1793, the fine physical appearance of the regiment was very
remarkable—a characteristic which it has been fortunate
always to maintain.

Guernsey, one of the Channel Islands, was the scene of its
earliest service on comparatively peaceful duty. Removed
from thence, in 1794, to Holland, it ultimately joined the
allied army, under the Duke of York, which vainly endeavoured to stem the tide of French aggression, then inundating
the Netherlands, and bereaving these provinces of their ancient

freedom. Engaged in the defence of Nimeguen, it contributed, by its excellent behaviour, to retard the progress of the enemy, whilst that fortress held out. Overwhelming might necessitated the evacuation of the place: the garrison in consequence retired with the army towards Germany. At Meteren our rearguard was overtaken by the advanced posts of the enemy, when a bloody action ensued. In the course of the fight the Seventy-eighth was charged by a regiment of French hussars, who, wearing a uniform similar to the regiment of Choiseul in the British service, and the better to deceive our troops, shouting as they advanced, "Choiseul! Choiseul!"—thus mistaken for friends—were permitted to penetrate our line, and were upon the Highlanders before their true character was discovered. Unmasked, in an instant the bold horsemen were met by a terrific volley of musketry, which, emptying many saddles, cooled the ardour of the assault, but could not arrest their progress. Piercing the intervals between the companies of the battalion, the cavalry furiously rushed upon the Highlanders, trampling them down, but, being warmly received, failed to overwhelm the gallant Seventy-eighth, whose firm, unflinching valour was very conspicuous, and altogether surprising from so young a corps in such trying circumstances. A column of infantry, which had witnessed the success of the cavalry, now advanced, big with high hopes, as they supposed, to complete the ruin of the British. Meanwhile the further career of the hussars had been stayed by the determined front of a company of the Forty-second Royal Highlanders, covering the village. Driven back in confusion upon the advancing infantry, both were finally repulsed, chiefly by the combined efforts of the Seventy-eighth and Forty-second Highlanders. The British resuming the retreat, retired to Bremen, whence they took shipping, and returned home. During this their maiden campaign, the Seventy-eighth was associated with the Seventy-ninth Cameron Highlanders and the Forty-second Royal Highlanders. The regiment was remarkable for its steadiness under fire, and its fortitude in enduring the hardships of a severe winter under canvas. On this occasion, too, a very melancholy and humbling testimony is borne by our foes to the prevailing sin of our British soldiers. The French, who had seduced the soldiers of the old monarchy by ministering to their evil appetites, sought by a like artifice to ruin our army; they accordingly bribed the infamous amongst the Dutch to sell liquors to our troops at a mere bagatelle, with a view to tempt them and intoxicate them. How truly lamentable to think that even then this national vice had acquired such a mastery, such a notoriety, as to be regarded by France as our weakness, and by the nation as our disgrace! Notwithstanding, we with pleasure record that the Seventy-eighth was faithful to its duty. Indeed, these seductions could not prevail against such a corps, whose history had ever been distinguished by sobriety; so much so, that while it was in India it was found necessary to restrict its soldiers from selling or giving away their own allowance of liquor to others.

Meanwhile a second battalion, raised in 1794, had sailed for, and participated in, an expedition against the Dutch colony of the Cape of Good Hope. After a brief struggle the colony was reduced and occupied by the British, the battalion remaining in the garrison.

The first battalion, with the army of Lord Moira, was engaged in a fruitless attempt to succour the Royalists of La Vendée, who yet withstood the ferocious assaults of the Republicans of Paris. Landing on the Isle Dieu, the expedition anxiously waited a favourable opportunity to gain a footing on the mainland. Alas! in vain. The time for action, frittered away, was not to be recalled. Returning to England, the battalion was embarked for Bengal. Calling on the way at the Cape of Good Hope, it was joined by the second battalion, and the two, consolidated into one regiment, proceeded to India. Arrived in February, 1797, nothing of importance falls to be recorded during its sojourn in the Bengal Presidency. Removed to Bombay in 1803, it joined the army of Major-General the Hon. Arthur Wellesley. With the Seventy-fourth Highlanders, the Eightieth Regiment, the Nineteenth Light Dragoons, and several native battalions, the Seventy-eighth advanced against the enemy—Scindia and the Rajah of Berar.

The strong fortress of Amednuggur was the first obstacle to be overcome in the line of march. For a while defended resolutely, the struggle was very severe, but the moment our Highlanders succeeded in scaling the high and narrow walls encircling it, to the enemy all seemed lost, defence appeared hopeless, and flight the only refuge. Thus this important conquest was achieved with comparatively little loss.

As in previous campaigns, so in the present, the business of the war seemed to be not so much to overcome but rather to overtake the enemy; who, sensible of his weakness in the field, strove to avoid the hazard of a battle, contenting himself with harassing our progress by a perplexing and incessant guerilla warfare. The persevering energy of the British commander was not, however, to be so duped of the prize he sought—the triumph he aspired to. By forced marches he overtook and surprised the foe by his unexpected presence on the banks of the Kaitna. Although not yet joined to the reinforcements at hand under Colonel Stevenson, from Bengal, and fearing the escape of the enemy under cover of the night, now approaching, the daring impetuosity of Wellesley at once ordered the attack. Reduced by detachments, the British army did not exceed 4,700 men, of whom the Seventy-fourth and Seventy-eighth Highlanders, and the Nineteenth Light Dragoons, were the only line regiments; whilst the Indian army, encamped in a strong position behind the almost dry channel of the Kaitna, occupied the village of Assaye, and presented a formidable array of 30,000 admirable troops, disciplined and led by European officers, the whole sustained by upwards of 100 guns. The Seventy-eighth occupied the left of the first line, whilst the Seventy-fourth, from the second line, ultimately took post on the right. But for the cowardly flight of the European officers commanding the Indian infantry, who abandoned their troops at the first onset, the resistance might have been far more formidable. The enemy's artillery was admirably served, and galled the advance of the British line with a terrible fire, which was only silenced by the death of the gunners, bayoneted whilst faithfully and steadily fulfilling their duty. In the ultimate retreat, one brigade refused to yield, although repeatedly charged by our cavalry; maintaining its order and retiring fighting, preserved the defeat from becoming a disorderly rout. The struggle was the most severe, and the achievement the most glorious which had hitherto marked our Indian warfare; illustrating the determined valour of which the enemy was capable, whilst anew it honoured the prowess of our soldiers in the result.

Strengthened by Colonel Stevenson's division, now arrived, including the old Ninety-fourth, or Scots Brigade, Major-General Wellesley continued to press the retiring foe, until, overtaken at Argaum, he made a brief stand. In the battle which ensued, whilst the Ninety-fourth occupied the left of the line, the Seventy-fourth and Seventy-eighth together upon the other flank, encountered the only considerable attack of the enemy; which, undertaken by a body of 800 furious fanatics, was sustained with exceeding valour, until the entire column had fallen before the veterans of Assaye. Notwithstanding the vigour of the assault, a very trifling loss was inflicted upon the British, and the enemy otherwise relinquished the field almost without a blow.

A quaint story is told by General Stewart of the piper of the Seventy-eighth, who, when the musicians were ordered at Assaye to attend to the wounded, esteeming himself included, had in consequence gone to the rear. This desertion his comrades attributed to fear, and the unfortunate piper, branded as a coward, felt the rebuke thus stingingly uttered: "Flutes and hautboys they thought could be well spared, but for the piper, who should always be in the heat of the battle, to go to the rear with the *whistlers*, was a thing altogether unheard of." Bitterly sensible of the unmerited insult, he gladly availed himself of a favourable opportunity at the battle of Argaum to blot out the stigma and redeem his fame. He played with such animation amidst the hottest of the fire, that, not only restored to his comrades' confidence, he entailed the commands of the colonel to be silent, lest the men so inspired should be urged too soon to the charge.

The war was soon after brought to a glorious termination by the fall of Gawilghur. Thereafter removed to Madras, the regiment remained in quietude till 1811, when, included in the army of Lieutenant-General Sir Samuel Auchmuty, it sailed with the expedition destined to operate against the valuable Dutch colony of Java. It required much severe fighting, especially at and around Cornelis—a very strong position, where the enemy, with concentrated might, maintained a resolute defence, only yielding when, with 1000 men killed, the post had become no longer tenable—ere the island was reduced. In this expedition the Seventy-eighth lost about 100 officers and men. Although the sword and the pestilence had each claimed its victims, still they failed to vanquish our Highlanders.

On the return voyage to India, a new enemy awaited the gallant Seventy-eighth, threatening even more fatal results— the sea, the ever-devouring sea. Six companies of the

regiment which had embarked in the "Frances Charlotte,"
transport, when twelve miles from the small island of Pre-
paros, on the 5th November, 1816, struck upon a sunken
rock. In this awful crisis, when the grim King of Terrors
confronted our soldiers, and this living freight of brave
men, women, and children, seemed about to be engulfed in
a watery grave, amid the consternation and wild dismay
inseparable from such a scene, the firm courage of our
Highlanders sustained them equally as amid the roar and
excitement of the battle-field. With heroic gallantry, the
soldiers, caring for the weakness of woman and the helplessness of childhood, nobly hazarding, prepared to sacrifice
their own lives that these might be saved, and so their duty
fulfilled. Instances of manly courage and true heroism like
these, tell us, in unequivocal language, that such are the fruit of
no mere idle sentiment and flitting emotion, but the result of
inborn, genuine character. Whilst the women and children
were conveyed in boats to the island, the men crowded upon a
small rocky islet, occasionally dry at low water, and situated
about 150 yards from the wreck. The ship, full of water,
soon after went to pieces, and disappeared beneath the waves.
The miseries of the ship-wrecked, from hunger and thirst, were
very grievous, and so cruel, that, although saved from becoming the prey of the sea, they seemed but preserved for a more
terrible doom. The gaunt visage of famine appeared to torment
the perishing multitude with the pangs of an unutterable woe,
and every ray of hope seemed eclipsed by the lowering darkness of despair and the dismal shroud of the grave. But a

merciful Providence was nearer to save. A vessel hove in
sight, and, responding to the hail of the men on the rock, sent
a boat to their aid, which took forty of the survivors on
board, but by a strange, unaccountable want of feeling, sailed
away without affording further assistance; leaving behind one
of its own boats, which, gone on the mission of mercy, and
whilst loading with a second instalment, had been upset by
over-crowding. Fortunately, all escaped safely, scrambling
back upon the rock. On the 10th of November, a large ship,
the "Prince Blucher," attracted by the vestiges of the wreck
which had floated seaward across her course, was drawn
towards the island, and embarking as many as possible, sailed
for Calcutta; from whence, on news of the disaster, other
vessels were immediately dispatched, which brought off in
safety the remainder of the survivors, who had endured the
severest pinchings of hunger with soldier-like stedfastness for
upwards of a month upon the island. It is interesting to note
how both the Seventy-fourth and Seventy-eighth Highlanders
should thus have encountered the disasters of the deep, and in
these vicissitudes evinced so worthily the qualities of the
soldier and the hero.

In 1817 the regiment returned to England, and disembarked at Portsmouth.

CHAPTER XXXVII.

" 'Twas a soldier who spoke—but his voice now is gone,
    And lowly the hero is lying;
No sound meets the ear, save the crocodile's moan,
    Or the breeze through the palm-tree sighing.
But lone though he rests where the camel is seen,
    By the wilderness heavily pacing;
His grave in our bosoms shall ever be green,
    And his monument ne'er know defacing."

GIBRALTAR—SICILY—MAIDA—EGYPT—WALCHEREN—
FLANDERS—1804–1817.

ALTHOUGH borrowing a good idea in pursuing a similar plan, we esteem ourselves excused, and not guilty of too slavish an imitation of General Stewart's account of the Seventy-eighth, in his excellent memoirs of the Highland regiments. Thus, having followed so far the history of the first battalion, we now devote a chapter to the annals of the second battalion, in which the distinguished officer above-named served with honour, exceedingly beloved by the soldiers; and to whom, as an author, we are largely indebted, having, by the vigour of his pen, rescued from the shades of oblivion and the crumbling ravages of time the history of our regiments and the peculiar characteristics of our clans, and so preserved ever fresh these endeared records of our brave clansmen and soldiers. Scotland had already largely contributed to the noble army of defenders which in 1804, during the momentous crisis in our national history of which that year was the scene, had gathered round the constitution and challenged the would-be invader.   Of the genuine Highlanders enlisted at this period, the following is a correct record:—

For the army of reserve,	1651
Militia—Inverness, Ross, Argyle, Perth, &c., &c.,	2599
Supplementary Ditto,	870
Canadian Fencibles,	850
Second Battalion of the Seventy-eighth Regiment,	714
Second Battalion of the Seventy-ninth Regiment,	618
Highlanders as substitutes in Militia regiments,	963
Recruits enlisted by the parties of the line, not exactly known, but estimated at,	850
Total,	8,615

The present battalion was the fourth raised by the family of Seaforth within twenty-five years.   It contained many Islesmen, especially from the island of Lewis.   Although to all appearance little else than a regiment of boys of very tender years, still they had within them the soul of the man, as after events abundantly proved.   Embodied at Fort George in the winter of 1804–5 with a strength of 850, it was by request of Major-General Moore placed under his command for purposes of instruction in the new system of light infantry drill.   This was a fortunate circumstance, and no doubt helped the battalion, not merely in the acquirement of a thorough military knowledge, but more especially served to instil a due confidence, which gave it that steadiness in action for which it was afterwards remarkable.   The urgent requirements of the

service having occasioned the removal of the battalion to
reinforce the garrison of Gibraltar, it was early deprived of
the benefits flowing from such an excellent course of training
under so able a master of the science of war. Nevertheless, it
had so improved the advantage which for a brief period it
enjoyed, as made it a valuable addition to the garrison.

From Gibraltar it proceeded to Sicily, to join the arma-
ment, under Sir John Stuart, destined for a descent upon the
mainland of Calabria, in favour of the exiled monarch of
Naples and the patriots of Italy. The expedition, which sailed
from Melazzo in June, 1805, included the Twenty-seventh,
Fifty-eighth, Seventy-eighth, Eighty-first, and Watteville's
Swiss Regiment, afterwards reinforced by the Twentieth
Regiment. Landing successfully in the bay of St Euphemia,
the British General strove to anticipate the attack of the
French under General Regnier, who, with a force lately
augmented to nearly 8000, stood opposed to the British, who
could scarce muster 4000 men, unsustained, moreover, by
cavalry. The enemy occupied a very strong position in the
vicinity of the village of Maida. Affecting to despise the
handful of British who had ventured to challenge the assault,
Regnier, forsaking his strong position, descended to the plains,
boasting he should drive the British into the sea. The two
armies advanced in hostile array in parallel lines across the
plain, halting when within a few hundred yards, and pouring
in a deadly volley upon each other. The precision of the
British fire so shattered the first line of the enemy, that,
broken, it retired in confusion upon the second line, and there

struggled to maintain itself against the attack of our first brigade, comprising the Seventy-eighth and Eighty-first regiments under Brigadier-General Acland. A Swiss regiment bearing the name of its commanding officer, Watteville, at this crisis of the fight advanced against the Seventy-eighth, and mistaken, from its similarity of uniform, for the corps of the same name, family, and nation in the British service, which held post in reserve, our Highlanders ceased firing, lest they should injure their supposed friends. When undeceived, a vigorous fire warmly hailed the enemy, and drove back the Swiss with great slaughter. Beaten thus in every quarter, General Regnier proposed, as a last resource, to try the effect of a flank attack upon the Twenty-seventh regiment. Providentially, the Twentieth regiment arriving on the field at this moment, hastened to sustain their comrades, and by their unexpected appearance so discouraged the foe, that the attack, languidly undertaken, was speedily given over. The French now gave way at all points, and retreated precipitately, so swiftly, that without cavalry they could not be overtaken—General Regnier falling a prisoner into our hands.

General Stuart had at first been grievously disappointed in the boyish appearance of the Seventy-eighth, 600 of whom were under twenty-one years of age; but now felt constrained to confess their gallant conduct unsurpassed; having vanquished the veteran troops of France, although fighting under great disadvantages in the front line of this their maiden engagement. Unfortunately, the British, unsupported, were

unable to do more than destroy the enemy's arsenals and
magazines at Monte Leon, ere prudence counselled their return
to Sicily.

Insignificant in itself, the result of the battle of Maida
exerted an important influence over Europe. Although the
numbers respectively engaged were small, still—occurring at a
time and in circumstances when European liberty groaned in
chains, and all the blessings which belonged to it seemed to be
eclipsed in the dark night of tyranny, and when the sovereigns
of the Continent had submitted to the imperious yoke of
Bounaparte, when the friendly light of hope, flickering, seemed
to die out—the battle and the victory of Maida revived the
drooping spirit of Freedom, restored to new life the palsied
pulse of Europe, and bade her many peoples awake from the
stupor of terror which the shackles of an iron despotism and
the cruel spoilings of rapacious might had imposed! It
required years of sore suffering and desperate struggling ere
the monster which so preyed upon the vitals of liberty could
be shaken off; and, emancipated from the oppressor's grasp,
the nations one by one once more breathed somewhat of the
blessed air of freedom.

Against their better feelings and judgment the Turks had
been cajoled into an alliance with France, and unwillingly as
our enemies, their territory in Egypt became the theatre of
strife, whereon a British army should again act. Accordingly,
in 1807, Lieutenant-General Sir John Moore arrived in Sicily
from England, and assumed the command of the enterprise.
In the army which set sail from Sicily for Egypt, the second

battalion of the Seventy-eighth Highlanders was included. Landed, the expedition, flattered by various successes, continued to advance towards Alexandria; but the Turks, in their peculiar mode of warfare, and their aptness in taking advantage of every favourable circumstance in defence, proved more terrible enemies than even the French, inflicting severe and heavy losses upon the British. In an attempt to gain possession of the town of Rosetta, the Thirty-first Regiment was nearly annihilated by the fire of the enemy from loop-holed houses in the narrow streets, who could not be dislodged. This attack in consequence failed; and the troops had to mourn the loss of its leader, Major-General Wauchope, whilst his second in command, Brigadier-General Meade, was wounded.

With hopes of facilitating and securing the friendly and promised aid of the Mamelukes, a detachment of 720 men, under Lieutenant-Colonel Macleod, was advanced on the 20th of April to an important outpost of the army at El Hamet, on the Nile. The detachment, consisting of a party from De Rolle's Regiment, two companies of the Thirty-fifth, and five companies of the Seventy-eighth, was divided into three divisions, and stationed accordingly. On the morning of the 21st, about seventy large boats filled with armed men were seen descending the Nile, whilst several corps of horsemen gathered around the detachment, and at once assailed the right of the three divisions, at the same time so surrounding the others as to prevent them rendering any assistance to one another, or drawing together into one. The right division, comprising the Highland Grenadiers and a company of the

Thirty-fifth, fought with the fury of lions at bay, and was utterly cut to pieces, along with its gallant commander, who, whenever he had perceived the peril of the post, hastened to rescue it or die with the brave. The little phalanx of heroes, reduced to eleven, attempted to break through the host of foes which beleaguered them, and so join their comrades in the centre division. Unfortunately, most of them perished in the attempt. Captain Mackay, the only surviving officer, was struck to the ground by a blow on the neck from the scimitar of an Arab horseman in pursuit. The blow failing to kill, by a miracle of mercy he was saved, and carried in by his serjeant. The remaining divisions, conscious how unavailing any resistance would be, surrendered, and after being brutally plundered, were conducted in triumph prisoners to Cairo, where the vanity and the hatred of the people were gratified in the parade of the captives through the principal streets of the city for seven hours; exposed, moreover, to indignities of the grossest kind—"These," said they, "are our British *friends*, who came from their ships to kill us and our children." The Pacha, however, sincerely sympathising, behaved with great kindness, and did his utmost to screen the prisoners from the blind wrath of the public, expressing his deep regret that Britain should have become so involved in war with his Government, which had been long accustomed to regard the British as friends and allies—never as foes.

In consequence of the disaster at El Hamet, the siege of Rosetta was abandoned, and our army, retreating to Alexandria, thence negotiated for the release of the prisoners, and

agreeing to evacuate Egypt, returned to Sicily. Of the captives thus released, a *drummer* of the Seventy-eighth, by name
Macleod, who had occasionally assisted the surgeon of the
regiment in applying poultices, etc., choosing to remain behind
in Cairo, by a somewhat extraordinary metamorphosis, set up
for a *physician*, and by consummate assurance attained a large
practice and acquired a larger fortune. From Sicily the battalion was removed to Lisbon, and thereafter ordered home to
England, where it arrived in 1808. Subsequently transferred
to Scotland to recruit, it forwarded large detachments of very
superior volunteers from its ranks to the first battalion, then
fighting in India.

In 1809 a corps of 370 men was battalionized under the
Hon. Lieutenant-Colonel Cochrane, and embarked for Zealand,
where it shared the disasters of the Walcheren expedition,
afterward returning to the Isle of Wight.

In 1813, as a small corps of 400 Highlanders, the second
battalion of the Seventy-eighth joined the army of Lieutenant-
General Sir Thomas Graham, afterwards Lord Lynedoch,
which endeavoured to expel the French from Holland. On
the 13th January, with the second battalion of the Twenty-
fifth and the Thirty-third regiments, it encountered the
enemy at Merexem, where it behaved with signal gallantry—an immediate charge with the bayonet by the
Seventy-eighth, ordered by Lieutenant-Colonel Lindsay,
decided the contest." The enemy was beaten with great
slaughter. At this period the juvenility of the battalion was
as remarkable as its valour—only 43 of its soldiers exceeding

twenty-two years of age. The battalion remained in the
Netherlands until after the battle of Waterloo, but stationed
at Nieuport, was deprived of the privilege of being present on
that memorable and glorious field. Nevertheless, it added to
its good name by its excellent conduct, becoming peculiarly
endeared to the Belgians, who spoke of the Highlanders as
being "kind, as well as brave;" "Enfans de la famille;" "Lions
in the field and lambs in the house"—so much so, that the
citizens of Brussels petitioned the mayor to request the
General-in-Chief to allow the Seventy-eighth to remain in
garrison in that capital.

Returning to Scotland in 1816, the battalion was subsequently incorporated with the first battalion as one regiment
on its return from India—conveying, with its few remaining
soldiers, a character for firmness truly remarkable in such
young soldiers, and adding the glories of Maida and Egypt to
those of Assaye and Java, acquired by the first battalion, and
now one in the Seventy-eighth.

CHAPTER XXXVIII.

But hark! what means yon dismal wail—
The shriek that's borne upon the gale?
It comes from India's sultry plain—
It calls for vengeance from the slain,
          Nor calls in vain to Scotland.

'Tis the destroying hordes of hell,
Whose hearts with fiendish passions swell,
Whose swords on ruined Beauty fell—
The Brave, the Fair, the Weak.   Farewell!
          Ye'll be revenged by Scotland.

Then Scotland, by brave Havelock led,
Rush'd o'er the field of murder'd dead,
Fighting for "bleeding Beauty's" sake—
The very earth itself might quake
          Beneath the wrath o' Scotland.

Haste ye to Lucknow's fainting brave;
Too long they've battled with the slave—
The weak and helpless Fair to save
From rapine, ruin, and the grave—
          Hope comes wi' bonnie Scotland.

And now brave Havelock's work is done;
He sets like to the evening sun;
By him the crown of glory's won—
His God, beholding, saith "Well done!"
          The Lost—the Loved o' Scotland.

PERSIA—INDIA—1817–1862.

ESCAPING from the tedious details of peaceful service which
for upwards of forty years mark the history of the Seventy-

eighth, we now follow that gallant regiment to India—the
scene of its early glory, and since embalmed in our memory,
as presenting the most splendid testimony to its heroic
character.

In 1857 we find it transferred from Bombay to Persia,
and engaged in the expedition destined to chastise its vain-
glorious and presumptuous monarch. An easy triumph crowned
the efforts of our arms. At Koosh-ab the Seventy-eighth was
present with credit; although that success was achieved rather
by diligent perseverance in long marches and battling with
inclement weather, than by any very remarkable feat of arms.
This name and that of "Persia" were gained for the regimental colour during the campaign, in scenery hallowed by
sacred memories, being supposed to be the site of the garden
of Eden.

But we hasten to look upon a darker picture—to find our
Indian empire on the verge of ruin, convulsed as in the agonies
of dissolution; its native military, whom we had trusted and
boasted, become traitors; their smothered vengeance, cherished
through years of duplicity, bursting forth to deluge our vast
dominion, and almost wrest it from us by a cruel rebellion;
all that once gloried in the very name of British doomed by
an unpitying and relentless revenge to utter destruction, consigned to be the subjects of a gigantic perfidy. The mine had
exploded, and awful were the horrors of the tragedy it
revealed! Helplessness consumed by the devouring sword;
beauty wasted by demons of lust and passion; hopeless
bravery sacrificed to satisfy a bloody appetite—whilst with

fiendish shouts the villains gloated over the murders in which their hands were embrued and which stained their souls, and rejoiced in the atrocities they had committed.

Never was the British soldier placed in circumstances so trying, and never did he display such heroism—a heroism which, equal to the emergency, was alone able to deliver him from the foul conspiracy of 150,000 armed and trained rebels, who encircled him and thirsted vehemently for his blood.

Delhi, the great central tower of rebellious strength, was the scene of months of hard fighting and sore privation; but over all these British valour triumphing, was rewarded in the reduction of that important stronghold, and the utter discomfiture of its daring defenders. But Lucknow reversed the picture. There we find the British besieged by a countless host of the enemy; there we regard a handful of brave men resolved to sell their lives as dearly as possible, rather than yield to the ruthless rebels who in multitudes encompassed the Residency. To save the brave garrison from the terrible fate which threatened them, and release the crowd of starving and emaciated women and children who, claiming the protection of the soldier, had found shelter there—to save and relieve these, a little army might have been seen advancing by rapid marches, encountering the greatest dangers, and eagerly pressing onwards to avenge their slaughtered friends. Stirred to marvellous achievements by the appalling traces of massacre perpetrated on the helpless and innocent, and which were too apparent all around—roused to heroic action, nerved to meet death or conquer in the awful and unequal struggle,

the little army of Brigadier-General Havelock pressed vigor-
ously forward to help and to avenge. It comprised of
European Troops: The third company of the eighth battalion
of Royal Artillery, (76 men); the First Madras Fusiliers, (376
men); the Sixty-fourth Regiment of Foot, (435 men); the
Seventy-eighth Highlanders, (284 men); the Eighty-fourth
Regiment of foot, (190 men); Bengal Artillery, (22 men);
Volunteer Cavalry, (20 men). *Native Troops:* Ferozepore
Regiment, (448 men); the Thirteenth Irregular, and the Third
Oude Irregular Cavalry, (95 men); Galundauze (18 men).

From Cawnpore the rebels had pushed forward to Futteh-
pore, purposing to destroy a small detachment of British under
Major Renaul, but these having succeeded in effecting a
timeous junction with the army of Havelock, the mutineers,
amounting to 3,500, were encountered by that chief, and in a
few minutes totally routed. The victory was ascribed by the
conqueror "to the British artillery, to the Enfield rifle, to
British pluck, and to the blessing of Almighty God."

On the 15th July Brigadier-General Havelock came up with
the enemy first at the village of Aeng, and next at the bridge
over the Pandoo Nudee, and was successful in each instance.
Anew in position under Nena Sahib (Doondoo Punt), the
rebels made a momentary stand at Ahirwa, but were immediately defeated by a brilliant charge of our Highlanders. The
arch-traitor Nena Sahib, finding himself closely pressed by the
British column, and unable to defend Cawnpore, retired from
that fortress, after having, with savage barbarity, massacred
the women and children who by the foulest perfidy had fallen

into his power. The remains of these victims of his cruelty were afterwards discovered in the bottom of a well; and the horrors of the tragedy are said so to have moved the soul of our Highlanders, that, vowing an oath of vengeance on the blood-stained spot, they were stirred to redeem it on subsequent occasions. Pursuing the enemy in the course of his memorable march to Lucknow, Havelock defeated a strong body of rebels gathered near Unao. Thrice he attacked, and thrice he routed the mutineers who had as often congregated at Busherut Gunge, and once at Bithoor. Cholera attacking the British troops, so crippled the little army that, surrounded by foes, Havelock was compelled to delay his further advance until reinforced by Sir James Outram. On the arrival of these fresh troops on 16th September, the command, by seniority, devolved upon Sir James Outram; but with a chivalrous feeling highly to be admired, that excellent officer waived his claim, desiring Major-General Havelock to finish the good work he had so well begun and was so nigh gloriously completing, Sir James serving in subordination as a volunteer.

"On the 19th and 20th of September, the relieving force, amounting to about two thousand five hundred men, and seventeen guns, crossed the Ganges. The Fifth Fusiliers, Eighty-fourth, detachments of the Sixty-fourth, and First Madras Fusiliers, composed the first infantry brigade, under Brigadier-General Neill; the Seventy-eighth Highlanders, Ninetieth Light Infantry, and the Sikh Ferozepore Regiment, made up the second brigade, under Brigadier Hamilton of the Seventy-eighth; Major Cooper commanded the artillery brigade, consisting of Captains Maude, Oliphant, and Major Eyre's batteries; Captain Borrow commanded the Volunteers and Irregular Cavalry."

Having distributed the army, Havelock resumed his forward march, and after encountering several powerful bodies of the rebels, and always with the same success as hitherto, Lucknow was reached, and the beleaguered and almost despairing garrison relieved. This happy result was dearly purchased by the death of Brigadier-General Neill, a most gallant and able officer. Colonel Hamilton, who led the Seventy-eighth amid these labyrinthian dangers, won a distinguished name by his valour and coolness in many critical moments.

Most deeply regretted, the hero who had achieved this crowning triumph fell asleep in the very arms of victory. The living exponent of all that was truly noble, generous, brave, and heavenly, entered into his rest, there to enjoy the better blessing of his God, to wear the crown of glory which cannot fade, and which is more to be desired than all the perishing treasures of earth, the gilded pageant of a world's renown, or even the fitful gratitude of his country. Such was the death of Sir Henry Havelock, which almost immediately followed the final relief of Lucknow by our deservedly favourite chieftain, Sir Colin Campbell (now Lord Clyde).

> "Brave Havelock's gone! let Britain mourn—
> Her brightest, boldest hero's gone;
> Strew Indian laurels round his tomb,
> For there he glorious triumphs won.

"There he accomplished deeds of might,
    Which stamp'd him bravest of the brave—
Cut through a host, put foes to flight,
    And helpless prisoners dared to save.

"A Christian warrior—stern, yet mild,
    He fought for Heaven, his Saviour's home,
Yet shrunk not from the battle-field,
    Where all his talents brightly shone.

"But now Death's mandate from on high
    His Father called; he was prepared
For mansions sure beyond the sky;
    Earth's honours could not him reward.

"And now he's buried with the brave—
    His battle's fought, his vict'ry's won;
His country's cause he died to save,
    Nor sunk until his work was done.

"Let England, then, embalm his name—
    'Mongst heroes he may justly shine;
For soldier he of nobler fame—
    His banner bore the stamp Divine."

In the latter defence of Lucknow the Seventy-eighth sustained a prominent and a very honourable part, cheerfully enduring the privations of a straitened and continued siege, and ever foremost in repelling the foe when he dared to attack.

The heart of the Scottish people followed with a yearning interest the movements of the Seventy-eighth throughout this memorable campaign. With gratitude our countrymen hailed the regiment, when a kind Providence recently restored it to its native land, where every grade of society united to do honour to that bravery which so conspicuously graced our national history upon the dismal page of the Indian mutiny, and in commemoration thereof a monument has been erected in Edinburgh, an Illustration of which is given in this work. We close our sketch with the feeling that words have failed to express the just admiration with which we must ever regard this, the "scion of the Seaforth," the "Saviour of India."

THE SEVENTY-NINTH FOOT;

OR,

CAMERON HIGHLANDERS.

CHAPTER XXXIX.

" There's many a man of the Cameron clan
　　That has follow'd his chief to the field;
He has sworn to support him, or die by his side,
　　For a Cameron never can yield.

"Oh! proudly they walk, but each Cameron knows
　　He may tread on the heather no more;
But boldly he follows his chief to the field,
　　Where his laurels were gathered before."

THERE is perhaps no name so deeply interesting in the annals
of the Highlanders as that of Cameron; no clan so truly the
exponent of all that is brave and noble, and none whose chief
has been so largely the exemplar in his life of all the god-like
qualities of the man, the patriot, and the hero, and whose
memory is so fondly cherished and so highly revered. Such
was the illustrious leader of the clan, Sir Ewen Cameron of
Lochiel—

" The crested Lochiel, the peerless in might."

The Camerons by their conspicuous patriotism, marching under the banner of the Lord of the Isles at the battle of Bannockburn, contributed to illumine the page of our ancient glory.

> " Bruce, with the pilot's wary eye,
> The slackening of the storm could spy.
> 'One effort more, and Scotland's free!
> Lord of the Isles, my trust in thee
>   Is firm as Ailsa Rock;
> Rush on with Highland sword and targe,
> I, with my Carrick spearmen, charge;
>   Now, forward to the shock!'
> At once the spears were forward thrown,
> Against the sun the broadswords shone;
> The pibroch lent its maddening tone,
> And loud King Robert's voice was known—
> 'Carrick, press on—they fail, they fail!
> Press on, brave sons of Innisgail,
>   The foe is fainting fast!
> Each strike for parent, child, and wife,
> For Scotland, liberty, and life—
>   The battle cannot last!'"

But the clan attained even a greater reputation from its devoted loyalty to the Stuarts, and its gallant efforts in their cause, especially when led by Sir Ewen Cameron of Lochiel.

This chief was born in 1629, and educated at Inverary Castle by his foster-father, the Marquis of Argyll. Fascinated by the chivalrous bearing of Montrose, at the early age of eighteen he deserted his early patron, mustered his clansmen, and proceeded to join the rebel army. Ere he could accomplish his intention, the tide of war had turned against the Royalists, and swept away the army of Montrose. Retaining his clansmen in arms around him, he most effectually protected his estates from the incursions of the soldiers of Cromwell.

In 1652, the Earl of Glencairn, setting up the Royal standard, received the ready co-operation of Lochiel against the Republicans. Jealousy and distrust estranging the Royalist chiefs, creeping into and distracting their counsels, breaking the bond of union otherwise so mighty an agent to success— Lochiel, keeping aloof from these troubles at head-quarters, acting independently, effectively shielded the Royal army in its consequent weakness, delaying the ruin which ultimately overtook this unfortunate attempt to restore the kingdom to Charles II. His exploits savour of the marvellous and romantic; nevertheless, they in truth displayed the heroism of his character and the genius of a master-mind in the business of war. On one occasion a party of 300 soldiers had been sent to ravage his estates around Inverlochy. Hastily collecting thirty-eight of his clan, with a fearlessness amounting almost to rashness, despite the remonstrances of the sager veterans of his little band, to whose experiences he replied, "If every man kills his man, I will answer for the rest," he descended upon the unsuspecting troops with the utmost fury, when a desperate and bloody struggle ensued. But nothing, not even superior numbers, could withstand so furious an attack by the Camerons. Steadily fighting, the soldiers slowly retreated to the boats from which they had landed, leaving 138 of their comrades dead on the shore, whilst the loss of the Highlanders only amounted to seven men.

By many such deeds of daring, in which he always

displayed prodigies of valour, to his foes he appeared a dread
avenger, but to his friends he was known as a sure protector.
When all other opposition to its rule had been overcome by a
victorious Protectorate, Lochiel remained in arms for his King,
unconquered, and seemingly unconquerable. Bribery could
not purchase the submission of so noble a spirit, and persua-
sion failed to gain over the allegiance of so faithful an
adherent of the exiled monarch. Fortunately, the good
policy of Cromwell effected an honourable compromise, consistent with the dignity of this brave yet haughty chieftain,
which put an end to the cruel war which had already
exhausted the resources, and if persevered in, must have
exterminated the gallant Camerons. Unable to win his
alliance, the Protector wisely contented himself with a simple
peace.

Consistent with his ancient loyalty, when the Revolution of
1688 had expatriated the last and degenerate representative of
the unfortunate race of Stuart, and set up a new and a better
order of things in the State by the installation of the family of
Orange on the British throne, Lochiel joined the party of King
James, and resolutely determined to uphold his standard as
unfurled in rebellion in 1689. Unsullied by the baser motives
of ambition and revenge which had driven Viscount Dundee
into rebellion, Lochiel devoted his sword to what he esteemed
the righteous cause of his rightful sovereign, who had been set
aside by the claims of a usurper. In the battle of Killiecrankie, the charge of the Camerons and Highlanders led by
Lochiel was irresistible, and contributed largely to the attain-

ment of the victory. It so happened (not uncommon in those civil wars) on this occasion that the second son of Lochiel commanded a company in the opposing army of King William. Attached to the staff of General Mackay, that commander, on viewing the array and position of the Highlanders, remarked to the young Lochiel—" There," said he, " is your father with his wild savages; how would you like to be with him?" " It signifies little," replied the other, "what I would like; but I recommend it to you to be prepared, or perhaps my father and his wild savages may be nearer to you before night than you would like." And so it happened. Dundee delayed his attack " till," according to an eye-witness, " the sun's going down, when the Highlandmen advanced on us like madmen, without shoes or stockings, covering themselves from our fire with their targets. At last they cast away their muskets, drew their broadswords, and advanced furiously upon us, broke us, and obliged us to retreat; some fled to the water, some another way."

This great chief died at the ripe age of eighty-nine in 1718, universally regretted.

His grandson participating in the rebellion of 1745, occasioned the ruin of his family, and to a large extent destroyed the military strength of the clan. Nevertheless, in 1775 we find the Camerons represented by a company in Fraser's Highlanders, and as " Lochiel's men " combatting with distinction in America, on the side of that Government which a few years earlier they had conspired to overturn.

In addition to the Seventy-ninth Regiment, now the only

living representative of the clan in the British army, the Camerons contributed, in 1799, a corps of fencible militia—the "Lochaber" Regiment.

The menacing aspect of affairs abroad, the political wrongs perpetrated by revolutionary France, and the dark cloud which threatened to envelope our own land in 1794, occasioned the augmentation of our army; and, in consequence, the Seventy-eighth (Mackenzie), Seventy-ninth (Cameron), Ninety-second (Gordon), and Ninety-third (Sutherland) Highlanders sprung into being about this period.

Immediately upon the completion of the Seventy-ninth it was hurried into action, and on the plains of Flanders made its *début* in arms. It was with the army of the Duke of York which vainly strove to arrest the victorious career of the armies of republican France, led by these famous soldiers, Pichegru, Moreau, Jourdan, and Vandamme.

Returning home in 1795, it was thence removed to the West Indies, and for two years was stationed in Martinique. After contributing variously to recruit other corps, especially the Forty-second Royal Highlanders, it returned home a mere skeleton, around which, as a nucelus, the officers succeeded, after many and persevering efforts, in raising a new Highland corps, under the old designation.

On attaining a strength of 780 men, chiefly by the zealous exertions of its original colonel, Allan Cameron of Errach, it was ordered on foreign service, and so, in 1799, joined the expedition destined to act against the enemy in Holland. There, placed in the fourth brigade under Major-General afterwards Sir John Moore, it was associated with the second battalion of the First Royals, the Twenty-fifth King's Own Borderers, the Forty-ninth Foot, and the Ninety-second Gordon Highlanders. In all the actions which marked this brief and ineffectual campaign, the Seventy-ninth was worthily distinguished, and won the memorial thereof now borne upon its colours—"Egmont-op-Zee."

In the Egyptian expedition of 1800, under Sir Ralph Abercromby, the Seventy-ninth was brigaded with the Second or Queen's and the Fiftieth Regiments, commanded by the Earl of Cavan.

Having helped to the deliverance of Egypt from the yoke of France, it returned to England in 1801. Whilst at home it was increased by a second battalion raised in 1804, when the vindictive wrath of Napoleon, roused into madness by the defeat of his armies by the British in Egypt, had gathered a countless host around Boulogne, whence, looking across, he longed but once to set foot upon our shores, and then he hoped to blot us out from the map as a nation, and so satisfy the bitter hatred of years. Whilst the tempest of human passion stood arrayed in portentous awfulness on the other side of the Channel, the Seventy-ninth was with our troops who anxiously waited the result. Suddenly the spirit of the imperial dream was changed, and the armed multitude, melting away, reappeared with a real terror upon the devoted plains of Germany.

Allied with Napoleon, the Danes, in 1807, once more were pressed into a quarrel with Britain. A British armament

appeared upon the coasts of Denmark. Our army, under
Lieutenant-General Lord Cathcart, consisting of the first battalions of the 2d (Coldstream) and 3d (Scots Fusileers) Foot
Guards; first battalions of the 4th, 7th, 8th, 23d, 28th, 32d,
43d, 50th, 52d (second battalion), 79th (Cameron), 82d, 92d
(Gordon), and five companies of the first and second battalions
of the 95th (Rifles), and several regiments of the King's German Legion, comprising a total of 28,000, of which 17,000
were British, advanced upon Copenhagen, overcame all opposition, occupied the capital, arrested the enemy's fleet, and having achieved this almost bloodless victory, baffled the deep-laid
schemes of Napoleon, charged with our destruction.

CHAPTER XL.

"Though my perishing ranks should be strew'd in their gore,
Like ocean-weeds heaped on a surf-beaten shore,
Lochiel, untainted by flight or by chains,
While the kindling of life in his bosom remains,
Shall victor exult, or in death be laid low,
With his back to the field, and his feet to the foe!
And, leaving in battle no blot on his name,
Look proudly to heaven from the death-bed of fame."

PENINSULA—WATERLOO—CRIMEA—INDIA—1808–1862.

In 1808 the Seventy-ninth was included in the army of Sir
John Moore, which endeavoured to aid the Spaniards and
Portuguese to rescue their country from the crushing tyranny
of France. But what could 25,000 men, however brave, do
against 300,000 veterans, concentrated under the command of
experienced officers, and now advanced to destroy the daring
handful of British who had presumed to penetrate the heart
of the Peninsula? We have already described the masterly
manœuvres which extricated our army from a position of great
peril when in presence of so powerful a foe, and at the battle
of Corunna gloriously arrested the further pursuit of the
French. The Cameron Highlanders were brigaded with the
Thirty-sixth and Eighty-second regiments, under Brigadier-
General Fane, but not actively engaged.

On the return of the regiment to England, it was shortly
ordered to Holland, there to be engaged in a new effort for
the deliverance of that country. Landed with the army of the

Earl of Chatham in Walcheren, it was soon found impracticable to force the position of the French, who, nearer their own resources than in Spain, were not so easily overcome. Fever breaking out among the troops, so thinned the ranks, that of near 40,000 effectives, scarce a half returned fit for duty.

Long and sorely had our soldiers struggled to overcome the gigantic tyranny of France, but like the many-headed monster of heathen fiction, no sooner was one head wounded, than a new one appeared to challenge the attack. So, scarcely had we succeeded in one quarter ere the foe arose in terrible strength in another. Thus we find our armies, sometimes in Flanders, sometimes in the Peninsula, sometimes in Egypt, sometimes in India, and sometimes in America, waging a desperate and incessant war with this Gorgon-headed enemy.

In 1810 we once more return to Spain, where happily more permanent results were to be achieved. Thither the Seventy-ninth had gone to join the army of Lord Wellington.

At the battle of Fuentes d'Onor (Fountain of Honour) the conduct of the regiment was beyond all praise. Occupying that village with the Seventy-first Highlanders and Twenty-fourth Foot, the Seventy-ninth was exposed to the most furious assaults of strong columns of French. Occasionally driven out of the village, yet always returning to recover it—which an indomitable perseverance ever accomplished—triumphing over all opposition, this key of the position was ultimately retained. These regiments thus deservedly acquired the largest share of the glory flowing from such a victory.

From the battle of Salamanca it advanced with the army

which occupied Madrid. In the subsequent siege of the strong
castle of Burgos, the valour of the regiment was most conspicuous, and in the several assaults its losses were very considerable. Unfortunately, the approach of a powerful relieving
force snatched the anticipated prize from our grasp, arresting
the further progress of the siege, and necessitating the retreat
of the British towards Portugal.

Although for the present retiring, the effects of these
campaigns were very different upon the combatants. The
British, elated with hope, incited to perseverance, brought a
new and living energy into the field when the rest of the
winter had passed away and the operations of the war been
resumed in the spring. On the other hand, the French—
depressed by the evil tidings of the Grand Army in Russia;
tired, moreover, with incessant yet fruitless fightings; disunited
by discontent, privation, and jealousy—when the season once
more invited action, found their armies dispirited and disorga-
nised. No wonder, then, that the forward march of the British
led to a series of victories ever gracing our arms, until, surmounting the natural barriers of the Pyrenees, our troops
descended into the plains of France in the day of that country's
humiliation. In the various actions of the "Pyrenees," the
Seventy-ninth was not seriously engaged.

It was present at the passage of the "Nivelle" and the
"Nive." On the latter occasion it was specially distinguished
for its well-directed fire, which caused great havoc in the
dense masses of the enemy which strove to defend the passage.

At the battle of Toulouse, in the brigade of General

Pack, with the Forty-second Royal Highlanders and the Ninety-first (Argyllshire) Regiment, the Seventy-ninth was engaged in a desperate attack which carried a redoubt strongly situated, and resolutely defended, on the crest of a series of heights on the right of the position. A French officer, witnessing the advance of the Highlanders, exclaimed, "My God! how firm these *sans culottes* are!" Another French officer in conversation said of them, "Ah! these are brave soldiers. I should not like to meet them unless well supported. I put them to the proof on that day, for I led the division of more than 5000 men which attempted to retake the redoubt." A British officer, high in command, thus yields his testimony to the valour of the brigade: "I saw your old friends the Highlanders in a most perilous position; and had I not known their firmness, I should have trembled for the result."

On the abdication of Napoleon, peace for a time dispelled the thunder-storm of war, and permitted the return of the regiment to Britain. His escape from Elba again threatened to crush out the reviving spirit of liberty beneath the iron heel of his sanguinary tyranny. Happily for Europe and for France, the convulsive effort by which he strove to redeem and avenge the past was utterly defeated by his total discomfiture at Waterloo, for ever dissipating his dream of conquest, and closing his ambitious career.

Purposing to sever the British from the Prussians, and beat each in detail ere the Austrian and Russian armies could arrive from Germany to resume the war, Napoleon, by one of those rapid marches for which he was so famous, suddenly falling

upon and defeating the Prussians at Ligny, turned with the
full weight of his power against the British, who were already
engaged in a desperate struggle with the corps of Marshal Ney
at Quatre Bras—fitly introducing the grander event of Waterloo. Although impetuously assailed by an immensely superior
force, and suffering a loss of more than 300 men, the Seventy-
ninth behaved with the utmost heroism.

> "And wild and high the 'Cameron's gathering' rose!
> The war-note of Lochiel, which Albyn's hills
> Have heard—and heard, too, have her Saxon foes:
> How in the noon of night that pibroch thrills,
> Savage and shrill! But with the breath which fills
> Their mountain pipe, so fill the mountaineers
> With the fierce native daring which instils
> The stirring memory of a thousand years;
> And Evan's, Donald's fame rings in each clansman's ears!'"

In the subsequent battle of Waterloo, it was included in
the fifth division under Sir Thomas Picton, and in the fifth
brigade of the army under Sir James Kempt. Here it was
associated with the Twenty-eighth, Thirty-second, and Ninety-
fifth (Rifles) regiments, and posted in defence of a hedge which
the Belgian troops had abandoned early in the fight. Against
this position three powerful columns of the enemy advanced.
"At this moment General Picton was killed, and General Kempt
severely wounded; but the latter never left the field. Like his
old commander, Sir Ralph Abercromby, he allowed no personal
consideration to interfere with his duty; and although unable
to sit on horseback from the severity of the wound, he would
not allow himself to be carried away from his soldiers, whose
situation, pressed by a brave and powerful enemy, required
every assistance from his presence and talents. The enemy,

anxious to gain the position behind the hedge, repeated their attempts, but every attempt was repulsed." The honourable conduct of the regiment on this occasion, as a matter of history, has been justly celebrated.

Occupying France for a while, the Seventy-ninth returned to Britain in 1818, and has long been peacefully employed.

In 1854, when the aggressions of Russia called upon the nations "to defend the right," the Seventy-ninth, with the Forty-second Royal Highlanders and the Ninety-third Sutherland Highlanders, formed the original Highland Brigade in the army of the Crimea.

At the battle of the Alma, co-operating with the Guards, this brigade, under Sir Colin Campbell, won a great renown. It was selected, with the other Highland regiments, under Sir Colin Campbell, to renew the attack upon the Redan. Fortunately, the retirement of the garrison to the other side of the harbour afforded a bloodless victory. The regiment was engaged in the successful expedition against Kertch.

Released by the conclusion of peace from the toils of war on the distant plains of the Crimea, the regiment returned home. Shortly thereafter, the outbreak of the Indian mutiny required its presence in that far-off province of our empire. Accordingly, embarked, it arrived there in 1858, and joined the army marching upon Lucknow. On the suppression of the revolt, it was retained in India; and we doubt not the presence of such staunch defenders of the British constitution will command peace—the military fire of "auld langsyne" still burning in the bosom of the Cameron.

THE NINETY-SECOND FOOT;

or,

GORDON HIGHLANDERS.

CHAPTER XLI.

The foe weel kenn'd the tartan front,
Which never shunn'd the battle's brunt—
The chieftain of our Highland men,
That led them on to vict'ry then,
    As aye he cried, " For Scotland."

THE GORDON—CORSICA—HOLLAND—EGYPT—COPENHAGEN—
SWEDEN—CORUNNA—1794–1809.

THE Duke of Gordon, rather as the proprietor of a vast domain than the chief of a clan, enjoyed an almost kingly power in the Highlands. Amongst his tenants were the Camerons of Lochiel and the Macphersons of Clunie, whilst his few immediate retainers were chiefly horsemen—almost the only cavalry known in Highland warfare. The Gordons have ever been distinguished for devotion to their king and country. The friends of the Bruce, they were ranged on the side of liberty at Bannockburn. Adherents of the Stuarts, we cannot but regret the mistaken zeal which so nigh involved in a like ruin so estimable a family. Happily, a better knowledge of the failings of the dethroned dynasty showed the worthlessness of the object of their attachment, and so estranged them from their cause, that, in 1745, the representative of the Gordons was found combating on the side of the Government, whilst the clans upon their estates followed Lochiel and other chieftains, and fought on behalf of Prince Charles.

Fortunately, Government succeeded in enlisting the loyal services of this powerful family; and by its influence regiments of Highlanders were successively raised in 1759, 1779, and 1793 (fencible), all of which have long ago been disbanded, or, more properly, are now merged and represented in the subject of our present sketch, the Ninety-second, raised in 1794. The efforts of the Marquis of Huntly, a captain in the Scots Fusilier Guards, helped by the Duchess of Gordon, were most active and successful in the business of recruiting. The Marquis was rewarded with the Lieutenant-Colonelcy of the regiment, embodied at Aberdeen in June, 1794, and originally numbered the 100th Regiment, afterwards the Ninety-second.

In September the regiment was embarked for Gibraltar, where it remained in garrison, completing its drill, until the following year, when it was removed to Corsica. With a detachment, in occupation of the island of Elba, it remained in Corsica so long as the natives were content with the British rule. When the rising fame of their great countryman, Napoleon, excited their admiration, and they desired to be merged in the glory of his "empire," our Government, convinced of the inutility of maintaining an expensive garrison in the island, and ever opposed to repressive measures antagonistic to the feelings of the people, wisely resolved to leave them to experience the bitterness of imperial tyranny. Accordingly, the Ninety-second was withdrawn to Gibraltar in 1796.

In 1798 the regiment returned to England, and thence proceeded to Ireland, where it was employed in suppressing the miserable attempts at rebellion got up by the disaffected, and encouraged by France. Although not actively engaged in the field, its good conduct in garrison was very commendable, occurring at a time when the disorders of the country presented many and powerful temptations. Fortunately, the corps was soon released from the painful duty of appearing in arms against those who should otherwise have been as brothers.

Under Lieutenant-General Sir Ralph Abercromby, who commanded the expedition of 1799 which proceeded against the French in Holland, the Ninety-second was included in the brigade of Major-General (afterwards Sir John) Moore, and associated with the First Royal Scots (second battalion), the Twenty-fifth King's Own Borderers, the Forty-ninth Foot, and the Seventy-ninth Cameron Highlanders. Landed at Helder, it was engaged in the actions fought around the villages of Crabbendam and Schagen, and commended for its "noble and steady conduct." At the battle of "Egmont-op-Zee," whilst escorting twenty pieces of artillery to the front, the Ninety-second was fiercely assailed by a column of 6000 French. Undaunted, the Highlanders stood the dreadful shock, when bayonet met bayonet, and hundreds, locked in the fatal embrace, fell the sacrifice of their own valour. Thus a horrid rampart of dead and dying humanity lay between the combatants. The carnage was terrible. The Ninety-second alone had to lament a loss of nearly 300, and amongst these its brave colonel, the Marquis of Huntly, and Lieu-

tenant-Colonel Erskine, both wounded. It was the charge
of the Ninety-second which began the action, their steady,
persevering gallantry which sustained it, and their unsurpassed
valour which completed the victory.' Major-General Moore,
wounded in the conflict, was carried off the field by two
soldiers of the Ninety-second. "We can do no more than
take him to the doctor," said they; "we must join the lads,
for every man is wanted." Grateful for this service, Major-
General Moore offered to reward the soldiers who thus
probably saved his life, but no claimant appeared; either the
superstition of the Highlander, dreading the curse which the
acceptance of such "blood money" was supposed to entail, or
his native pride, would not allow the acceptance of the gift, or
else, what is more likely, the men, by a glorious death, were
now beyond the rewards of this world. Thus disappointed,
Major-General Moore found another means of commemorating
this act of generous devotion, in selecting a soldier of the
Ninety-second as one of the supporters of his armorial bear-
ings. By the convention of Alkmaar, the army abandoned
Holland to the French; and therewith the Gordon Highlanders returning to England, were stationed at Chelmsford.

In 1800 the regiment was engaged in a fruitless enterprise
intended to aid the Royalists of France by a descent upon the
coast of that country. The remainder of the year was spent
unaccountably wandering up and down amongst the garrisons
of the Mediterranean—Gibraltar, Minorca, and Malta.

In the spring of 1801 a definite purpose was assigned to
the regiment, as part of the expedition assembled in Marmorice

Bay, destined, under Sir Ralph Abercromby, to deliver Egypt from the usurped dominion of France. Accomplishing a successful landing despite the assaults of a powerful enemy, whose artillery from the heights above swept the bay of Aboukir, the Ninety-second, placed in brigade with the First Royal Scots and the two battalions of the Fifty-fourth Foot, advanced with the army towards Alexandria. On the 13th of March the French were encountered at Mandora, where, forming the advanced guard of the left column, the Gordon Highlanders shared the glory of the action with the Ninetieth Perthshire Volunteers. "Opposed to a tremendous fire, and suffering severely from the French line, they never receded a foot, but maintained the contest alone, until the marines and the rest of the line came to their support."

The Gordon Highlanders were honoured in being selected to furnish a guard for the head-quarters of the Commander-in-Chief. Sadly reduced by the inroads of sickness and the sword, the regiment had been ordered to Aboukir, but the battle of Alexandria occurring ere it had scarce begun the march, arrested and recalled it to its place in line. The campaign was closed by the surrender of Alexandria and the submission of 24,000 veteran troops, who, under General Menou, yet remained to France of the "Army of Egypt."

On the 15th of October, the Gordon Highlanders, embarking from Alexandria, returned home, calling on the passage at Malta, and finally arriving at Cork in 1802. The corps remained in the United Kingdom for the five following years, peacefully garrisoning various towns, during which period it was increased by the addition of a second battalion, raised in 1803, but disbanded in 1813.

In 1807 the first battalion was included with the Forty-third, Fifty-second, and Ninety-fifth regiments, in the reserve brigade of the British army of Lord Cathcart, which, invading Denmark a second time, occasioned the capitulation of Copenhagen, and arrested the Danish fleet. Returning from this almost bloodless victory, a body of 600 men of the battalion was shipwrecked in the "Neptunis," but rescued after enduring many and sore privations.

During the following year the Ninety-second was employed, under Lieutenant-General Sir John Moore, in a vain expedition to Sweden. Our aid being rejected, the army returned home.

It afterwards proceeded to the Peninsula, where it arrived in time to learn that the Convention of Cintra had delivered Portugal for the present from the thraldom of Marshal Junot, the Emperor's Lieutenant. Placed in the division of Lieut.-General Sir John Hope, the Gordon Highlanders advanced therewith into Spain, where a junction was formed with the army of Sir John Moore. It endured with firmness all the hardships of a disastrous yet successful retreat, crowning its perseverance by its gallantry at the battle of Corunna, where it was called to regret the loss of a gallant officer, Lieut.-Colonel Napier, and, further, to mourn over the fall of the hero of the campaign, Lieut.-General Sir John Moore, who terminated a life of honour and a career of glory on that memorable battle-field.

This victory secured the unmolested embarkation of the army, which accordingly sailed for England.

CHAPTER XLII.

"And, oh! loved warriors of the minstrel's land!
Yonder your bonnets nod, your tartans wave!
The rugged form may mark the mountain band,
And harsher features, and a mien more grave.
But ne'er in battle throbbed a heart so brave,
As that which beats beneath the Scottish plaid;
And when the pibroch bids the battle rave,
And level for the charge your arms are laid,
Where lives the desperate foe that for such onset staid?"

WALCHEREN—PENINSULA—WATERLOO—1809–1862.

In 1809 the Ninety-second was engaged under the Earl of Chatham in the unfortunate expedition to Walcheren, wherein a splendid army in a few weeks was discomfited by the poisoned breath of the pestilence. Of 1000 men comprised in the Gordon Highlanders, only 300 returned effective to England.

In 1810 the regiment embarked for the Peninsula, and joined the army of Viscount Wellington in the lines of Torres Vedras. Brigaded with the Fiftieth and Seventy-first regiments, under Major-General Howard, it advanced with the army in pursuit of the French under Marshal Messena, shared the glories of "Fuentes d'Onor," accomplishing the fall of Almeida.

The brigade was afterwards detached as part of the second division of the army, commanded by Lieutenant-General Hill, which covered the operations of the grand army under Wellington against the fortresses of Ciudad Rodrigo and Badajoz. This division, pursuing the enemy towards Merida, overtook and surprised the bronzed veterans of the fifth French corps,

under General Gerard, when about to decamp from Arroyo
del Molinos. The honour of this feat of arms is mainly due
to the Seventy-first and Ninety-second Highlanders, who,
during the raging of a fearful tempest, and screened by a thick
mist, charged into the village. In the confusion the loss of
the enemy was immense; of 3000 only 600 escaped to tell
the tale of the catastrophe. It is said the enemy was first
made aware of his danger by the scream of the bagpipes as
they appropriately played—

"Hey, Johnnie Cope, are ye waukin' yet?"

Driven out at the point of the bayonet, the French were
utterly broken and dispersed. Few events reflect greater
credit upon the Gordon Highlanders than this exploit.

It was the business of Lieut.-Gen. Hill so to engage the
attention of Marshal Soult, that he should be prevented assisting the army of Marshal Marmont, opposed to Wellington.
By the capture of Forts Napoleon and Ragusa at "Almaraz,"
gallantly accomplished by the brigade, the separation of the
two Marshals was effected, and each forced to follow his own
line of retreat, at every step widening the breach.

The battle of Salamanca having cleared the way, the
British advanced to Madrid; and, whilst Wellington proceeded against Burgos, Lord Hill occupied the capital. The
concentration of the French armies for the relief of Burgos
occasioned the abandonment of that enterprise, and, for the
last time, compelled our army to retire towards Portugal,
evacuating Madrid. "From the 27th October to the 20th
November, we were exposed," says Lieut.-Col. Cameron, "to

greater hardships than I thought the human frame could bear.
In most inclement weather, with the canopy of heaven for our
covering, wet, cold, and hungry, we were generally marching
day and night. Fifteen poor fellows of the Ninety-second fell
down, and were lost. My heart bled for them."

On reaching Alba de Tormes, an old Roman town, defended
by a ruined wall, it was deemed necessary to make a stand
against the pursuing enemy, who, urged forward by the vigorous Soult, sorely pressed our army. Here the brigade, entrusted
with the honourable yet difficult duty of maintaining the rear
guard, behaved with extraordinary gallantry. The scene is
thus described by Lieut.-Col. Cameron :—"We did what we
could to improve our situation during the short time left us.
I threw an old door across the place where the gate once had
been, and barricaded it with sticks and stones. . . . We
had not a single piece of ordnance. Just as the clock of Alba
struck two, the French columns moved to the attack, and,
from that time until night, we sustained a hurricane of shot
and shell from twenty pieces of cannon! Their riflemen
threw themselves into ditches and ravines round the walls,
but their masses never forsook the protection of their artillery,
which was most dastardly for Soult, with ten thousand men!"

"It is said, that on the 8th, a French officer of high rank
approached so close to the position of the Ninety-second that
several muskets were levelled at him, when Cameron, disdain-
ing to take such an advantage, promptly forbade the firing
of a shot. It was Soult who was thus saved."

Thus arrested, the French did not again disturb the

retreat. Both armies going into winter quarters, the campaign of 1812 terminated.

With the first dawn of spring Wellington was again on the move. Having re-organised his army, and been strengthened by considerable reinforcements from home, with 78,000 excellent troops, he proceeded to drive the enemy before him. The French, on the other hand, discouraged by evil news from Russia, and denied that assistance they needed, because of the more urgent necessities of the Grand Army, could not be expected to act with the same energy as heretofore, yet did they exceed these anticipations.

At "Vittoria" King Joseph and Marshal Jourdan having gathered together their utmost disposable force, ventured to try the fate of battle, hoping to check the progress of the British, or at least secure a safe retreat, laden, as they were, with the spoil of the Peninsula. But the battle of Vittoria fatally disappointed them, and rescued the treasures of Spain from their avaricious grasp. In this battle, the Ninety-second Highlanders, having been ordered to seize the heights whereon the village of Puebla was perched, and hold the position to the last, with persevering valour overcame a determined resistance, pressed up the sides of the mountain, entered the village with an impetuous charge, and, after a fierce struggle, drove the enemy out.

Having gained this great victory, the British now addressed themselves to the Herculean task of forcing a passage through the defiles of the "Pyrenees" into France. Notwithstanding the stupendous efforts of Marshal Soult to retrieve the losses

of Vittoria and defend these natural barriers of his country,
the British still pressed "forward." On the 20th July, 1813,
whilst the brigade was threading its way through the pass of
Maya, it was vigorously attacked by a corps of 15,000 French,
who, forcing back that "fierce and formidable old regiment,
the Fiftieth," upon the Seventy-first and Ninety-second Highlanders, very nearly drove them out of the pass. These,
however, for *ten hours* stood the shock of this formidable
assault. "So dreadful was the slaughter, especially of the
Ninety-second, that it is said the advancing enemy was
actually stopped by the heaped mass of dead and dying.
Never did soldiers fight better—seldom so well. The stern
valour of the Ninety-second would have graced Thermopylae."
Of 750 Gordon Highlanders who were engaged, only 400 survived it scatheless, but these returned in the truest sense
"conquering heroes," having, when every cartridge was expended, and in presence of succour, decided the victory as
their own by a desperate charge. Throughout the many conflicts which it needed to clear a passage through the Pyrenees,
and thereafter drive so terrible a foe successively across the
"Nivelle" and the "Nive," the Ninety-second always displayed
the same desperate resolution and valour.

At the sanguinary action of St Pierre, which raged with
exceeding fury for three hours, cumbering a little space of one
mile with more than 5000 dead and dying, the Ninety-second
impetuously charged and destroyed two regiments of the
enemy. Pressing onwards, the Highlanders were arrested by
a fearful storm of artillery, and forced to retreat upon their

comrades of the Seventy-first; who likewise yielding to the iron tempest, both found shelter and rallied behind their brethren in brigade of the Fiftieth. "Then its gallant colonel (Cameron) once more led it down the road, with colours flying and music playing, resolved to give the shock to whatever stood in the way. A small force was the Ninety-second compared with the heavy mass in its front, but that mass faced about and retired across the valley. How gloriously did that regiment come forth again to charge, with their colours flying and their national music playing as if going to a review! This was to understand war. The man who in that moment, and immediately after a repulse, thought of such military pomp, was by nature a soldier."

Excepting at the battle of Toulouse, the Ninety-second was daily engaged with the enemy, and always with equal credit.

The abdication and exile of Napoleon spread the calm of peace over the face of Europe. Alas! that it should have been but as some sweet vision of the night, doomed to be dissipated by the dawn of the morrow, when the sterner realities of life, its toils and its wars, anew presented themselves. The night which had shrouded the destiny of imperial France was succeeded by a new day happily; but, as a brief winter's day, when for a moment a glimpse of sunshine shone upon the spirit of the old empire, as it seemed to revive beneath the influence of the great Magician, who was wont to conjure up kingdoms and dynasties by the mere fiat of his will. Soon we shall find the day-dream of ambition eclipsed in a darker night. Already, we can almost read the mysterious writing, prophetically pointing to Waterloo, as more surely sealing the fate of imperial France.

In 1815 the rude blast of war once more summoned the Ninety-second to the field, as the gathering hosts of France and the Allies accepted the dread arbitration of war on the chivalric field of Flanders.

In this campaign the Ninety-second was brigaded with the First Royal Scots, the Forty-second Royal Highlanders, and the Forty-fourth Foot, under Major-General Sir Denis Pack, and placed in the famous fifth division of Lieut.-General Sir T. Picton. The same tide of imperial power, which rose upon the Prussians at Ligny, rolled along towards Quatre Bras, and dashed its stormy billows in foaming wrath upon the living rocks of British valour there. As the Gordon High-landers encountered the furious onset of the corps of Marshal Ney, Wellington himself was in their midst, and beheld their splendid valour. Concealed in a ditch by the road-side, they waited the charge of the French cavalry, as it ventured to sweep past them in pursuit of the Brunswickers. Here, however, the pursuit was stayed by a fatal volley from the Highlanders. At length the Duke gave the word, as he observed the enemy pushing along the Charleroi Road, "Now, Cameron," said he, "now is your time; you must charge these fellows, and take care of that road." Soon the massive columns of the foe were broken and hurled back in confusion, as the Ninety-second emerged from the awful conflict a bleed-ing yet victorious remnant, having lost its brave commander, Lieut.-Colonel Cameron, and nearly 300 comrades. Colonel

Cameron was deeply lamented by the regiment, and the whole army. Temporarily buried in the vicinity of the field of his latest glory, his remains were afterwards removed, by his family, to the churchyard of Kilmallie, where his sacred dust now reposes beside the chieftains of Lochiel. No funeral in the Highlands was ever so honoured—the great, the noble, the brave, and upwards of 3000 Highlanders were there to pay the last tribute of respect to the beloved soldier, now no more.

But the great event of these "hundred days" was at hand, as the 18th of June dawned upon the plains of Waterloo.

It was late in the day ere the Gordon Highlanders were brought into action to recover the farm-house of La Haye Sainte, lost by the Belgians, and which the First Royal Scots and Forty-fourth regiments had failed to regain, from a column of 3000 French At this critical moment Major-General Sir Denis Pack said, "Ninety-second, you must charge, for all the troops to your right and left have given way." Although mustering scarce 300 men, with characteristic dauntlessness, the Highlanders rushed impetuously to the attack, and in another moment seemed lost amid the dark masses of the foe. As if moved to help their countrymen, the Scots Greys came to their aid, or rather to witness and complete the victory the Highlanders had already won. Together, shouting " Scotland for ever," these splendid corps renewed the assault, which utterly ruined the column of the enemy, the survivors being only too glad to seek refuge in flight. Sir Denis Pack having witnessed this magnificent charge and its glorious effects, commending the Ninety-second, said,

"You have saved the day, Highlanders." Meanwhile, beholding with unfeigned regret the discomfiture of his troops, the
Emperor, at the same time, felt constrained to admire the
valour of the Highlanders, which had so signally triumphed,
exclaiming, "the brave Scots."

> And on the plains of Waterloo
> The world confess'd the *bravest few*
>   Were kilted men frae Scotland.

Pursuing the enemy, the allies entered Paris in triumph,
and thence, on the surrender of Napoleon, dictated peace.

Returning to England, the regiment was employed in
various home garrisons, until the year 1819, when it was
removed to the West Indies. During its sojourn there it was
almost destroyed by the dreadful ravages of fever among its
soldiers, and returned to England a mere skeleton in 1827.
In 1834 it was removed to Gibraltar, and thence, in 1836, to
Malta. Whilst stationed at Malta, it was reviewed by Prince
Maximilian of Bavaria, and further honoured in furnishing a Guard to Her Majesty the Queen Dowager whilst resi-
dent in the island. In 1841 it was removed to the West
Indies, and two years later returned home. In 1851 it proceeded to Corfu. Removed to Gibraltar in 1853, it embarked
thence to the Crimea, arriving a few days after the fall of
Sebastopol. Returning to Gibraltar in 1856, in 1858 it was
despatched, *via* overland route, to Bombay. In the suppression of the Indian mutiny it was engaged at Rajghpur, Mon-
growlie, and Sindwah. It still remains in India.

THE NINETY-THIRD FOOT;

OR,

SUTHERLAND HIGHLANDERS.

CHAPTER XLIII.

"Trust in the Lord, for ever trust,
And banish all your fears,
Strength in the Lord Jehovah is,
Eternal as His years."

CAPE OF GOOD HOPE—NEW ORLEANS—CRIMEA—INDIAN
MUTINY—1804–1862.

GENERAL STUART writes of this most respectable corps:—
"None of the Highland corps is superior to the Ninety-
third Regiment. I do not make comparisons in point of
bravery, for, if properly commanded, they are all brave; but
it is in those well-regulated habits, of which so much has been
already said, that the Sutherland Highlanders have for
twenty years preserved an unvaried line of conduct. The
light infantry company of this corps has been nineteen years
without having a man punished."

Unfortunately, it has not been so highly favoured as many
of its predecessors in having the same rare opportunities for
displaying in the field the sterner qualities of the soldier.
Nevertheless, in the few enterprises in which it has been

engaged, it has always shown itself to be equally meritorious, possessing the same heroic valour which has so signally glorified the Highland regiments in every corner of the world.

It was raised in the year 1800, on behalf of the ancient and honourable family of Sutherland, by Major-General William Wemyss of Wemyss. Of its original members, 460 were Sutherland men. It still retains its Highland character, perhaps more so than any other corps, and like many of them, the Channel Islands witnessed its maiden service.

When the Peace of Amiens seemed likely to continue its blessings to the country, and supersede the necessity of an extensive military establishment, our Government proposed to reduce the strength of the army, and the Sutherland Highlanders were accordingly ordered home to Scotland in 1802 for the purpose of disbandment. Ere this could be accomplished, symptoms of unquiet became too painfully evident in the political horizon of Europe, which fortunately occasioned the retention of this excellent regiment intact among the stalwart defenders of our land at a moment of peril such as never before had threatened our independence as a nation.

As the danger for the present somewhat subsided, the Ninety-third, in 1805, was included in the expedition which, under Major-General Sir David Baird, proceeded against the Dutch colony of the Cape of Good Hope. With the Seventy-first and Seventy-second regiments it formed the Highland brigade of Brigadier-General Ferguson, which landed in Lespard Bay. On this occasion, thirty-five of the Sutherland Highlanders were drowned by the upsetting of a boat in the surf. The only opposition of any consequence made by the Dutch Governor, Lieutenant-General Janssens, was encountered at Blaw Berg, or Blue Mountains, where the irresistible charge of the Highland Brigade decided the fortune of the battle in our favour. After this experience of British valour, the Governor relinquished the contest, and surrendered the colony.

Retained in the garrison, "being anxious to enjoy the advantages of religious instruction agreeably to the tenets of their national church, the men of the Ninety-third Regiment formed themselves into a congregation, appointed elders of their own number, engaged and paid a stipend (collected from the soldiers) to a clergyman of the Church of Scotland, and had Divine service performed agreeably to the ritual of the Established Church." Consistent with this excellent conduct, so gratifying to every thinking man who claims a patriotic interest in the soldiers of his country, no matter what be his creed, we quote a further illustration of the godly character of these true soldiers. On their return from the Cape of Good Hope, when "disembarked at Plymouth in August, 1814, the inhabitants were both surprised and gratified. On such occasions it had been no uncommon thing for soldiers to spend in taverns and gin-shops the money they had saved. In the present case, the soldiers of Sutherland were seen in booksellers' shops, supplying themselves with Bibles, and such books and tracts as they required." Mindful of the wants of the "old folks at home," "during the short period that the regiment was quartered in Plymouth, upwards of £500 were lodged in one banking-house, to be remitted to Sutherland, exclusive of many sums sent home through the post-office and by officers. Some of these sums exceeded £20 from an individual soldier." We may well expect great things from men of such a stamp, no matter what be their profession—truly in them is exhibited "an honourable example, worthy the imitation of all."

In the eventful times of which we write little rest could be granted to the soldier. Thus, we find the regiment, within a month after its arrival at Plymouth, on its way across the Atlantic, as part of the expedition under Major-General the Hon. Sir Edward Pakenham, destined to operate against the city of New Orleans. Rendevouzed at Jamaica, the expedition proceeded thence on the 27th November, and landed at Cat Island, at the mouth of the Mississippi, on the 13th December, 1814. The unfavourable nature of the ground, the immediate presence of an enemy greatly superior in numbers, and having an extended line of formidable entrenchments whither to retreat, rendered the enterprise one of difficulty and danger. Commanded by able officers having every confidence in their soldiers, perhaps overrated as they overtasked their capabilities, the army fearlessly advanced, surmounting all the obstacles which lay in the way ere they confronted the citadel of the American position. Nothing could surpass the heroism of the Commander-in-Chief, who fell whilst leading the troops to the assault, nor the gallantry of the officers supporting him, of whom Major-Generals Gibb and Keane (afterwards Lord Keane) were wounded—the former fatally. Nothing could excel the dauntless bravery with which the troops followed their leaders through the murderous tempest of musketry and artillery, which carried death and destruction into their very midst; yet all was unavailing, save the attack of Colonel Thornton upon the right of the enemy—everywhere else these formidable entrenchments proved impregnable to so small a force, unaided by an adequate artillery. Thus, after a fearful loss of life and limb, Major-General Sir John Lambert felt constrained to abandon the attempt and sound the retreat. Weakened by a loss of upwards of 1500 killed and wounded—nearly a third of which was sustained by the Ninety-third, proof of the valour of the corps in this fiery trial —the troops were re-embarked, and bade adieu to the scene of so terrible a disaster.

On their return home in 1815, the Sutherland Highlanders were peacefully employed; for the long period of nearly forty years its history presents a comparatively uninteresting record of military stations occupied from time to time, lightened by such glimpses of character as these:—One inspecting officer reports the Sutherland Highlanders to exhibit a "picture of military discipline and moral rectitude;" another declares them "altogether incomparable;" and the colonists of the Cape of Good Hope lament their loss as "kind friends and honourable soldiers." Such are the men whose good conduct in quarters and in peace evince a sterling character which, never failing in the day of battle, is capable of sustaining a great renown.

Passing down the stream of time, we arrive at the year 1854, and follow the Ninety-third to the Crimea—

When despot power in pride sent forth
Her slaves from empire of the North,

To crush in her gigantic fold
The nation who its own would hold,
    And wad be free like Scotland.

On leaving Plymouth *en route* to embark for the seat of war, whilst other troops in like circumstances manifested a fearless indifference, striving to kill the thoughts of long farewells by marching to the tune of "Cheer, boys, cheer," in keeping with their past history, the Sutherland Highlanders unostentatiously preferred to chant a hymn of praise to the God of battles. What a lovely and impressive sight!—lovely in the sight of God and man, to behold these brave men going forth as Christian British soldiers beneath the banner of their country, at the same time the banner of the Cross.

Thence we learn the secret of that Samson strength, deep-rooted in the soul, which fixed them like a living rock of Gaelic valour at Balaklava. They feared not to die, for death to such was welcome, not to satisfy the cravings of a mere earthly heroism, but because in that grim messenger they could recognise the herald beckoning their immortal spirits on high, opening the portals of a bright hereafter to an emancipated soul.

In our army, which after a variety of anterior and unimportant movements landed in the Crimea in September, 1854, with a view to the humbling of the aggressive might of Russia, the Ninety-third with the Forty-second and Seventy-ninth formed the original Highland Brigade, so justly celebrated. No higher compliment to its worth could have been accorded, than that of being associated in the same division with the brigade of Guards. Advancing towards Sebastopol, the enemy was discovered in a

very strong position, prepared to dispute the passage of the
river Alma. It needed all the skill of our officers, and a
desperate exercise of bravery on the part of our troops, to
drive the enemy from the position; and the occasion called
forth the native energy of the Highlanders, led by their
deservedly favourite chief, Major-General Sir Colin Campbell.

"Balaklava," than which no name is more expressive of
glory dearly won, is commemorative of the triumphs of our
cavalry—the irresistible charge of the Heavy Brigade, and
the "death ride" of the dauntless Light Brigade. But
another and, if possible, a grander event immortalises the
scene. The story of "*the thin red line*" which the Sutherland
Highlanders presented when, isolated from the army, alone
and in line, they withstood the desperate charge of the
Russian cavalry, is an exploit which must stir the soul of
every Scotsman. The cool intrepidity of Sir Colin Campbell
in such trying circumstances, and his unbounded confidence in
the mettle of his Highlanders, most remarkably glorify the
victors in the marvellous result.

> Like billows dashed upon the rock,
> Unmoved, ye met the dreadful shock;
> When horsemen furious charged your line,
> Brave Campbell cried, "These men are mine—
> " Ye needna fear for Scotland."

The brigade was increased to a division by the addition of
the Seventy-first and Seventy-second Highlanders, and was
chiefly employed in reserve, covering Balaklava. In the final
bombardment of Sebastopol, the Highland regiments were

selected to make the second assault upon the Redan, but in the meantime the place was abandoned by the enemy. The subsequent fall of Sebastopol brought about peace, when the Ninety-third, released from the stern duties of war, returned home laden with many honours.

The awful tragedy of the Indian mutiny, which cast its dismal shadow over the history of the year 1857, once more called forth the services of the Ninety-third. It followed its favourite leader, Sir Colin Campbell, to the plains of India, visiting with a terrible vengeance the murdering villains, the traitors, and the rebels, as with the army it advanced to the relief of the beleaguered garrison of Lucknow, yet struggling for very life. In every instance where the foe was to be encountered, the Sutherland Highlanders were most conspicuous for their gallantry. Having finally captured Lucknow, the regiment was engaged in several harassing conflicts with the enemy, sharing in some of these, such as Bareilly, with the Ninety-second. Its last action was fought in December, 1858, near Biswah. It still remains in India, and is now stationed at Peshawar.

Thus we close our History of the Scottish Regiments with this latest illustration of Highland valour, and we think our readers will admit, however faulty the writer, the theme at least is worthy of their best attention, nay, is entitled to their truest sympathy.

GLASGOW: PRINTED BY THOMAS MURRAY AND SON.

Printed in Great Britain
by Amazon